Praise for *The Winged*

"All of it is harrowing—and written in such
there's a good chance readers will ignore the pl
ing on the words, slowly, to draw out the flavor. ɪ ɪɪᴄɪɪ ᴛɪɪᴄy ɪɪ ɪɪᴄᴄᴅ ᴛᴛ
Fortunately, this is a short book; also fortunately, there's a lot of novel packed into
relatively few pages. A highly recommended indulgence."
— N. K. Jemisin, *New York Times Book Review*

"A faceted jewel of a book that looks at the land of Olondria from the perspective
of four of its women: One is a soldier, fighting a war of independence; one is a
scholar, musing on sectarianism, violence and loneliness; one is a poet, singing her
people's songs, and one is a socialite struggling to survive. Their lives cut across each
other like scripture on a stone, written in stunningly beautiful language that left me
breathless."— Amal El-Mohtar, NPR, Best Books of the Year

"For every moment of power and adrenaline, an equally crushing or lovely or strange
occurrence is offered. But then, such is war, and life."— Jessi Cape, *Austin Chronicle*

"Throughout it all, Samatar ponders weighty questions. 'What is the difference
between a king and a monster?' Tialon asks; 'What is music?' wonders Seren. But
Histories isn't a book about easy answers, any more than it's driven by plot. . . .
Samatar carries a great deal with her in the pages of *The Winged Histories:* beauty,
wonder, and a soaring paean to the power of story." — Jason Heller, NPR

"Told by four different women, it is a story of war; not epic battles of good and
evil, but the attempt to make things right and the realities of violence wielded by
one human against another, by one group against another. It's about the aftermath
of war, in which some things are better but others are worse. Above all, it's a story
about love—the terrible love that tears lives apart. Doomed love; impossible love;
love that requires a rewriting of the rules, be it for a country, a person, or a story."
— Jenn Northington, Tor.com

"An imaginative, poetic, and dark meditation on how history gets made."
— *Hello Beautiful*

"If you love stories but distrust them, if you love language and can also see how it
is used as a tool or a weapon in the maintenance of status quo, then read *The Winged
Histories.*" — Marion Deeds, *Fantasy Literature*

"Samatar's use of poetic yet unpretentious language makes her one of the best
writers of today. Reading her books is like sipping very rich mulled wine. The
worldbuilding and characterization is exquisite. This suspenseful and elegiac book
discusses the lives of fictional women in a fantasy setting who fear their histories
will be lost in a way that is only too resonant with the hidden histories of women
in our own age." — *Romantic Times Book Reviews* (4.5/5 stars, Top Pick)

"A brightly moving narrative that crystallizes into scenes as delicate, hard, and changing as ice, that rises up to meet four women in the midst of warfare, and the most devastating kinds of devotion and rebellion."
— Amina Cain, author of *Creature*

"A nuanced and subtle tale of war, love, duty, family, and honor. It's like polyphony—a chorus of voices singing different melodies, sometimes at odds, but ultimately harmonious. And moving. And exciting. Have I mentioned exciting?"
— Delia Sherman, author of *Young Woman in a Garden*

"Sparse and magical, beautiful and terrible; *The Winged Histories* is a story spun out of stories and the lives of fierce women, each a warrior in her own right."
— Nalo Hopkinson, author of *Midnight Robber*

Praise for Sofia Samatar's first novel, *A Stranger in Olondria*

WORLD FANTASY AWARD WINNER · BRITISH FANTASY AWARD WINNER · CRAWFORD AWARD WINNER · LOCUS AWARD FINALIST · NEBULA AWARD FINALIST

★ "A rich, strange landscape, allowing a lavish adventure to unfold that is haunting and unforgettable." — *Library Journal* (starred review)

"Gloriously vivid and rich." — Adam Roberts, *The Guardian*, Best Science Fiction

"The rare first novel with no unnecessary parts—and, in terms of its elegant language, its sharp insights into believable characters, and its almost revelatory focus on the value and meaning of language and story, it's the most impressive and intelligent first novel I expect to see this year, or perhaps for a while longer." — *Locus*

"Books can limit our experiences and reinforce the structures of empire. They can also transport us outside existing structures. The same book may do both in different ways or for different people. Samatar has written a novel that captures the ecstasy and pain of encountering the world through books, showing us bits and pieces of our contemporary world while also transporting us into a new one." — *Bookslut*

"The novel is full of subtle ideas and questions that never quite get answered . . . such as what is superstition and what is magic? How much do class and other prejudices affect how we view someone's religion? . . . Samatar gives us no easy answers and there are no villains in the book—simply ordinary people doing what they believe is right." — io9.com

"As you might expect (or hope) from a novel that is in part about the painting of worlds with words, the prose in *Stranger* is glorious. Whether through imaginative individual word choices—my favourite here being the merchants rendered "delirious" by their own spices . . . Samatar is adept at evoking place, mood, and the impact of what is seen on the one describing it for us." — *Strange Horizons*

The Winged Histories

I T H V A N A I

NISSIA

FIADUORON

Adein

IAVAIN

Belenduri KELEVAIN

Berevias

Telunith

Sinidre

Velvalinhu

Blessed Isle

Bain

I T H N E S S E

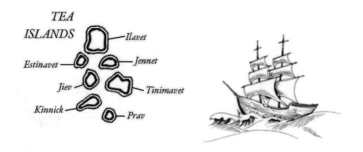

TEA
ISLANDS

Ilavet

Estinavet

Jennet

Jiev

Tinimavet

Kinnick

Prav

The Empire of Olondria with Nissia & the Tea Islands

The Winged Histories

by

SOFIA SAMATAR

Small Beer Press
Easthampton, MA

Small Beer Press
150 Pleasant Street #306
Easthampton, MA 01027
smallbeerpress.com
weightlessbooks.com
info@smallbeerpress.com

Distributed to the trade by Consortium.

Names: Samatar, Sofia, author.
Title: The winged histories : a novel / by Sofia Samatar.
Description: First trade paperback edition. | Easthampton, MA : Small Beer
  Press, 2017.
Identifiers: LCCN 2017001065 | ISBN 9781618731371 (paperback)
Subjects: | BISAC: FICTION / Fantasy / General. | GSAFD: Fantasy fiction.
Classification: LCC PS3619.A4496 W56 2017 | DDC 813/.6--dc23
LC record available at https://lccn.loc.gov/2017001065
                          2015029662

First published in hardcover (ISBN 9781618731142) and ebook (ISBN 9781618731159) editions by Small
Beer Press in 2016. First trade paperback edition 2017: 1 2 3 4 5 6 7 8 9

Text set in Centaur 12pt.
Printed on 30% recycled paper by the Maple Press in York, PA.
Author photo © 2015 by Peter Duffy.
Map © 2015 by Keith Miller.
Cover illustration © 2016 by Kathleen Jennings (tanaudel.wordpress.com)

To the Reader:
Give me your hand.

Family Tree

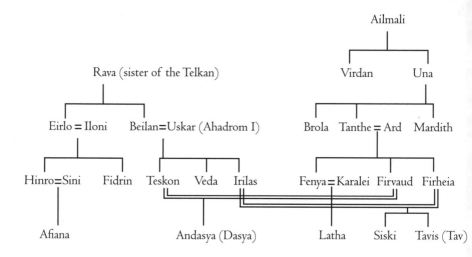

Ailmali

Virdan   Una

Rava (sister of the Telkan)

Eirlo = Iloni   Beilan=Uskar (Ahadrom I)   Brola   Tanthe = Ard   Mardith

Hinro=Sini   Fidrin   Teskon   Veda   Irilas   Fenya=Karalei   Firvaud   Firheia

Afiana   Andasya (Dasya)   Latha   Siski   Tavis (Tav)

Contents

⚭

But those on the border write no histories.
Their book is memory. Their element is air.
— Karanis of Loi
The Eighth Meditation

BOOK ONE

The History of the Sword

Everywhere the sound of wings.

I. Secrets

The swordmaiden will discover the secrets of men. She will discover that men at war are not as men at peace. She will discover an unforeseen comradeship. Take care: this comradeship is a Dueman shield. It does not extend all the way to the ground.

The swordmaiden will discover her secret forebears. Maris the Crooked fought for Keliathu in the War of the Tongues. Wounded and left with the high-piled dead, she was rescued before the pyre was lit by the man who most despised her: her second lieutenant, Farod. "Farod," she said to him, "what have you done?" And he answered: "Do not thank me, General. I am like a man who has preserved his enemy's coin; and I am like a man who, having seen his enemy safely submerged among crocodiles, has drawn him out again."

The swordmaiden will discover that her forebears are few. There was Maris, and there was Galaron of Nain, and there was the False Countess of Kestenya.

The swordmaiden will hear rumors of others, but she will not find them.

Her greatest battle will be waged against oblivion.

— Ferelanyi of Bream, *The Swordmaiden's Codex*

I became a swordmaiden in the Brogyar war, among the mountains.

I was fifteen when I went there to school. Fifteen, and a runaway. The old coach swayed, the pink light of the lantern bounced against the mountainside, and I sat with my hands clenched in embroidered gloves. My furs were cold. I made Fulmia stop the carriage at the officers' hall so that I could give them my letter. This hall had once been a temple of Avalei; now fires burned among its smoke-stained pillars, and battered shields lay stacked up in the porch. Nirai stood in the doorway and cried in the wind: "What news from the Valley?" Then he peered closer and started. "It's all right," I said. "I have a letter from the duke." Inside they were all there, Uncle Gishas, Prince Ruaf, and others. They passed my letter around the great stone table.

Sparks flew in the wind; an orderly tossed a branch of pine on one of the fires. High above, shadow-faces grimaced from a frieze.

"The other rooms have crumbled," Uncle Gishas said. "Inside the hill." He pinched my chin with bare cold fingers protruding from his glove.

"Forgive an old man," he said, and they brought hot wine stewed with raspberries and I sipped it slowly and watched the candle flames torn by the wind.

"Well, Lady Tavis," Prince Ruaf said. "Are you pleased? You are the first woman to have tasted camp wine since the days of Ferelanyi."

Such cold wind, such heat from the thick sweet wine and from the fires, such elation and bitterness, such a vastness of stone. They believed my letter, every word. I took it as a sign. At last I lay down on a pile of skins and blankets in front of the altar.

"Sleep, my lady," Fulmia said. He lay down near my feet and began to snore. The others were talking, fires danced, orderlies walked by. I thought of the school and what it might be like and how soon I would die and how it would feel, but these thoughts made me more excited and more awake. So I began to think of horses. It had become a habit of mine after leaving home and had never failed to soothe me to sleep. I began with the first one, Nusha the black pony, feeding her in the dark and the blue doorway and holding the lantern up and afraid of her teeth. That would be in the early morning, the season of sour apples. After Nusha I

thought of Meis although she was only a carriage horse. I realized that I had forgotten Felios and went back for him, my uncle's
dusty farm, the smoking stove, the tents by the road. In the midst
of apparent disorder, the horse: slant-eyed like a fox, disdainful,
his mane full of ribbons. I went on counting horses but did not
want to think about Tuik, and while trying not to think about him
I thought of the Angel Horse, and how Nenya said she had seen
it coming down to drink from the fountain at dawn. We made
her call us early and crept out to the cold terrace in our furs and
peered between the branches of the rose tree. Siski bit a rosebud
off and chewed it to prove she could—she had once eaten candied
rose petals at Grandmother's house in the north. But we never
saw the Angel Horse, nor did we see the Snow Horses that came
down every winter to graze on the plain. Where they passed they
left the snow. Sometimes there were stampedes, the whole world
blanketed in the morning with their whiteness. At other times
they passed lazily and gracefully and nuzzled the trees. Nenya
threatened sometimes to send us away with the Bad-Luck Horses.
Look Taviye, the Snow Horses have come. Frost on the window, the sound
of servants stoking the chilly fires, and next door Malino in his
cloth cap.

The school perched on the mountain above the officers' hall, a
great honeycomb of stone that had once held the nessenhu, the
domain of Avalei's women. From the ledge you could look down
on the ancient temple and the statue of Avalei that had fallen and
lay awkwardly on the roof. One arm was broken, the other raised
and holding a shattered vulture. The goddess looked embarrassed,
as if hiding behind her arm. On a clear day you could see the
smoke from the villages far below and we would sit chewing on
our knuckles and dreaming of pears. That was after we had passed
to the second grade, after we had slaughtered the herd of screaming pigs in the inner courtyard. In the first grade we never sat out-

side, we ran in the outer court and washed the clothes and cooked and scrubbed the floors. And Nirai pulled me aside one day and said: "Your aunt is here." I stood up, holding a dripping rag. My breath roared in my ears. "Go to your room and make yourself presentable," he said, irritable. "She's waiting in the officers' hall."

Of course she had come herself. I had not expected it—I had thought she would send Uncle Fenya—but once I realized she was there I saw that it was right. It was perfectly right that Aunt Mardith should come herself. She had set out from Faluidhen before dawn; they must have changed horses at Noi. Now, just at dusk, she sat before the fire in the officers' hall. The whole room looked guilty: someone had cleared the omi cards from the table. As I came in, a noisy clinking erupted in the far corner of the room, where Uncle Gishas was shoving some bottles out of sight.

"Well, Cousin Tavis," he cried, giving the pile a last hurried kick, "you have a most illustrious visitor. Some wine, Aunt?" he asked Aunt Mardith. "We've nothing too fine to offer—not what you're used to—but a warm glass, at the end of a journey—"

"No," Aunt Mardith said.

Uncle Fenya sat beside her, gloomily twisting his gloves in his hands. He half stood, as if intending to embrace me, and then sat down.

"Well," said Uncle Gishas.

"Gishas," Aunt Mardith said, in the special tone she reserved for inferior branches of the family, "you may go."

She waited for him to go out. Her eyes glittered. She wore a gray cloak trimmed with white squirrel fur. Her hood thrown back, her hair in place, she was like a pillar of snow. "May Leilin curse and cripple you," she said.

"Oh, Aunt," said Uncle Fenya.

I tensed my legs to stop their shaking and gripped Ferelanyi's book close to my chest. *The Swordmaiden's Codex.* I had brought it with me as an anchor, and it anchored me: I stood motionless. Aunt Mardith, too, was perfectly still.

"If I understand matters correctly, you spent less than a fortnight in the capital, where you had been sent, at no little expense, to stay with your uncle the duke. The idea was to introduce you to the best society—though I hardly consider Bainish society to be of the best. In Bain—and please correct me if I am mistaken in the details—you forged a letter of application to this school, signed your Uncle Veda's name, and stole his seal to complete the trick. You then lied to your manservant and induced him to drive you here. You have practiced a deception not only upon your family and your servant, but upon the staff of this school and indeed the entire Olondrian military. You have now spent three weeks in the company of soldiers, chaperoned by none but an aging manservant. Am I correct?"

"Yes."

"Again?"

"Yes," I said, louder.

"Fenya. Strike her."

"Oh, Aunt, really," Uncle Fenya cried, staring.

"Do as I say."

"I'll defend myself," I said.

"For the love of peace!" exclaimed Uncle Fenya. "We're not going to start sparring with one another, surely?"

He stood and shuffled toward me. When he reached for my shoulder, I flinched, but he was only patting me. "There, there," he said. He reeked of ous. His eyes watered; the bags under them were swollen. "There, there, now," he said, "it's all right, we're just going to take you home."

He turned to Aunt Mardith. "Isn't that right, eh, Aunt? We'll take her home and forget all about it. Why, it's no worse than the escapades Firvaud used to get up to! Stealing all the pencils—you remember that, Aunt, don't you?" He turned to me. "She stole all the pencils once. Our governess was in tears!"

"Fenya, if you are going to be useless, sit down."

"I only meant to say, now that we're taking her home—why, everything will be forgotten. I'll buy her a gown myself. You'd like that, wouldn't you, Tavis? A gown in the latest shade—butterfly's heart, I believe they're calling it. We might even have them put a pattern of shields on it—eh?" He chuckled, beads of excess spittle at the corners of his mouth. "That's often how fashions get started. You'll be our little swordmaiden, with shields all over your gown. A red gown! Pretty as a sunrise!"

"I won't go," I said.

"Oh, come—" he began.

"No?" said Aunt Mardith. Her eyes two flawless mirrors of black ice. "Look at your niece, Fenya," she said. "Defiant still. She does not appreciate our kindness, our willingness to take her back."

"You call it kindness?"

"Quiet," she said. She never raised her voice. "If you come with me, Tavis, you must not expect new gowns. You must expect a year of seclusion—enough, perhaps, for the world to forget that you have lived with soldiers. That you are irrevocably damaged."

"Oh," Uncle Fenya said, "not—"

"I'm not at all damaged," I said. "I'm like Ferelanyi."

I held the book toward her, hating myself for trembling. She rose and took it. She was so upright, despite her age—taller than me. She glanced at the stamp in the book. "Ah. Stolen from your uncle's library."

"Yes, but—"

"*The swordmaiden*," she read, "*will discover the secrets of men.*"

She looked up. For one breathless moment she met my eyes. A moment that seemed to hold everything: war and passion and Faluidhen and snow. Then she flung the book into the hottest part of the fire.

"No!"

I bruised my knees on the stone floor, scorched my hands in the flames. Uncle Fenya pulled me back. Aunt Mardith stood above us, brushing her fingers on her cloak. I shouted that I would not come home, and she told me her offer would not come again: she had only come to see me for my mother's sake. If I refused her, I would take the path I had chosen: I would finish my studies and join the army like the other students. "That's what I want!" I screamed. I was on my back, Uncle Fenya trying to cradle my head, hopelessly in the way. Aunt Mardith loomed above us, the long sweep of her traveling cloak hiding her feet like a bank of fog. *She advances by weight*, I thought, *like a glacier.* She said I would have what I wanted. She said it would make my mother suffer. She hoped I would die in the mountains. To her, I was already dead.

"If I'm already dead then why did you burn my book?" I was on my knees now, sobbing. The book a black architecture in the fire.

I did not realize then what I learned soon afterward: that I could recall the entire *Codex*, word for word. What Siski called my "prodigious memory for stupid things." Now I think I could tear one leaf from Ferelanyi's book and place it at the head of each chapter of my life. For the mountains, secrets. For Siski, loyalty like a necklace of dead stars. For the desert, blood. For Seren, song.

Aunt Mardith put up her hood. She pulled on her gloves, adjusting each finger. "Come, Fenya. If we leave now, we can break our fast at Faluidhen."

The next day, Master Gobries struck me because I had fallen asleep in my boots. I stood and turned my back to him and lowered my head toward the others. In the frozen air the stroke on the back of my neck was almost loving, opening out like a brush of fire and warming me to the roots of my hair. *This is pain*, I thought. It was warm and reminded me of the feeling in my tongue and lips after I had eaten Evmeni peppers. *Where is the rest of the pain?* I thought. I went and joined my line and felt that I was warm and more comfortable than the others.

"You looked like a demon," Vars said to me later, admiringly. "You looked as if you could strangle him with a curtain." And I was astonished because I had not felt the desire to kill him but only wonder, and disappointment because I could not find the pain.

That night there was a celebration for those who were going to Braith and we were invited into the masters' drawing room. A fire blazed on the hearth and we were given teiva and honitha and permitted to argue and organize games in the courtyard. I ate my honith too quickly, the cheese scalded the roof of my mouth. I stood by the wall and watched the clusters of those leaving for Braith. They wore clean scarlet sashes and stood carelessly, a foot propped on the fender or a loose hand waving a pipe. One of them looked at me strangely, suspiciously, and then he realized who I was and smoothed the lines out of his face. I smiled at him. Of course, if Aunt Mardith had come, it meant everything was in the papers, they would have heard of me everywhere. The man looked away from me, stretching his legs. Because of my high rank, he would not shout. He would not stand up and say: *"A woman? Here?"* He would not even stare at the young soldier he had just recognized as Tavis of Ashenlo, the Telkan's niece.

Outside the night was cold and there were screams where boys were running in the torchlight, a ball skidding across the stones. I went upstairs and down the gloomy hallway, counting the doors to reach my own. Inside it was dark with a smell of boots, there was no one there. I knelt on my bed and opened the shutters. The window was so small that I could barely rest both elbows on the sill. The cold wind blew, the night was immense and silent, and the peaks of snow shone rich as curdled milk under the moon.

Dear Siski, I wrote, *I wish I were going to die at Braith.* I wrote this inside my swordbox as there was no paper in the room. I thought I would use it later, but when we had passed to the second grade, and they let us write letters for the first time, I no longer wished to die. And by that time it seemed impossible to write to Siski, to come up with answers to her letters crammed with parties and flirtations, and if I wrote to Mother, I knew she would cry. So I wrote to Dasya instead. *You should join the army. There's good fun up here.*

In the mountains in winter the peaks disappeared in the air, so vast and white that they became part of the sky. We craved warmth like bread, we fought the frozen trees for kindling and at night the hills were dotted with small red lights. It was a foolish way to camp and when the Brogyars came they slid down on us screaming and hurling their heavy axes toward our fires, and we ran and slipped and ran again and turning to fight I saw like a burst of shooting stars a sudden fountain of teeth. They scattered beside me, and there was an axe in the snow and a faceless man. The trees shrank, a blue light shuddered over the snow. The Brogyar was huge, an inarticulate figure of hair and shadow, and it was only his own weight that pushed my sword through his leather armor. He fell heavily and twisted my wrist and the sound of his harsh breathing became mine as I struggled to turn him and free the sword. There were black shapes and red shapes, sudden screaming and wet snow soaking through at my knees, and we were all running toward the gorge. Sparks flew over the snow, we ran like beasts for the thin forest. Kestau turned back for his sword and an axe removed one of his arms. It happened as if on a stage, there was a white expanse and a glow from one of the fires and black blood spouting, and he fell. Someone was screaming in the gorge. A Brogyar rushed to Kestau and knelt to cut his throat, bent over and wrapped in scarves like an old washerwoman. I thought I saw the flash of the knife. And only when they were gone did we find Vars lying in the gorge with a broken leg.

Then I realized that I was warm at last, as we were dragging the bodies into a heap, making long dark tracks, and afterward as we were burying them while the sun came up and the scene of the ambush appeared, ashes and blood in the snow. Vars fainted when they set his leg and Nirai stood above him making a list of the dead and wounded in the White Book. Most of us were smoking. Odra squeezed my shoulder, squinting in the light, and said: "Now you've tasted iron."

That was the world of the mountains where we stumbled endlessly in the snow, dragging the wounded on sleds of wood and hide, always trying to meet another line of the army that never arrived or waiting for them in the ice-blue winter forests. We were always late or early. If we met them at all, the captains would scream at each other and throw their caps down in the snow. The rest of us sat in silence, watching. At night I wriggled down in my sleeping sack and thought of horses. The horses were marching across the sky and I saw that this was the swordmaiden's life, filth and starvation and cold and the hills to come. When I couldn't sleep I would get up and offer to take sentry duty for someone or smoke with Odra who also slept poorly and often sat up counting the stars.

"I've lost the talent for sleep," he would say, and despite the cold he would pull down his scarf and show me the lines on his neck, running his finger along the grooves. I could see the scars clearly in the starlight reflected from the snow and he would tell me how he had awakened to find a Brogyar at his throat.

"Sarma preserved my life, but at a price," he would say, resettling the scarf. "A priestess told me that the goddess had taken my sleep. What she wants with it I don't know, but it's true enough that it's gone. I don't mind, my life will be twice as long as the lives of men who sleep."

When the snow fell we were forced to march so as not to be buried by morning and we tramped in the whirling darkness side by side, Odra and I with the straps over our shoulders pulling Vars on the sled and whenever we stopped to smoke Odra would talk. He told me about his daughters in the Balinfeil who were both unmarried weavers. The elder one rolled her stockings down because they pinched her knees, and Odra was sorry for her because she was *moik*—a Nainish word meaning silly or strange. "My life, my poor *moikyalen*," he said. I laughed, and his gaze deepened in the faint glow of our pipes. He asked me if I felt well and I nodded and made myself stop laughing. Beyond the rock where we sheltered there was a blackness filled with screams where all the gods unknown to us had been released. And we would plunge into it and be pursued by those black winds and find ourselves up to our thighs or armpits in snow, and struggle out of it again and shout to the others and turn and get entangled with those who had failed to receive the order. "The dance of the mountains," Dasya called it later, with a sneer. And truly it was like being part of a dance. It was like a dance in a dream in which one had a part but did not know what it was, a dance of strange and dreadful figures. When I was convalescent I had a dream of a splendid ball in an unfamiliar house: my partner was a woman with a tall headdress, with much black paint around her eyes and in one figure she gave a graceful bow and clasped the top of her hair and removed her head from her neck. That was a dream about the mountains, it showed the life of the mountains, that new life. At times we were seized by a sudden and absolute happiness. It happened most often when we were beating back an attack and then we howled and dismembered the bodies, choking with joy.

There was joy, too, when we sighted villages in the gorges: a glimpse of cottages huddled among the pines and snow, and sometimes even a light or two through the cracks in the ancient shutters or a lantern wavering toward a dark mud barn. Then we would come down shouting. They were lost villages abandoned by priests with names like Waldivo and Unisk and Bar-Hathien, separated by blizzards so that they thought they belonged to something larger, forgetting that each had only ten or twelve families. So there was High Unisk and many leagues away, Low Unisk. Dark villages where they melted the snow because the wells were frozen. The peasants were pale and heavy in their movements and wore amulets of straw and some could hardly converse in the common tongue. The women sat in the corners and wept or hovered around their few possessions, muttering, guarding the old tin pitchers and apples of colored wax, while the men sat on the floor morosely wrapping and unwrapping the linen strips they wore in layers around their legs. Sometimes there were immobile children lying in osier cradles. We sat by the fires and smoked the peasants' winter stores of tobacco, we drank their gaisk until the firelight swam with secret signs, we made them slaughter their beasts and give up their flour and potatoes.

In one village there was only a donkey and everyone gathered to weep for it. Vars said: "If they take any longer I'll murder the beast myself." His leg was still bad then and he was lying against the wall and sweating; his face was pinched and exhausted and I could see that he needed the meat. The room was full of people, it was warm although the door was open and more were crowded around the donkey outside. A stinking old man, perhaps a village elder, in a sheep's-bladder cap, offered up uncouth prayers to the gods of the hills. I pushed my way to Odra and asked him what they were praying about and he turned on me, tears glinting in the lines on his face, and swore at me, what did I think, the last animal in the village and we were killing it. The women had covered their heads with coarse wool shawls. And firelight shone on the wooden shutters with rags stuffed in the chinks and on the broken lantern hanging on the wall, and beneath the smells of dirty skin and hair and ill-cured leather and burnt potatoes there was the delicious odor of carrots. These were the villages of our desires where we would sleep at last and feel a pleasure even in vomiting gaisk and donkey meat: how clear the air was when I retched outside the door on the crust of snow and saw a few bird prints there, like writing.

When I was made captain they gave me a horse, a brown mare called Loma. She was quiet and strong and reminded me of Meis, and how Siski had said that Meis's neck always smelled of strawberries so that one could pick her out in a dark stable. Sometimes at night I stood and put my face against Loma's neck, closing my eyes to shut out the strange glow of the hills. Perhaps another soldier, also sitting awake, would begin in a mournful voice to recite a sein of the *Vallafarsi* such as "The Kingdoms." *Balinu, whence cometh fruit.*

As always this phrase reminded me of the ring my mother wore on a chain at her throat. Something had happened to me, perhaps I had fallen or been scolded by Malino and she was comforting me by showing me her ring. She unfastened the chain and showed me how the opening phrase of the sein was engraved inside the ring, in both Olondrian and Nainish. Her soft hands, the side of her dress, on the table an ancient knife with a chipped handle. Outside the fruit fell from the trees.

I clung to Loma's neck in the storm that almost buried us in the Month of Lamps. I screamed at my men, for there was a village below us, all dark, and we left the sick and wounded on the rise and rushed down on the houses and broke the doors open and shattered the rotting shutters with our sword hilts. Rotting, the shutters were rotting and the beds inside were strewn with rotten sheets. We stumbled into the empty silence of the rooms. Even the cellars were empty and at last we gathered and stared at one another, trailing our clean swords in the snow.

"It's deserted," Vars said hoarsely. Suddenly I could hear him and I realized we were sheltered from the wind, in the lovely sleeping village with the blueness of the snow at night. The stars were breaking the darkness one by one. The others were looking at me and I spoke gently, hearing my own voice without screaming for the first time in seven days. "Bring the others down," I said. My voice came out so beautifully, simple and full of reason in the silence. Later the same voice said softly and clearly: "Kill the horse." She was the last one, I did not need to say her name. She was the one who ended the habit of thinking about horses, Tuik had not been able to end it but it ended that night with Loma. After we had eaten I thought, I will have to choose something else to think of at night. It did not worry me, I felt sure I would think of something. We were all together in one house and warm at last with a fire of broken furniture crackling on the hearth.

Softly the snow fell, and the men died softly. We dragged them out and buried them in the snow, for the earth was frozen. They died against the walls of the cottage in attitudes of sleep, their cheeks faded and their hair brittle with frost. Those of us who were well enough would totter into the brightness, seeking firewood, tugging feebly at doors and shutters. Once Vars and I came back together, and Odra, lying against the wall with his eyes very bright, said something about the sea and its thousands of angels.

"Don't talk, Uncle," Vars told him. "Save your strength."

And Odra breathing quietly gave a bright and secretive smile. It hung motionless on his bloodless face so long that I thought he had died with it, and I bent and shook him roughly by the shoulder. But no, he was not dead. He died much later and before he died he made us listen to him and obey his orders, swearing at us, cursing us because his blanket was caught beneath his arm and because he could not bear the diet of snow and horseflesh.

"Take me out," he snapped. "This air, a man can't breathe in here. Look." He slapped his neck and rolled a louse between forefinger and thumb. "Look at this filth. These aren't soldiers, they're animals." And we carried him out and built a fire for him under the pines.

The low red flames, the blackness of the earth under melted snow, Vars hunched miserably in his dirty jacket, and Odra in his blankets propped against a tree, thin-lipped with scorn, staring out at the hills, at the snow that trapped us. His voice was harsh, he spoke of his seventeen years in the mountains and pulled down his scarf to show us his scarred neck. "A man is not expected to live for more than three years up here," he said. "But I've lived nearly twenty and killed more men than the fever. They took me into Amafein six years ago and gave me the Order of the Bear, my daughter has it in her basket at home. The duke himself presented it and we were sixty-eight at table that night and everything paid for by the Olondrian Empire."

He drew his breath in sharply, sucked his teeth and darted a glance at me. "Yes, I remember, you're the Telkan's niece. You're his niece through both Houses and nobody ever mentions it and most

of the men are afraid to speak to you as to an equal. Even you"—
he jerked his grizzled chin at Vars—"you're some sort of nobleman but you're afraid to approach her ladyship, really approach her.
Only I am not afraid and that's because I know my worth and I'd
proven my worth ten times before you were weaned."

He stopped abruptly and leaned against the tree. Something
went flying overhead, perhaps an eagle, its blue shadow streaking
the snow. And then he began to speak again in bitterness, cursing
the Telkan and this war that was not even a war. For many days he
cursed us and then suddenly he stopped, he grew listless and no
longer demanded to be taken outside, but we still took him out for
Vars insisted the air would do him good. And we built a fire and sat
with him in silence.

Sitting there, I breathed on my cold gloves and tried to find
a train of thought I could use to sleep at night. I tried so many,
and finally I found that simply letting my mind drift was often the
quickest way to the dark. I remembered Siski singing "The Swallow in Winter." She was standing with her hands clasped and her
thin feet on the rug. There was the knocking sound of Uncle Veda
emptying his pipe and I was watching her mouth as it opened and
closed. *Poor lost bird, you flit from place to place but cannot find your home.*
The green curtains in the parlor smelled of tents. Yes, and under
the chair we found a dagger and an ivory comb. On the sheath of
the dagger, a drawing of Tevlas in spring.

All at once I realized that Odra was saying something, he was
saying "No, let's stay here a little longer." And it was night, and
the stars had come out thickly within the circle of the peaks: they
pulsed in the dark, as if trying to break through.

"That's a beautiful sky," said Odra dreamily, "it reminds me of
the song, *Let's stay a little longer, the evening is so fair.*"

"Then you're feeling better, Uncle," Vars said eagerly. His teeth
were chattering and the firelight flashed up strangely on his face.

When he said these words, Odra began to weep. He was lying
on his side and the tears coursed down his gaunt creased face. "My

poor *moikyalen*," he sobbed.

He wept for a long time. Vars was biting his lips and tears were on his cheeks. Then Odra grew calmer and smiled. He reached out feebly and Vars seized his gloved hand and pulled the glove off, pressing the rough hand to his lips.

"You're a good child," said Odra. Then he raised his head with difficulty and looked at me, stretching out his other hand. "You're a good child too," he smiled, "but why are you so shy?" I had taken his hand, I was kneeling by him in the snow. Vars was weeping openly and I looked at Odra's face in the light of the fire, searching his eyes which were like two coins.

"He's dead," I said.

Vars was sobbing, bending over the corpse to kiss the sunken cheeks, pressing his living brow to the brow of the dead, and then he rose and rushed into the drifts, thrashing his arms, snatching snow in his hands and hurling it into the dark. While he leaped and screamed I closed the dead man's eyes and stripped the body, piling the boots and clothes to be sent to the daughters in the south. And very poor and small he looked when he was laid out naked on the snow. And we left him there in a tomb of ice.

"You could, if you wanted to," Vars whispered to me later. "You could get us all released with honor. You could send to some-one, maybe not the Telkan himself, but someone."

"No," I told him, "it's not true, there's no one."

"Yes, there must be," he insisted in a breaking voice.

I found that I was smiling at the ceiling. "That's the strange thing," I said. "Sometimes I can hardly believe it myself. But in fact, there is no one."

He turned his face to the wall and began to moan. And I lay ordering my thoughts while someone stirred and shuffled his feet and someone else kicked Vars and whined for silence, and I put my thoughts in categories such as Games and History and tried to choose something to think about. The memory of Dasya among the pillars beckoned, black eyes, bright face. But no, that thought was too strong and would keep me awake. Instead I thought of the Ethenmanyi and going to visit our grandmother's house in a country not very far from the Lelevai. It was not far, but how different it was! I remembered going with Mother and Siski in spring with all of our finest clothes in trunks, and wearing my new green traveling cloak as we jolted along the mountain road with the sunlight flickering through the carriage windows. Always there were things to see in the hills, the narrow gorges and then apricot trees in flower among the rocks, and the funny herders' cottages whose thatched roofs came down almost to the ground, and the children selling milk from pails. We stopped at Mirov and then at Noi. After that the road began to slope downward and the enormous valley opened below the mists, and Mother grew suddenly pensive, letting her jeweled prayer book fall into her lap and watching the land drift by. I believe there is no country more beautiful than the Balinfeil in spring. Great meadows slumbered beneath the soft pink haze of the fruit trees. We would see again the straight white houses standing up with their conical roofs and the fat tame musk deer tied to fence posts. There were the graceful and ordered fields separated by bands of sunflowers, and the peasants' houses almost smothered in bushes of dark pink aimila. Also the smell, peculiar and fresh, drawn from the mountain winds, and also the strange and inescapable silence.

It was the silence more than anything else that showed me we had arrived. Waking at night in an unfamiliar bed in a roadside inn, I would become aware that although the window was open, the world was sleeping so soundly that there was no noise at all. No dogs barked, no midnight horseman jingled by on an errand. Even the mattress, firmly stuffed with goose feathers, did not crackle beneath me like the leaf and straw-stuffed mattresses of Kestenya. And there were no night guards playing kib on the doorstep. I am in the Balinfeil, I thought. And for a long time it was a pleasant thought, like the thought of an adventure: it meant that I would play with my cousins and eat honitha and watch the puppet shows and laugh as my uncles danced the klugh. And ride the fat and stupid pony Mertha, whom I liked to treat with scorn, assuring the stable hands that she was nothing to Nusha. And allow Hauth the assistant cook to terrify me with tales of the Bilbil crawling out of the hearth to make mischief at night. But after several summers had passed I no longer woke to the silence with that feeling of excitement: rather my heart sank. Ah, I'm in the Balinfeil, I thought, and the stillness of the inn and the roads and countryside in the dark oppressed me.

Even the inns, where we were awakened early by the severe bright ringing of a bell and the sheets and tablecloths shone with a daunting whiteness, even these seemed to possess the watchful and disapproving air of our grandmother's house, of our own house, Faluidhen. That mansion of eighty-two rooms in which the important halls were known by color, Nainish-fashion. The silver room and the lilac room and the gray. The blue room where my Uncle Brola had died and still communicated by slamming the shutters viciously when it rained. The rooms opened southward whenever possible and the north side was shut against the summer dust and the ruthless winter winds: a dreary arbor of birch and cypress and winter plum survived there, along with the old iron chair where my grandfather used to sit. This chair was wrought with curious forms of dragons, dogs and rabbits and stranger creatures, goat-headed lions and winged dolphins. It stood alone beneath the trees, a little away from the house, covered with dust and dried leaves. Siski cleaned it off with the hem of her skirt. Beside it stood the timeworn brazier with which our grandfather had warmed himself in the winter months, where we once made a fire with the idea of roasting nuts and Dasya burned his arm and Siski blew on the injured spot to cool it. Dasya did not tell anyone but sat very stiff and pale through dinner, saying nothing and eating with his left hand. The next day the old brazier was blacker than ever as if it had never been used. "There must be a curse on it," Siski said. And Dasya said that if it was cursed, so much the better, for we had gone to that strange place on the north side to play Drevedi, knowing that no one would look for us in our dead grandfather's lonely patch of trees on the unlucky side of the house. Siski sat on the chair: she was Oline, the Dreved of Dolomesse. Dasya was always the Dreved of Amafein. Usually they made me a soldier or peasant or ill-destined king to be put to death repeatedly under the trees.

Afterward we went back to the house and into the silver room where the adults sat talking quietly in groups. Their chairs and couches seemed so far away, under the lamps. "How restless you children are," Grandmother called. And sometimes everyone was restless or the weather was hot and we would go for an evening walk around the grounds, walking up and down the rows of flowers and along the pitch-dark banks of ivy, which gave off a bitter scent. Down the avenue of limes, everyone keeping to Grandmother's pace. Voices floating in the evening hush. "Why don't you keep dogs?" said a visiting neighbor, and Grandmother said, "My dear boy, because we are not under siege." And when we turned we saw the lights of Faluidhen in the darkness of the grounds, and working by smell I found my way to Mother's dress. I touched the folds of cotton and took her hand. "Is that you, my love?" she whispered, squeezing my fingers. "Come and walk with Mother."

Later I thought of Dasya, when it seemed that I would never have the chance to think of anything again. At first I thought: *How tired my arms are!*—and I was glad my sword had spun away and lay distant in the snow. Yes, and it was pleasant simply to lie there with my arms at rest in the dazzling whiteness, flung back on the slope. The others seemed suddenly quiet, they had lowered their voices as if they were talking privately and did not wish to disturb me. The swords struck one another with a tinny sound, like that of children playing at dakavei in a neighboring courtyard. The air was fresh and sparkled in my lungs and then the Brogyar rose up suddenly and blocked the brilliant sun, and a moment later when his face grew clearer I recognized his sagging eyelid and his mouthful of rotting teeth. So then I had not killed him. He was breathing raggedly and the sound thrilled me, for he was close now, very close. His hair stuck out from underneath his cap, it had no color except at the edges where the sunlight made it glow. I noticed the iron studs along his leather jerkin where his coat fell open and I could see his gilded belt when he raised his arms. Then the arms descended, and there was pain. There it was, it was the pain of which I had heard, it had arrived. It was the rest of the pain which I had waited for when I had fallen from my horse or been struck by the masters at the school, it had simply been waiting for me too and now it stepped from behind a screen, clad in majesty like the body of a god. When I could breathe again I opened my eyes and saw the Brogyar through a veil of light and he was smiling at me, and I knew his smile for it was the smile of the mountains. There, his eyes were alight, he was biting his lip, unable to speak for joy.

Soon he would laugh as we had laughed as children in the inner courtyard of the school when the door was raised and the pigs came clattering in, their smooth backs and bobbing ears passing us in the torchlight as we stood trembling and holding our bare swords. "A pig screams like a man," we had been told by Master Gobries that afternoon, "and also he has flesh similar to man's." We struck them clumsily across the eyes and along their bony heads and they cried out as the blood began to flow. And after a moment we began to laugh. A tall boy slipped in the blood and fell and Vars had a stripe of black gore on his cheek. When we caught one another's eyes we crouched with impossible laughter while an unearthly clamor of woe rose to the sky. Stumbling over bodies, sliding, chasing the last survivors. At that moment I thought, *Joy is one of the secrets of war.* And now I saw that exultation on the Brogyar's face and thought, *He is going to kill me. This is death.*

And if it was death, then why not think of dancing in the avla, of my mother's ring, of milk, of Uncle Veda? But only one thing came to me and it did not come with pleasure but with regret, such

sharp regret that my eyes flooded with sudden tears. I remembered
our camp along the Firda, near the end of autumn, when the sable
geese were flying in long arcs. The wind came from the north bringing the gusts of early snow and there were dark leaves massed on
the surface of the river. I went up to the hills alone. Riding along
the stony paths I heard the wind as it sang in the dry grasses, bat-
tering the little oaks so that they threw their acorns to the ground.
A few hawk-apples withered on the crags. And I was lonely and
happy going up to where the snow lay in the grass, urging my
horse through the rocky passes, camping by myself under the trees,
making my fire and cooking beans and drinking bitter gaisk from a
flask. Sitting by my campfire I would take the letter out of my coat
and read it again while the pines creaked in the wind. *If it is possible
make haste for I have much to tell you that I cannot write and will not be able
to say in front of others* . . . Deep blue skies with the mountains sharp
against them and a sad twilight that promised an icy storm out of
the north, and I was riding upward with my mantle wrapped about
me when I saw the first broken pillars, gray in the dusk.

A smell came toward me, stone walls under the rain. There was
a hissing sound and rain streaked down my hood and over my face.
I had not seen Dasya in four years. There were no lights in the
school and I supposed they had camped beyond it in the gorge.
But a red glow touched the old pillars of the temple. I rode in
through the archway, throwing back my hood in the sharp thunder
of hooves on the stone, the sounds of the snorting horse and the
jingling reins enormous under the lofty roof, and then I had slipped
from her back, and he was there.

We greeted one another in whispers, standing back from our
embrace to stare, and then he laughed and shook my shoulders.
And I was laughing too. "Tav," he said. There was a fire on the floor
and a bottle of Nainish wine on the stone table.

"*Vai*, my life," he said. He looked older and he had put on flesh
and he moved with energy like an athlete, a soldier. He sat on the
table and rested his feet on the bench and put the bottle between

his knees to open it and passed it to me, and I drank.

"So you're alive," he said. He was still laughing and I thought how proud and joyful he seemed in his scarlet tunic trimmed with gold, and how as always he wore such finery easily, careless of how the wine dripped on his rich Feirini velvet. He passed the bottle to me again. My cloak steamed in the warmth. And we spoke of the war and our regiments and our losses, and that was when he sneered and spoke to me of the dance of the mountains and his laugh turned hard and rattled in the dark hall. For he had been at Gena when a regiment of new recruits had died in a snowstorm under the Miveri Pass. "They swallowed the snow," he said. He waved his hand. "They just lay down and it closed over them. They were lying in rows like corn . . ."

We passed our bitterness back and forth, our years in the Lelevai, Dasya listing the errors of Uncle Gishas and Prince Ruaf: "Stupid old men," he said, "who only wish to prolong the war because they're tired of life at home and burdened with debts." And we did not speak of the past, which seemed so distant now, but only of the future. His strange pallor in the firelight, his brooding eyes. "All this death," he whispered. "It's as if we're eating—eating them. These men. As if Olondria can't stop eating."

We were sitting against the wall. The bottle rolled on the flags. I searched inside my jacket for my leather flask. I opened it and drank. The gaisk was strong and had a flavor of bruised grass and cleared the air of uncertainty. I looked at the smooth flames of the fire piercing the air in long clean waves and the shining bottle empty on the floor, and I thought of the dance of the mountains and how it had gone on since the days of worshiping milk, the same steps over and over. Generations now in rows like corn. And with a twinge, a shift in my heart, I thought of Olondria for the first time. I thought of it as a living thing, not a place to go or settle but a vast entity that grew and breathed and ate. Faluidhen in summer, all those rooms of empty luxury, and then, in Kestenya, the feredha tents pitched on Uncle Veda's land. Uncle Veda sweating with fury, shouting: "Call me a traitor to Olondria if you like, these people have nowhere else to go. Nowhere, nowhere, we've hounded them into the waste and waterless places, it is a crime and Olondria must answer."

"Olondria must answer," I said.

And Dasya turned to me in eagerness and whispered: "Yes, you see it, you're not afraid."

But I was afraid, and I laughed and my hands were shaking for I knew his mind and that once lit it burned like a dragon's entrails. I heard myself speaking, half frightened at my own words: "Why should we die for these hills, when we might die for an independent Kestenya?" I said the words in Kestenyi: *Kestenya Rukebnar*. Forbidden words. And Dasya went pale and then red, and his grip on my arm was fire. And lying in the snow with the axe flashing again in the sun I wept because I had lost the chance to die that way, because I was dying in the mountains after all, dismembered in the snow, because I was dying the death of a pig. And in the spring, I realized, I had planned to leave the army, but I did not know it until I lay under the axe. The plan had created itself in the dark of my mind and only now had it come to light, and I recognized it, and I wept. For I had thought to go down to Ashenlo and to the plains. And now, I saw, I would bleed to death in the snow. And all Kestenya blazed before me, flashing across the blue-gray sky, the desert like a ray among the clouds. The axe bit my thigh as the Brogyar fell, pierced by arrows, but the pain could not erase that gleaming sight. And still it glows before me and I see those shining mountains in another landscape, and in another war.

2. Loyalty Like a Necklace of Dead Stars

The swordmaiden will rise each day with the knowledge of her death. This death is a fair coin, which must be spent for a worthy purpose.

It is said that the sword is nobler than the arrow, because the sword extends the body, and to fight with it is to dance. It is said that the sword becomes its bearer's soul. Thul the Heretic only believed in his body because he saw it reflected in his sword. In the Temple of Tol, it is common to say: "O Scarred God forever gone a-hunting, Thou has left me the pin from Thy hair."

This pin, claim the priests, is the sword.

Such ideas are poetry and not history. The sword maims and kills. Evil is its essence.

The swordmaiden will hold evil in one hand, or, if she fights with a Nainish blade, in both. Consider then the purpose of each stroke. Maris the Crooked was asked on her deathbed: "What led you to turn against your king?" She answered: "Ask the women of Oululen." This was a people who had been destroyed by the armies of King Thul: it is written that "their very names became dust." When the men of Oululen had perished, the women took up arms. The last of them died defending herself with a harrow.

The swordmaiden wears her loyalty like a necklace of dead stars. Their worth is eternal, although they no longer shine.

Maris was a renegade general, Galaron a rebel, the False Countess a bandit. Which of these now reclines on a couch of light?

∞

When I came down from the hills that rainy spring with a shattered thigh they had already sent most of the servants away, and the east and north wings of the house had been shut off and locked and the unused keys hung in a row in Mother's cabinet. Even from the window of the carriage the house and grounds looked lonelier, as if an expected visitor had failed to arrive. At the time I thought the gloom was caused by the unseasonable rain that dripped from the eaves and darkened the sand in the court.

Mother came out to greet me with a shawl over her head, tripping lightly across the mud in her felt slippers. "Oh Fulmia," she cried, "have you brought her?"

"Yes, sudaidi," Fulmia called, "and the two of us can take her, she weighs no more than a chicken."

"Don't be a fool," I said. "Get Fodok and Gastin."

Mother had climbed into the carriage and she knelt beside me and kissed my cheeks and brow. Her hair was loose and her face was wet with rain or tears and she wanted to embrace me but since I was lying down she could only squeeze my shoulders.

"Drive on," Fulmia shouted.

Mother's shawl had slipped and fallen onto my chest. The carriage shifted, getting closer to the door.

"Don't try to lift me yourselves," I said. Her hair blocked the light and the pallor that was her face moved slightly as she raised her hand to her eyes.

"Do you hear her, Fulmia?" she sobbed. "She says we're not to do it alone, we must bring Gastin. Call him, Fulmia. Call Gastin."

The carriage stopped, the doors opened, and as they eased me out the rain dropped on my face and I blinked in the cold rain-light.

The servants gathered by the door, the children staring at me and sucking their fingers as I was carried across the court. "Don't let me fall in this mud," I said, and everyone laughed. They carried me under the lintel into the warm air of the amadesh. There was the same soft yellow glow and the odor of roasting apples and I closed my eyes and let my head roll against Gastin's shirt; I could hear him breathing and feel him gripping me carefully as they took me down the hall where there was less light. I opened my eyes.

"Not so quickly," Mother was saying.

"And look at your slippers!" Nenya cried. "All over the carpets too."

At the end of the hall stood Father. He stood very straight at the foot of the stairs where the glassed-in porch opened into the hall and looked down on me sternly and held his pipe. As we lurched past he turned his head aside and muttered something. I craned my neck as we started up the stairs, catching a glimpse of his slightly rounded back and the shawl about his shoulders as he went back to the gray light of the porch.

I lay in that room all through the spring and they brought up my meals on a tray. Outside a milky froth of blossoms came out on the trees, pink and then white, and I rested propped on pillows and watched the changes in the section of orchard visible from my window. When it rained Mother came and read to me, her voice keeping back the thunder. We read Hodis the Solitary and *Tales from the White Branch*, and the whole *Romance of the Valley* and a number of similar stories, all the tales I had loved and listened to as a child. Mother searched in Malino's old library for the books and she would burst into my room with a happy cry, with dust and cobwebs in her hair, brandishing a book whose leather binding had split and was hanging down in strips.

"Look at this, you loved this one!"

At such times she reminded me so much of Siski that I was almost startled. She leaned in the doorway, laughing, wiping the book on her skirt. Once my father shouted from the foot of the steps, "Firheia!" And as she called back a promise of silence, her eyes twinkled just like Siski's.

She crossed the carpet noiselessly in her slippers and sat in the chair beside my bed. "Look, you remember this one, don't you?"

The book had fallen open at a picture of the boy Istiwin watching the Queen of the Bears emerge from the hill. His round eyes, his hands thrown up in horror. At his feet crouched the ragged, long-eared hare we had named Atsi as children.

"You don't feel well," Mother said. Her hand was cool against my cheek, her face reflected in the bowl of the lamp.

"No, I'm fine," I said. She smoothed her skirt out on the chair, the same brown velvet skirt she had worn seven years before. Now the golden pattern in it was faded and the swirling leaves could only be seen in the lamplight on her knee.

"What's happened to the forests?" I said.

She frowned and turned the pages, biting her lip. Then she said: "Let's not talk about that now."

"I know he's sold them," I said. "To Uncle Fenya."

She turned another page. "Please not now, the doctor says you must rest."

I turned my head on the pillow and looked at her, her wide sad eyes and the delicate skin around them where blue shadows lay. She tried to smile. She did not look like Siski anymore but only like herself. She turned back to the book and tried to find her place. And I thought of her through all those years at the table in her sitting room, her neat accounts, everything slipping away from her like sand. I thought that she must have put her head down sometimes in despair and rested her forehead on the glass of her writing table, and as she had done so I had moved through snow on horseback, killing, killing, watching men die for the glory of Olondria. It seemed right to me that the house was in decay, the avla shut up. I remembered earlier times, and what we had called "the unrest": how we rode across the bridge on the Oun and heard an insolent song in the meadow: "*Down goes the house! Fire, fire, fire!*" I don't think we knew they meant our house. The song was in Kestenyi and we were Kestenyi, Dasya and Siski and I. But to be Kestenyi, I thought, no longer hearing my mother's voice, it can't mean the blood you're given, it must mean how you give your blood away.

Give it away. But not to Uncle Fenya, who acted for Aunt Mardith, obeying her orders, pouring our precious forests into her coffers. I wanted to shout: *Don't you see how we're changing masters? The Laths have ruled Kestenya with swords and the Nains will rule it with gold.* But I couldn't say it. Not when Ashenlo had been my mother's life. Not when this was her work: finding a way to pay the herdboys, to have the carriage repaired, to scrounge up decent clothes for Siski and me as our father sold everything to pay for the bolma he ordered from the south. As he sat like a king in his glassed-in porch. He was the true son of a traitor, the heir of my grandfather who had signed the Treaty of Tevlas. Thinking of it, rage filled me and I ached to crawl out of bed, to hurl myself down the stairs and accuse him to his face. *You. You.* You have supported my grandfather's act of treason, that disgusting treaty that crushed Kestenya's chance at independence. And now you're selling Ashenlo to the Nains so that you can stuff yourself with bolma. I twisted in the bed and my mother touched my brow.

"You're warm," she said. Her hand was as soft as gauze. I closed my eyes and remembered the forest, driving out there in the winter long ago. I remembered Mother exclaiming how hard the servants must have worked to clear the road. "Oh, you shouldn't have," she said.

"First you complain that I do nothing for the children," Father said, "and then you complain about what I do."

"No, I don't mean to complain." She put her hand on his arm and he shrugged it off and turned and shouted, "Who can see the Snow Horses, eh? Who's seen them?"

We crowded to the sides of the wagon and gazed at the snowy stillness of the wood, and the shadows of trees moved over us like the shadows of bars, and the trees themselves stood arched above the road or glided by like sentries deep in the long blue corridors of night. The horses kicked up mist and the wagon jolted. In the carriage behind us men were singing, the little red lantern swinging in the dark. "Go on," Father shouted. Some of the children were playing in the straw and Mun Karalei was afraid they would burn themselves on the bricks. "She hisses like a gander," Siski said. We stood close in the smell of our coats and looked for alien hoof-prints where the moonlight fell. The wagon stuck when the horses turned and everyone had to get out. Uncle Veda carried Siski on his back.

"Come on, Meisye, pull," she screamed, kicking her feet in excitement, her thin legs flashing in a shaft of moonlight.

"Please don't let her down," said Mother, "she'll soak her stockings and catch a chill."

"My dear," Uncle Veda said, "she's stuck to me like a crab."

While they struggled with the wagon I wrestled Dasya in the snow and struck my face on a hidden root and began to bleed, and I fell asleep on the drive back to the house and the snow they had pressed against my eye slid down my face and soaked my collar. I woke groggily under the lights of the house. They seemed so high, as if the windows opened onto the stars.

"Look up there," I said.

"Yes my darling," Mother said, but it was Father who held me and carried me up the steps.

"Take care how you play," he told Dasya. "She's only a girl." In the hall everyone was laughing and giving their coats and furs to the footmen.

"Acres of trees," said Uncle Fenya. "It's a silent fortune. I congratulate you." Firelight filled the mirrors.

Late that summer, I woke in the night to a pounding on the stairs, an urgent clatter that could only mean Siski had come.

"I'm awake," I called.

"You see," she cried. She dashed into the room and threw her traveling case down in the corner. And then she was kneeling beside my bed and had flung her head down on my chest and her arms in the tight black coat were about my shoulders.

"Oh, it's me, it's me," she said. "You didn't think I was coming but I came. I'm sure I got here faster than a letter. I came all the way from Nauve without stopping once, we slept in the carriage."

Nenya came in with a candle and lit the lamp, grumbling. "It's not the way to treat an invalid, disturbing her rest." Light flared up, revealing Siski's sharp, pale face.

"Don't look at me, I'm the image of death," Siski said, tucking her hair behind her ear. Her coat was dusty, one button hanging. "I came so fast I'm wearing all the wrong clothes. It's warm here, isn't it? Oh Taviye, we're home again and it's going to be delightful!"

Looking at her I could see that she believed it. "No, don't look at me," she said. "Do I look older? Yes, I must, I'm five years older. And you, you're lovely but so thin."

I did not know if she looked older, but certainly she looked different in some indefinable way. Her hair had fallen down on one side, but her embroidered collar gave her an air of refinement and hidden wealth. It was a Nainish look, and her face despite the narrowness and the tiredness had a new and elegant cast.

"We'll do anything you like," she said. "Riding, bathing, anything. Can you get up?"

When I told her I could not, she put her hand over my eyes.

"What am I seeing?" I asked her, smiling. An old game. Her voice came clearly and with a fierce undertone: "It's our rowboat on the Oun."

"We couldn't row on the Oun right now," I said. "It'll be dry."

"You're not playing right. You're supposed to see it."

"All right," I said. "I see it."

And I did. Sun on the chipped white paint, sunlight on the water under leaves.

The next morning I realized Kethina had come as well. As soon as I saw her, I knew what had made the difference in Siski's face. The two of them came in together, Siski in yellow, Kethina in rose. They had washed their hair and tied up the long damp plaits. "For the heat," Kethina explained. "It's not hot now but later we'll be so glad we put our hair up early, believe me." She bent and pricked my cheek with her arrow-shaped mouth. Her fingers strayed in my hair. "So pretty! Siski, you never told me about her hair. Almost blue—a real mulberry black."

She turned, sighing, swinging her arms. "So what are we going to do?"

"What about breakfast?" Siski said.

"Splendid!" Kethina cried, snatching Siski's shoulders. She pressed her brow to Siski's, her eyes laughing. For a moment they whirled with their foreheads together, giggling, their fresh gowns lifting and swaying around them. "What would I do without you? I'd never eat!" Kethina cried. "But now I'm terribly hungry. What shall we have? Please not fish or cucumbers."

"Let's go down to the amadesh and see," said Siski.

"We'll be back to report," Kethina cried out over her shoulder. And they were gone in a patter of pale house slippers and bubbling laughter and floating gowns and scent, and that was the way they were all summer. Laughing in corners, embracing one another and making journeys which, from what they said, were always perfection itself. On the journeys they wore wide hats and carried baskets. They would come home dusted with chalk from the hills and burned by the sun on their slim arms, Siski's hair grown wiry and Kethina's lank with the heat and their dresses creased from sitting on banks or old stone fences. And always they would explain about the wonderful day they had had, and indeed the excitement on their faces suggested extraordinary delights, as did their dusty boots and drooping ribbons and the odor of sweat, like that of pea flowers, which rose from their damp clothes. Siski had moved the two red chairs from Malino's old study into my room and she and Kethina would collapse on these, their legs stretched out, the toes of their boots turned up, fanning themselves with their bleached silk hats while the scent of burnt grass drifted in at the window. Then they would tell me what had happened. Sometimes they had been charged by bulls, sometimes received from a peasant a gift of butter tied up in a cloth. Later still I would smell their tobacco and hear them whispering out on Siski's balcony as the moon rose over the orchard. And while I could hear their sudden giggling and even the jingle of Kethina's charm bracelets and sometimes, I thought, a bare toe rubbing the iron grating, I never heard what they talked about. And the sound of their chatter exhausted me, they talked without ceasing all through the day and night.

My sister despised silence. She had a willful and hectic happiness with which she was determined to conquer the world. Sometimes I would hear them screeching, her and Kethina, swinging on the boughs of the Lathni chestnut tree by the well. The house grew quiet only when my father shouted for peace and then I would hear again how it was when we were absent, the growing hush of solitude in the halls where no one walked and the lifeless parlors and the rows of abandoned bedrooms. Then it seemed like our house again with the alien element banished. And for a few days the girls would slip out early, whispering in the hall and returning only when the sun was setting to lock themselves together in Siski's room. But irrepressibly the laughter would burst from her balcony and soon it would spread through the house again, into all the corners. Once she dashed upstairs and shouted as she passed my room, "We're eating out on the terrace, I must put on my shawl."

Whirling past my door again with the shawl about her shoulders she paused, the black and scarlet fringes settling slowly against her dress. "Don't you want to come outside?" she said. "They could bring you in a chair."

"No," I said.

She did not move, she stood by the door.

"What's the matter?"

"Nothing," I said.

She stood there for a moment. Then she said: "Then why won't you look at me?"

I told her that I was tired and when I glanced at the door again she was not there, she had slipped away without making a sound. And I felt my bandages under the blanket and struggled to sit up. I'd work, then pause, holding my position, propped on trembling arms. Work, then pause. Work, then pause. Thinking of the last time I'd seen her, five years before, when our happiness had shattered. Her horse, the beautiful Tuik, had died. Siski mourned through the corridors, knot-haired like a bereaved woman in a song. We all supposed she'd get over it, it was terrible, of course, but after all not the end of the world, everybody said. I remember the intense darkness of the house that autumn, the way the halls seemed to lengthen when you stepped in with a candle. I didn't like to go up the stairs alone. Dasya was silent and morose—he too seemed wounded by the death of Tuik. And I was outside, subtly abandoned, too young for them, for the first time. On the day of the first snow they went out alone. No one knew they were gone until Siski returned without our cousin, chilled and filthy and with blood upon her cheek.

Work, then pause. Work. When I swung my legs out of the bed the pain slammed into my gut and nearly made me retch. I sat there sweating and shaking like an overworked mule but I would stand up, I was going to stand. I clasped the bedpost. I had never asked my sister what had happened that dreadful day. It seemed impossible. They bathed her and put her to bed in Mother's room. The doctor was called and prescribed a draft of oinov. Nenya stopped me when I tried to go in: "My heart, get back, don't you know your sister is ill?" Her eyebrows, flecked with gray, stood up like the quills of an angry goose. But what was wrong with Siski? No one would say. And when Dasya returned, very late I learned from Gastin, they dressed him in traveling clothes and sent him down to Klah-ne-Wiy in the coach.

Work. Work. I stood up, gasping, my weight on my good leg. It is possible for the world to change in an instant. Siski needed to be alone, she needed peace and quiet, Mother said. My sister who thrived on noise. I was to go to Bain, to spend the season with Uncle Veda, who had recently been called upon to take up his role as duke, to leave his dogs and horses, his dusty carpets, the stedleihe brewery in his cellar, and go into the west. Before I left, I visited Valedhara. Uncle Veda's former steward—now the owner of the house—met me at the door. He clung to the doorjamb with small, alert fingers; his eyes had grown very bad. "It's cold in here," he said, "since the old man left."

Late in the summer Siski and Kethina's friends came from Nauve. I was walking then, I had even ridden Na Faso in the meadow, and we had heard of a slaughter in the Valley, unarmed peasants massacred on the orders of the Priest of the Stone. I had had no letter from Dasya, but I knew what he must be thinking: that this was our chance, that for the first time the Valley was divided against itself. That if the anger simmering in Kestenya could be released now, swiftly, we might see freedom in the east at last. At Ashenlo no one spoke of such things: Siski's guests arrived laughing, their scabbards ringing as they hung them on the wall. They poured in led by Siski who was radiant and triumphant in a pink silk bodice cut low and tight in the arms.

"This is the informal parlor, the oldest room in the house," she explained, her face aglow above the rosy silk. She put her hand on a young man's arm. "Don't smoke those things, we'll never get the smell out of the carpets. Let me fill you a nice pipe." I thought of her as a child, collecting apricots and standing on a stool to watch the jam boil on the big stove, and I thought of her riding Tuik into the desert outside Sarenha and coming back with her hair in tails and her skirt shredded by thorns. She used to be so happy there, especially in the mornings, giggling over her breakfast, making herself

choke, then laughing harder. No one could understand her. And
Nenya, spooning out the porridge, would say: "Some people eat
crow berries during the night."

And now, in the evening: her smooth face like a china dish,
black brows and lashes starkly painted, a crisp light laugh. "I never
did that, did I?" she said, looking around her wide-eyed. "I don't
remember, it sounds terrible, not like me."

"Do you mean to say you're not terrible?" said Kai of Amafein,
leaning over her chair.

It was just what she had wanted him to say. Her tinkling laugh,
the others closing in on her, the pipe smoke and her bright expectant face looking up at them.

And I was far away. Sometimes a guest spoke to me—it was clear
Siski had told them not to shun me—but mostly I sat by the wall
and drank. First we drank Eilami brandy and then we drank mountain wine and gaisk from my father's cellar. "I knew how it would
be," Siski said bitterly, on one of the evenings—rare after her guests
arrived—when she came into my room. "First he says he won't have
anyone and won't pay for anything. But then he can't bear to have
others pay for it. I told him," she said, lifting her chin and glaring
at the closed door. "I told him, they've brought everything from
Nauve. If you don't want us we'll sleep in the hills." She was wearing
a thin gray shawl and she drew it about her shoulders as though she
were cold. Then she gave a hard laugh. "He's with us now. He can't
help it." She turned toward me and her face grew soft in genuine
amusement. "He's going to give a party for you. To celebrate your
recovery. A garden party with lamps and singers, everything."

I said I did not want a party.

She grimaced fondly and tweaked my hair. "Don't be silly. Why
shouldn't he give parties for us, if he wants to? I don't care if he
gives us some of his money."

"He doesn't have any money," I said.

"Nonsense, where does he get that bolma from, and the wine?
No no, don't be stubborn." She drew her legs up onto the bed

where we were sitting and covered my eyes with her cool hand. "See your party."

I took her wrist and pulled her hand away. "He has nothing," I said. "Do you understand me? Nothing."

And on the evening of the party, when the lamps were lit in the garden, she passed with her skirts whispering against the leaves, and with light falling over her shoulders and hair she knelt to give me a glass and grinned and said, "Have a sip of our father's nothing." I took the glass and smelled the gaisk; it reminded me of the mountains. In the garden all the voices and laughter were soft. It was not like being inside where the noise became unbearable; the loudness was drawn away and absorbed by the night. The feathery trees swayed above us, hung with round-bellied paper lanterns, and a wooden arch decorated with roses bristled above the musicians. We sat on wicker chairs and smoked. "Look, everything is the color of smoke," said Siski. Talk and laughter rose in the thin trees. Gastin came out with a tray of difleta, and Armali took two glasses at once and winked at me. He braced one foot on the rung of the table. "Thank you, I'd rather not sit. Sitting too much is no longer restful. If only the heat would break we'd amuse ourselves with a hunt."

Kethina shook her head in passing, wrinkled her nose and prodded his thick arm, crying, "Always in such a hurry!"

"Like yourself," he boomed out after her. His smell was fresh and strong as if he had bathed himself in lemon verbena.

"Look, fireflies!" cried Siski.

He looked vaguely toward the garden and made a humming sound in his chest. "Yes, delightful!" Then he turned back to me. "What are you planning now? Going back into the army, I hear." He gulped his second glass.

"No," I said. "Into the desert."

"Tav is going to visit a cousin of ours, Prince Fadhian," Siski said quickly. She took a brief sip and added: "A very good friend of our uncle the duke's."

"Not so good," I said, and at once felt foolish.

"Well, you told me they were friends." She frowned, tapped her foot on the gravel and looked away toward the musicians under the arch, and everything gathered in me, the misery of being with her and being estranged from her, and I said: "He is a prince of the feredhai."

Later, up in my room, I thought that I could easily have escaped, I could have avoided everything that came afterward, I might have said "He is my uncle's friend," I might have danced, I might have bowed to Siski's request that I take off my sword. Instead I stood harsh and awkward in an old-fashioned frock, too tight across the shoulders now, with my old scabbard half smothered in its folds, and leaning on my cane I looked like a clown, Siski told me afterward. *A prince of the feredhai.*

"*Do* they have princes?" Kethina asked brightly, looking around at the others.

Armali swallowed hastily in order to answer: "Not as we do. Not at all. There's no—" He put down his empty glass and snapped his fingers, looking for the word. "No sense of continuity, of blood."

"But they have such dreadful feuds!"

"Well, but in that case the bloodline is just an excuse. All of their squabbles really take place over cattle. Cattle and horses—it's what they have instead of politics!"

Laughter.

"And what's *your* politics?" crowed Kethina.

"My dear, gaisk and good weather!"

He motioned to Gastin for another drink. His foot restless on the rung of the chair. His calf pulsing and swelling. And Morhon was still talking about blood. The lamplight on his spectacles hid his eyes. "In order to have proper royalty, that is, princes of the blood, or as it is more genteel to say, princes of the Branch, one requires history, and in order to have history, one requires a means of recording history, and the feredhai, possessing no writing—" Kethina was helpless with laughter. Kai of Amafein nuzzling her ear. Something had fallen into her dress—a spider. And Siski sat under the spreading mimosa tree, a pattern of leaves falling over her face and dress, gazing up at Armali, nodding and smiling. Her plaits in a knot on top of her head, small curls escaping and glinting like black fleece. The greenish radiance of her gown. And on the side of her brow a small contraction, the hint of a frown, a pulse beating angrily, signs only I could read.

"Feredha politics are clean, at least," I said.

Armali looked at me, surprised. "My dear girl."

"Cleaner than ours. Look at the Lelevai. A feud over horses, a feredha feud—that's a feud over something. The Brogyar war is a feud over nothing."

"But think of—"

"Nothing."

He laughed. A sound like a cough. "Hrrm, hrrm," deep in his chest. His eyes glittered, chips of broken enamel. "I should think someone like yourself—you are, after all, of a Nainish House— would see the sense in protecting our northern border."

"You are, after all, of a Kestenyi House. I should think you'd respect the feredhai, your own—"

"Don't start that!" he barked, putting his glass down hard.

"Come," laughed Siski.

"Lady Siski," he said, breathing hard through his nostrils, "my respect for you is absolute, but I will not stand to be called a feredha by anyone."

"But you *are* one," I said, "if we trace your lineage back far enough! So am I. So are we all."

It was like running downhill. I waited for him to say it, and he did. "If you weren't a lady, I'd—"

"Stop!" cried Siski, leaping up.

She seized my hand as I started to draw my sword, and I let it slide back into the scabbard, afraid of cutting her. "Stupid!" she hissed. "You're making fools of us all!" She was so close I could smell her skin: liquor and summer rain. There was a brief silence, and then the music again, the singers' repetitive song. The hum of voices resumed, but excited now, subtly energized, Kethina's eyes sparkling under her pointed brows. "Drink!" Ermali shouted. "Where's your idiot footman?" And Gastin hurried toward him over the gravel.

Siski caught her breath and gave my wrist a pinch—a single, childish gesture, a brief word in the language of boredom and the schoolroom. It startled me so thoroughly that I laughed. At once I wished I could take my laughter back, for her eyes widened and I knew she would not forgive me. Then she laughed, too. She leaned forward, embracing me gently, her breath warm at my ear, and for an instant I was transported back in time, and the cheap Tevlasi music wrenched my heart, for it was home.

She pulled me close. "You look like a clown," she whispered.

Very well. I looked like a clown in my old frock. She was right. But I would not be a clown. I would not dance to a Valley tune like our hapless Uncle Veda. When I thought of him in Bain, in the stuffy rooms of the ducal residence, I knew that I had been right to run away. Siski had depressed me with her mysterious illness, Dasya had cut me with his desertion, but it was Uncle Veda who truly broke my heart. He met me at the door smelling of hair oil and fresh steam, squeezed into a figured coat, and I wished that I was dead. I wished I had died before I saw his anxious, sweating face, his lopsided mustache decorated with a pair of beads. He only owned carriage horses—"It wouldn't be right to keep a proper horse in the city"—and dosed his "cold stomach" with Eilami brandy. Because he was a bachelor, and considered too stupid to deal with young ladies, my Aunt Firvaud had come from the Isle to help me settle in. The two of them led me upstairs to a bedroom crowded with lamps and couches. The window, my uncle informed me, over-looked the gardens.

I put down my things, and he noticed the swordbox. "Oh! Ha, ha! Did you bring that thing? Ha, ha!" he wheezed, leaning on a couch. "A joke," he explained to my Aunt Firvaud, who regarded me with a searing stare. "Our Tavis used to be so fond of swordplay."

"I still am," I said, though I did not feel fond of anything. I thought I would never be fond of anything again.

"So I understand," said Aunt Firvaud. Small, with painted lips, she flashed like a jewel in the setting of her elaborate beaded cape. "Veda," she said then, in a deliberately careless tone, "please leave us. We have things to discuss. As ladies."

"Naturally!" Uncle Veda said. And he went out, receiving a tiny shock when he touched the doorknob, because of the way his buffed slippers rubbed against the carpet.

Aunt Firvaud, my sharpest and most scornful relative, who hardly allowed us any intimacy with her although she was my mother's sister, who always insisted on being called "Teldaire Aunt" because she was Queen of Olondria, advanced on me with a blazing face. "What has happened?" she demanded. "What is the matter with him?" And I knew that she meant Dasya, and it was as if my heart had dropped into my boots.

"Why?" I asked. "Is he ill?"

"Ill!" she cried, flushing darker still. "He's weaker than a gnat; his heart is broken!"

I stared.

"Don't stand there like a stump! Your sister has crushed his hopes, that's clear enough; does she think herself too good for the future Telkan?"

"I don't know," I faltered. My head was spinning, and the edges of the room seemed to fade. I thought of Dasya and Siski going away together into the woods without me, and Siski coming home alone. The blood on her cheek, so dark in the instant I was allowed to see her, the instant before they whisked her away upstairs. I felt like a fool for not having seen the signs of romance between them, for thinking them depressed by the loss of Tuik. As if horses were everything. *Kad shedyamud*, I thought in Kestenyi. What barbarism. I felt, in that moment, like a barbarian, someone who was only good for riding and hunting and fighting, and then I almost wept for desire of such a life. My aunt was screaming in my face, her elegant little hands tearing the air—"I want to know what happened! Nobody tells me anything! What did they quarrel about? Whatever it is, she must forgive him!"—and I gave up the effort of standing and sat down on a plump silk couch.

The cushion was harder than I had expected; my teeth clacked together. Outside the window, just past my aunt, spread the windswept sky of Bain. Gulls swung between the towers. The sun struck a distant window that glittered so brightly I thought, for a moment, it was a tear in the corner of my eye. How quickly the world comes down, as if it were only made of paper. I thought of Uncle Veda pacing downstairs, his thumb and forefinger stained with ink, his ankles throbbing from dancing the arilantha and other intricate Valley dances. And everything was gone, the house, Valedhara of the high cupboards which even my uncle's valet stood on a table to reach. The pearl-knobbed doors, the antelope horns that were taken down and polished with wax, and the great collection of weapons in the study. This room that was called a study was really a storage room for no one studied there and the old wall lamps were empty of oil, so that one always carried a candle inside even during the day because the windows were blocked by enormous old armor cases. I remembered the odor of dust and leather and the glow of the candle revealing the buried wonders of that chamber. "Somewhere here," said Uncle Veda. Suddenly he had decided to look for a hawking glove that predated the War of the East. Metal clanged, shields slid to the floor. "Help me look, my dear," my uncle said. His robe trailed in the dust and caught on boxes, his hanging sleeves became tangled in a collection of Panji hunting bows. At last he said: "Ah, look. There it is." He held the glove up in the light of the candle. It seemed huge, misshapen, a monstrous gauntlet trailing moth-eaten ribbons. "I knew you would enjoy that thing," he chuckled. "How we loved our hawking parties then, when Ranlu was alive!" And downstairs in the parlor I sat with the great glove on my knee and gingerly touched the ribbons and strands of beads, while Uncle Veda lit his pipe and told me of the hawking they had done in the golden days before the war. First they would choose their birds, walking quietly in the early morning among the hooded cages of the lokhu. Then they would go out among the hills, riding on the shaggy, stalwart ponies of the plain, and at last release their falcons to the sky. "We would catch foxes, yellow hares, even ermine," he said. His eyes grew moist as he began to laugh, remembering how Ranlu's hawk had perched on the roof of an aklidoh and the hermits had refused to let them retrieve it. "They were so kind to us, that was the worst of it!" he sputtered, wiping his eyes. "Yes, suddi! Welcome, suddi! Giving us curds and butter! We squatted in the yard and ate while Ranlu eyed the roof and they gave lectures on the sanctity of their walls . . ." He laughed, his face as red as mahogany in the dusky parlor. How wonderful it seemed to me as I sat on that hard silk couch, how wonderful, the soaring birds and galloping hooves, the wheeling space of the plain beneath the blueness of the hills. And rage welled up in me like icy water in a thaw: rage at Dasya and Siski for allowing some stupid lovers' spat to spoil our autumns; rage at Uncle Veda for accepting the title of Duke of Bain and submitting to a society he loathed; and rage at my Teldaire Aunt who, tired of shouting, realizing I knew nothing, picked at the shoulder of my gown on her way out of the room. "Cheap," she pronounced, standing over me, smelling of some expensive scent that reminded me of nothing but her own apartments in the Tower of Pomegranates.

"You'll have to dress better in Bain," she added. "This isn't some highland barn."

I raised my eyes, and she took a step backward, her fingers against her throat. For a moment I exulted at having frightened her, but then her expression cleared. She even smiled. "That's it," she murmured. "You'll do very well."

∽

I often wondered what she meant. Did she recognize something in my murderous look? Did she, too, dream of murder every day? Did Siski? Do they still? Is that how they survive, these bright society women—by chewing on visions of violence as if on milim leaves? But I would not, could not; I would follow Ferelanyi; I would run away to military school. In the stolen carriage—borrowed, as I put it to myself—I flew eastward along the Ethendria Road. A kind of terror oppressed me, the sense of having done something irrevocable, of having set myself apart from my world forever. Autumn had come to the Valley: the vines lay rumpled and brown and fallen leaves blew over the road in the cold wind. And then there was that blue and misty morning when the horses seemed so fresh and stamped so prettily on the bricks of the old inn yard. The air was crisp and smelled of smoke and coffee and roasted chestnuts and the laughter of the girls in the kitchen rang from the lighted window. The porter ran out with my great trunk: he was a crooked old man and grinned with strong white teeth as he heaved his burden up into the carriage. And I stood smiling back at him and he smacked his palms together and exclaimed something about the chill in the air. Why did he suddenly strike me as such a handsome and wonderful old man? All that day we flew past empty fields; there were a few horses and children squabbling over the last of the apples, and when the sun came out the frost glittered. We crossed the Ilbalin on the ferry and I stood by the rails and smelled the air and listened to the shouts in the blunt accent of Nain. My happiness and impatience grew as we climbed into the mountains and I had to wear my wool vest and heavy mantle. "Raise the window, my lady," Fulmia said. But I closed my eyes and let the wind scour my face, burning with joy and cold. I would not be a clown, I would not dance. *Goodbye, Uncle Veda!* It was the end of ribbons, the end of bouquets.

Years later, when my sister told me I looked like a clown, that moment sustained me. The carriage climbing higher, into rare air. My swordbox at my feet. In my excitement, I drummed it with my heels. It was the beginning of the dance of the mountains.

⊂⊃

I still carry the letter my sister sent me from Ashenlo three months ago. It found me just before I left the great plateau. I was with the feredhai then, and the young boys crowded around me with huge eyes to watch me read the piece of paper. "What does it say?" they asked. "No news," I told them. I folded the letter and tucked it into my shirt. There it stayed as I traveled westward with a small company of men, into the clement autumn of the Valley. It crossed the country with me and now it has taken up residence in the forest. I carry it still, in this chilly camp where we wait to make our move. Surely it no longer possesses any virtue. Its letters smudged, its creases near-transparent. Still I carry it and sometimes I unfold it by the lamp.

> *My own dear Taviye,*
>
> *If you knew how dull we are without you, you would come back at once. Even the horses are pining for you! Poor Ustia will hardly eat his mash, and when I took him across the Oun this morning he wouldn't gallop, but ambled like an old workhorse. All of the dogs are terribly jealous of Farus. Noni told me that she will not speak to you when you come unless you bring her an emerald collar. You know how she is, so you had better comply. As for Fotla, when I mention your name he acts as if he's never heard of you!*
>
> *To speak from my heart dear Taviye, come back for the feast if you can. It will be so wonderful for Mother. I've told her to try not to think of it but she says she dreams of you in those wild mountains surrounded by criminals disfigured by the black needle! So you see how it is. Father is the same as ever, exactly the same, only more so if possible, taking most of his meals alone in the porch. One never knows what mood will take possession of him from one moment to the next. I hate to leave them alone together.*
>
> *As for me, I'm bored almost into the grave. Kethina has gone back to Nauve and never writes, as she says she is "caught up with life." I*

suppose she means new gowns. I have given up on all that myself and go about in a blue dress like a peasant. What is the point? Mother and Nenya force me to dress in the afternoons, as we have not, apparently, sunk so low as to appear at the table in slippers. How stupid everything seems! Even my shell combs have grown heavy; when I put up my hair, I swear to you, my arms ache.

Taviye, how has it happened that we are scattered all over the country?

Well, they are calling me to dress. It's already cold in the mountains and all my gowns are Valley ones, thin silks with open backs. I freeze nightly. Taviye, dear Taviye, do you remember when we were children, how we used to slide across the floor of the avla? Suddenly I remembered that. I think of those days so often and have so much pleasure from it that sometimes I actually burst out laughing. I remember even the terrible things with nothing but fondness now, like Grandmother's burial day and how we fell into the gorge. Do you remember that? Nenya tells me I'm too old now to be giggling or sighing to myself over my embroidery. "Alas my heart, sudaidi," she says (for she is a true Kestenyi though she will never lose her pride in calling herself a "daughter of Nain," and if a new tradesman comes to the door she still looks at the ceiling and snaps her fingers as if she can't recall Kestenyi words—what nonsense!)—"Alas my heart, sudaidi," she says, "be sensible and break this habit of laughing and crying all the time, it's not right for a lady!" As if one's rank should prevent one from feeling anything in life! But it's only the memory of those days that makes me feel anything. So come back soon, and let's go riding over the Oun like we used to, and have wine and raush under the trees by the bridge. You know it was funny when Kethina was here, she said you'd always seemed so stiff and proud to her and without any lightheartedness at all. She said she used to be afraid of you, you were so serious, and I said you were the merriest person I knew. Vai, here I am with nothing but memories, like an old woman. Come soon and make us all cheerful.

Love, Siski

∞

On her last night, the night they all left for Nauve, she came upstairs and stood by my bed in her dark gray traveling clothes and a cherry-colored scarf. Her face severe above the brilliant silk bunched at her throat. She held a little round case in front of her with both hands. When she shrugged, it tapped against her knees and stirred her long dark skirt. She looked at me and smiled and then looked at the window.

"After all, it's been a wonderful summer," she said.

Dogs barked; the light of carriage lamps gleamed behind the curtains.

"Siski, don't," I said.

"No, I have to go," she said. She bent down and kissed me, smiling. "I don't know what's the matter with me." Her breath struggled for a moment in the tightness of her coat and then she was calm, at the door, touching her hair, and gone.

3. Blood

The swordmaiden will bleed.

All bleed who fight with the sword. All confront, with greater or lesser difficulty, the worship of their own flesh. The swordmaiden faces particular obstacles in this matter: she will have seen, in the temples and elsewhere, many images of unscarred women.

The swordmaiden, like all warriors, must transform aversion into pride. She will be aided in this by the knowledge that her path to this achievement, being rougher and less moon-lit than the paths of her companions, endows her triumph with a superior glory.

Consider: the unscarred women depicted in the temples are gods.

Consider: very few overcome the worship of the flesh. Bardo of Weis, an exceedingly arrogant brawler, whose skin was so tortured it resembled a carpet, wept in his dreams once a year for the loss of his former body.

There is also the small matter of the swordmaiden's monthly blood. It is advisable to stanch the flow with rags, and to wash these rags in privacy, if at all possible, as one's companions may find the subject cause for jest. It is also acceptable to follow the example of Maris, who slew two men in duels prompted by such insults, or of the False Countess, who used to discuss her flow openly in her camp, as she and her men together discoursed on the issue of their bowels.

The question is unlikely to arise except in times of peace; the swordmaiden at war will often find that her flow has

stopped. Consider Galaron of Nain, who bled for the first
time in her life at the age of thirty, and mistook the pangs and
blood for signs that her food had been poisoned.

When my wound had fully healed and I no longer needed the cane,
I went into the desert. I dressed in the highland way, in wide trousers and a sheepskin jacket; with my hair loose on my shoulders
and the sword worn openly at my side, I was taken everywhere for
a young man. Even Fadhian, who met me, as my letter requested, a
few miles south of Tevlas, thought I was a boy. He was seated on
the fence outside the inn, his horse cropping the weeds nearby, and
he nodded to me without expression.

Then I smiled, and his hard face rippled into understanding.
He jumped down, I dismounted, and we clasped hands.

"Tavis," he said.

"Tav."

He bowed. We rode together in silence until firelight appeared
against the dusky sky.

"There's the camp," he said. We quickened our pace. Several
boys came out to meet us, bearing torches and one broken lantern
that gave off an evil smell. They swung the lantern in my face,
exclaiming in a dialect I found difficult to understand. I was struck
by the rowdy noise they made and the way they did not try to hide
the fact that they were talking about me, and also by their jostling
closeness, the way they all rode in a knot, which I recognized as a
skill but did not like.

Tumbling and clattering, we rode into the camp. Fadhian
smiled as girls ran up to greet him and tug his stirrups. He dismounted and embraced everyone and kissed each boy and girl on
the top of the head and the women kissed him on the shoulder.
Everyone laughed when he kissed Lunsila, who was so tall she had
to bend her knees in order for him to kiss the crown of her dark
head, and she laughed more than anyone and everyone made jokes

that it was clear they had made many times before. The children crowded at Fadhian's knees and then he was carrying two of them and continued to hold them as he introduced me. I clasped hands with everyone and was overcome by loneliness. Later the boys told me they had feared my angry face. And Fadhian ducked into a tent to greet his wife while I sat by the nearest fire and someone brought me coffee in a tin cup. The coffee, boiled with goat's milk, had a strong, musky taste, but I drank it all while the boys crouched around me and stared. The men sat with us too and gave me tobacco and asked questions in gruff voices. There were long pauses between the questions, and sometimes the boys broke in with piercing voices, all in the dialect that refused to arrange itself in my mind.

I can speak Kestenyi, I said to myself. *I have spoken it all my life.* And it was true—in a few days everything would be clear: I would hear the familiar words under tricks of pronunciation, but on that first night the language seemed encased in a thicket of thorns. I heard my own voice, strained and weak like the voice of a Valley official who believes that learning the language will endear him to the highlanders. Some of the words even came out with a strong Olondrian accent, such as I had never affected at home.

That night I slept poorly in the tent they gave me, thinking of how Fadhian's son Redos had pulled me aside. Thinking of his arrogant face and figure in the black jacket and his question asked with such deliberate slowness.

"Why have you come here?" he said.

I could not pretend not to understand. "To forget," I answered him, "and to begin."

His black hair, the blackened silver at his throat, and there, at the door of the tent, a string of prayer bells ringing in the wind.

At the end of the Month of Plenty we struck camp and began to move. The sunlight was brilliant, falling in sheets of whiteness.

It glittered on the roofs and fences covered with new snow and the leagues of hard flat country under the bird-speckled sky. In the morning we rose and grimaced and worked the stiffness out of our limbs and beat the blankets, throwing off flakes of frost. The boys ran out calling the herds with the curious hollow cries I could not imitate. And the girls crouched under mantles squinting in the smoke of the fires or clicked to call their milch goats, strange thick-haired creatures with cross-eyed stares, who gave off a fierce odor and whose heavy yellowish milk made the crumbly cheese the feredhai carried on journeys. Sometimes the girls called to their ponies too: for this they had a high and trilling cry like the sound of the black eagles of the Tavroun. I watched the girls run, crying, catching up the folds of their mantles with one hand and mounting the ponies with a sudden sideways leap. I was always amazed at how fast they rode, sitting cross-legged and seemingly off-balance but never falling. They would ride to the neighboring farms with hides to trade for coffee and tobacco and, if the trading went well, perhaps a handful of grain.

"So now you have seen the barbarity of the plains," Fadhian smiled.

He sat back under the femka, his features indistinct in the gloom.

I watched the glint of his teeth and said: "It is not barbarity. True barbarity exists only in cities."

"Really," he said, still smiling, and I knew I had spoken clumsily. He bent to refill my cup from the silver pot. "I realize," he said, "that you are spending only a season with us. Please refrain from any custom that does not suit your tastes."

And I wanted to tell him that everything suited my tastes, everything, riding and living in tents and always seeing new parts of the country, eating cheese and hoda in the saddle and the way the boys, with their rough, easy ways, had made me one of them. I wanted to tell him that I could live for days on nothing but raush, that I grew sick unto death on teiva, rich food and wine. I wanted to tell him that my desire was only to sleep in a tent or beneath the stars and never again to have silk or muslin against my skin. But I was silent. After a moment I asked if he regretted accepting me. Then he laughed and reached out to clap me on the arm.

"Sensitivity!" he cried. "It's the curse of settled folk. By the end of winter you'll lose your fear of words."

But he was wrong. I have never lost my fear of words, nor have I learned to master them and bend them to my will, to meet them with confidence and strip and twist them as I saw him do on his stool of judgment under the red femka. His decisions grew from hours of talk and the quiet pronouncements of his wife, Amlasith, who sat beside him in a leather chair, while two girls tossed sweet sandalwood into the brazier at her side. These decisions were final and I never saw them questioned. An unhappy man could ride away if he liked. The feredhai were never anxious unless women were involved in the disputes, for an unhappy woman would take with her the male relatives of her ausk and all their flocks, a blow to the larger clan. This never happened while I was there, but I heard of Nith Rudasa who in the year of the yellow rams had cut herself off from Fadhian's people. They still remembered her and spoke of her sadly, while the men who had abandoned them were referred to as used shoes.

Winter came after us and we rode faster. We hurried eastward, the wagons clacking over the frozen ground, fleeing into the Duoronwei where the winter camp awaited us and the secret pastures among the folds of the mountains. There was no time to pause on that long run and the women cooked on the moving wagons and cured raush in the flying smoke. The farms we passed were white and still, the doors closed. Bildiri horsemen watched us over the fences, holding their coiled whips. I rode with the feredhai through the stinging sleet and later over the whitened plains, peering through the slit in my wool headscarf, the scar on my thigh aching and my limbs burning with the desire for speed, cold, hunger, and oblivion. After three days the men were silent and no longer stared at me with secretly mocking looks as they had done at first. But the boys who had always loved me for my spurs and my sword in its embossed scabbard remained my closest friends after Fadhian himself.

"Well," said Redos, when I had brought down the great white ram among the Lihoun, "so the lady can shoot."

The snow was falling thickly. The women, with yells of exultation, descended on the silver beast and in moments had skinned and gutted and quartered it. The children were given handfuls of fleece dipped in the blood to suck, and tottered about in their heavy clothes, sometimes falling and dotting the snow with pink. Around me the men sat on their horses and watched. Weafan rode up on her pony and presented me with the liver.

They watched me cut off a piece and nodded gravely when I had swallowed it.

I had been afraid but did not feel ill.

"You've eaten it before," cried Finor, smiling in amazement, and I laughed when I remembered Loma struck down in the north.

I dug my heels into my horse and dashed away over the snow. I knew that I had a reputation for eccentricity, strange for me who, as a child, had been considered so ordinary that my parents had once forgotten me on a journey to the Valley. Yes, they forgot me, they left me behind with the servants. I laughed as I galloped over the snow, remembering Nenya's sandals scraping over the flags. She opened the lid of the chest and cried out, "Oh, what are you doing there?" I heard her breath and her soft moan of distress. She reached into the chest and pulled me out, the keys clinking at her belt. My traveling clothes were covered with sawdust, and she dusted me off in haste, sometimes slapping me so that it hurt. I could hear that the house was entirely empty.

"They're gone," I said.

She snatched me up into the floury smell of her dress. I clutched her collar as she ran out to the lane, bouncing in her arms, her breath about me and the patches of sun in the lane and the trunks of the trees all leaping madly.

"Here she is," she cried.

Mother was standing outside the carriage and she clasped me tight and I breathed her different smell of violet perfume. "Why can you not control her?" said Father. I looked up and Siski was at the window, making an evil face against the glass.

I rode until it seemed my horse's hooves had trampled that face into the snow. Two days later we were at the winter camp, Fadhian filled with satisfaction because we had reached it on the second Tolie of the month of Mur in the season of Earth Ringing. In the cave we slaughtered a bull and drank its blood by torchlight, and that night the boys were restless and could not sleep, knowing that all the married men were lying with their wives. In the morning we ate fresh meat and a pudding of blood and went back to bed. That deep sleep of satiety and weariness under furs and blankets in the tent that was full of the breath of youth. A child woke me in the afternoon and summoned me to Fadhian's tent where I sat among cushions and drank hot milk with sama.

I told him that I wanted to go with the boys, eastward into the winter pasture, and not remain with the women in the camp. "It will be very hard," he said. He waited for me to answer, and when I did not he clapped my shoulder in his companionable way. "Forgive me," he laughed, and when the boys departed into the Duoronwei I went with them, treading on the edge of the world. The rigid frost, the blue air, and the animals linked with rope on the treacherous ice took me back to my days in the northern war.

"Are the Lelevai colder than these mountains?" Mantia shouted.

"No," I shouted back, and we were overwhelmed with echoes. Finor stalked back down the line and hissed for us to be quiet: he was afraid of the avalanche, the shifting dragon. In silence we plodded along the ridge and after three days we saw the valley, a gash in the mountains filled with a whirling mist. It took us seven days to get the animals to the bottom and my hands bled and I ached and was very happy. There was the day when without the slightest warning the sun struck down on us and illuminated a valley of black flowers, of black fir trees and cold streams and enormous birds that rose up honking, blocking the light with the spread of their huge wings.

"Iloki!" I cried.

I had heard that they came from the mountains but had never seen them in the wild, where they feed on sleeping fish. The famished cattle cropped the tall black lilies and Amantir smiled and said: "Here is the Paradise of Oud."

I thought of Dasya then, how he used to speak of the outlawed Kestneyi goddess Roun: he believed she was only another name for Avalei, and that her paradise, called Oud, was a paradise of song. "Song," he said, "not sign. Speech, not writing." I wondered where Dasya was, if he was still at his secret work in the Lelevai, carefully testing captain after captain, pulling together the structure of a war. Or perhaps he was in the Valley now, where peasant unrest was growing. Already it was spreading into the highlands: rumors reached us of a carriage waylaid on the road to Bron, two Olondrians slain, tiny bells found in their mouths. Bells, for prayer. I wondered how Fadhian had received the news—if he, so cautious, was ready to hear the words *Kestenya Rukebnar.* Delicious motto of the traitorous dead. Sometimes I could not sleep, thinking of how I would say those words to him. *Kestenya Rukebnar.* In their silver resonance I would be revealed: not merely an eccentric noblewoman amusing herself with highland games, but a link between rebellious Kestenya, the rebellious Valley, and the rebellious north—a key, a chance, a bell, a sword.

Kestenya Rukebnar. I whispered the words with joy in that cold valley, where I left my sadness among the frosted leaves. All of it, abandoned. It slipped from me in the ache of the rushing streams, in the harsh cries of the iloki. "Do you like *hesensaï?*" Mantia asked me, grinning, and I said yes, only realizing a moment later why he laughed. *Hesensai*: to drive the cattle to their winter pasture. Literally, "to travel without women."

In the spring we climbed out of that valley, forcing the animals up the rocky slopes, shouting and clacking sticks behind them, driving them over the sun-touched snow that broke under their hooves into the camp where blankets were hung to dry on lines. Girls ran out, holding up their mantles, embracing their brothers and cows and horses without any kind of order, and crying with happiness. Their faces glittered dark against a landscape covered with mud and dirty snow and they were bright and warm and alive. I was dazzled by them, by their light voices and quick hands, their odor of wood-smoke and roasting coffee and wool blankets, the flash of their heavy silver anklets and the beads in their tangled hair and their bold movements as they shoved one another and hurried to build up the fires. I felt that I had never seen women before. Amlasith approached me, her arms spread out, and I leaned to kiss her shoulder. The fleece of her jacket made me sneeze and she laughed and pulled my head down and kissed my brow and patted my cheek with her warm hand.

"Did you bring back my Tras and Su?" she asked.

"Yes," I said.

She narrowed her eyes and looked across the snow. "Ah yes, there they are," she said, and I watched her brightening face as she caught sight of her two favorite russet cows.

That night a sheep was slaughtered in our honor and we drank stedleihe from a gourd smeared with pitch that usually hung in Amlasith's tent, passing it ceremonially around the fire, the boys composing their faces into sternness before they drank. The wind came up and the night grew very cold and the sparks flew and all the children were put to bed in the big tent, except for those who insisted on sleeping in the artusa among the cows and went off dragging their blankets over the snow. Rumios sang a part of the

Song of Lo and then a girl in a white cloak recited half of the poem, "When Tir Rode Out from Eilam's Halls." When she had finished, Amlasith said to me: "Come, Tavis. It is time you sat with the women for an hour."

"Tav," I said, my throat dry.

She bowed her head slightly, but did not repeat my name. *My name is Tav*, I thought as I rose to follow her and the girl in white, feeling suddenly heavy and awkward, not wanting to answer or even look at Mantia and the others who called to me across the camp. I stalked silent in my boots, the light of the lantern brushing my dirty herdsman's trousers. Amlasith's tent was the largest in the camp. There were several lamps inside it, and girls and women and children lounged about on low beds covered with stretched hide. Some of them sat up when they saw me, curious, ready to laugh. The girl in white set the lantern on the floor, and Amlasith sank down in a clinking of gold, crossing her legs under billows of red cotton that filled the air with a smoky scent. Her wealth of gold flashed in the light of the lantern. She lit an ivory pipe patterned with dragons, a relic from the south. Her hand curved about the bowl, the fingers delicate and smooth, with sharpened nails and many golden rings.

"Welcome, Tav," she said.

"Thank you, sudaidi."

Titters pricked the air, and Amlasith threw an amused, warning glance at a clump of girls. She looked at me again and smiled, a coil of smoke at the corner of her lip. "Do you smoke?"

"Yes, thank you, sudaidi."

Another burst of giggles, rough as a fall of gravel.

The girl in white, the reciter of poetry, passed me a small enameled pipe. She did not raise her eyes; she looked angry and ashamed, like me. She threw off her white cloak to disclose a leather vest, shiny and supple with grease.

Another girl passed me a tinderbox. I lit the pipe and smoked the heavy Evmeni tobacco, bartered for at the back door of a barn, and Amlasith said, "Seren, give us a tale," and the reciter of poetry spoke the invocation: "People of the House . . ." Then she told the story of Bel Marfunya, whose blood had dried up. Children gathered as she related the tale, kneeling on the ground, their legs ashen with a mixture of dust and the sparkling goblin silver of the hills. The smaller ones crept close and nestled against the breasts of the women, who stroked their soft hair absently and watched the teller, and Nask fell asleep in the crook of Amlasith's arm, gripping her finger tightly and trailing saliva on her fiery sleeve. When the story was over Amlasith smiled and snapped her fingers to show her appreciation and her bracelets jingled down the length of her arm. The thinner chains moved slowly, caught on the hairs. "Now," she said, "does anyone have a question for our visitor?"

"How can you tell if the white snake has struck?" someone cried, and laughter, quelled by the story, burst out everywhere. The feredhai called love "the white snake" and a lover was one who had been struck or one, it was said, who had swallowed dragon's milk.

"I don't know," I said. Hot light beat up from the lantern into my face.

"Are you engaged?"

"Have you ever been struck?"

"Will you have a green or gold wedding?"

Suddenly the storyteller, the girl in the leather vest, interrupted, claiming that people in love were unable to eat hoda. She spoke over the protests of the others, telling of somebody she knew, a distant cousin of hers beyond the Uloidas, a man with a beard down to his chest who had gone for a year without eating hoda until he gained the woman he loved as his bride. This cousin had survived only on milk and fish and sama. In the end he grew so thin that his own horse failed to recognize him; it bit him on the shoulder, and the wound went black and he lay in his tent on the brink of death beneath a carpet of flies. Then his uncle, who had refused to support his suit, rode out on his stallion, weeping enormous tears that streamed in the wind, and brought back the girl with her tent on the back of the horse. "That is how it happens," she said, drawing their laughter toward her, leaving me safe.

To swallow dragon's milk. The next day she came to me where I sat with Fadhian, once again clad in her pale cloak. She must be in mourning, I thought. My throat thickened strangely when she stopped and looked at me, dark eyes under curving brows. She said Amlasith wanted me: the women were going to bathe. Fadhian watched the cows, half smiling into his coffee. I followed the girl, feeling like a broken, sideways creature, the owner of a body that would not serve.

I told myself that this was a lie. I thought: *My body has fought and lived.* I thought: *I could seize this poet's arm and break it behind her back.* I thought: *The unscarred women depicted in the temples are gods.* Yet misery covered me like a rash.

At the stream, I removed my clothes as if before an executioner. First the sword. Then the jacket, and then the boots. Some of the girls already splashed in the water, shrieking in the cold, but most stood gazing at me unabashed. Vest, shirt, undershirt. Here then is my map. On my shoulder, a slash received at Orveth. Bar-Hathien across my ribs. One arm is also Bar-Hathien, the other Godol. Now the trousers. This leg: the foothills of the Lelevai.

I stood shivering under their stares. An exquisite self-loathing frothed in me like wine. And then something brown and galloping seized my hand. The poet, whooping in the raw air, pulled me down the bank till we crashed in the stream, like running into a sheet of lightning.

Her name was Seren. She had memorized countless lines of poetry. She spoke the *che*—the secret language of feredha women. It was the language they used to call the goats, a barrage of clicks and humming, but there were words in it too: *klasn* was water, *niernetsa* was thread. She told me, laughing, that she had met me before. She would not tell me where. I thought she must have been one of the girls who came riding to Ashenlo, whirling up to the fence like crows, and my mother would tell Nenya to take them a handful of onions and a sack of rice. Seren wore the white cloak, not to mourn the dead, but to mourn the living: her elder brother had fled and was hiding in the mountains. "Yes, we lost him," Fadhian told me one night. His jaw tightened in the smoke of his pipe.

"Lost him how?" I said.

We could hear the jingling of anklets and the laughter where the boys and girls were dancing. Seren passed in the firelight, stamping, thin-shanked like a bird. "Lost him to a feud," Fadhian said.

He glanced at me and gave his hard smile and told the story of how Seren's father had died in Tevlas, fighting over a horse. And how Seren's brother stood among the women of his ausk while they wept and each gave him a gold bangle or a ring.

"It was a great misfortune," Fadhian said. "He had no choice." Later they had heard of his bloody revenge, how he had crept into the tent, the struggle, his wounds, and his triumph. And he was alive and had fled to the western hills.

"But he can never come back," Fadhian said. "We lose so many that way. Or worse, they are caught and we lose them to the prisons. *My clipped hawk*, our song says." He raised the pipe to his lips again and we watched the dancers through the swirling dust.

Dust, darkness, and fire. But soon a subdued air came over the camp, for we had begun to travel among farms. Fadhian forbade dancing and singing, and sometimes we all grew silent as a carriage rumbled past in the dark. It was strange to hear those wheels, or footsteps along the roads. One night the sound of hooves approached, and the boys all mounted quickly and rode out to the edge of our firelight and we heard them talking and soon they returned with a group of black-coated horsemen. Later I learned that there had been eight soldiers from a nearby town as well, but they had remained out there in the dark, beyond our circle. This was according to Fadhian's law, Fadhian who now slowly put his bowl aside and wiped his hands on his trousers and stood.

He greeted the strangers, courteous and tall in the firelight. The sovos was pale and wore a round straw cap. He did not dismount, nor did his seven horsemen who were armed with whips and long bildiri knives.

The horses shifted nervously as the sovos cleared his throat and explained that we could not camp here, it was forbidden. Where could we camp then, Fadhian asked, and the sovos said he did not know, this was a settled area and a private road.

He waved his hand southward. "Perhaps there," he said. He did not know, he knew of nothing beyond his master's lands.

"That is a shame," Fadhian said, smiling.

The sovos looked at him but could not decide if he had been insulted.

"I must ask you to move at once," he repeated.

Listening to him I realized that I had not heard Olondrian spoken since the autumn, and also that I had never heard Fadhian speak it before. He spoke very well, with a soft accent, and his smallest children looked at him in dismay. And I, too, looked at him with a pang. He was so polite and deferential. Yet no one moved until the sovos had gone. Then we began to take down the tents and kick dirt over the fires and I heard women explaining to the children that they could sleep on the wagons.

We rode all night, there was nowhere for us to camp. Lights appeared in the houses as we passed, lanterns in the dark fields. Through everything the scent of a spring night and the beauty of the stars and the sad clang of a pitcher against the side of a wagon. Mantia rode up beside me in the dark and told me about the soldiers and then I thought of them, of their well-fed horses, of how they had probably left a game of londo or even an entertainment in the town: Evmeni singers or dancing girls from the Valley. There would have been an argument and at last those who had been chosen to go had stood up grumbling, securing their belts and buttoning their jackets. I wondered where they were from and if any of them had served in the Lelevai and lost a thumb to frostbite or languished in the hospital at Giva. Outside our circle they had stood, talking softly about the women in town, pausing to spit on the side of the road. At last they had ridden back complaining, bursting into the tavern again. "These idiot farmers don't know what they want. He called us for nothing . . ."

Sunrise broke out tenderly in the east, through a gap in the mountains. Birds awakened in the trees by the road. We breakfasted on cheese and hoda without dismounting and after an hour we finally stopped and crawled into the wagons to rest. The women who had been resting rose and drove the animals on and I lay under the shelter of the moving wagon, rocking from side to side in the noise of hooves and wheels and cries, watching the points of light through the gaps in the hide roof. Lulled to sleep at last I dreamed of orchards. When I woke it was almost dusk and we were still moving among the farms. I crawled out of the shelter, and Seren, sitting on the back of the wagon, smiled and passed me a pitcher of water.

I splashed my hands and face and drank. "Will we stop soon?" I asked.

She shrugged and gave me a piece of raush from her pocket. We were passing a villa where, by the light of the lamp on the terrace, two girls clad in muslin worked on their embroidery. I watched them until they were small white shadows in the darker blur of the house. And perhaps it was the sight of them, or perhaps the sound of Olondrian still ringing in my ears, that made me suddenly say to Seren: "*Niernetsa.*" I mimed the act of embroidering, the pull of the thread. She laughed and shook her head.

She crawled into the shelter and beckoned me after. It was dim and noisy inside, the wagon jolting with us toward the noon country. When she whispered to me, the motion made her nose bump gently against my ear. "Never give away the *che*," she said.

"I didn't mean to," I told her.

"I know."

She kissed my cheek. "*Elu,*" she whispered. "Do you know that word?"

I said no, and she told me it meant love. Up close, she smelled dry and fragrant, like wheat. Her eyes were frightened, my legs like water. "Love," she whispered. "Loving. In the *che*."

For many days it was dry, our lips grew white and we moved among the wells and traveled by night and there was no sound of singing; then suddenly we would come upon a sacred grove with a woman's name where we swallowed the soft and fragrant air like milk. Coolness breathed from the wild mimosa trees and the pink acacias and the white and waxy bark of the karhula. We slit the nalua bulbs and drank the juice and dug up asphodels and ate them and peeled the spines from the aiyas leaves. Only we did not cut the trees for fuel, this was forbidden. The cattle wandered and chewed the flowering broom, looking comical with their broad muzzles smeared with yellow when they had browsed among the heavy golden tras. And then one night there was rain, a hard cold rain, and we stood under it and gasped for a moment of agonizing sweetness. The children screamed for joy and in the morning we all looked brighter with the dust beaten out of our clothes and our crisping hair.

How empty it was, how silent in the desert. There was a happy delirium in being with others, in laughter, in song. The notes of a diali under the stars with a scent of clouds on the wind brought me an unfamiliar joy that clenched my throat. Seren and I set snares for rabbits far away from the camp, and we walked out together to check them twice a day. We lay on her white cloak. She rested her head on my arm as I unfastened the long strings of her leather vest. Each string slipped through its hole with a soft *shirring* sound, then the knot at the end caught for a moment, it wouldn't pull through, I had to pull it harder, her fingers in my hair and at last it gave. They gave one after the other, all released, and I breathed and breathed her skin.

Once I asked: "What if someone discovers us?"

She shrugged, stretched, laughed. A bitter note, for the first time. She said they'd scold and laugh at us. They'd tell us to find men, to get married. "*Chff!*" she said, wrinkling her nose, slapping me on the arm. The gesture of someone reprimanding a child who has soiled itself. "*Chff!* At your age! Shame on you! Susa!"

"They'd call you a susa?"

"A susa's not just a bird. It's a wrong girl, one who won't grow up. But the bildiri use it to mean all feredha girls . . ."

Susa. The bird of the desert, with its brief serrated voice.

"But it's all right," I said awkwardly, "if you're young?"

"You'd have to be younger than we are. We're too old now. It's for children."

"Well," I said, "at least they won't shut us up in a temple."

I told her of Bain, an excursion to Avalei's temple, and how I glimpsed, in the upper story, a jeweled hand tugging a curtain. That hand seemed, for an instant, the sign of paradise. In Avalei's holy house, any person may love any other: love overflows all forms. But a moment later I knew it was not for me, that luxurious hidden life: Avalei's servants never leave the temple except on feast days. They adorn her crown like insects in a lump of amber. "It's a kind of half life," I explained.

She touched my cheek. "Not the life for a soldier."

"Stop, you're getting sand in my eye."

She slapped my face gently, twinkling. "*Chff!*"

"*Chff* yourself." I grabbed her wrist.

"*Chff! Chff!*"

"For shame!" I rolled onto her.

"Susa!" she wheezed. A storm of giggles.

It was there in the desert that my blood returned, there that Seren taught me to seize black ants and snap them between my teeth, there that my heart came open in two halves and words poured out of it: my heart had not been empty after all. I talked night after night until I was hoarse. There was a curl of whiteness in the dark sky, what the feredhai call the track of the goddess Roun, the wake

of her boat in the sea of the heavens and this is what was coming
out of my heart, memories pouring out in waves. All of my life. I
told Seren about the dance of the mountains, about Ashenlo, about
my sister and how she had called me a clown, about Dasya, about
my father, how he was forever a traitor and the son of a traitor and
so he hated himself and everyone else, about my uncle the Telkan,
so weak he allowed himself to be stretched out and then collapsed
again like the sail of a boat controlled by the Priest of the Stone,
about my Uncle Veda, the Duke of Bain, who also hated his life
but with more resignation than my father. I told her about Aunt
Mardith in the north, about Uncle Fenya and his money, how I was
certain they were buying up land in Kestenya, how the desert was
changing hands without anyone knowing, becoming the property
of the Nains, as if you could buy this wind and light. I worried that
it was too much, this blizzard of words. She said: "No." She said
she would give me a field. "This field is wide enough to contain
everything you say." She told me the field would never be filled. Her
hair above me, swinging. She said it was mine. She said she'd never
take it back.

There was one thing I could not tell her. I had to tell Fadhian first.
    I told him to come with me, alone, through the Land of
Flints. We traveled at dawn and dusk through the blackened plain
and in the afternoon we slept beneath the white summer femka
stretched on wooden poles. The country was very bad and often
we walked to spare the horses. I picked up a few stones and rolled
them in my hand. Very black and rough they were and stark in
the sunlight, painting their outlines on my eyes, their inescapable presence. The feredhai said that a dragon had scourged this
country, and I believed them. At the site of the aklidoh there were
a few bowed wild mimosas, all dead. Dead palms, dead acacias
black and hard as iron, pieces of dead wood scattered on the
ground. But the aklidoh was standing, square and silent with its

gray domed roof. Inside we found a few bits of ancient straw. We entered the cool of the inner chamber and sat on the mud benches carved into the wall, facing each other in the light from a hole in the roof.

"Now," said Fadhian.

I took a deep breath, and then I spoke. I told him that I was a Kestenyi. I told him that there was nothing more precious to me, or more fragile, than *Kestenya Rukebnar*, and that this was the reason I had asked him to follow me to this abandoned place. I told him that the war in the north, the Brogyar war, was a ruse, a trick to keep Olondria docile, and he smiled. I told him that the Telkan had made mistakes, that he was weak, the pawn of a priest. I told him that this priest, too, had made mistakes. I spoke of the riot at the Night Market: Valley peasants crushed on the orders of the Priest of the Stone. Fadhian's face grew quiet; I could see him thinking. I told him that my cousin, Prince Andasya, was gathering disaffected generals in the far north. I told him I wanted men from him, a force that would sail westward; I would claim I was taking them to trade horses in Nissia. That winter, on the Feast of Lamps, Dasya and I would converge and take the Isle. And Fadhian would free Kestenya.

"I know you can do it," I said.

I knew he could do it: he would know just whom to ask. He listened in silence, sometimes glancing up at the sky through the hole in the roof. Sky of the desert, Kestenyi sky. He listened until I was empty, spent. Rubbing his jaw, his face as still as noon.

Then he told me a story. I had heard it before but not that way, not from the lips of a man like Fadhian. I had not heard the story told so plainly and with quiet energy and pauses in which the afternoon slowly turned. Sometimes he raised his hand. His eyes were fixed on a spot in the darkness of the crumbling wall but I knew that he did not see it. It was as if we had been abandoned at the bottom of a well, a well that slowly filled with the blueness of night.

"It won't be like that," I whispered, my voice huge in the broken room.

"Won't it?" Fadhian said. I could feel him smiling. Then he sighed and said that my grandfather Uskar had not been a monster or a fool but simply a man of incomplete passions.

"My grandfather knew him well," he said. "He used to speak of what an excellent dancer Uskar had been before he joined the rebels. You know he was terrified of wasps. You see, these are the things we remember. These, and the little children burned alive on the Karafia. Uskar was running up and down the streets of Tevlas shouting and weeping, everyone has heard that part of the story. But who knows what he thought afterward, after he betrayed the rebellion, after he gave his brothers to the noose?"

Fadhian shrugged and crossed his legs, his heel scraping on the sandy floor. He leaned on the wall and looked up at the damaged roof. A single star hung there in a dark blue circle, shifting slightly as if breathing, bright and unguarded and alone.

"Why did they fail?" Fadhian murmured. He said that it was not because they were cowards nor because of feuds among the feredhai. He said that in the end men like my grandfather had not been able to murder their own and so they had been defeated.

"I'm not afraid."

I could feel him smiling again. "This is what worries me. Do you know what it will take to remove Kestenya from the empire? They have grown together, a tree inside a wall. Separate them and the wall is likely to crumble, the tree to die."

"Do you think so? Will it be hard to remove the feredhai from laws and fences, from those who are buying and selling the desert?"

"You have misunderstood me," he said, but when I asked him how he would not answer and for a long time we were silent.

Later, out on the plain, he touched his heels to his horse's ribs and shot off swiftly with his mantle flying behind him, dark blue in the starlight, and I followed at a gallop in the cold air drifting from the edge of the world.

"Spare the horses!" I shouted. My face was hot with anger but the thin sound of my voice shocked me and I did not shout again. Fadhian had heard me and he slowed his horse and proceeded at a walk. And I was listening to the night.

I listened but could not hear anything for its sound was an absence of sound, a deep absence in which the crunching of hooves over stones was lost, and the stars stood very solemn and bright in a circle and seemed so alive that their silence was uncanny, as if they were holding their breath for their own strange purpose. Their whiteness struck me in the face and I bowed my head. That night I spoke without stopping, although Fadhian did not answer. I told him again and again that this time was different, that I was not my grandfather Uskar, that I was loyal to Kestenya, whatever he thought. I spoke again of the fires in the Valley, the anger of people there, and how that anger was singing the song of Kestenya in a different key. And there was a third note: the anger of soldiers in the north. "Only imagine," I said, "if we should sing together."

We slept in the lee of a ridge of hills and I had a dream in which Seren asked me to go with her into a cave: I followed her, and not until she released it did I see that she was bearing with her an enormous dark-furred bat. We stood on the edge of a pit inside the cave and watched the bat fly down in slow circles to join the others. There were cats there too, at the bottom, gliding among the stones. "You'll never get it back now," I told her.

In the morning we made a fire of dried dung and boiled coffee in the shade of the hills while the sun came flooding in silver over the plain. I remember Fadhian's crouch, his fingers lightly touching the handle of the pot, his eyes fixed on the level of the coffee. A little wind came up and raised the dust about our camp. The horses stood with their legs in the whirling cloud, their bellies gray. Fadhian poured the coffee and we shielded the cups with our mantles and drank, chewing the grounds and spitting onto the rocks. He glanced up at me, and his face looked young, young and thin and tired. His smile was a crooked knife hung on a wall. How it cut my heart.

"Well, Tav," he said. "Let's try it. Let's have *Kestenya Rukebnar.* Let's have war."

"Don't go," she said, when I told her.

"I must."

"Going to Bain," she sneered.

"I'm not going to Bain."

She shrugged. "To the Valley, then."

"I'll come back."

I leaned close and told her all our plans. I told her to be ready for independence. She shook her head, her earring trembling against her neck. A silver ring adorned with a red glass bead. Cheap glass from Tevlas. She said that this war would not be mine, I would never triumph. She, who knew nothing of war, told me that I, a woman, would never be remembered, that any victory would be Dasya's and not mine. They would call it Prince Andasya's War. I told her it didn't matter. "We'll be free," I whispered. "Free. Even if I'm killed, you'll live on in a free Kestenya."

She bowed her head. When she raised it again, her eyes had turned silver. "You still don't remember where we met," she said.

She stalked to the fire where the boys sat playing the diali and took up the instrument. The look she gave me turned the air to ice. She sat cross-legged and played. She played and sang in an exaggerated manner, tossing her stiff plaits, rolling her eyes where a few tears still clung. And I knew. She had been among the hired singers at my going-away party in the garden at Ashenlo. She had been there, beneath the wooden arch, while I imagined life in the desert and engaged in a stupid argument with Armali.

"Stop it," I said.

She didn't stop. The flesh crept on my neck. She sang of the dead who wander among the caves, the dead who haunt the ruins of the aklidai and the girls who meet them there and are transformed into birds and slaughtered and eaten. *She strayed among the stones,* she sang, *and he was waiting there.* Such a terrible song for her pure voice. I listened, enraged. I wanted to smash the diali, to strike her face. I would have swallowed her whole if it meant I could take her with me.

4. Song

The swordmaiden will sing as she rides and the song will cool her spirit. She is happiest when singing the songs of the road. Songs of the hearth may make her body heavy and uncertain: it is difficult to manage a sword at a feast.

All songs that tell of brave deeds are useful, especially those in which the hero is slain. The False Countess was accustomed to prescribe melodies like physic. A man overtaken by trembling would be ordered to sing the ninth verse of the Vanathul. *For self-hatred, the Countess recommended "The Pass of the Doves."*

Songs sung in childhood may also be used, but with care.

Melancholy music is appropriate only in peacetime, never in war.

At night, wrapped in her cloak, the swordmaiden murmurs the song of her unknown comrades, swordmaidens past and future: a song without words.

If I live, I will find Seren again.

The camp is silent. In three days, on the Feast of Lamps, we depart for the Blessed Isle. Dasya will meet me there, and together we will take Velvalinhu. We'll have surprise on our side: everyone will think we have come for the feast. My Telkan Uncle and his priest will fall, while in the north whole battalions forsake the army, charging down from the hills to take the Valley, and in the east, Fadhian rides at the head of the feredhai. This is what I think of now at night.

If I live. If I live.

I lay on the sand with Seren and named the stars, the way Malino had taught me in the observatory. Firelight touched my wrist as I pointed: the right wrist, overdeveloped like the whole arm. I told her she ought to call me Tavis the Warped.

She clicked her tongue at me in disgust.

"Is that *che?*"

"Yes. It means who asked about your arm? What's that one— the bright one to the right?"

The feredhai have their own names for the stars, their own con- stellations. What we call the Bee they call the Clasp.

If I live.

She told me she had dreamt of me on the night I first arrived. She dreamt I was holding water in my cupped hands. "Look inside," I told her, "it's a taubel." She bent and peered into the circle of water. It was completely black.

"This field is for you," she told me once, "I'll never take back." But she did take it back. The day I left she stood apart, near the artusa, while the others kissed me and patted my shoulders and wished me luck on the road. Her sunburned arms crossed and her gaze trained on the mountains. No white cloak today, no sign of grief. She was taking it back. Her hair and her voice and her breath and the scar where she had been bitten by a wild dog. "I yelled like fever," she'd told me. She was taking it all back. I wanted to be the first to turn away. I lost.

So many memories. But one is missing, because it never arrived: Seren performing at the garden party at Ashenlo. It lies like a needle in the back of my mind. I grope for it, desperate to draw it out. I see again the lamps among the sparse-limbed trees. Gowns brushing over the gravel and the musicians under the wooden arch. Were there three or four? Four, say four, Seren and three others. Guitar, diali, and drum. They glance at one another and nod, the drummer taps his calloused fingers, and it begins. Seren in the center, her strong face and supple, easy bearing, her hands in her lap. The light glints on the parting in her hair. Her plaits are tawny where the sun has burned them. She tosses her head and sways from the waist, using all the coarse, familiar movements. It's not the feredhai style, but a parody of it, something sold all over the empire. She sings the old songs: "The Swallow in Winter," "The Rose of the East." Curling one hand in the air, opening and closing her great black eyes. People are listening, drawing chairs closer, mouthing the words. When she finishes a phrase a clatter erupts among the crowd, a burst of snapping, rings clicking on glasses, cries of *"Bamanan ai."* The words begin as something maudlin and meaningless but repetition gives them power, and she repeats each line in fifty ways. Sobbing and swaying as if overcome by the music. And under the sound of the words comes the true meaning, the one they possessed long ago. How sad they were when they were first composed.

Where are you? I am waiting.

And once again: *I am waiting. Where are you?*

When we were small at the Feast of Lamps the lanterns were lit in the avla and our mother sat at the table smiling and handing out the glasses. Each glass had a flower tied to it, a jasmine bloom or a sprig of mint, and the women fastened them in their hair and the men put them in their boot tops. Our mother sat in her chair all evening and never danced though she loved the music. In those days, I remember, we found it simple to be extraordinary. Everyone watched when I danced a sadh for Father or offered him his pipe on the beaded cushion when he was tired of dancing and sat by the window. And Dasya and Siski clasping hands in the corner would swing in circles until they fell and Siski's boots left marks like tea stains across the floor. And when they carried me upstairs at every window I saw the lights of the hunters down in the forest where they lived on raush and snow. And she was my dear, my dear. And she sang underneath the wooden arch at a party to celebrate my recovery from my wound. Who can understand the sadness of this? She was singing and I was whole and her song was a wound and the money we paid her was a wound. And all the lamps were wounds, and the beaded cushion, and the avla, and the music. When I was eight years old, still inside the enchanted circle, a strange little boy who had come to play with the servants' children tripped me in the courtyard and I fell and cut my chin. "Down goes the house!" he sneered. I remember his hard, shiny lips, and how cold he looked. He did not have a proper coat, and his earlobes were red as coals. Fulmia came running around the side of the house, waving a rake and roaring terrible curses in Kestenyi. The boy ran off, and Fulmia helped me up, but not before I saw, in the eyes of this man who had served my House since my father was a child, the eyes of this man looking after the fleeing boy, an expression, not of anger, but of some secret satisfaction. It was gone by the time I was on my feet, and I never saw it again. But I know what I saw: hope, like a desert aloe. Hope, stubborn and bitter to the taste. That hides water. That bears the drought. An ugly plant with the power to heal.

Now often at night it seems as if there is something abroad in the wood with wings or something that breathes as it sits upon my chest. I get up in the night and go to the flap of the tent and open it. Farus is instantly awake and rubs against my knee. "It's only the rain," I tell him, patting his head. The wind blows in my face and shakes the trees and powders me with rain. The cold rain and the warm dog by my leg. And far away in the dark the lights of the bridge. Everywhere the sound of wings.

From Our Common History

Olondria, land of almonds. Land of myrrh.

In the words of wine-tongued Ravhathos, our greatest poet: "the gods' garden."

In a cave on the northern tip of the Blessed Isle, they say, lies Olondria's navel: the exact starting point of history. Naturally, also, a door to the Land of the Dead. There the poor shepherd Hernas slew a white deer, which revealed itself as the goddess Avalei. Bleeding, weeping, and happy—for she was now free from the spell of the Dead King her brother—the goddess crowned her deliverer with a garland of straw. A symbol of marriage ever after. She kissed him on the mouth: "a breath of incense," says the Book. From their union came a line of kings.

Yet this was not the only line to descend from Avalei, Ripener of the Grain. For in the form of a deer, running wild through the Iavain, she had been stung by Karos, the God of Plague, in the form of a fly (hence one of her names: *Velkosri*, the "Plague Lily"). The site of the sting swelled for eight months, and when it burst, a pair of twins leapt out, creaking to the sky with slobbering blue lips. They were winged and horned, and spoke no human tongue. They were the first Drevedi, blood drinkers and flesh eaters of the woods.

And so, as the shepherds of the Valley, a rough people who had all but forgotten the gods, were united under a divine line of kings, a menace brooded and multiplied in the forest. This mystery, writes Fanlewas, expresses the essential duality of Avalei, the goddess of love and death. "In her white form," he explains, "she is snow and mourning: she gives birth to monsters, children of Karos whose color is white. In her red form—the red of her blood, when she is slain by Hernas—she gives birth to kings and roses." Imrodias prefers to view the Drevedi as a type of warning, even a prophecy of the war that would be waged by the offspring of Hernas. "For that war is known as the War of the Tongues; and the primary characteristic of the Drevedi is that they cannot speak."

Whatever our interpretation, certain facts remain: that the people of Hernas, who called themselves Laths (from the ancient *lak-thet*, "vine grower"), sought forcibly to unite themselves with the Kestenyi and Nains, their neighbors to the east and northeast, who spoke languages related to their own; that their justification was their common ancestry, and the favor shown the Laths, through Hernas, by the goddess; that the ensuing War of the Tongues was the longest and bloodiest in our history; and that it was effectively ended by the Drevedi.

"They appeared in the western sky like a storm of claws," writes Von.

"The first to die in their clutches," Besra adds, "was Natho of Ildei. Seated on a saddlebird, his bow drawn to shoot down at the ground—where he thought his most dangerous enemy to be—he was torn from the saddle and devoured face first, as if in a diabolical mockery of the act of love, by an ogress of piercing beauty."

"Like blue leaves of a murderous autumn," writes Hailoth.

"The earth is poisoned now," writes an early, anonymous contributor to the *Dreved Histories*. "We all go about in white cloaks. My heart is sore: a bruised and seedless fruit. And a salt wind blows endlessly in the empty streets."

The *Dreved Histories*, perhaps the most painful chronicle ever written, gathers accounts of the reign of these monsters, who, not satisfied with anthropophagy, put on clothes, established themselves in palaces, and married the sons and daughters of noble houses. The *Histories* also tell of the eventual human rebellion, the fall of the vampires (who were variously burned, drowned, and battered to death with bricks), and their reemergence here and there in the coming centuries, in the form of horned or curiously insect-like children. As recently as the reign of Varon the Petulant, a boy with horns was executed at Ambrelhu. But the era of Dreved domination is, happily, long over. Iloki, or "saddlebirds"—once the war steeds of noble Laths— are kept in the palace, but never ridden. We will have no winged lords.

"The project undertaken in the War of the Tongues," writes Imrodias, "a project of unity (and there is, surely, no greater or wiser aspiration), was interrupted by the accursed Drevedi, but not abandoned. In the course of time, it would be completed, and called Olondria."

This expresses a popular perspective among the Laths, who eventually conquered Kestenya and Nain under Braud the Oppressor. What we now call "the common tongue," or simply "Olondrian," is in fact the language of the Laths. In Nain and Kestenya, due to a centuries-long series of political marriages, those who hold titles often carry, as well, a strong strain of Lathni ancestry: "the higher the branch, the closer to the trunk," being a common saying. Genealogy is a national obsession. The *Hath Harevu*, a book containing the names of all those who can trace their ancestry, however distantly, to Hernas the Shepherd, is updated every year, and consistently outsells the *Vallafarsi*, causing Odrid of Eal to quip: "Our true Holy Book is the *Hath*." The most exalted bloodline, of course, is that of the Telkan—a title meaning "King Over All." Olondrian inheritance passes from a man to his sister's son; if he has no sister, and names no heir before his death, it passes to his own son—that is, to a different family or House. As the proverb goes: "A house without sons, a house without windows; a house without daughters, a house without doors." The betrothals of kings, particularly those with no sisters, are watched with great anxiety: the House of a queen may, in such cases, seize the kingship through an accident of fortune or judicious poisoning.

The noble Houses of Nain and Kestenya are generally considered "too far from the trunk" for marriage with the Telkans. They are not quite Olondrian enough; yet for all that they speak the common tongue, dance the arilantha, and play the limike. It is thus possible to speak of "our common history": a history briefly blocked by the Drevedi and then permitted to run its course. This is not the only way of seeing matters, however. Faska, the Kestenyi rebel, is said to have spat, while bound to a post: "For this the gods cursed you with monsters."

"And the years pass like clouds."—Karanis of Loi

Olondria swells and shrinks. It gains Nain and Kestenya, then it loses them both. It wins Kestenya back, then loses it after the Olondrian army is weakened by a protracted war with the Sea Kings of Evmeni. Olondria gains Evmeni and the hitherto independent kingdom of Panj. The justification of a common ancestry is no longer thought necessary. The only justification now is power. Goods flow north from Evmeni: ivory, oranges, bolma, musicians, and salt.

Nain, threatened by the Brogyars to the north, enters into a treaty of fellowship with Olondria. Olondria gains

Nain. "Not by force of arms," laments the historian and Nainish patriot, Ailmali of Faluidhen, "nor even by some treachery did we fall, but through our desire for wines, silks, dyes, and other seductions of the insidious Laths." The greatest seduction, it must be admitted, is that of the vast and well-trained Olondrian army, which enters into a war with the Brogyars north of Nain. "War," writes General Aren of Deinivel, "breeds war." His mood is cheerful, his sword hungry for conquest. Olondria gains Kestenya.

Rebellions wrack that mountainous waste, which is called the Intractable Province. "Then they must be made tractable," insists Aren. "We must accustom them to the bit." The aklidai—houses of lonely ascetics which serve the highland people as temples—are emptied, and the mystics put to the sword. Roun, the Moon Goddess, patroness of Kestenya, is declared a blasphemous figment. "*Woe, woe,*" runs a popular song of the times. "*Woe for my little bone thimble. It lies broken in the gorge. And woe for my little bone finger, pricked to death.*"

An uneasy peace. An outbreak of war. An uneasy peace. An outbreak of war. An uneasy peace. And then an organized rebellion in Kestenya, a revolt that unites the cities and the desert. *Kestenya Rukebnar*, they shout— "Independent Kestenya"—nomads, farmers, aristocrats, they all cry out together. This revolt almost succeeds, but is broken by that cruel attack, the Karafia—in Kestenyi, "The Night of Tears"—on which the city of Tevlas is burnt to the ground. During the reprisals, the desert is so thickly strewn with corpses, the crows grow listless.

Uskar of Kestenya, heir to the destroyed city of Tevlas, cannot bear it. When he joined his cousins in rebellion, he was drunk on stedleihe, singing in a café. Now, smearing his tears on his sleeve, he gives in. He betrays the rebels to the king.

The young Telkan, Eirlo the Generous, is generous indeed. Once the last rebels have been captured and strung up by their heels to die (*"like songbirds on a wire"* as the Kestenyi lament has it), the Telkan gives his sister in marriage to the loyal Uskar. That marriage shocks the empire: the next Telkan will be half Kestenyi. Princess Beilan, the Telkan's sister, thinks it a fine joke. A tall, broad woman, her hair dyed yellow as Nainish apples, her face weather-beaten from a life lived primarily on horseback, she throws herself into what she considers the customs of her new home. Having been a passionate hunter of deer, she switches to hunting shambus, the wild sheep of the highlands. It pleases her, once a year, on Tanbrivaud Night, to throw a ball to which she invites the most notorious bandits in Kestenya: "I won't cut your throats," reads the invitation, "if you don't cut mine."

Wine flows, and the princess lights the outlaws' cigars with a candle.

She bears three sons. Teskon, heir to the throne. Veda, heir to the valuable duchy of Bain. And Irilas, who will inherit the Kestenyi estate of Ashenlo and the duchy of Tevlas.

Three sons. No daughters.

A House without doors.

The princess develops a passion for raising doves. Her skirts crusted with guano, her eyes encircled by rings of dark green paint, she reclines in her aviary, blowing pipe smoke toward the rafters.

Princess Beilan and Lord Uskar were sadly unsuited to one another. Where the princess was bold, the duke was timid. Where she was hale and ringing as a bronze bell, he was pallid—for a Kestenyi, unusually so—and short of breath.

He loved wildflowers, but because of his asthma could only enjoy them in pictures. He began to suffer from night terrors after the Kestenyi War—he kept hearing the glass in the windows of Tevlas shatter in the heat, the children scream, and his betrayed, dead cousins curse him before the gods. For a time he attempted to live in Tevlas, but his health was so affected by the ash in the air, the dust of renovation, and the gloom of the gutted buildings, that he retired to Ashenlo. There, one winter, his health and spirits were restored by a visit from a saint.

"The old man came out of a snowstorm," said one of Uskar's footmen, speaking on condition of anonymity. "Half naked and with that great stone on his back. We never thought he'd last the night. He'd no more flesh than a stick of raush."

The old man, however, did live. He was Hudra, First Priest of the Stone. Led by a dream, he had ventured into the deadly region beyond the Duoronwei, where even the feredhai dare not go, and returned with a huge black rock, magnetic and apparently covered with writing. Uskar engaged a doctor for him (saving his life, but not his frost-bitten toes) and soon the old visionary was settled in a small room at the back of the house, where, aided by Uskar, he devoted himself to copying down the lines in multiple languages and scripts inscribed on the Stone. The two men became convinced that what they possessed was a message from the Nameless Gods, those who were before Avalei or any of the others, the architects of Time and Space, distant, inexplicable, and inexorable, who are referred to collectively as Nieb. The earliest lines deciphered by the two enthusiasts instructed them to burn their garments and put on robes of raw wool. Never had Nieb shown an interest in such trivial human matters. The two men wept. Thus began the Cult of the Stone.

Hudra changed his name to Elarom: "Bearer of the Stone." Uskar became Ahadrom: "Face of the Stone."

His eldest son, Teskon, who was extraordinarily like his father, tall, black-haired, and inclined to melancholy and coughs, joined Ahadrom in his work and was soon indoctrinated into the new faith. Neither of the younger boys, however, could be prevailed upon to spend his time squinting at a stone and being lectured by an old windbag mottled with frostbite. Veda, who had inherited his mother's passion for sport, spent his days outdoors, while Irilas plagued his tutors and pillaged the liquor cabinet.

Princess Beilan, absorbed in the lives of her birds, was nearly oblivious to the changes taking place under her roof. When her husband spoke of his work, she was overheard to say: "Pssht!" To her brother she wrote: "We are all as healthy as cockroaches and as merry as thieves."

Years later, when her son Teskon took the throne, he changed his name to Ahadrom II. The princess was then in mourning for her brother, Eirlo the Generous, who had died at table, collapsing into a bowl of mutton soup. The news of her son's decision startled her from her thoughts for a moment; she is reported to have asked: "Is it so serious with him, then?" At once she lapsed back into her reverie, playing absently with a feather and murmuring: "I had no idea. I had no idea."

Her ignorance might be excused, as she had not seen her son for some years: he had moved to Velvalinhu after his marriage. That marriage, to Firvaud of Faluidhen, a Nainish noblewoman, had been celebrated all across the empire. Eirlo, the Old Telkan, overjoyed at his nephew's choice, had ordered sweetmeats and festive ribbons distributed in the streets. The ribbons read: "Olondria's Love Match," "The Greatest Green Marriage in History," "A Braid of Three Peoples," "Unity at Last." Now, however, Eirlo was dead, and the new Telkan seemed more preoccupied with the Cult of the Stone than with promoting the unity symbolized by his marriage. He had the Stone transported to Velvalinhu, along with its priest and Ahadrom I, who could not bear to be parted from his master. The first Ahadrom, who had been Uskar of Tevlas, was aging fast: he found it hard to speak, and even writing had become an arduous task. From the ship, he wrote to Princess Beilan, left behind in the highlands: "Lord. Burnt. Thunder. Where. Lament."

The Cult of the Stone grew. We hardly noticed it at first: the fading of the old priest, Elarom, and the rise of Ivrom, his successor, a man who used his tongue like a riding crop and gained several thousand converts with the fire of his eye. We failed to take note of the priest's growing power, the success of his books and pamphlets; we were too much occupied with the question of the throne. Who would take it after Ahadrom II—who was, as certain voices never tired of repeating, only half a Lath himself? Could Olondria bear to see, on the Horsehair Seat of her ancestral kings, that dream of Eirlo's: a living "Braid of Three Peoples"? For not long after his coronation, Ahadrom introduced the empire to his son and—as he had no sisters—his heir.

There were other living members of the House of the Old Telkan, of course. It was expected that one of them would lay claim to the throne. Hinro, Duke of Ethendria, was the most likely candidate: not a young man, but strong, and of impeccable lineage. No one expected that Prince Andasya, the son of Ahadrom II and his Nainish bride, would so thoroughly bewitch the public. "My pet, my pig," goes a bul composed in his honor, when he was but an infant: "my bully, my bee, my bud, my cherry-sweet."

"Impossibly handsome," wrote a journalist for the Bainish newspaper the *Starling*, when the prince was nine years old. A lady who was fortunate enough to glimpse him astride a white pony on the Isle of Ban declared that she could have eaten his velvet breeches.

At the age of twelve, the prince posed for Ferulei, then First Court Painter. Engravings of his portrait sold by the thousands. The boy, black-haired, with pouting lips, holds a kite in one hand and leans on a leafy oak. The title: *Death, with Kite.*

By the time he was sixteen, it was clear that no one in Olondria would refuse to have Prince Andasya for their king. He was not only the most beautiful youth in the country, but a superb dancer and rider, a budding scholar, and a wit. "His charm perfumes the air for a hundred miles," gushes a writer for *The Watcher.* Hearts flutter when he enters the army: if he should be injured or killed! But then—how heroic of him to enlist! When he puts on his scarlet guardsman's jacket, his lips look redder than ever.

He is charmingly old-fashioned—a proper Prince of the Branch, despite his questionable lineage. In opposition to his father, Ahadrom II, he declares himself a devotee of the goddess Avalei, now the primary enemy of the Cult of the Stone. "I could never bow to a rock," he is quoted as saying, "and I have too much taste to go about clad in a blanket." He is the monarch of our dreams. He is seen at Loma in a green coat, at Feirivel in gray. No one imagines that, with his cousin Tavis, he is planning a war.

Suddenly, in the Valley, the peasants are armed.

It is the Feast of Lamps, and all the roads are blocked.

They travel in groups of ten. They wear red cloaks, red woolen caps, sometimes only a red rag pinned to a shoulder. Even the poorest have hennaed their beards.

They are singing the songs of Avalei on the roads. *The hunting knife is within my heart. The hunting knife is the ornament of my heart.*

Such a moon! The dogs bay as if wild with joy.

Fighting breaks out in Bain. Within hours, the garrison is set on fire.

Fighting in the Balinfeil. It begins in the mountains and spreads to the woods and farms. Soldiers are bleeding out of the hills. They knock on doors, they are found asleep in haystacks. Their stories are garbled, excited. "No, it's not the Brogyars," they keep repeating.

The first refugees from Kestenya have crossed the Ilbalin.

In Bain, the duke, Veda, is trying to control the rioting in the Old Quarter. During a brief retreat to the Ducal Residence, he receives a note from the Isle. *Dear Uncle Veda, I have decided to take the throne early!*

He stares at the card, his bones filling with ice.

Smoke drapes the windows.

Outside, figures huddle in the walled garden. They are devotees of the Stone, seeking refuge at the Residence. Their lives are in danger in the streets of Bain.

Veda drops the card and runs up the stairs.

He runs up stair after stair, panting, until he reaches the flat roof. As he has often done over the last few days, he peers toward the Blessed Isle, his eyes prickling in the smoky air. He looks toward Velvalinhu, the Holy City, his royal brother's seat, where he has sent so many frantic letters, asking for help, for counsel, for armed men.

Today, for the first time, he sees flames in the distance. Velvalinhu is burning.

BOOK TWO

The History of the Stone

Yours is a negative kingdom.

"The towers are all aflame and I, I skim the air between them, defiant in my feathers of burnt lace." Lines by the great queen Fanleshama the Poet, who recited them long ago from the Chrysoprase Seat. In this poem, the *Seventy-Fifth Elegy*, she speaks in the voice of an owl. "Oh pines, oh rain of opals, oh curling ice." The owl laments the loss of its home in the north but refuses to leave the Blessed Isle, where its mate is trapped in a burning aviary. Today I repeat this elegy over and over through numb lips, for the towers are burning. Smoke pours thickly from the Tower of Mirrors; the Tower of Lapis Lazuli is visible only as flashes of murky light in a vast pall of ashen fog.

The railing of my balcony has gone black. When I grip it, it stains my gloves.

It is the ninth day of Fir, the Month of Darkness. On this day, the Telkan hears reports from the Master of Granaries and seed samples are presented on beds of raw wool. The Telkan tastes the winter wine and pronounces it either Sloe, Amber, or Earth. Based on his choice, his rooms are refurnished in purple, red, or black. He hears reports from the Master of Prisons. His chief scribe, known as the High Engraver, records the number of prisoners in each province of the Empire.

A priest of Tol enters in a pair of otterskin slippers and touches the ears and throat of the Telkan with white ash. Bells are rung in the ninth room of the Temple of the Storm God; the iron boar on the doorstep is rubbed with resin. The Teldaire hears reports from the Keeper of Gardens and the Master of the Reservoir, who recites the height of the water in all the wells. The Teldaire wears either plum-colored or rust-red garments. In either case, she wears gold jewelry, because the silver is being cleaned.

If the Telkan has children at home, they are dressed in scarlet and scented with bergamot. Tonight they will listen to stories about foxes.

The worms have entered their deepest sleep. The gods favor dogs and ravens. The stars bend low, trailing their long beards.

So says the palace almanac, the one I keep in my bed, in between the sheets. I have always kept it there, for fear my father would discover it. He would have sneered at me—perhaps raged at me, depending on his mood—for keeping this trash in my room, this compendium of palace life. It was the life he had sworn to destroy. He used to refer to all rituals as "bears' dances." And Velvalinhu he called "the den." But I found meaning in the almanac: in the light of its brief and graceful descriptions, the life of this Holy City became legible. My reading, too, grew richer: Fanleshama's poetry called out to me with new urgency when I realized that the "wind-battered owl" of the seventy-fifth elegy, written on the last day of the Month of Lamps, undoubtedly refers to the pair of horned owls released by the Telkan and Teldaire on that day. "Oh pines, oh rain of opals," she writes—references to the Grave King, the Lord of the Dead, whose steed is a horned owl. While the refrain sings over and over of "perfect love." The poem captivated me; when I turned the page of the almanac, I left a streak of blood . . . I had been chewing my nails as I read, a bad habit that grew worse in times of excitement or distress. I closed the book and kissed its garish cover splashed with poppies. Lunre had given it to me that afternoon. "Read the Month of Lamps," he told me, smiling. He did not say, did not need to say, "Don't tell your father."

And now my father is gone and I am alone and still I keep the almanac under my sheets, with my drawing pad, my brushes, my charcoal pencils, my private notebooks, my mother's hand mirror, dear gods, after all these years I do not think I could fall asleep on an even bed.

Yet the rituals mean nothing now. Nothing. My father's purpose is achieved: Velvalinhu is broken like a cup. Horses clop through the halls; figures hurry across the courtyards with chests and bundles; the air swells with the odor of smoke. Enemy soldiers lounge everywhere: strange, ragged rebels in mismatched uniforms, some of them speaking only the rasping tongue of the Kestenyi highlands, that language which, Firdred wrote, makes it sound as though all of one's teeth have been shattered. They play londo on the roofs, rings-and-arrows in the gardens; their bonfires paint the night. Dirty, flea-bitten, drunken, and happy, they sing vanadiel until dawn, decked with spoils: gold earrings, bangles, rich scarves fashioned into turbans. My father's vision is achieved, in a sense, the rituals of the palace abandoned—though it is his enemies who have stopped Velvalinhu's heart.

Even how I hear soldiers singing down below.

The one assigned to my door is a Valley boy with a snub nose. His name is Vars. He brings me bread and olives, but no news. "Be easy, teldarin," he says. His eyes are red; perhaps the smoke irritates them, or perhaps, like most soldiers, he drinks.

One day I tried to push past him and escape. I brushed against him and he stepped back, probably conditioned by his upbringing, for he has the air of the minor nobility or that tradesman's class whose manners are even more impeccable. He could not at first bring himself to seize a lady—and so I ran down the hall, my slippers skidding on the dusty tiles, and he shouted and caught up to me before I even rounded the corner, for he is younger than I as well as stronger.

"Now, teldarin," he said reproachfully, his hand on my arm. His breath had not quickened, while I was gasping like a carp.

I think it is possible that they will kill me. This is, after all, Velvalinhu, where as Olirei puts it, Death wears dancing shoes.

Vars took me back to my room. Now, when he brings me something to eat, he is careful to block the doorway with his body.

It is possible that they will kill me. *Write, write,* it rings in my head, remember, quickly, before it is too late.

Write.

My name is Tialon of Velvalinhu. I am the daughter of Ivrom the Priest of the Stone, who brought to Olondria the message—

My hand goes slack. I find myself drawing flowers in the margins. I draw spikes and a small woman among the thorns. The woman is ugly and wears a black dress. I lick my finger and smear her to create shadows, but only succeed in ruining the page.

Get up. Go to the door. Listen for Vars. My stomach grumbles; the light fades. What if they plan to starve me in my room? Blow out the lamp and step out onto the balcony (I am afraid to appear there after dark, with a light at my back—they might use me for target practice). How dark it is down below! I can scarcely see the Alabaster Court, where I walked as a child, or rather trotted along behind my father, awkwardly trying to match his long strides, carrying his writing box. It was so hot I sweated dreadfully in my wool frock. I remember the day I noticed a bitter odor from under my arms: an attacking smell, fiery and somehow shameful. I scrubbed myself almost raw with our brown soap, coveting the florets of scented toilet soap the maids carried through the halls . . .

Write. Write. My name is Tialon of Velvalinhu. I am the daughter of Ivrom the Priest of the Stone. If only he would come back and stand over me again, in the way I hated so much when I was a girl!

The sound of his breath when I made a mistake. His disgust. I want it back—that short, irritated sigh—I want to crawl inside it.

I think I could make a home there, in that angry, hollow place.

I'm wasting ink. I must write of his vision, of the Stone.

My name is Tialon of Velvalinhu.

I draw a woman with a beak. A woman with the feet of a hare.

Forget yourself. Crawl inside, crawl inside him—not into the sound of his breath which is lost to you but into his message, the treasure he wanted to give the world. For certainly he did not wish to give it this tall, round-shouldered woman, going gray, whose jaw aches dully because she grinds her teeth together. She, I feel sure, was an accident. Yet if the accident could speak. If the beads of a ruined necklace could arrange themselves to spell a word. *Father.* I will not allow them to bury you as a heretic.

Write. Remember. This is the History of the Stone.

I. You will sever all ties and pass from your bondage into light.
914

When he had shed his name, left the capital, cut off relations with nearly all of his family and friends, when he had become this harsh young man, *Ivrom*, "the Mirror of the Stone," he still remembered the pink peppercorn tree in his aunt's garden in Bain. The old lady scattered pink peppercorns over everything: the meat, the flavored ice. And the cloth on the garden table, which had once been red, had been left outside in the sun so long—held down at the corners with bricks to keep it from blowing away—that it echoed that marvelous dry, pink, summery color. A color that at once recalled the little handheld fans, made of paper or wicker, or, in one case, seagulls' feathers, which his aunt kept in the desk by the terrace doors and always offered to guests before they went out in the garden to take the air. "Don't go without a fan, it's so hot." And when Ivrom, on one of the Telkan's barges, was crossing the Ithvanai to the Blessed Isle, and first caught sight of Velvalinhu in the splendid evening light, its walls throbbed with that same vibrant peppercorn color. It made him uneasy—or perhaps that was only the motion of the boat—he had always hated boating—his cousins used to tip him out on purpose—but no, most likely he felt uneasy at being reminded so strongly of his aunt's house, now, on the eve of his new life. The Isle grew closer and closer, and with it those scintillant pink towers. Their color oppressed him, as did the complex, salty smell in the air, and most of all the muted snuffling of his pregnant wife, Tenais, who was crying bitterly among the bags.

The barge drew up at the pier. A pair of young boys were light-
ing lanterns, their voices bouncing back from the calm sea. And
Elarom, the Priest of the Stone, rose from the bench where he had
been sleeping and faltered forward, hands outstretched for balance.
Ivrom took his arm. "Thank you, my boy," the priest said with a
smile that pierced the younger man's heart. Ivrom helped his new
master onto the pier. Faintly he heard Tenais calling behind him:
"Ivrom, Ivrom!" Like the cry of a gull. He held tight to Elarom's
arm. "Lean on me, Master," he said.

Ivrom and Tenais moved into a pair of bare rooms in the Tower
of Aloes. Tenais tacked a few of her paintings to the wall: wobbly,
watery creations on heavy paper, made on excursions to the Isle of
Songs with her sisters when she was a girl. She owned enough of
these pictures to cover the walls with representations of blurred
fountains, crooked mares, and dropsical squirrels, but she soon lost
heart and left them in the box, and sat at the window all day eating
raisins from a bowl balanced on her stomach. From the window
she could peer upward at the sky between the towers, or down into
a complex system of drains. On the Feast of Birds, when doves
and pigeons were released, panicked flocks clattered overhead, and
a bird fell down past her window—dead, no doubt, of the shock.

"The windows are too small," she complained to her husband,
who spent his days studying with the Priest of the Stone, absorbed
in the tenets of a bright new faith, a faith that seemed to him deli-
ciously cold, stripped of impurities, serene as a winter dawn. He
would come back to their rooms from his days of study wrapped
in a freezing and holy cloud. And there was Tenais, complaining the
windows were too small. "The daylight can scarcely come in!" He
brought her extra candles to quiet her, and one night he returned to
find she had lit them all.

She had prepared a stew. They ate in the profligate glow of
twenty candles—two would have sufficed, as the sun had not yet

set. Tenais ate slowly, her round face seeming to pulse in the light, a moon. Ivrom was sweating; the dye of his robe would run, leaving marks on his skin like bruises.

Bruised by the Nameless Gods, he thought. A potent image. He would use it in the tract he was writing for distribution on the Feast of Plenty. If only he wasn't so hot! Then he could think . . . how to connect the image of the bruise to the notion of prayer . . .

Tenais wore no shawl. Her plump arms gleamed in the blaze.

"It's warm," he said.

"I am very glad," she said softly. "You were so late, I feared it would be cold."

"Not the stew," he snapped.

She raised her eyes. She knew perfectly well what he meant. Her eyes were flat, hostile, like two circles of black paper . . . And he began to shout at her, amazed at how easy it was to step through into rage, as if it were an open hall inside him, a hall with no door, or more accurately, an abyss, an empty space into which he hurtled, exhilarated by the plunge. Let the whole Tower of Aloes hear him shouting—he didn't care! He was already lost, deprived of the refined, austere atmosphere of the room of the Stone, where the glow of the small green lamps enveloped him as he studied with the old priest, reverently copying the words of the Nameless Gods. They examined each mark on the Stone with care, observing it through a glass. The old priest had a number of special brushes to remove the dust from the lines. They could spend whole hours, whole days, on a single scratch. Time disappeared—and now he was plunged in time, in heat, in the vicious stare of this woman Tenais! The smell of the stew rising from the table was making him ill. He knocked his bowl to the floor—he'd fling the candles—he'd set the place on fire! And Tenais was standing and shouting too, red in the face as if ready for a brawl, despite the bulge underneath her apron.

"You'll break my mind! You'll break it!" he shouted, jumping up and down and snatching at his hair, which was already growing thin, and he knew he looked absurd, and the thought enraged him so that his temples throbbed and he feared that his mind really was going to pieces. He gazed at his wife with hatred. She waved her fist, her face shining with sweat or tears. Of course she wanted to undermine his work, having no real work of her own, only the Temple of Heth Kuidva in Bain, where she used to go every Tolie to dole out rice to the poor. That was where they had met—he, a priest of Heth Kuidva, the Oracle God, already aloof, touched in advance by a marvelous destiny, with the sharp, proud profile that made him look noble and withdrawn even when his stockings, as Tenais would soon discover, were falling into rags—and she, delicate-featured and shy, the eldest of four sisters, the only unmarried one, fond of songbirds and the romances of Korim, scrupulously devout and committed to serving the hungry once a week, her hair demurely bound up in a pale green scarf. They had walked by the harbor together, and he had bought her a caged cricket. She told him he had the nose of Baron Murei. And this was the same Tenais who now tore off her apron and threw it on the candles so that he—he!—had to beat out the flames with his hands.

"I hate it, I hate it!" she sobbed, while he tried to burn his hands as badly as possible. "I want to go home! There's no one to talk to here, nothing to do!"

"No one to talk to!" he cried, looking up. "I've never enjoyed more splendid conversation in my life!"

"Oh," she said, gazing at him scornfully. And she called him by his old name, the one he had left behind in the capital. And she said that he was a dupe and a toady, tricked by the old priest and drawn to the Isle by his longing to sit at the table with kings. She said he was dazzled by the young Telkan—when in fact he despised that silly oaf! And this was Tenais, whom he had married in the Garden of Plums. He would never, never forgive her. He clung to his anger like a spar while, quiet at last, she daubed his burns with medicinal honey.

☞

Write. Write how they sat on the floor together in their little room, a single candle burning on the table. It shone on her brow as she bent over his hands in concentration. A faint reek of drains came in at the open window. Tenais, Tenais. She would be his enemy always. He felt almost cheerful. She was binding up his hands in linen strips. When she had finished she looked up and gave him a single, searching look, her eyes quivering darkly. She would die that year.

And I want to stay with them, for the sake of the child who will be born in a thunderstorm just as the hunting season begins. For the sake of the child who will grow up in the dark, accustomed to torches and lamps, expert at snuffing out candles with wet fingers. This child will possess no images of her mother. She will have to peer into a mirror and dismantle her own face. Her high, flat cheekbones—they can't be from her father. Her curly hair, her verdigris eyes, she must have gotten them from the other place, from Tenais.

For the sake of that child I want to go back to Bain and walk by the harbor with the young couple, accompany them to their cramped rooms behind the temple. Rooms so small Tenais propped the window open with a pair of tongs when she used the stove, even in winter, in rain. Ivrom, who had a different name then, would stand on a chair to help her hang the clothes to dry—they couldn't be hung outside, or they'd be stolen—the dark blue robe with the silver trim he wore when interpreting dreams in the temple porch, and the rich sash, the keilon, weighted with silver beads.

He loved his vestments, Tenais knew—how he fretted if he dropped wax on the cloth! He would pick it away himself with one of her needles. That robe was his reward, a sign of the gods' approval after his terrible childhood, his years of torment at the acolytes' school. She knew so little of those miseries, though he had told her how, at the age of five, he had been set to work in his father's shop, how his aunt took pity on him and sent him to school, and how, at school, the other students blindfolded him and pinched him till urine flowed down his leg. These things she knew. She read others in the way he treated his robe, his tenderness toward it. And so a dreadful bell began tolling in her heart, a bell that said *finished, finished*, the night he came home from attending a lecture and calmly placed his robe and keilon in the fire.

"What are you doing?" she screamed.

He stood shining in his rough undergarment, a shift that ended slightly above his knees. His eyes glittered, his cheeks were drained of color. While she dragged his robe from the fire with the poker, he stood on a chair as if intending to help with the washing. He raised one hand in a strange, jerky gesture. He had met the true priest. Olondria's one true priest. Why did he hold his head on one side that way? As if he were listening. "Get down," she cried, trembling, weak with fear. She called him by his name. "Don't call me that," he said.

He had been hollowed out, transformed by the Stone. This holy gift. The Nameless Gods blew it from Their palm like a dandelion seed. It floated, then hurtled to earth, white and then black, obliterating everything, harbors and candles and crickets and peppercorn trees. It tore through his mind like lightning as he sat in the gloomy lecture hall at the temple, in the tiny audience that had gathered to see the priest, this priest of an obscure new cult, which, it seemed, the Telkan favored, an old man hobbling in his great square boots. The windows were open; there was a smell of cut grass. Gnats circled the lamp beside the speaker. In the audience people whispered and passed bags of sunflower seeds. The young priest who would be called Ivrom gripped the back of the empty chair before him, his eyes fixed on the old man's mild, wrinkled face. When the talk was over he stumbled forward, rushing, trapped in the crowd, and only afterward did he realize that in fact there had been no crowd, that no one was trying to keep him from seeing the priest, they were going the other way, it was only his fear of missing this chance that made him see obstacles everywhere, and he reached the old man and grasped his hand, a cold dry hand like precious enamel, and he said he had always felt in his heart that the gods would send a new book, a text more eloquent and absolute than any dream, and he begged to go with the priest, to go to the Isle, to see the great Stone. To see.

"Strength to you, my son."

"Thank you, Master," he said. Something was wrong with his mouth; he thought he might be thirsty.

"Come closer, child."

He approached the hard chair where the priest sat with his legs stretched out on a stool.

"I should die," said Ivrom.

"That is blasphemy," the old man answered kindly.

"I should suffer."

"You are suffering, are you not?"

"Not enough."

"*Consider the sufferings ordained by the Nameless Gods,*" the priest quoted. "*A cupful weighs as much as an ocean.*"

In fact—as Ivrom would discover later—a cupful weighs much more. When the time came, he would be able to bear more terrible things with less pain, less anguish than he felt that night, the night he became a father and a widower, the night of my birth, of the death of Tenais. He could not yet say the words to himself: *She is dead.* Instead, in the priest's room, he staggered toward the great black Stone against the wall, a block as tall as a man, its surface glimmering faintly in the firelight, and he embraced it, something he had never done before. He had barely touched it. Now he laid his cheek against its darkness. He could feel its etched surface against his skin. The priest did not reprimand him. His cheek pressed hard against the lines: *You will sever all ties and pass from your bondage into light.*

At times she came back. Strangely, she did not come when he looked at the child, who was less an object of pity than a generator of duties—the nurse to be hired, the letters from his wife's relatives to be dealt with—and who grew into a sober, alien little creature, nothing like Tenais. If he thought of Tenais when he looked at the child, it was only in the abstract: what would the dead mother think of her daughter's progress? But at night, in the room of the Stone, Tenais would come, more often after the old priest's death, when Ivrom himself was Priest of the Stone, a man of power. Then she came. She was lying on the bed, her face turned toward him. Women were weeping. The air smelled strongly of edlath and jasmine oil. Her face on the pillow, the eyes sunken and withdrawn. Someone put a bundle in his arms: the child. Her eyes sunken, accusing, withdrawn.

He remembered holding the child to his chest. And how he carried it out onto the balcony while the women of the leilinhu mopped the floor. He was going to jump. He was going to kill them both. It would be quite simple. He gripped the railing, the newborn child tucked almost carelessly in one arm. Then he paused, distracted by the notes of a hunting horn in the wood. He stood motionless, breathless; the child began to wail. One of Leilin's women came onto the balcony and scolded him. What was he doing, what did he mean by it? Look at the rain.

It was something he would discuss often with his fellow scholar and Stone worshiper, Lunre of Kebreis, the only man he ever called friend. These tricks of memory. Pink peppercorns in the towers of Velvalinhu, his dead wife's face at night in the room of the Stone. Lunre felt that such shadows represented the two forms of pain: the loss of happiness and the coming of grief. Such experiences caused lumps to form in the ventricles of the heart; at times of stress, the lumps swelled, causing a slowing of the blood, and with it depression and illness. In addition, the swollen lumps secreted memories into the blood, which carried them to the brain and the inner eye.

"You will make me out to be nothing but a pudding of blood and fat," said Ivrom.

"So are we all," Lunre answered cheerfully.

Lunre was a passionate reader of the physician Ura of Deinivel, known to her enemies as the Bloody Imp. Hers was a happy philosophy, in which any sorrow, however great, might be diagramed and treated with some combination of herbs and baths. Her optimism suited Lunre, Ivrom thought, as the wind blew across the terrace where they sat, lifting Lunre's dark hair out of his eyes. The younger man leaned back on his elbows, tilting his head to catch the sun on his face. No doubt he believed that lumps in the heart could be cured with mallows.

Ivrom's idea was different. He held that the phantoms of memory, like ordinary shadows, only appear in the presence of light. Events are lamps of varying strength: a strong lamp, such as a painful or dangerous event, causes shadows to spring out on the wall of the mind.

His daughter, who sat on the floor with her knees drawn up, listening avidly to the two men, decided she agreed with Lunre. She, too, preferred the interpretation of Ura, the Bloody Imp, because, she reasoned to herself with a child's practicality, all the others were useless. What good was her father's talk of lamps and shadows? But a swollen heart could be treated, with, for example, oinov to thin the blood. She rubbed idly at the terrace wall with the tip of her finger so that the dried dust, gold in the sun, crumbled away like a morsel of cake. She did not yet know (and it would take her two decades to admit it) that she approved of Ura's philosophy in part because Lunre liked it, or (and this would take her even longer to admit) that she approved of it because it was a philosophy of the body. Ura's conclusions were thick with blood and with time, her instructions unwinding in strings of numbers: a five-minute bath, a cupful of edlath, two blows to the chest. The child's blood had recently begun to obey the moon's calendar and she felt herself in the realm of flesh and time, the realm of Tenais.

Tenais, who swelled. One month, two months, three, up to nine, and then death. The child dreamt that her mother was an animated clock. Its belly stuck out angrily. Her father was dashing to and fro, small as a dragonfly, dressed in white for some reason, crying "Eternity." Waking, she found that her sheets were damp with blood. Her father would never make her feel that she was not worthy to study the words of the Nameless Gods, he would never suggest that she was too timebound to touch eternity, he would never even mention that she was a girl. Yet she felt it obscurely, always, this sense of heaviness, of torpor. As she grew older she suffered from headaches and insomnia. On the terrace that day, as she picked at the wall, she experienced the first twinge of a strange resentment. She put her finger into her mouth.

"Think of history," her father was saying. "Think of the Drevedi, Avalei's curse. They disappear in times of peace, and resurface in times of unrest. They are the memory of the Olondrian Empire. And war is a lamp."

"They might be lumps in the empire's heart," Lunre said.

A lump in his heart. A shadow in his mind.

You will sever all ties, he thought. He whispered it to himself the night Tenais died. The words of the Nameless Gods, revealed on the great black Stone drawn out of the desert, scored in it by the Architects of Time. *Sever all ties.* The words in his mouth like ash. It was not the coldness of the words that horrified him, their utter opposition to anything human, but rather his own affinity for them, the way he was drawn to this vision of solitude with a feeling almost of nostalgia. He had the kind of loneliness that battles everything, that makes a person strange forever. If only he had seen it before, he would never have married Tenais or produced the tiny child now pressed against his heart. *Sever all ties.* And he had severed Tenais and she was dead.

He'd jump from the balcony, he thought suddenly, taking the child with him. He was a monster that should not live. Her face on the pillow, oh Nameless Gods. He was choking, something terrible was happening in his throat. The misery of his wife's last days! Without habit, he would explain to Lunre years later, we should all of us run screaming out of doors. It was habit that made life possible, both for individuals and for the empire. For this reason one must be careful to take things slowly. One could not simply outlaw the worship of Avalei outright; one must teach the people, lead them by stages, allow them to keep their rituals as long as possible. Habit is a curtain. It dims the lamp. As he stood on the balcony, he heard horns: Ahadrom II was riding in the rain. Thin, merry shouts rang out like the clinking of jewelry as the whole company of idiots passed on horseback far below, the Telkan and his wife's insufferable family, invisible to Ivrom but no doubt clad in gaudy cloaks that glistened in the torchlight. His jaw tightened; how he loathed them! And it was this bracing hatred that brought him back from the brink of death that night, that allowed him to think of the vase he would have commissioned in his wife's memory, a white marble vessel engraved with her name and the dates of her birth and death. It was the sound of those shouts, so bright and ephemeral, quickly erased by a roll of thunder, that saved him even before the child began to cry, and before one of Leilin's women came out and scolded him. And in fact he did commission the vase, as Telkans commission memorials of war. For the memorial does not preserve the memory of suffering, but rather transforms it into habit. At first he kept a bundle of blooming sage in the vase. But after some time, this gesture toward the afterlife was abandoned. The child would know the vase as the place where they kept the pens.

∞

"Vars, what is happening?"

I went so far as to grip his sleeve, almost upsetting the pewter dish he had brought me, the olives and cured meat. He managed to put the dish down on the table. I never let go of his arm. His fingernails, I noticed, were very black.

"What's happening? Tell me something, anything! It's cruel to keep me locked up in ignorance."

"You are not in prison, teldarin," he said.

"Am I not? Yet I can't go out."

"For your safety."

"Safety from what? The fire? Or a hanging?"

He winced at that and briefly massaged his ragged beard. Vars grows rougher by the day, his jacket stained, one shoulder tearing. Does he bathe?

"Is everything in ruins?" I asked him. "The fountain in the Alabaster Court is choked with rubbish—I see it from my window. Have you done the same to all of them?"

"The water I bring you is all right, I hope?" he asked anxiously.

"I don't care," I cried. "I wish you'd poison me. What does your prince mean to do?"

He drew himself up then, and a high color came into his cheek.

"He has already done it," he said. "He has returned us to Avalei."

A chill ran down my limbs. I dropped his arm. "Very well," I whispered.

It was his turn to take my arm now. He led me to a chair. He fetched a knife and fork from the cupboard and cut up the meat he had brought me, saying something about preserving my strength.

My laugh was a sob. "For what? So I can abide the torture longer?"

"Nonsense, teldarin." He crouched before me, stabbed at the meat, and held the fork toward me. I took it; the meat was tough and salty, so delicious it brought the tears to my eyes. Vars nodded, encouraging. "There, you see? It's just hunger."

While I chewed he sat cross-legged and told me he came from the estate of Ollahu, near Feirin. He was the youngest of eight brothers, and his inheritance was so small he could only survive with any honor by joining the army, which he had done at the age of fifteen. There he had met his captain, Lady Tavis of Ashenlo, the Telkan's niece. As he spoke of her he grew at once more animated and more serious. He and his captain had endured torments in the Lelevai, he told me, such as he would not recount while I was eating. "We understood then that Olondria was going to ruin," he said. "People were unhappy all over the empire. The Kestenyis had been miserable for generations, of course, kept under the Telkan's boot, as they put it, but now there was rage in the Valley as well. My mother sent me letters saying our Temple of Avalei had closed for lack of funds . . ." Here he trailed off and gave me an embarrassed glance, no doubt remembering that it was my father who had closed Avalei's temples.

I smiled at him coldly. "It's all right. I feel quite well now. Please go on."

"Well," he said. He cleared his throat. "Well, teldarin, it wasn't right. That temple was nearly as old as the War of the Tongues. We'd all been dedicated there—myself, my mother, my grand-mother, going back into the mists of time, as it were. You can't take something like that away from people. And they were saying the High Priestess of Avalei was imprisoned here on the Isle, and it was against the law to interpret dreams or even to read the taubel, and soon the Feast of Birds would be outlawed, dancing, wine—even weddings! And there we were in the Lelevai, dying for the empire like sheep. We couldn't stand it." He lowered his eyes and passed me the dish.

"So you all banded together against us," I said.

"Against the Telkan."

"And against my father."

He met my eyes again. "Yes."

I nodded. My strength was returning; perhaps he was right, and I had been hungry without realizing it. I tried to speak in an even tone, but my voice came out tight and scornful. "You must not think I am surprised to learn that we were hated."

He inclined his head, acquiescent. An absurdly elegant and formal gesture, something out of a different era.

I looked toward the balcony doors, which are streaked with grime and rimmed with frost. I thought of how, at the end, my father had made an error of judgment. He, who had once advocated caution, had pushed the people too far. And they had broken on him like a wave.

"Today is the twelfth day of the month of Fir," I murmured. "On this day, the Telkan hears reports from the Master of the Hounds. The Telkan's nails are cleaned and trimmed and the wax removed from his ears. The High Priestess of Avalei examines the wax and predicts the coming year's harvest."

Vars stood up and poured a cup of water from the jug. "Drink, teldarin."

I took the cup. "Our Telkan gave up this ritual," I told him. "I suppose your prince—your Telkan—will bring it back."

Vars hefted the water jug, drank from the lip, and wiped his mouth on his sleeve. "He'll do what's right," he said.

2. For they have set forth in a ship of fools.
917–922

Avalei. Love. Ripener of the Grain.

When Ivrom was small he dreamt of gorging himself, as rich children do, on pigs made of almond paste. One year on the Feast of Birds he stole a handful of nuts from a vendor's cart and was beaten and locked in the coal cellar for two days. The sweetness of cashews, their unctuous buttery flesh, the way they collapsed between the teeth as if in longing to be eaten, combined in his mind with the darkness and cold of the cellar and the struggle he waged with his body before he gave in and relieved himself in a corner. The shame of it, the stinging scent of the lye his father made him use to scrub out the cellar afterward, his terrible helplessness, his rage—all of these insinuated themselves into the atmosphere of the Feast of Birds: into sweetmeats, the worship of Avalei, and the spring. So much so that when he saw plum trees in flower, it gave him pleasure to imagine them shriveling or in decay. And when his aunt asked which god he would serve, he chose Heth Kuidva, whose voice is the knell of doom, and who is no friend to the Goddess of Pigs.

During school holidays he stayed with his aunt in her quiet, leafy neighborhood between the Savra Mai and the Quarter of Sighs. The peppercorn tree presided over games among the cousins, all of whom were handsomer and better dressed than he. There was a game with a key on a string; one of his cousins, shaking with merriment, hid it in the bosom of her dress. There was sweetened lime juice, so bright and cold he couldn't stop drinking it. And someone pushed him and sent him sprawling among the azaleas.

And on the Isle, on the Feast of Birds, the Teldaire approached him with a star on a chain, her black eyes flashing wickedly, and she stood on her toes—for she was a very small woman, a journalist had once named her the Mantis—and raised her arms as if she would favor him with the star. When he flinched, she lost her balance and placed one hand on his chest. He flinched again. "I am sorry, Your Highness," he said gruffly.

She laughed. "Dear, dear," she said, swinging the star so that it sparkled. "Are you really so frosty? They told me it was warmer in the Valley, but, by the Rose, you'd make a stone shiver."

"I am sorry," he repeated. Was she mocking him with that reference to a stone? "I do not wear jewelry of any kind, Your Highness."

Again a peal of laughter, like glass breaking. "I can see that; my eyes are quite good. I don't expect to go blind yet, at my age!"

She spun the chain on her finger. It came so close to his face that he stepped back. She did not appear to notice. "I thought you might wear something festive, just to please me. It can't be entirely forbidden. My dear Ahadrom is wearing his great uncle's medallion—though, between you and me, it suits him very ill! How can something so precious contrive to look like it's made of tin? I told him to wear his rubies, you know he owns half the rubies in the empire, he has perfectly splendid ornaments, some of them nearly as big as breastplates, but he wouldn't do it, even for the feast. I suppose that's your influence?"

"I hope not, Your Highness."

"Why? Surely you hope to influence him, as his priest? I understand you've been made a priest now—a priest of the Stone."

She said the words slowly and carefully, with the shadow of a smile, like a child repeating a lesson and hoping for praise.

"Yes, Your Highness."

"You grit your teeth—are you ill?"

"No, Your Highness."

His legs were trembling. She gazed straight into his face, malicious and amused. He avoided her eyes, looking instead at the amethysts in her high black hair, at the dancers whirling behind her under the lights.

"Veimaro."

"Yes, Teldaire."

"Look at me. Yes, that's better. It's not so terrible, is it? I'm not entirely repulsive to look at, I hope? No, I know you can't answer that, don't bother. I wonder what you know about me? I mean, besides what the papers say—that I'm pretty and know how to dance. I don't suppose my intelligence comes up in the newspapers much—not that I read that trash. But I assure you, veimaro, I am not stupid. My husband is a very young king. Very young. He requires guidance. Do you know what the Old Telkan said to me before he died?"

He thought: You are even younger than the king. She was only eighteen. In her little face, her eyes glowed like a blacksmith's tongs. "No," he said.

"He said: 'My dear, you are more than decorative, and this union is more than political. My nephew is but a man of dough. He needs fire to bake him.' I can only suppose he meant that I was to play the role of the oven. He said it to me in this very room. At my wedding."

She smiled sweetly. "The Old Telkan was a very cautious man, though people remember him as a pleasure-loving prince. He was careful to make sure that people thought of him in that way. Olondrians like a king who is large and strong and cheerful. I know this, although I'm Nainish. And you—you're from Bain, aren't you, veimaro? So you must know it even better than I. Olondrians rule the world, but their national character is essentially weak. Isn't that odd? They're like children. Now, look at Ahadrom."

He looked. Across the room, the young king sweated under the lamps, buttoned into a black coat that shone like a beetle's carapace.

"Gray as a cod," the Teldaire said, "and miserable as a victim of the toothache. I suppose he looks happier when he's tucked away with you? With you and your High Priest and his old father. And the Stone, of course. Is he happier? Tell me. Does he ever smile?"

"Our work is not done for pleasure, Your Highness."

Her eyes widened. "You snap! Very good! I knew you had it in you. I think we might become friends after all."

She slipped the chain with the star over her own head. "I'll wear this for you, as a token. And you," she concluded with her bright laugh, "will leave the bread in the oven."

Leave the bread in the oven! As if Velvalinhu were a kitchen! And it was, it was, he thought as he stamped out of the ballroom in fury: a stinking kitchen, begrimed with soot, where the empire's wealth poured in the back door, and princes, like dirty scullery boys, stood with their hands in the pots. But he would not be part of it—he'd starve first! "Who is she?" he raged in the little room where his High Priest sat beside the fire, and the Stone stood heavy in the corner, covered with a black cloth, and Ahadrom I drowsed in his low chair.

"Who is she? This chit of a girl—she dares—! Where did she come from?"

"Nain," the old priest said mildly.

"Yes, but how did she get her claws into the Telkan?"

"You are very angry, my child," the priest observed. "Remember: *A quiet heart is a clear doorway, through which may enter the horsemen of the gods.*"

Elarom's puffy, discolored hand wandered over his chest, found the strings of his robe and drew them tight. Even in the spring he felt the cold. His trembling sent a pang through Ivrom's heart. "Forgive me, Master," the younger man said.

Ahadrom I made a snuffling sound and jerked upright, looking blearily about him.

"You," said Ivrom, turning to the Telkan's father. He would not say "my lord"; such words had been banished from this holy place; in this room, he did not even call the Telkan "Your Highness."

"Yes?" Ahadrom I said, startled.

Ivrom knelt in front of him, bringing his face level with that of the former Duke of Tevlas. Ahadrom I had a round old face and a pitiful straggling beard; his head was bald, his eyes poor; he rarely managed to speak two words of sense together. But he will speak sense to me, Ivrom thought grimly, if I have to slap him awake. "Tell me about the queen," he said.

"Iloni," Ahadrom I murmured with a hint of fondness. "Eyes like grapes. Such watercolors . . . on the terrace . . ."

"Not that one. I mean the new queen, Firvaud."

"Oh, *that* one!" the old man chuckled. "Graceful. Like a little black goose."

"How did she meet your son?"

"It was . . . they came to Ashenlo. All the family together. For the—was it a wedding? In winter. Tanbrivaud, perhaps."

"They came from Nain in winter?"

"Yes, in a . . ." Ahadrom I skimmed his hand across his robed knees.

"A sleigh?"

"Such handsome children. The girls had very sharp feet. Marks in the parquetry, you know, from dancing. Then the falcon died. Beilan was so sad. The grave, all afternoon, digging. The ground was frozen . . ."

"Tell me about Firvaud."

"Oh, that one! A little veil. Little quick hands. In the parlor for hours. The needle flew . . ."

"She made herself look industrious."

"Eh?"

"And what else? About Firvaud."

The old man yawned. "A good girl. Came to look at the Stone."

Ivrom turned to the priest. "She saw the Stone?"

"Oh, yes," Elarom said, smiling. "In those days we had more freedom. We worked in a little lumber room in the west wing of the house—do you remember that, Ahadrom? The corridor was very long and dark, but anyone who got to the end of it could find us. The servants used to visit at night sometimes. We'd make them tea, Ahadrom and I. Young Firvaud came several times. She seemed quite interested, as I recall."

That flint-eyed, shiny-haired, dancing wretch. With the Stone.

"What did she wear?" Ivrom asked hoarsely.

Elarom hesitated, but Ahadrom spoke up with sudden confidence. "White. All white. She and her sister and brother. White jackets, white frocks for the girls. White shoes. They'd lost their father that year, you see."

Ivrom left the room. He was finished with the two old men. They had given him enough to begin. And then, the room of the Stone was windowless, stuffy with the fire burning, and he felt the need of expansion now, of distance. In his own apartment, the nurse was asleep on her cot with the child beside her. He passed the solid darkness of their shapes in the airy darkness of the room. He stepped out onto the balcony, into the smell of rain. His new apartment, bigger than the one he had shared with Tenais, commanded a view of parks and gardens flecked with lamps. He breathed the sweet, humid air, filled with the exaltation of hate, remembering the night his child was born. A company had passed on horseback then, hallooing in the dark. She had been among them—Firvaud of Faluidhen—probably in the lead, her little boots snug in the stirrups.

He saw her. In her dark green cloak. Her face turned in the torchlight, the laughing mouth. He saw her three years ago, before he knew she existed: demure in her white mourning frock, in the formal parlor at Ashenlo, white ribbons in the black cream of her hair. She was doing needlework—very fine, with her fine sharp fingers! She would be sure to put on an attitude of sadness. Her father had died of a catarrh in the autumn. Perhaps, when she spoke of it, she managed to produce a tiny tear. He could see it all so clearly! Her father had been a general in the Olondrian army, fighting the Brogyars along the northeastern border; the handsome award of appreciation the family had received from the empire upon his

death had financed this trip to visit the Prince of the Realms. That
money had purchased the girls' exquisite lace stockings, which made
it look as if some snowy nymph had breathed upon their calves;
their dresses were of the softest wool; their cloaks, in typical Nainish style, were richly embroidered with silver on the inside. Who
could doubt that Firvaud, with her sinuous dark beauty, appeared
to advantage in her mourning clothes, like a black flower in a silver
vase? And then the way she widened her eyes—the way she took
the prince's arm, when they walked among the trees of the frozen
gardens! Her vivid face, rosy with cold, peered out of her white fur
hood. "Tell me about the Stone, I am so interested!" And Ahadrom
II—Teskon, as he was called then—the great, slow, credulous fool,
with his mouth half open—he had been taken in!

Nothing Ivrom discovered about the queen's family afterward
caused him to alter this initial vision. And he learned a great deal
about them, for he made it his business to know all that could be
known about the House of Faluidhen. He knew their names by
heart: Mardith, the reclusive matriarch, never married, who controlled the family finances from her castle of Rediloth; her sister
Tanthe, petite and pretty, her hair dyed fox-red, who often visited
Velvalinhu, her slight frame brilliantly clad in the latest fashions;
and Tanthe's three children: wine-loving Fenya, a bachelor with tea-
colored eyes that were large and "full" like the eyes of the heroes in
Lindioth's paintings; Firvaud the queen; and the tall, timid younger
sister, Firheia, whom a journalist had nicknamed "the Nainish
Rose." Ivrom knew them all. He endured plays and celebrations,
sitting stiff and often too hot in his black robe, in order to observe
them: Lord Fenya dancing a stamping Nainish klugh, Lady Tanthe
cooling herself with a peacock fan. He observed the pained expression of Lady Firheia, blushing fiercely in a gown that was far too
tight across the bust, as her mother surreptitiously prodded her
toward the table where Lord Irilas, the Telkan's brother, tossed back
a cup of wine. Ivrom smiled coldly. The Teldaire glided up to him:
"Welcome, friend! Look, I am wearing your token." She pulled the

jeweled star from between her little breasts. Let her laugh. That night, in his room, he pored over her history in a book called *The Nains*, written by her great-aunt:

The lords and ladies of Faluidhen are descended in a direct line from Braud the Oppressor, the conqueror of Nain: not from his first union with the unfortunate Nardis of Lokhond, but from his second, with Singheia of Bar-Oul. His kingly relations disputed his choice, for which we are thankful: for their stubborn opposition to the match, their prejudice against the Nains, sparked an investigation in which Singheia's exalted lineage was revealed.

"Have we forgotten," asked Dardh, her cousin and primary defender at the open council held in the fortress of Niva, "the scourge of that accursed folk, the Drevedi, and the manner in which they captured and bore away the daughters of Nain?" Thus did the Nainish princes scorn to seek a link with the conquering western nobles; they claimed the goddess Avalei as ancestress, she who was also the mother of Elueth and of the Drevedi whose wickedness had once shattered the countryside. Naturally there were many who cried that one could not join with the line of kings by claiming to be descended from a vampire; however, only two years previously, Nerod of Beal had proved his rights to that princedom through the same cunning logic. Singheia's curiously colored fingernails, which a historian of the time compares to "fragments of brown crystal," were displayed as proof of her heritage, and the wedding took place at Niva without delay: the first between a noble Lath and a noble Nain.

In addition to her strange fingernails, the bride is said to have possessed "eyebrows like ravens' feathers" (though she probably combed them upward), an army of nine thousand skilled warriors, and a weathered castle crumbling on the shores of the Inland Sea. Her son was that Gara whose true name was either Mavelok or Mavedok but who took the name of the mighty fortress he built in the Haramanyi, from which he defended his lands against the Brogyars, slaying with his own hand the terror of the north, Muisegh of the Boars. Able in war, he was also a brilliant diplomat in times of peace, and successfully protected his domain from the ever-greedy Laths through a combination of diplomacy and belligerence.

"And they who possess the sweet lands of the west," reads his epistle to his cousin, Aurik of Bain, "with its vineyards and noble breezes, can scarcely be tempted by this country of burning dust and savage hills of ice; though if they please, they may come and take it from me."

The veiled threat did its work, and in a generation, as the Laths had feared, the Balinfeil was in the hands of the Nains. They did not hold it continuously; they were harried from both the north and the south, and fought many bitter battles in self-defense. Hargilu, the eighth descendant of that house, which had already become known by the name of the Gara-Hiluen, was defeated and slain at Ora, his sisters were forced into shameful exile, and his followers went into hiding in the mountains. For many years we find it hard to trace them, though they always record new births in the precious Book of Singheia's Children. We see them taking to ships for a time, finding sanctuary with Dauvor the Wielder of Iron, fighting in mountains and drinking out of their helmets. This sad period was ended at last by Merva the Dog—so called by his enemies, though he accepted the title with laughter—who, having prepared the army for rebellion, slew his Lathni lord and claimed his lady, Queen Vaihar, as his wife. Several happy generations followed ("happy" in the sense of those distant times, when kings maimed themselves at games of rings-and-arrows and sustained themselves on pigs' feet). It was during this period that the fruitful lands in the foothills of the Ethenmanyi became known as "Faluidhen." Here, in the twilight of

Nain, King Brom visited, and was astonished by a purple tablecloth purchased in the west.

He was that great lord known as Brom the Last, not because he was the last of that name but because with him an era passed away, the era of Nainish independence, ancient and warlike values, and the wedhialsu that were once sung every evening. For the reign of his nephew Tandrus coincided with that of Ilherin the Sunny Prince, whose mighty army destroyed the gods of Kestenya, and who attacked the Nainish princes not with arrows, but with objects of fine make, such as the fatal tablecloth of Faluidhen, which now hangs in the castle of Rediloth. Conquered by greed, the Nainish princes fought one another for places in a foreign court and competed to stamp out the language of their fathers. Ilherin's army was welcomed with banners, and the noble Princess Ridh, who had sought to poison him, was flogged to death. Within three generations the Nainish nobility were speaking the Olondrian tongue, and the word "Telkan" was used as a matter of course. There was great peace and prosperity. "We are all conquered," wrote Nabien of Bar-Theil, "whether by force, by strategic unions, or by the pleasure of the gods."

Ivrom closed the book and turned on his back. In the next room his child wailed briefly and then fell silent, soothed by the nurse. He thought of the House of Faluidhen, the House which— if the queen bore a child—would one day see their issue on the throne. A bitter, resentful, grasping House, humiliated by the submission of the Nains, riding toward power on the twin horses of money and marriage. They traded in fruit, in opium, in livestock, in silver, in Nissian slaves, in tobacco, in wool, in timber, and in their own daughters. Ivrom was not surprised when, three years later, the younger daughter of Faluidhen married Irilas, the dashing Duke of Tevlas, adding another knot to the family's bond with the Royal House—"They've been planning it since the girl was born," he crowed. He shared this opinion with the nurse, as there was no one else about—no one but the child who, though she could talk, was not yet capable of reasoned argument, and knelt at a little table, her drawing pencils before her in a row.

He slapped his desk. "The second goose is slaughtered," he shouted, "and sizzling in her fat!" His own vulgarity delighted him; he felt impatient when the child stared at him in dismay and the nurse replied with a barely perceptible nod. This nurse was a pale, awkward peasant from among the king's olive growers—capable, Ivrom thought, but very dull-witted. It was his fate to be surrounded by people who did not understand him, to never, never discover his own people. . .

"A winter goose," he cried coarsely. "For Tanbrivaud!" It was the Feast of Lamps; Tanbrivaud Night was only five days away. The windows were closed against the chill, but still the sound of the wedding celebration seeped in from the Tower of Mirrors. The child could hear it as she lay in bed. Her nurse lit the little red lamp and told her a story about an enchanted goose. While in the next room her father paced alone, laughing and shouting. "Breast meat! Oh, so tender!" It was her first memory.

But we are not concerned with the child's memories. We are concerned with him, with his genius. He had begun to write. He had begun, carefully and with pain, to collect the lines written on the Stone and record them in a white book. He submitted each phrase to Elarom for discussion, and to the small group that had gathered around the old man: volatile, nervous, yearning people, mostly failed priests and priestesses of one sort or another, who looked lost, like strange paupers, in their black robes. When the weather was fine they sat on a terrace, arguing and sweating. The devotees of the Stone had pockmarked skin, dandruff, bad breath, bad teeth. There was an exquisite thrill in watching their faces in the shade of a rare fern tree whose starry blossoms were meant to adorn a noblewoman's sash.

And there was an exquisite humiliation in asking them to critique his work, to correct his usage of one of the many languages found on the Stone, to offer suggestions which Elarom might approve, nodding quietly, his eyes melancholy and full of light. Sometimes, when they worked in the room of the Stone, one of Ivrom's colleagues discovered a line of writing—then Ivrom would rush forward, pushing the others aside, pushing aside even the one who had found the frail, etched trace, in order to put his hand on it, to mark it with his touch. This was his right, because he felt more than the others, he suffered more cruelly. The others read, yes, they studied—but they also laughed. Sometimes, from his high window, he saw them playing at dakavei on the lawn, gawky as crows running over the grass.

And if his lip twitched in contempt when he watched them chasing a ball, how much more did he despise Ahadrom II, who rode, hunted, attended obscene comedies at the theater, and danced, holding his wife gingerly as if he feared she would sting! *The blood of their souls floods the marble ballroom—when they dance there, they shall slip.* These were the words of the Nameless Gods! Words carved into the Stone and flung down into the wastes of Ulunith where Elarom had found them in the snow. Elarom had nearly died in retrieving these words. And Ahadrom II, Telkan of Olondria, who had had the great good fortune to be born at Ashenlo, who had crept, as a boy, into the room where the flower of the age lay recovering from frostbite—Ahadrom danced because, he said, he was king. "I can't get out of it," he said, seated on a stool in the room of the Stone with his knees splayed out, turning and turning his skullcap in his hands. His big, pallid, sad young face with the firelight playing on it, the cropped black hair already growing thin . . . and the robe he wore when he came here to work, but not to official functions, not to parties: on those occasions he put on his plain black suit. The iron ring of the Telkans shone on his finger. *And the lifeless metals with which they adorn themselves will avail them not, though they flash like a dragon's scales.*

"We shall work late," Elarom said gently. "You may join us after the ball." Ahadrom wriggled off the stool with a little sob, knelt on the floor, and kissed the old man's hand. And the other Stone worshipers looked up from their books and murmured in sympathy. Ahadrom, who had been more sensitive than usual since the death of his father, remained bent over Elarom's hand, his great shoulders shaking, while Elarom, who ought to have spurned the king, kicked him, spat upon him—Elarom smiled, and a faint blush of pleasure warmed his withered cheek. "Your burden is great, my child," he said. And if the old man was warm from the king's tears, Ivrom was hot, white-hot, gripping the seat of his wooden stool in both hands, the pressure of his seething blood mounting into his temples so that the figure of the kneeling Telkan swam before his eyes. He must leave the room; he was choking; he was falling into a fit. But he stayed. And mournful, traitorous Ahadrom shuffled toward the door. Useless, stupid Ahadrom, who contributed nothing to their work, slumped off to dance with his barbed and sparkling queen. "A man of dough," she had said; and she was right. And she would mold him with her fingers and her teeth. She would dip him into a vat of caramel and roll him in colored sugar till he gleamed. And still Elarom would say, "my child."

But I'm your true child. I'm your child. Ivrom passed a shaking hand over his eyes. His body felt enervated, as if after a long illness. He turned his gaze to his notebook and the words heaved before him. *For they have set forth in a ship of fools.* "A ship of fools," he murmured. He was tossing on the sea. He clung to his hatred and it bore him through the waves. Gradually, he discerned the shape of land, the shape of the message: a condemnation, vast and final, of the worship of Avalei.

"It occurred to me that night," he explained to Lunre, shortly after the younger man had joined the work of the Stone, "that there was a wonderful consistency in the statutes of the Nameless Gods. They condemned wine-drinking, gambling, adornments, gluttony . . . and many other things, such as popular divination and the interpretation of dreams, which are associated with the cult of Avalei. They condemned all forms of the worship of the body. They condemned superstition and the pursuit of invisible spirits. They urged us to read, to write, to think. To live simply and with grace. In that moment, I saw the future."

He saw it alone, without the aid of his master or his colleagues. Utterly alone. Impossible to comprehend the burden of that vision. He told Lunre of it quietly, almost casually, seated on the floor of his apartment after a meal. Evening light came through the open door that led to the balcony and glinted on the strings of the limike against the wall. Ivrom was peaceful, leaning back beside the instrument, his throat elongated, vulnerable and still. A small vibration when he spoke. "I saw it, not as a blinding flash, but as an accumulation of solid truth. It rose up like a mountain. It was as real to me as the stool on which I sat. As tangible as the Stone itself."

He did not speak of the violence that accompanied the vision. How he gnawed his sleeve. The bruise where he struck his fist against the door. The nurse coming into his bedroom with a taper, fearing disaster, the terrified child clinging to her skirt. "Get out, get out!" he roared. He was half naked, streaked with sweat and ink. Broken pens were strewn across the floor. He flung the heavy inkwell at the nurse; it hit the wall, and she retreated with a shriek, dragging the child. His shouts reached them from behind the closed door, muffled, inarticulate. The nurse muttered prayers— prayers to Avalei—she was, after all, a peasant. The words took up residence in the child's heart; they would be uprooted later. "*Protect us, merciful Ripener of the Grain . . .*"

"Insect! Scum!" he yelled. Everywhere his shadow appeared it took the form of a woman in a rich dark gown. He spun, but could not catch her. He would tear off her jewels, tear down her hair, grind the roof of her House beneath his heel. He would see her people sober and bowed in contemplation, or dead. These noble descendants of the gods, these pigs, these vampires! He would burn their theater, shred the canopies above their scented beds, put out the lights of Velvalinhu one by one. What is a mantis? It is well known that the female of the species is larger than the male, and that, when she is finished with him, she eats him. The queen had taken offense when a journalist nicknamed her the Mantis; that journalist now languished in Velvalinhu's dungeons. The king had put him there, though he knew it was wrong. He wept, but he obeyed. And Ivrom craved that power over the king. He craved it, and he would get it. Many years later, the Telkan, whimpering softly, would write the order to burn a school in the village of Nerhedlei. At this school, in the depths of the Valley where the worship of the Ripener was most entrenched, where the half-civilized peasants lived on bais and mushrooms, the eunuchs of Avalei were teaching the autobiography of Leiya Tevorova in defiance of the new law written by Ivrom. The book, considered a classic of Olondrian literature for the writer's refined and effervescent prose, was among those he had banned because it encouraged a belief in angels, and therefore in spiritual voices other than that of the Stone. Violaters of the new law must be punished. The Telkan would weep at the thought of destroying the school, but he would obey. Ivrom would stand behind him with his narrow hands clasped; their shadow, cast on the wall, resembled an insect's spiked forelegs.

On the night of his vision he had no such power. He was wild, feverish, desperate.

Write. Write. One day he would teach the child: Writing is power. He leaned on the table and added a scrawl to the page. Such pain. He was tearing down walls. He was trampling their starry chains and cashews and peppercorn trees. The Teldaire had wasted away and he broke her sternum and she was dust. He ground her aunt, Mardith of Faluidhen, to a smear of chalk. This woman he had never met but who faced him across the country from her castle in Nain, manipulating the Teldaire, laughing at them all. She had orchestrated the farce of the Telkan's marriage; she wanted to see a

Nainish prince on the throne. She sought power only for wealth—
not, as Ivrom did, for change, for a transformation in Olondria's
deepest heart, for the start of a new, quieter, more pious era. He
had gathered from his research that this Mardith was regarded as
a woman of principle, self-denying, almost ascetic, that she went
about clad in the palest colors as if in perpetual mourning, and he
hated her even more for this posturing. She was no ascetic—but
she'd know asceticism soon enough, when the temples of Avalei fell
and demands for wine dried up, when she could no longer make a
fortune from her vineyards and frankincense trees, when she was
forced to exchange her theatrical white for black! Then she would
cry—in his vision the smear of chalk wept icy tears. He was surrounded by a chorus of weeping women. And Time was defeated,
and Death. When his book was finished, he'd mock the queen in
the title. Wear these jewels, my queen, just to please me. *Jewels from
a Stone.*

∞

Today when Vars came in I was holding my father's book in my
hands. That little white leather volume, the edges of the pages
touched with blue gilt, has been until recently a bestseller in the
capital, ostentatiously displayed on shelves and tea tables throughout the empire. "Even if they don't read it they have to buy it," my
father said a few weeks ago, triumphant, upright in his chair. I was
silent. I never liked his attention to power, so naked—it humiliated
me to hear him crow. I felt his ambition threatened the book itself.
Those words Lunre called "a healing rain." *And if you find a stone along
the way, pick it up and set it aside. It will leave dust on your fingers but cause no
pain. And in this way you will proceed to the Mount of Clouds.* The last words
Lunre said to me, the night before he left the Isle forever. Under
our favorite stone archway in the Tower of Aloes. The air pulsed
blue and his eyes were full of shadows. I thought it was the beauty
of the words that made us weep.

Vars unpacked his satchel onto the table with some pride. A heel of bread. "You can soften it in water," he said.

"Vars, have you read my father's book?"

He glanced at it, uneasy. "No, teldarin. My sister's read me a few lines."

"Really? She's sympathetic?"

He blushed.

"Ah, I see. She read it to mock at it. Is that right? In the garden, after a glass or two of wine? No, no, you mustn't apologize," I went on, talking over him, "you mustn't think I'm offended, why should I be? I know how we are used. But Vars, did you never think that we are really on the same side, you and I? We are both rebels after all."

"Well. But we came to restore the Goddess."

"Yes. You are rebels who look backward, and we are rebels who look forward."

I rose and walked toward him, smiling. There was a prickling behind my eyes. The truth is that my morning had been very bad. Had it not been so, I doubt I would have tried to push the book into his hands. He recoiled, of course—as if a moth had flown at him in the dark.

"It's only a book, it's only a book," I soothed him. I reminded him of Uskar, known as Ahadrom I, the grandfather of the prince. How Uskar, like Vars, like all the rebels, was wounded by Olondria, by its violence, the ruthlessness of its ceaseless wars. Like them, Uskar had tried to free Kestenya. But in the end he had relinquished his sword and become a man of peace. He had found another way to turn his back on the Olondrian Empire. He had turned his face to the Stone.

All morning I had been thinking: *I am now the High Priestess of the Stone.* I had been thinking: *How can I survive without my father?*

For a long time, it seemed, I tried to make Vars take the book. Its white leather binding nosed feebly at his hands.

At length he took me by the sleeve and led me to the chair. He was saying something—words of comfort, I believe. Something about the prince. That the prince had guaranteed my safety. "No one is to touch you," I think he said.

The room was coming to pieces. I opened the book, I don't know where. I don't need to see the words. I read without seeing: "*Yours is a negative kingdom.*" I thought of my father and how he was like a bird who flew through a window by mistake. Ultimately, we Stone worshipers are a homeless people.

This did not keep us from cruelty. From murder. The children at Nerhedlei dead. Farhal dead. My argument with Vars was flimsy, I see now, hollow. Ahadrom I may have been a man of peace, but everyone knows my father was not. And even Ahadrom, when he was Uskar, betrayed his own kin to their death.

It is the twenty-first day of the month of Fir. On this day the Telkan puts on a blue robe and yellow slippers. He drinks rose-colored sherbet made with snow from Porcelain Mountain. He meets with the representatives of the White Council. They come to see him on the Isle and sit in the Chamber of Midday Reflection, their feet submerged to the ankles in a rug made of white lion's manes. The rug has been laid down for the occasion; afterward it is combed by the servants and wrapped in seven leaves of waxed paper.

Such polished ceremonies. And the end of it is blood. Such graceful language in my father's book. Blood.

I have been thinking that I don't know how to be Priestess of the Stone. I don't know where our followers live, I don't know their names. I can't convince a single soldier to read our book. My father prepared me for nothing. Why did I think that he would never die?

The fire sinks. Vars is gone. The room goes colder. I put on my gloves. The sky is dark today: they are putting out the fires.

No one is to touch you. The words seem terrible, profound.

Only one person could mourn my father with me: Lunre, who is lost.

3. And gentle from the edge of night the blue.
928–936

Look at his face. This is the face he will wear until his death. A grim face, beardless, chiseled out of jasper. Every morning he washes and shaves the face. The hair grows thinner and whiter and he is the Priest of the Stone and his master is dead. Elarom, whom the gods favored, is dead, and Ivrom still dreams of the chilly morning he entered the room of the Stone, feeling his way toward the lamp and the flint on the table, and he had never lit the lamp himself because Elarom was always awake and reading in its light, and he fumbled with the flint and knocked the lamp over, spilling the oil, and he could just see the white, almost dead log lying on the hearth, but he couldn't see his master's bed at all, and at length he realized that the strange, shrill voice crying for help was his own.

Look at his face, at the funeral on a hill overlooking the sea. The king is weeping, as are most of the worshipers of the Stone. The sea wind tugs their robes. Lunre and Farhal, two young men who joined the work of the Stone two years ago, are digging the grave. They are scholars, slender, unused to the work. It takes them half the morning. When the child, now thirteen years old, sinks down to sit on the grass, her nurse quietly pulls her up again. Slowly the light changes from the gray of a dog's coat to the gray of a coin.

Ivrom's profile becomes ever sharper, more rigid, more heroic. He does not weep. He notices that the child does not weep either. He is proud of this. He cannot see her young heart shuddering under her ugly homemade frock, in panic, in anguish, in a kind of horror. No one speaks as the body, wrapped in Elarom's black robe for a shroud, is carried forward in the arms of three sobbing women. They can't keep hold of it once they've sunk down, they don't have any ropes, the body tumbles into the hole like a sack of rice. Everyone looks at Ivrom. Look at his face, it might be carved on a granite doorpost at the entrance to a temple, except that there is no Temple of the Stone, and if there were it would be without images, decorated only with words. For the image is vulgar, the gods have said; it coarsens the spirit and dulls the intellect. Who but an infant needs to receive the world through pictures? The wise use words. But Ivrom does not speak, and the Stone worshipers are at a loss, for they possess no traditions, no funerary rites.

Look at his face, like a blade. At length Lunre clears his throat. He draws his wrist across his sweating forehead, leaving a smear of mud. He steps forward and begins to shovel earth into the grave. Soon Farhal joins him. And the others watch.

Walking back to Velvalinhu through the fields it grew colder and colder and they stumbled in the stony aisles among the faded vineyards, and had it not been for the child's nurse, who knew these paths from childhood, they might have lost their way altogether. For though Velvalinhu, with its vast and complicated towers, its hanging gardens like cuffs of precious lace, was ever in view, the way toward it was not direct, but involved a series of unexpected turns and sometimes even reversals around a house or copse. And this, Lunre said afterward, was an apt metaphor for the process of deciphering the message of the Stone, in which so many promising trails had to be abandoned. Indeed, he said, it might serve as a metaphor for any worthy endeavor. This was in Ivrom's apartment, where the nurse served tea while the child went into her bedroom and curled up, trembling, with Nardien's *Tales for the Tender* (and when her father came in to say good night he would frown and ask if she could not find something less babyish to read). It was after they had reached the Court of the Sands, vast as a battlefield, where the sentries watched them steadily and in silence, as the Telkan paused and cried out with a loud voice that he had no anchor now, no adviser, no friend, no counselor but Ivrom. "Both my fathers have passed away," he said, "and I must depend upon my brother." And Ivrom's heart, frozen in sorrow, shook itself awake, and he held out his hand to the tall, clumsy, black-robed king of Olondria who knelt on the stones and grasped and kissed that hand. The king had a bald spot on the top of his head and his kiss was repulsive, slick with grief, and the new High Priest of the Stone wore his usual knife-hard face. When Lunre mused about their circuitous journey home, the priest laughed. "Oh," he said, "but we might have cut the vineyards down."

Here was Velvalinhu, with its courtyards, its gardens, its mighty towers, its light and darkness, always light in one place and always dark in another, and how strange it seemed, now, that Tenais had been so oppressed by the darkness, that she had lit a fortune in candles one night long ago. How strange that he himself had been disturbed by the salmon-colored stones, half-blinded by the glitter of the ballrooms—half-blinded, if the truth be told (and why not, there was no harm in admitting it now) by the brazen, jetty, taunting eyes of the queen. He looked back in astonishment at his nights spent poring over the *Hath Harevu*, and that idiotic little book *The Nains*, by the queen's great-aunt, with its anguished clan sensitivities and the bloated, rubicund figures on the cover, who looked less like knights than the inhabitants of a sanatorium. How small the palace seemed now, though they called it a city! It was so little he could balance it on his palm; it reminded him of nothing so much as the music box in the shape of a castle that stood on his aunt's writing desk in Bain. This castle, manufactured in Feirin or Deinivel, where such trinkets were churned out in great numbers, was graced with gardens of green baize, with trees of wire and felt, balconies of such fine filigree they might have been earrings, and windows of real glass. When the key was wound, the box played

the popular vanadel "Bain, City of My Heart," and the mechanism
inside rotated, so that, peering through the windows, one could
see tiny smiling ladies and gentlemen passing in a row, in a kind
of eseila. Now, bending down and squinting through the window,
he could see the queen, no taller than his fingernail, passing with
a fixed smile, her paste jewelry glinting as she moved jerkily in the
path she must travel forever. Her black hair looked freshly painted
(and he knew for a fact that she had begun to dye it, although she
was not yet forty, because one of her ladies-in-waiting, a secret
devotee of the Stone, spied for him, and even copied out the
queen's letters). She passed to the plinking of the keys. Behind
her, holding her hand, came her son, Prince Andasya, now eight
years old, stiff as an effigy in one of his marvelous outfits, so thick
with embroidery and pearls that he might have been tossed down
the stairs without injury. He bumped along in his mother's wake;
he was already unhappy; his eyes brimmed with resentment in his
candy-colored face. He would come to the Stone. Ivrom wound
the key as tightly as possible, then released it, and the whole company whirled around to the sound of the keys. *Bain, city of my heart!*
All the colors blended together; it was no longer possible to make
out the black stains on the queen's teeth (she had begun to chew
milim), the red marks on her fingers (she slammed the lid of her
writing-box on them deliberately every time she received a letter
from her tyrannical Aunt Mardith); the young prince's glowering
brows had disappeared, the melancholy jowls of the Telkan, and
the sumptuous oiled shoulders of a thousand court ladies, and
the gentlemen's jeweled scabbards, and all of their boots, wine-
glasses, prize-winning roses, londo debts, racehorses, intrigues, and
affairs. The ballroom was nothing but soup. It looked like the gray,
gelatinous, peppery soup he had once eaten at one of the queen's
dinners, back when he had felt that he must always be where the
Telkan was, that he must watch over the king to maintain his power.
The noxious soup was treacherously threaded with melted cheese,
which clung to Ivrom's spoon, his lips, and the side of his bowl;

he found himself in a desperate battle with this cheese, though he tried to copy the cunning manner in which the others spun their spoons in order to break it. At the head of the table, the queen's eyes glistened with tears of mirth. Muffled laughter ran up and down the room. But they were not laughing now. If they were not careful, he'd make them dance until they fainted; he'd wind the key until it snapped.

No one laughed now, for vineyards might be cut down, and it was not only the Mantis who could have people thrown in prison. *Jewels from a Stone*, Ivrom's collection of the words of the Nameless Gods, had appeared in print in the winter of 931. It was a particularly cold winter; there was snow on the Isle, and many went hungry in the east. "It soothes me," choked the Telkan, wiping his face, cradling the little book against his chest in the room of the Stone, "it soothes me to read these blessed words, when things are so difficult!"

The priest bowed slightly. His hard face did not change. He dwelt in a different realm, one infinitely more exalted: the realm, not of those who are soothed by the truth, but of those who draw it forth—those who are torn by its brambles and battered by its stones. It had wrenched his heart (whatever Lunre supposed) to have Farhal imprisoned in order to keep him from spreading his inferior translations. He had wept when Farhal, whose health was poor, had perished in the dungeon after his usual winter cough spread to his lungs. The inner lamp had blazed out at Ivrom then, and his heart, he told Lunre, had nearly stopped. And Lunre, seated at one of the desks in the room of the Stone, with a barricade of dictionaries and prayer books around him, had looked up calmly and said: "Peace, Ivrom."

Ivrom stared at him. "Peace?"

"Peace," Lunre whispered. Somehow, though his hair was cropped short and his cheeks clean-shaven, he looked disheveled; something about him suggested that he had been rubbing his face, or trying to tear his hair. His eyes glinted flatly.

Ivrom looked at his own papers, but found he could not work. He spent a few moments trimming his pen. "Farhal was ill," he said. No answer.

Ivrom tried a sigh. "Perhaps you are right, and this feeling of depression comes from a slowing of the blood . . ."

With a sudden, violent scraping, Lunre thrust his stool backward over the stone floor and stood. The oil lamp on the table lit his face from below; the shadows made him look aged, almost a skull. "Everyone has left you," he said in a strange rough voice. "Everyone save poor Ahadrom, who cannot go anywhere, and Tialon your daughter. You have chased everyone away; Farhal you have killed, yes, murdered; I am still here. I am still here, and I hate myself. I hate myself. But Ivrom—"

Here he stepped out from behind the desk, his hands outstretched, his voice breaking with tenderness, and clasped both of Ivrom's hands. "I cannot go. I *will* not go. I will not leave the Stone, and our work, and you. Not yet."

The two men embraced. Lunre was shaking. "Only," he said, stepping back, his face warped with grief, and with something else, something dreadful, a kind of warning—and his voice grew in strength and harshness—"only we will never speak of Farhal's illness again. We will not speak of Farhal at all."

Ivrom nodded, speechless. And he kept that bargain. It was Lunre who failed, Lunre who went back on his word. Lunre, whom he called friend. They quarreled when Ivrom banned the heretical autobiography of Leiya Tevorova—a monstrous act, Lunre said. They quarreled again, more bitterly, when Ivrom forced the Telkan to burn the school at Nerhedlei and three little children were killed. Have you seen the Ethendrian grottoes? Neither have I; I was happy with the stone arcade in the Tower of Aloes, where Lunre gave me the almanac.

"Read the Month of Lamps," he said. His smile.

It seemed impossible that he would leave us. But it had also seemed impossible that we would lose Farhal. Things were becoming more possible. The world was growing larger—terrifyingly so. The Priest of the Stone traveled back and forth to Bain. Everywhere he drew crowds. They came to heckle, then to engage him in serious debates, then to buy his book. Once while he was away, before Farhal died, the priest's daughter crept down to the dungeons with a copy of *Jewels from a Stone*. She ordered the guard to let her through in a piping, imperious tone. A young girl, only fifteen, her face as green as glass. The guard hesitated; she told him to unlock the door at once or she'd tell her father. The guard obeyed and gave her a paper sealed with black wax. This was her pass to show to the guards on every level of the dungeons as they admitted her into the bowels of the palace. After a certain level the floor was flooded, her slippers soaked. Farhal lay on a bench; she could see him through the bars.

"Farhal! Farhal!"

"Here, little mistress, let me," said the last guard. He banged on the bars with a dented pewter cup. Holding his lamp aloft in the horrible din. Farhal jumped up, trembling pitifully. He stared toward the bars, shielding his eyes from the light.

"Farhal, it's me, it's Tialon."

He stood and came toward her, his bare feet in the cold water. His beard had grown and it seemed as though one of his eyes would not open. He coughed against his shoulder: a deep, full sound. The priest's daughter was losing strength in her knees. She slid the book through the bars. "Here . . ."

"It's all right," said the guard. He had checked through the book for hidden weapons. "There might be a needle in here," he'd explained to the girl. "Someone swallowed a needle once."

Farhal took the book and looked at it wonderingly. "Is this from your father? He asked you to give it to me?"

"Yes," she lied.

His beautiful sloe-colored eye, huge in his starved face, brimming with light.

"Thank you!" he whispered.

The guard caught the girl's arm before she fell. He took her to his chair by the door and rubbed her temples painfully with his great thumbs. "You'll want to wear boots next time," he said.

Stop. Don't go. In the foothills of the Tavroun there is a marvelous rainy valley overgrown with purple gentian. The air tastes of herbs. And we never had to go there, because we had our little hillside above the sea. We had the narrow walkways running through the palace orchards and the parapet overlooking the garden of the iloki—the huge saddlebirds with their raucous honking and prehistoric heads, who give off a terrible odor of decay. Once a day the sentries toss them the carcass of a pig. We used to watch the creatures moving through their gloomy garden, the chains on their necks clanking, their dusty tail feathers trailing in the weeds, till they reached the carcass and shredded it like silk.

Everything. We had everything, it seemed. Sooner or later, we thought, my father would forgive Farhal and let him go. We thought this, Lunre and I, even as our little circle dissolved, the other Stone worshipers leaving us for the mainland. They became leaders of reading circles in the capital, in Ethendria, in Sinidre. My father never mentioned their names again. It was forbidden to speak of them in his presence. The way he'd look up, crackling with rage. The red-hot orb of his eye.

I think of Farhal lying on his bench in a dark room. Did he even have enough light to read? Did he beg the guard to hang a light from the bars? Did he need the light to read *Jewels from a Stone*, or did he just run his hands reverently over the lines? Some of them were his own transcriptions. Some of them were Lunre's. Some belonged to other Stone worshipers. Three of them were mine. But the book was my father's because my father had drawn them together into a coherent vision, he had forged meaning out of scraps. At a moment when two powers were struggling for Olondria's soul—the cult of Avalei with its mysticism, more magic than religion, and the wealthy barons of Nain, who cared for no religion at all—my father raised a two-edged sword against them both. *Jewels from a Stone* is divided into three sections of equal length. The first attacks Avalei's cult: superstition, dream interpretation, communication with spirits. The second decries ostentation, greed, the accumulation of wealth. And the third sets forth an argument for reading as prayer. The words seem to glow as if wrought in adamantine. The book is perfect. It is perfect because it admits of no contradictions. It is perfect because a great number of the words written on the Stone—more than half, in fact—are absent from its pages.

"Orphans," my father called these writings. The ones that contribute nothing to his vision. Minor scratches, marginal, like vestigial wings. The love songs, the lists of horses and camels bought and sold, the detailed accounts of events in long-lost villages. There is a prayer for an ailing cow. There is a message in plain Olondrian that might have been written yesterday: "*I've gone up the pass with luck we'll meet on the other side.*" My father's theory on the "orphans" was that they were recent defacements, scratched into the Stone by those who were ignorant of its value. In the terrible conditions of the desert, he thought, people used the Stone as a rough signpost, almost a way of exchanging letters. He raged at these scrawls for complicating our efforts, quoting a line from the Stone itself: "*A curse on these orphans darkening my path!*" But Lunre felt that the orphans were worthy of study. If we agreed, he said, that the Stone came from the Gods, that They directed the hands that touched it, then we must attend to even its smallest, most crooked lines. "After all," he added, half smiling, "one could build an entire theology on '*with luck we'll meet on the other side.*'" And Farhal—Farhal loved the orphans, especially the ones that seemed to contradict my father's theory that they were only recent marks, the ones that were deeply scored in the rock, written in the Ancient Tongue yet cryptic, senseless. "*And gentle from the edge of night the blue.*"

Useless, my father said. A waste of time. And then, as time passed: dangerous. The orphans might weaken the true message of the Stone. He forbade us to work on them. Farhal did not listen. Secretly, he published a small pamphlet of his transcriptions in Bain.

This pamphlet no longer exists. All the copies have been destroyed. Farhal too.

His enormous eyes. The way he looked at my father with love. So eager to sweep the floor, to carry my father's writing box. He had moles on his neck; when my father felt cheerful (affectionate, cruel) he called him "Spots."

Ivrom and Lunre quarreled for the last time when the priest found Lunre's private notes on the orphans. Lunre was the last of Ivrom's disciples, the most intelligent, the most gifted, the most beloved. "How dare you?" Ivrom roared, louder than the autumn storm that thundered outside. His heart was breaking. And we never visited Nain, where the little houses glow red among patchwork fields and tame musk deer are tied up at the gates. We never needed to go any-where. We had poetry. Lunre made me a crown of aimila blossoms from one of the gardens. "Fallen star," he said.

Fallen star. He crouched at the hearth, throwing his notes on the flames while my father watched to make sure that every shred was ashes. It was the end, it was ending, Lunre was leaving, the next day, forever. "You might as well kill me," he whispered. "As you did Farhal."

Farhal lies in an unmarked grave on the hill, beside Elarom. Lunre—who knows?

Ivrom's follwers were weak. He brushed them off like burrs. He maintained his precise activities, his routine. Every evening, wher-ever he was—on the Isle, on the mainland to give a speech—he sat down to a soup of herbs. In Bain the soup was ordered in a hotel. "No butter please." On the Isle it was composed in the tiny kitchen in his apartment, first by his daughter's nurse and then, once the nurse had been sent away, by the daughter herself, who was then nineteen years old. The soup required that the bones of a goat be boiled for seven hours. All the fat had to be skimmed off, the thyme and mint chopped very fine. The single narrow window in the kitchen whitened with fog. Not too much salt, no pepper. The daughter cried and cried.

Lunre, she wrote. *Come back.* She hid the letter under her mattress.

The daughter grew pale and sluggish. She, too, was weak, Ivrom thought regretfully. He attempted to strengthen her with the example of his own upright carriage, his thin hard mouth, his unrelenting poise. *Clink, clink*, went the spoon on the edge of his bowl. The daughter cried in her soup. He asked her if she was taking a course in amateur theatrics. No answer, of course—she was sulking. As usual he left his robe on the floor outside his room so that she could scrub it and hang it to dry.

Lunre, she wrote. *Don't come back.*

In her room she took off her clothes. She could not see herself whole; she did not have a large enough mirror. She had only the little silver-backed mirror embossed with mourning doves that had belonged to her mother: her nurse had given it to her before leaving Velvalinhu. "I kept it," whispered the nurse. She had found it in the old apartment, in the chaos of the death and burial of Tenais, and had tucked it in her own bag. She had been afraid to give it to the girl before, she explained: she did not think the old man would like it. Now the mirror flashed in the light of the candle on the table. "Mother, come fetch me," whispered the girl, but no one came. She drew a picture of her hand in charcoal, a picture of her face. Both pictures were ugly, distorted. She burned them at the candle.

❧

I want to stay there. I don't want to go any further. I want to stay. I can't remember who it was—one of the poets, perhaps Tamundein—who said that all of our happiest hours must pass away at last, even those in which we believe we are unhappy.

∞

Look at his face.

The fire dies down, the air grows clearer, but everything looks bleak. How quickly Velvalinhu has fallen into ruin. Without its servants, who have been permitted to leave the Isle—chambermaids, gardeners, footmen—the palace is as desolate as a cave.

Thunder. Racing clouds. Across the Alabaster Court, a great painted cloth ripples in the wind. The rebels put it there, I know, so that I can see it, though Vars insists they do not know where I am. My kind, cruel jailer—he pretends the fires were started by accident—lamps knocked over in panic, bed-curtains alight. I know better. They set the fires on purpose, this gleeful, jeering rabble, as they raised that rough painting outside my window. *Rabble*—a word my father would have used. I see his face on the painting. Though the colors are crude, the brushstrokes hasty, the artist is not without talent. The pigs in the foreground look healthy, like ripe peaches, the mint-green grass appears soaked with rain, and the children seated nearby gnaw their maize with obvious delight. In the center, a peasant youth in a blue robe dances in a mire that is meant to represent grapes, or perhaps blood, with a girl, also in blue, on whose upright breasts and sunburnt calves the artist has expended considerable effort. How the rebels yelled as the painting went up, waving their wineskins! In the right-hand corner—the corner of law—the artist has painted my dead father. Dangling from a tree with his mouth open. His eyes bulge, but it is his face. Jasper. Hard. It is his face.

When Vars came in I was lying on the floor. "Get up, teldarin," he said, alarmed. I obeyed, though I could not see why it was important. What does it matter where I am? Bed, chair, floor. I could lie on a table. I could curl up in the big washbasin.

It is the thirtieth day of the month of Fir. Today the Telkan. Today the Teldaire.

No. Today the old rituals do nothing for me. I opened the balcony doors while Vars was building up the fire. I made sure no one was below, then dropped the almanac over the railing.

"What are you doing?" Vars cried.

The book unfolded in the air as if trying to fly, then crashed in the branches of a plane tree in the courtyard. I came back in and closed the balcony doors, but not before I caught sight of my father's painted face streaked by the rain.

Vars had brought nothing but olives and water. He told me to conserve whatever oil I have. For light. His fingers trembled.

"Sit down," I told him. There are two chairs at the table, but he's never sat with me. He seemed nervous, awkward, pulling everything close to the fire, arranging, fussing. At last we both sat down. My slippers and stockings began to grow hot. He rubbed his face and hair with both hands, as if he were washing.

"What is happening?" I asked him.

He looked up, tired, rumpled, reddened. "The duke is coming."

"Which one?"

He laughed briefly at my ignorance. "Veda of Bain."

I thought of how the palace has seemed quieter lately—less singing, fewer revels. At intervals, shouts ring out in the distance.

"I thought it was me," I said.

"Hm?"

"I thought it was me. The way everything's getting quieter."

He did not understand, but was too distracted to ask questions. He told me the fires in Bain had died down, the city was under the duke's control once more, and warships were filling the northern harbor.

"They can reach the Isle in a day," he said.

"What will you do?"

"Fight them, of course."

His voice was frayed; it did not match the confidence of the words "of course." After a moment he added: "I hope you'll tell them we've treated you fairly. That we've done only what's necessary to hold the Isle."

Perhaps because I have been eating so little, it took a moment for what he was saying to reach me, but finally I said: "You expect to lose."

He crossed his arms on the table and held his elbows tight. "No. We'll win, with Avalei's aid. But the prince—the prince is ill."

The prince is ill. He is lying on a rooftop under furs. He does not speak. His eyes are fixed on the wintry sky. If they try to move him, to take him indoors, he stiffens his limbs and groans through clenched teeth—a high-pitched sound, terrible, almost a shriek.

For a week he has eaten only black foods: raush and hard black bread. He takes almost nothing now. Sometimes he lets them spoon a little olive paste into his mouth.

"Nobody knows what's wrong with him."

And the Duke of Bain has reclaimed his city. The rebels are falling in the Valley, in Nain.

"I tell you this," said Vars, "because the prince said you were his friend."

I should have screamed with laughter. I should have flung the olive dish at his head. I should have snapped my fingers in his face and gloated: *The duke will unstring you like a harp.* I should have wept. *My father. My father.*

Instead, I ate. Rava, sister of the twentieth Telkan, said that the Isle possesses two things in abundance: music and clarity. I too will look at the world with clear eyes. I will see my own part in this. When Vars had gone I stepped onto the balcony and looked at the painting again. In the left-hand corner of the picture—the corner of passion—a table in an arbor. There the prince drinks wine with the High Priestess of Avalei. Dappled sun on his claret coat. His black hair like a wing. His mouth a bloom. His eyes obscured by a ray of light.

4. A curse on these orphans darkening my path!
939–942

"It is time," said Ivrom, "for the young prince to come to me."

"Ah, yes," said the Telkan, rubbing his knees. He glanced uneasily at the priest's daughter, who sat in the corner turning the pages of an enormous dictionary. In the opposite corner of the room gleamed the Stone.

"Yes, well," the Telkan stammered. "It is difficult to find time. There are his riding and music lessons, and the calligraphy. He is practicing advanced swordplay now. And then, in the autumn, he goes to stay with his aunt and uncle in Kestenya . . ."

The priest sat with his arms crossed, wearing a sardonic smile. He knew very well why Prince Andasya traveled to Kestenya. Redis, one of the Teldaire's ladies-in-waiting and a recent convert to the Stone, copied out the queen's letters for him. Sometimes Redis wrung her hands and yanked at her layered skirts: she ought to be wearing black, she said, not this gaudy stuff. And the priest replied unctuously: "Calm yourself, my child. The gods understand the requirements of your service. Remember—this is the work of the Stone."

So, dear sister, he had read the previous night, *I intend to send Dasya to you again before the Feast of Plenty, for though it tears my heart to be parted from him, I cannot bear the thought of his falling into the clutches of Ahadrom's wretched priest.*

Now the "wretched priest" gazed at the Telkan. His hips ached, his spine twinged, but as usual he ignored the pain. He was only five years away from the wheeled chair in which his daughter would maneuver him through the halls of Velvalinhu to the end of his days. The Telkan had no such fortitude: tears of sweat gleamed in his brows. He was not made to rule—but then, Ivrom reflected, neither were his brothers: sunburnt Veda, Duke of Bain, who always smelled so strongly of saddle oil, and the fiercely handsome Irilas of Tevlas, a nervous recluse and bolma addict. Olondria's Royal House was like a gambling den, Ivrom thought, whose members would gladly forfeit both wealth and honor, if only they could have (for Irilas) a cup of wine, (for Veda) a horse, and (for the Telkan) an hour of peace. No doubt the young prince was equally feckless; the sooner he was taken in hand, the better, for the cult of the Stone was still small and required the next king's support.

"There is the month of Lunre," the Telkan admitted at last, "but during that time he is always fitted for new clothes . . ."

The priest's smile, like a sword cut, remained in place. His daughter drew in her breath audibly at the sound of the word *Lunre*—an irritating habit, for it was, after all, a common word, a month of the year, and one must expect to hear it. The Telkan wiped his brow with his wrist. In his mind, Ivrom basted the younger man and turned him on the spit. Then he increased the heat. "And are these things," he asked quietly, "more important than the well-being of his soul?"

"Believe me," the Telkan cried, "if I could, I would bring him to you at once—you would be his tutor—you must know that nothing on earth would please me better! But the Teldaire is very firm, very attached to him, very excitable—truly excitable—she has not been well."

"Has she not?" the priest asked dryly.

"I think not," said the king. "She is always on her couch when I arrive."

"*And harshness is no crime!*" snapped the priest, quoting the Stone. "Leave her be, or yank her up by the roots of her hair, but bring me the boy."

∞

And harshness toward the self is no crime, Lunre thought it was. A question of the translation of an ancient word.

Years later, Ivrom's daughter would say: "You care more for the prince than you ever did for me." One of her rare arguments with her father. And her father would stare, taken aback that this slip of a girl, this shadow who owed him everything, could attack him. His first impulse was to shout, but he thought better of it, and raised his chin proudly. "In the War of the Tongues," he declared, "King Thul sacrificed his daughter. He threw her into the sea as a gift to the goddess Ithnesse. A painful act, yes, but honorable. And he won the war."

The Telkan, however, was selfish; he would not make sacrifices; he shrank and whined; he sat up all night, according to Ivrom's spies, not studying or praying, but watering, sniffing, and crooning over the plants he grew in pots in the Tower of Lapis Lazuli. Plants! The priest longed to run up the stairs and hurl every one of them over the balustrade (but he would not—that would happen many years later—and it was the young prince who would send those pots crashing into the courtyard one by one, to the cheers of his rebel army). And then, one rainy winter, when the fog lay so heavy on the Isle that lanterns were carried about even in the middle of the day, and the servants' children rang bells on the landings to drive away melancholy, the Nameless Gods smiled on their priest at last.

"Oh, very good," he whispered. "Very good."

What have I raised, Firvaud? he read. How did I manage to fail so completely with both you and your sister? What was the purpose, I ask you, of all my care with your education, if it is to result in nothing but dishonor? Those sessions in the white parlor when you were a child—wasted, wasted! I might have been working! I might have been devising some alternate plan for success. Instead I placed all my faith in you children, all of it! And this is how you reward me—the trap sprung too early, and the pheasant flown!

A letter from the queen's aunt, Mardith of Faluidhen. Ivrom had a moment of fellow feeling for the rigid, power-hungry old lady. He could picture the white parlor where she had taught her nephew and nieces herself, forcing them to add up long columns of figures. He knew that she kept no steward; she alone managed all the business of the estate. She was formidable, formidable! But now something had happened—he could not quite tell what—something had gone awry, and the time had come to grind her people to chalk.

To make matters worse, Firheia has allowed Dasya to start home, so he is on his way to you, though he ought to have come directly to me. I would have cured him; I would have made him sensible of his duty, if I had to wear out Fenya's riding crop on his back! That, I know, is the sort of image that usually makes you laugh—your old aunt whipping a boy of seventeen. I hope you laugh, Firvaud, I hope you have your fill of laughter before your son comes home, trailing our name behind him through the mire! Perhaps, then, you will look at him without smiling. Perhaps you will begin to take your duty seriously. But no, I know you—wine, milim, lovers, I know it all, your escapades are notorious even here in Nain.

"How did the queen look when she read this?" asked Ivrom.

"Sallow," answered Redis. "And when she had finished, she struck her head on the wall."

"Did she indeed?"

"She did. It will leave a bruise, that's certain; tomorrow she'll have her curls arranged on her forehead."

"I see, I see," the priest murmured. Firelight shone through the paper and he lowered it to his lap to read it better. *I expect you will go on spoiling the prince, while your sister spoils her daughters in the highlands, and Faluidhen shatters like a glass on the stove. I expect no one will listen to me. But if you did, this would be my advice: the children must be kept apart. They must be kept apart, far apart, until even the servants have forgotten that there was ever a hint of impropriety between them. (The servants at Ashenlo must be bribed, of course, to encourage the process; I am sending Irilas some money for the purpose, so that he cannot plead destitution. I have never seen a person less able to keep his wealth in hand, though he sells more land every year, and not cheaply.) Tavis must go to Bain, as she is old enough to go into society now. She must be kept free, if possible, from the taint of the whole business, for if we should lose Siski, Tavis will be our only weapon. And Siski—if only Firheia listens!—Siski must come to me.*

Impropriety. A taint. The priest folded up the paper and absently pressed a corner of it against his teeth. He gazed into the fire. The trap is sprung, the pheasant flown—what could it mean? *The queen struck her head against the wall.*

Redis had taken out a little ivory filigree fan and was cooling her face with it. The firelight gleamed on her hard young skin.

"What do you think has happened?" he asked her at last.

"Isn't it obvious?" she smirked. "They want the prince to marry his cousin."

Of course. Of course.

Faluidhen spread before him. The linden trees. The white parlor where Lady Mardith turned the pages of her prayer book. She had raised her nieces and nephew to know the common prayers and a good third of the *Vallafarsi*, but not to be particularly devout. Don't over-salt the soup! It was not genteel to pray too much, to talk constantly about the state of one's soul. Look at Uskar of Tevlas, who now called himself Ahadrom I—he was a laughingstock, a bumbling, earnest clown in woolen robes. His son was going the same way. "Make sure you ask them about this Stone!" she advised her niece Firvaud, smoothing the girl's lace collar. That collar was not more intricate, more cunningly conceived, or more elegantly executed than her plan. Slowly she drew the threads into marvelous flowers. Firvaud married Ahadrom II, Firheia his brother Irilas. Firvaud bore a son, her sister a daughter. The marriage of first cousins was frowned upon, but there were precedents in the royal line. If those children married, the throne would belong to Faluidhen.

"Brilliant," he said.

"Do you think so?" Redis sniffed.

But something had gone wrong. *A hint of impropriety between them.* Every year, the queen sent her son east to Ashenlo, to keep him from

Ivrom, but also, he saw now, to encourage the boy's attachment to his cousin. Siski, that was her name—barbaric—surely chosen by her father—the name of an ancient princess of the highlands. Had the young people become too attached? Had they consummated their love too early, unlawfully? *The trap sprung, the pheasant flown.*

Yes, that was it. The priest chuckled. Ah, youth! He remembered the faint stink of the canal in Bain, the streetlamps reflected in the oily water, and himself, on one of his rare visits home, flinging a handful of gravel. The object was to hit the windows on the other side of the water; perhaps one of the harlots would look out. "Open up!" he shouted, and the boys with him (urchins he only played with when home—they introduced themselves by bloodying his nose) clutched themselves laughing. And one night a window opened and a coarse word was hurled out, along with a glimpse of a fleshy, radiant, naked arm. And afterward, back at the temple school, such remorse! He shook his head, smiling. "Redis," he said, "we must prepare to receive our prince."

He came. He wore a black suit and black skullcap like his father. Pearl earrings gleamed against his skin. It was the eighteenth day of the month of Mur; the prince had bathed in the Tower of Aloes that day, and his hair had been fumigated with apple-wood smoke. In the Temple of Sarma, he had walked three times around the ancient, blackened mirror representing the Waters of Destiny, and his face had been painted with silver flowers. He had washed, but a scrap of metallic paint still clung to his cheek as he sat in the room of the Stone. The prince's eyes had a strange, lifeless glitter; his spine curved. In the afternoon he would put on indigo and flame-colored garments. It was the day the Teldaire tasted the new wine. The prince would escort her and open the ceremonies by blowing a swan-shaped horn.

He sat hunched at the table, and the priest's daughter saw at once that he was like her father: a person of absolute loneliness.

The air around him seemed red, as if he dwelt in a different atmosphere. He awaited instruction with apparent indifference.

"Well," said the priest in his stinging, sarcastic voice. "You have come at last, eh? You have left off digging for truffles in Avalei's mud patch."

The priest's daughter flushed, but the prince said nothing.

Ivrom laughed rustily, then coughed. "Sulking, my prince? Perhaps you are missing a riding lesson? How sad for you. Or perhaps my tone offends you? You are accustomed to flattery, no doubt, and to hearing the words 'Your Highness' from noon to midnight. But you are in a different place now. In this room your blood and accomplishments mean nothing. Please follow me with the lamp."

He turned his back on the prince and approached the Stone. The prince took the lamp from the table and followed, his movements oddly smooth and subdued, as if he were floating. Obediently he held up the lamp and listened as the priest explained the work and showed him where the dictionaries were kept. Then Ivrom gave the boy a stack of transcriptions in the Ancient Tongue. "I hope you read it?"

Prince Andasya nodded.

"I see! They have not wholly neglected your education. You read the Ancient Tongue and also dance the arilantha! Dear me, you are drenched in knowledge like a pear in syrup."

The prince returned to his table and set down the papers. He went back to the dictionaries with the lamp and selected Ainoe's *Coastal Lexicon* and Muir's *The Harpist's Tongue*. Armed with these, he sat down at his table and began to work. In the green lamplight his hands looked attenuated, fragile.

Ivrom watched him for a moment. No sound but the scratching of the prince's pen and the soft slap when he opened a dictionary. "You will find it very dull," the priest said at last, in a voice that sounded forced, even to himself. "Our work takes more concentration than a game of londo!"

Silence. The prince wrote. And the priest, discomfited, turned to his own work. Throughout that strange season when the prince worked in the room of the Stone, Ivrom found no way to reach him, no barb that could pierce his armor of almost somnolent impassivity. Each day the boy arrived precisely an hour after dawn. He always walked from the Tower of Pomegranates, accompanied by a gaggle of gaily clad courtiers provided by his mother: gorgeous men and women with antimony-stained cheeks, their jewelry and beaded clothing clinking, many of them stinking faintly of wine. He was a prince; he could go nowhere alone. When the priest's daughter opened the door for him, she would catch a glimpse of his elegant companions in the hall, yawning, whispering, or rolling their eyes, evidently glad to be rid of him. Once one of them led a small wildcat on a chain.

The prince worked. His throat was a pale arrow. He still possessed the famous winglike lashes that graced the portrait *Death, with Kite*, but the color had abandoned his cheeks and his skin had lost its wonderful elasticity, so that it was more like granite than (as the journalists said) almond butter. It was rumored that his lungs were diseased. It was rumored that he had contracted an ignoble illness and was being treated with mercury. He worked every day until sunset, foregoing all daylight duties and pleasures. Gloom hung about him like fog. His translations were excellent.

Ivrom spent a great deal of time on the mainland that autumn and early winter, proselytizing and debating in the temples. It seemed strange, considering the time of year, the dampness, and the increasing pain in his hips, for him to choose that season for travel, but only to those unaware of the heavy numbness that had taken up residence in the room of the Stone, a numbness in the shape of a prince. Though the prince did nothing to offend, his presence acted on the spirits like an eclipse. At this time, the priest's daughter, who was often alone with him, took to roaming in the palace gardens. She'd run up and down the outdoor flights of steps in her mannish boots and circumambulate the Long Gardens in rain, underneath her white umbrella. Sometimes she held the umbrella aside and let the rain beat on her face. After one such journey, she entered the room of the Stone and heard the prince's voice. A half-strangled whisper, caught in the moment before he knew she was there. "Will it change," he muttered. "Will it change will it change will it change."

Will it change. The door clicked behind her. The prince looked up.

His heavy-lidded eyes like a pair of dead coals.

She busied herself shaking out her umbrella. She propped it against the wall and pushed back her damp hair. Her nervous fingers caught in the strings of her coat.

When she had hung up her coat and brushed off her skirt, he was still looking at her. She gave him a half-smile. "Good morning, Your Highness."

For a moment he stared, and she feared she had insulted him somehow—should she have bowed? But then he answered: "Good morning."

His voice was surprisingly deep, gravelly, unused. And somehow this low, rough voice reminded her that he was still a boy. He was a boy, and that day, the sixth of Brome, the month of Melancholy, he had kissed a jade stone in the Temple of Heth Kuidva. A day of wind and reluctance. In parts of the empire the frogs were already going to sleep. His head looked terribly heavy, bowed on his slender neck. A few nights ago, wandering the halls, as she did more and more often these days, the priest's daughter had happened upon the Dedication of Instruments. No, that is false—she had not happened upon it, she had gone there deliberately. Why lie, why now, after all this time? She knew what was happening every day, she had the almanac by heart, she was familiar with the draped galleries above the Hall of a Thousand Tapers. She knew she could hide there unobserved and look down into the hall where the Teldaire sat on a pale blue throne as magnificent as a cake, her black hair shining, her laugh ringing to the ceiling as musicians, seated around her on the floor, presented their instruments. Talk, laughter and fractured notes of music filled the air. The Teldaire inclined her head to each limike and harp. Because she was queen, she was said to have the best ear in the empire. If an instrument pleased her, she blessed it by rubbing a bit of her spittle into the wood.

At her side, standing, the prince. He wore white boots and a beryl-green suit. His bowed shoulders were swathed in a violet cape. His plaited hair sparkled under the lights, studded with chrysolite pins. His face looked devastated. His face was like a wilderness.

Now in the room of the Stone she rose and approached his table. "What have you been working on?"

He spread his papers out and showed her the work. As she looked at the even lines of script she forgot, for a moment, her compassion for his sufferings, for his rigid, barren, and ritualistic life. She forgot that she had intended to speak to him of reading as prayer, of work as sustenance. She had planned to use herself as an example, hoping to break through his reserve. "Sometimes I want to die," she was going to say. But reading his papers her heart thudded. "This is all wrong," she said.

"Wrong?"

"Yes, yes." She shifted the papers, searching them. "This isn't what my father gave you. It's not in the Ancient Tongue."

"No, it's in plain Olondrian."

"But how—he didn't give you this."

"No. I found it myself. On the Stone."

She drew in her breath and let it out slowly. "You're not supposed to do this. You've transcribed an orphan! You were supposed to do what my father asked."

"I did," he said. "I finished it. I didn't have anything to do. I took some impressions—look." He showed her papers covered with pencil rubbings. He had laid the papers against the Stone, collected the markings with this crude method, and then transcribed them in his elegant hand. "*On the seventh day of the Month of Mur the*

Abomination of which we shall speak appeared upon the borders of this our village of Ambrelhu . . ."

The priest's daughter covered her face. "All this work. I'm so sorry."

"What's an orphan?"

She explained, quoting her father's favorite line.

The prince repeated it with a faint smile. *"A curse on these orphans darkening my path."*

"So it won't do any good. This work. I'm sorry. It's useless."

The prince was silent for a moment. Then he said: "Look at me."

The priest's daughter looked. In the green radiance of the lamp his face had a mineral sheen. A face like a desert. A smile like a broken mirror. "Do you think," he said stiffly, "that any amount of writing will do me good?"

"I don't know," she heard herself saying. But it was a lie.

Her father's voice reached them from the hall, harsh, disapproving—he must be speaking to the Telkan. Their fathers were coming: one soft as jelly, the other a hard knife. The prince held her eyes, and she wanted to tell him: No. No. She wanted to say: No, this work won't do you any good because in the end you will be claimed by whoever is stronger. My father, your mother, your aunt. The one who wins. And that person will wield you like a scepter to rule the empire. You will appear on feast days, she wanted to tell him, in gold brocade or a black wool robe, but you will appear as a sign of power.

There was no time to say all of this, so she bent down and whispered a single word, the one she did not have the courage to say to herself: *"Run."*

Perhaps this is why, years later, the prince referred to her as his friend. At any rate, he never returned to the room of the Stone. He began to be seen at parties instead, loud, mocking, careless. He collected a fortune in paintings. He ran off to Bain and explored the Evmeni Quarter. Then he ran farther: to the Lelevai and the army, after receiving a brief letter from his cousin Tavis, who had herself recently escaped to military school. "There's good fun up here," she wrote. The prince stowed away on a merchant ship on the northern sea. When his mother learned of it, she tore down her curtains, screaming.

Ivrom, of course, was furious, humiliated. The trap sprung, the pheasant flown.

His daughter did not run away. She stayed. She stayed to carry on the work of the Stone, to convey her father through the halls in his wheeled chair, to organize his notes. She stayed to listen to him grumbling over his bowl of soup. His monologues grew fiercer when the prince returned to Velvalinhu after years in the military, not to rejoin the work of the Stone but to take up ostentatiously with the High Priestess of Avalei, whom Ivrom kept virtually a prisoner on the Isle. "I must get him back! I must get him back!" the priest fumed. One night, when he and his daughter had quarreled because he would not permit her to attend a limike concert, she startled him by bursting out as she knelt to build up the fire: "You care more for the prince than you ever did for me."

Sometimes she took out the prince's orphaned text, which she had secreted in her own writing box. His looping handwriting progressed like fine embroidery. She would read his work and think of him bent over the table, trying to put some meaning into a life weighed down by duty. Not everyone reacted that way to the life of the palace; some thrived on it; the Teldaire was one of these. But for the prince Velvalinhu was a place of torture. Suffering throbbed in every line of his cold face flecked with ceremonial silver. She thought she could read this misery even in his handwriting. *"We mention in passing that the weather was cruel . . ."* How strange to look at his text again after all these years have passed, now that I know the prince for what he is: a butcher.

On the seventh day of the Month of Mur the Abomination of which we shall speak appeared upon the borders of this our village of Ambrelhu. It was first observed by shepherds and other humble folk, always at night, and was taken for a figment of Dream rather than a deadly actuality. The Monster was blamed for the disappearance of sheep—and this, too, in the minds of the judges and responsible men of Ambrelhu, seemed to support the idea of its being merely a Phantom, devised by the shepherds to excuse what their negligence had brought to pass. It is true that a boy of twelve years was so terrified by the Apparition, that he became nearly demented and had to be carried back to his hut, and that no amount of threats and violence on the part of his uncle could induce him to return to the fields. But this was seen as an isolated incident, and we deemed it best to proceed as usual, issuing no warnings or commands, but continuing quietly to supervise the daily life of this our town, until some event of note should take place.

It is thus that we date the appearance of the Creature from the seventh of Mur, though it had almost certainly arrived before that time. On that day, or rather evening, a certain Meirin of East Ambrelhu was returning from a visit to her father's home in the country. Dai Meirin is an educated woman and a lady's maid in the house of the Honorable Simyas of Ambrelhu, and her employers vouch for her truthfulness, further stating that she is given neither to drunkenness nor to fits. It was after dusk, for Dai Meirin had spent longer than expected at her father's house and was returning later than she had intended. She affirmed in a private interview that she was walking quickly and with her head bent low against the autumn wind. The kerchief with which she had covered her hair came loose, and she stopped to tighten it, setting down for that purpose a basket of foodstuffs which she was bringing from home. It was upon raising her head that she saw, in a stand of trees beside the road, "a boy in torn clothes with horns growing out of his forehead."

Dai Meirin states that the boy was of an astonishing beauty, despite his unnatural pallor and the unruliness of his clothes and his uncut hair. This hair was black and curly, but, though it fell over his brow, it was clearly parted by the marks of pollution. Forsaking her basket, Dai Meirin ran for the village, arriving half dead with terror to receive the kind ministrations of her employers. She glanced behind her only once, to see that the Creature was not pursuing her, but examining the contents of her basket.

Following this incident, steps were taken to preserve the security of the village. Sentries both stationary and ambulatory were posted, and armed escorts were provided for the protection of travelers and all those, such as woodcutters and shepherds, who were required to leave the town. Some days passed without incident, but on the eighteenth of Mur, the Abomination, driven no doubt by hunger to attempt to cross our borders, was surprised in a peasant's pigsty by the owner of the pigs, one Koivan the Juggler, so called by his neighbors for his proficiency in that art. Aroused from sleep by the clamor of his pigs, Koivan, carrying a torch, arrived at the pigsty to find the Creature seizing a suckling. The lusty peasant shouted for assistance while the Creature, perhaps surprised by the strength of the other's voice, fled into the darkness. In so doing, it stumbled over a fence and released the stolen piglet, which was afterward burnt alive in the Temple of Avalei at Virna. A search was conducted by torchlight, but the Creature was not discovered. It was assumed that it had escaped into the Aravain.

Realizing our peril, we now proposed to destroy the Monster before it was able to cause further harm to our citizens. We mention in passing that the weather was cruel, crows *thronged the village in numbers, and many of us had fallen victim to accidents. To rid ourselves of evil, we set iron traps in several barns on the outskirts of the village, leaving these places apparently unguarded, while posting obvious sentries in other locations. The traps were moved every twenty-four hours and regularly anointed with blood and milk by the priestess. But the cunning of the accursed Beast enabled it to avoid these snares—nor did it cease to torment and harass us. It was seen in the very center of the village, by several witnesses, exiting a broken window of the bakery.*

On the second day of the Month of Ami we followed a peasant tracker into the Aravain. A recent snowfall assisted the tracker's efforts. Accompanied by dogs, we traced the Creature to its lair, where we discovered the remains of a fire and the carcass of a squirrel. There was also a pile of cloth, roughly in the shape of a swallow's nest, which was found to be composed of garments stolen from the village. The Creature, however, was not there. We divided our party into three and spread out through the precincts of the forest. The Abomination was discovered, pursued, and at last brought to bay in a snow-drift where the valiant Lord Avras shot it in the shoulder. This writer can uphold the testimony of Dai Meirin, that the Creature was young, beautiful, and clad in assorted rags. Bleeding from the shoulder, it uttered the words "I am a Lath" before our courageous villagers brought it down with the blows of their cudgels. Its remains were burnt in the forest, and the village and countryside purified by the priestess. And may Avalei never fail to protect Her own.

What is the difference between a king and a monster?

A tremor is moving through the palace like an earthquake. A sense of fear. At night, torches waver across the Alabaster Court, but they look lonely now, fugitive, with no spirit of celebration.

Vars brought me a few more bitter olives and, unbelievably, two letters. I explained to him that the letters could not be for me, that I'd never received a letter from anybody in my life, not once. "Nobody knows me as a person," I said.

He smiled, insisting: "Look." He's so worn down with poor diet and worry I thought he might be delirious, but in fact my name was on both letters. "To the Daughter of the Priest of the Stone, Velvalinhu." I stared at the yellow paper. "They came in soon after we took the Isle," said Vars.

"But who can have sent them?" I whispered.

"Why not open them and see?"

I looked up at him, clutching the letters to my chest. He is gaunt and his lips are cracking but still he wore the curious expectant look of a person for whom it is normal to receive letters.

"I can't," I croaked.

"Oh, come!" he said, disappointed. "I thought it would please you."

I sat down slowly, still gripping the letters. "How is the prince?"

"Bad," he replied. He told me the prince had been unconscious for two days. He smiled as he spoke, his face open and almost boyish in its despair.

"I am sorry," I said, and it was true. I was sorry he had carried his passion for the goddess Avalei up out of the Valley, sorry that he had put that passion into the service of a cruel and mercurial prince who now apparently lay dying. I wondered how long the prince had been ill, how long he had known of this illness. Was it illness that had forced him to seize the throne instead of waiting to inherit it? Was he unable to wait for the Telkan to die a natural death because his own death was slavering at his heels?

If so, then he is not only a parricide. He is not only guilty of hanging my father from a tree. He is guilty of killing Vars and all his companions, of leaving these loyal and eager young men to the mercy of the Duke of Bain. The withdrawn, unhappy boy I knew so briefly is a monster, as surely as if he had horns growing out of his forehead. "Can't you get away?" I asked. It seems I am fated to tell others to escape, to advise everyone to flee.

Vars lifted his chin. "We will defend our prince to the last man."

"Don't be stupid," I said. But before I could argue further, wind rattled the balcony doors, shouts reached us from the courtyard, and I glanced at the window smeared with melting frost. It was then that I saw the ilok.

It rose above the Alabaster Court, huge and clumsy as a vulture, chains swinging from its neck. Its beak shone dull bronze. Its wings, impossibly vast, cast a shadow over the roof on the other side of the court. At first I could only stare and gasp and stutter—for the iloki never leave their garden, they are creatures of ancient history, incarcerated like dusty archives in a library, and no one has ridden one of them since the War of the Tongues, yet this one had a rider—two riders—no, three!

"Look!" I cried at last.

Vars turned. When he saw the creature, he opened the casement and leaned out with such violence I feared he would fall. "Captain!" he shouted. Other shouts rose from other windows and from the court, while the ilok circled, tentative, as if learning to fly.

"Captain! Captain!"

It was hard for me to make out the faces of the riders, but Vars knew them, and when the bird dipped down for a moment, I recognized two of them: Lady Siski of Ashenlo, and, clasped in her arms, secured with ropes, sagging, apparently unconscious, Prince Andasya. The foremost rider, who seemed to be guiding the creature with his knees, I did not recognize, but this was the one Vars addressed as "Captain," and when he cried "Captain Tavis!" I understood that the black-haired rider in the military jacket was the prince's other cousin, Tavis of Ashenlo.

Only she, of the three riders, seemed to hear my companion's cry. She turned her head. Her face was both sorrowful and forbidding. It was clear what was happening: the prince's war was indeed lost, and now the rebellion's leaders were making their escape.

"No!" screamed Vars.

He thrust himself back from the window and ran from the room, not forgetting, even in his panic, to lock the door, good soldier that he was, and he pounded down the hallway and then the stairs, those shallow stairs of Velvalinhu that resemble floodwaters and take forever to get down, and he had to go through several gardens, at least it was faster that way, though he may not have known that, he may have stayed inside the walls, in which case he would have had to go up stairs as well as down, and through several empty galleries and pointless antechambers until he spilled out at last, lungs aching, into the Alabaster Court—and there, I could see him from my window, a small figure among the others who were clutching their hair and wailing as if at the greatest of disasters, but the ilok had already flown, it had winged away eastward over the sea and Vars was left spinning in circles, as if at the foot of a cataract.

5. For in a field you have found a hidden treasure.
950

What is the difference between a king and a monster?

It was the Feast of Lamps and the towers of Velvalinhu blazed like torches, prefiguring the fire that would rage through them in the coming days and turn the bright halls to a wilderness of ash. The Tower of Mirrors was particularly splendid, strung with lights, colored light spilled over the balconies of the ballroom, and sometimes, from across the Alabaster Court, you could see (if you were a lonely young woman sewing) a lady in brilliant clothing smoking a pipe. Everywhere, on every available body of water (in some places they broke the ice to reach it), Olondrians were setting little boats afloat, each loaded with a tiny lamp or candle and a twist of shiny paper on which was written a name and a message for the dead. *We miss you. Rest easy, the horses have not been sold.* My nurse gave me these examples, for the followers of the Stone do not participate in this ritual, and I never sent my mother a little lamp. "Never?" asked my nurse. "Never," I replied. She was a kind woman, and shrewd, whatever my father thought. She knew how to arrange her face to hide her feelings, how to change the subject, to spare me the knowledge of how small and sad a life I lived. How often I must have been protected by her bland, circumspect face, which my father said resembled a boiled potato . . .

Write it. Write.

The ships came into the Inner Harbor, floating fountains of light. The prince made no attempt at stealth: that was the trick.

He arrived as if on parade, in the sort of ostentatious gesture one expects from a merry, sportive, and profligate prince. To run away to the army, to come home again for nearly two years, enough time to lull everyone into thinking his restless spirit had been tamed, to run away again, and then, on the Feast of Lamps, to arrive with an army of revelers—what roguery, what a prank! I am told they cheered when he entered the ballroom: those fools who would soon be led away in chains. Some of his cousins began a chorus of "Gallop, my little black mare." His mother was so overcome with joy she leaned on the wall for support, and her beauty turned blue, as if it had been preserved in brine.

Then misery came; then joy was turned to dread. "Kneel!" cried the prince, and "Kneel! Kneel!" echoed the jostling crowd of his followers, and the dancers knelt, laughing, still thinking everything was a joke, save Baron Fidrin of the Isle of the Poet's Daughters. An elderly man with aching joints, he leaned on the wall, irritated, lips pursed, the Order of the Lamp shining on his chest. And then someone (perhaps Vars, who knows) struck him across the shoulders with the flat of a blade. The old man crumpled, groaning.

An instant of silence. The flutes and guitars of the orchestra dying out.

From music to silence, and from light to darkness.

"Ha!" cried the prince, swelling with exultation, his cheeks as red as his military sash. And he drew his sword and ran around the edge of the ballroom, leaping and striking at the lamps, putting them out one by one—*crash! crash!*—while the revelers cried out in terror. He could not, of course, reach the great chandeliers that hung from the domed ceiling; these dispensed a dim, uncertain, gold-tinged light, which glinted on the drawn swords of the rebels and on the prince's hair, which glittered with powdered glass as if with frost.

The scene swirls before me like a ruined watercolor, everything blending. These hints I managed to gain from Redis, before she left the Isle. I lay facedown on the tiles and she whispered to me under the door while my father hissed at me impatiently from his chair.

"What is she saying?"

"Shh!"

"And they've taken the nobles and locked them up," Redis murmured hurriedly, "and nobody's tried to do a thing about it, because all the palace sentries and everyone, everyone's glad to see Avalei restored, there's celebrations everywhere, bonfires and noisy dances, and the High Priest and Priestess of Avalei go about like a king and queen, showered with rose petals, it's disgusting, they go out on pleasure boats and hunts, they're quite happy to see Velvalinhu burn to the ground around our ears! Whole sections of the Tower of Aloes are gone, and the library—"

"Don't," I whispered. "What of the Telkan?"

"Locked away, like the others! And rumor says he'll be executed."

"The prince wouldn't kill his own father."

"Wouldn't he?"

"What does she say?" my father snapped.

"Nothing, Father. Redis—have you heard anything about us?"

"No," she whispered. "But everyone with a robe has taken it off. Naris of Ethendria stripped it off as soon as they came to her in her room. Yanked it over her head and stood before them in her shift. At her age. They let her put on a coat, then they took her away in chains. It's dangerous for you . . . dangerous, I tell you . . . I've brought some things for you and your father, clothes—"

"No use," I told her, "the door's locked." (And even if it had not been locked, I knew my father would never give up his robe, and I—I've never worn anything but black wool in my life.)

"Be cautious, then," said Redis. "Don't say anything to anger the prince, tell the priest not to shout at him! He's drawn tight as a bow, everyone says; sometimes he seems delirious; he is as strange a lord as anyone has seen since Wuol dined on his enemies' eyeballs!

He went through the Gallery of the Princes and tore down all the portraits that looked like him, and set them on fire in the Garden of Sated Ambition; and the other night, when it rained so hard, some of his men found him lying at the feet of a stone angel near that hill called the Girdle of Avalei. An evil place, and he is an evil prince, in an evil mood! And Lady Tavis, his cousin—the military captain—she terrifies everyone! A face like the bars of a jail! They say the two of them are planning all sorts of horrors . . . they might set the dungeons on fire, or throw people into the sea . . ."

"She cannot be saying 'nothing' all this time!" my father interrupted.

Redis was babbling still, and I stopped her. I told her she must find a way to leave the Isle. No one knew her for a follower of the Stone; she must go away at once, to Bain, to safety, to another life.

"Tell your father I'm sorry," she sobbed. Then, with a small rustling noise and a flicker of shadow under the door, she was gone.

I sat up, resting on my knees.

"Well?" my father said testily.

The light from the window. The curve of his brow. His hands.

In the War of the Tongues, the war that established for all time (or so we have always been taught) the superiority and centrality of the Olondrian language, King Thul sacrificed his daughter Solin. He bound her hands behind her back and hurled her from a window in the Tower of Pomegranates. A direct plunge into the placid waters of the Outer Harbor. In the *Vanathul*, Ravhathos creates a touching scene from this historical fragment. The girl begs her father to leave her hands free. *"No,"* he answers, weeping, *"for I would have thee suffer little and die swift."*

Alas for the king. Alas.

No one knows what Solin thought, or what she said. We only know that her death was a step on the road to victory. A victory that seems less and less certain now, as I sit alone, drinking my water sparingly, nibbling at the last of the dried fruit. I light no lamps, hoping the rebels will forget me, as they roar through the night, smashing vases and furniture in their despair. The moon gleams between the towers and I long for the Stone, its solidity, its dark weight, the solemn cadence of its words. *For you are following a thread. For you are cloaked in dawn. For in a field you have found a hidden treasure.* It occurs to me that perhaps we did not understand its message, that this message may have been concealed in plain view. Why so many languages? Different tongues, different scripts, some of them dead. The hours we spent poring over dictionaries and grammars. We thought the message of the Stone, arriving in such a spectacular form, would unite us. But perhaps its true message was one of disintegration . . . Or perhaps it spoke a message of unity we could not understand, one that did not unfold in language as my father thought, but rather in the way the lines crossed over one another, cutting across each other, one word into the next. If the message is not in the words but in the cutting. How flint etches stone, how diamond enters. How flesh intersects with flesh. Newer languages digging themselves into old ones, accounts of vampires into the meditations of some nameless saint. How we are written into one another. How this is history. Then the meaning of a line like *"Sever all ties"* is not in the words themselves, but in their entanglement with the words written underneath them: *"For in a field you have found a hidden treasure."*

Alas for Solin, drowned in the waters of the Sea of Songs. Alas for me, that at my age I still weep when I think of my father's words. *A painful act, but honorable. And he won the war.* Useless to record this for posterity; he probably forgot about it himself. I'm cold, and I can't remember what I meant to write. *Writing is power,* he said. Standing over me in the bare room at the center of our apartment. His robe in the corner of my eye. Always in the corner. And his silence. And his breath, tight, irritated, impatient. I risked a glance up at his face; he was staring out of the window. So much distance.

But I'm your child. I'm your child. Fanlewas informs us that the Ideiri believed the Sea Goddess rescued Solin. For them, the dead girl was a minor hearth goddess. Her symbol a chain.

And as for the priest's daughter: she was a bird that flew into a window by mistake, a ragged creature among the fine ladies of Velvalinhu, ignorant as an owl, she knew nothing, no one had taught her, she had only her peasant nurse and of course her dour inflexible father, and she was stunted somehow, stunted and odd, very odd indeed it was whispered, able to converse fluently about anything that had been written in a book, but completely lost when it came to ordinary daily activities like plucking one's eyebrows or even riding a horse. She only left the Isle once in her life: she went to her maternal grandfather's funeral somewhere in the Valley with none but her nurse for company, and she ought to have been thrilled at the adventure but instead she cried every day, because birds that are raised indoors lose their tolerance for the sky. The girl had lost her tolerance for the hugeness of the world, or rather she had never developed it at all, and she cried at the horses and cried at the cities and cried at the strange beds and cried at the fields and cried at the people, her relatives, who tried to make her stop crying. She said she would never leave the Isle again, and she never did. But you must not entertain the idea that she was innocent as well as naïve. No, she was crafty, in fact a thief, and she stole her father's papers and rifled through them when he was working or at a council with the Telkan. And between these thefts and the almanac under her mattess she knew a great deal about the palace even if she could not select a good bottle of wine or tie a sash: she knew that there was a patterned silk called "twilight" that sold for seventeen droi a span, but that a friend of the queen's had managed to get some for fifteen, and she knew that Evmeni pearls are far superior to the ones brought up around Bain, which are only pitiful little bits of greenish marble, and she knew how very boring Lord Fenya was when he got to talking about rare porcelain, and that Lady Tavis of Ashenlo had run off to join the army, making it impossible for her to be received in decent society ever again, and that this was a shame because she might have made a good marriage. For even though Lady Tavis was very clumsy and her mother let her go about in horrid Kestenyi getups that made her look like a trained bear in clothes, she had the Faluidhen coloring, all of the women of Faluidhen have it, that dazzling dark skin that makes them glow like lamps in the middle of the day, and Lady Siski had it too, and was the only hope of the family now, and the queen was introducing her to one bachelor after another, because she must do something, her sister Lady Firheia was so hopeless, such a peasant really, years of life in the highlands had coarsened her, in fact she had begun to smell distinctly of animals and coffee, and Siski must be spared that awful fate, and the sooner the better, she was not getting any younger, though she was admittedly a vision when she arrived at the Isle in her gorse-yellow traveling suit.

The priest's daughter read about the life that was going on in the palace. She drew pictures under the beam of her single candle, pictures of ladies and gentlemen walking and dancing and sitting down to meals at elegant tables. She knew all the styles of dress, how bodices changed from year to year, the fashions of hairpins, and whether the gentlemen were wearing their hair short or long, and sometimes she drew herself in the midst of the dancers, in a light carmine frock with a necklace of tourmalines and Evmeni pearls. She read the geographers, Elathuid the Voyager, Firdred of Bain, and she drew herself aboard ships, in hotels, in tents, on the pinnacles of mountains, and then sometimes in cities, in little parlors, among cousins, in the garden of an aunt who passed her an ice decorated with pink dust. She had to imagine the colors, as she possessed only charcoal. She drew in a frenzy of self-loathing and a sick, irresistible craving. Sometimes she made herself eat the charcoal as a sort of penance and vomited ecstatically over the balcony.

At dawn the sky was so clear and almost green. And she felt bright and light. She always burned the drawings before she left her room.

How quickly the feeling dissipated. As she walked to the room of the Stone her bones seemed to sigh. *You will sever all ties and pass from your bondage into light.* She repeated these words to herself. She repeated: *Yours is a negative kingdom.* She felt herself becoming stranger, her loneliness irrevocable. But she never tried to go anywhere else, she never tried to change anything, she only committed one grand act of betrayal, when she helped a little foreigner, an enemy of her father's, escape the Isle, so that he could deliver her letters to Lunre. Once again she told someone: "*Run.*" And now alone in her room she wonders if she is somehow responsible for the howls and crashes outside, if by telling the prince to run away, and later by setting that foreigner free to aid the prince's design, she woke this dragon, this new war, its wings blazing, and she wants to run outside, as she did just once when a man named Vars was her captor, pelting down the abandoned hallway only to be caught and brought back in minutes, because Vars had told her her father was dead, hanged by the prince from a tree in the Garden of Quinces, and she wanted to see his body.

(And how he would have hated the Garden of Quinces— the fussy little benches, the anemic statues, the carefully cultivated moss to make the rocks look "natural." It was raining, but not hard enough to douse the fires. One could hardly breathe for the smoke. The prince—broader now in the shoulders, and taller—was grimy with soot. He was shouting something, jabbering about the Stone, about how it was an abomination, he was condemning the Stone worshipers as foul heretics, as mockers of Holy Avalei, and the people around him were cheering, all of them rough and muddy and smoke-smudged in the rain. And look, there, between the walls: a wash of vivid color, a perfect pink. *My peppercorn tree!* the priest thought, smiling. In his radiant solitude he did not recognize the fire. I think he did not recognize the fire. I think he went easily to the noose, slipping earthward like a leaf, and gave the prince one stern, cold look before he died. I think he died so quietly that the crowd was awed for a moment and fell silent, and the prince himself quaked with fear. I think he did. No, I think my father begged for mercy. I think they dragged him from his chair and made him crawl to the foot of the tree. I think he loosed his bowels and his murderers laughed. I think he thought of me and feared for me and thanked the Nameless Gods that I was not there. I think he cursed and threatened them, he swore the gods would smite them. I think his bones were so light he took a long time to die. I think he is still hanging there. I think they cut him down. Let me go, I begged Vars. Let me see him. Let me go.)

Geography.

Nothing distant, not the grottoes of Ethendria or the blue paradise of gentian-covered hills, but a tree-lined street in the harbor district of Bain. Discreet, yet determined, I shadow the steps of a young priest of Heth Kuidva who walks with his wife on his arm. He wears the gray robe of his order, tied with a belt of braided leather instead of the keilon—an off-duty priest, a priest on holiday. And there is a holiday air to the crimson cap, decorated with faience beads, that sits jauntily atop his wife's brown hair. It has rained recently; a watery sun peers hesitantly through the catalpas, and the priest tugs his wife's arm to keep her from walking directly under the branches, because drops of water are shining on them and sometimes falling off, and it would not do for her to get wet in her condition. Sometimes, in his efforts to maneuver her around café tables and people rushing in the opposite direction (in Bain people always rush, they never just walk, something the couple has discussed many times), he pulls her sideways so unexpectedly that she stumbles, and he gives her a glance of wide-eyed alarm, for it is well known that the ankles of pregnant women are exceedingly unsound. And Tenais, who is not at all vain (he was drawn to her, when he saw her serving a meal to the poor at the temple, by her uneven dress, one sleeve rolled up, one down), nevertheless insisted on wearing for this outing to the harbor a pair of Dueman shoes with scarlet heels. Her swollen feet are obviously suffering in these shoes, but she smiles at her husband and gives his arm a reassuring squeeze. Still, he is annoyed at her choice of footwear, which is keeping him from enjoying their walk . . . at the corner, he will refuse to buy her an ice . . .

Lies. The truth is, Bain is on fire. The spice markets have gone up in a plume of incense. The trees crackle in the heat.

The truth is, I don't know if my parents ever went on an outing to the harbor. I have had to imagine everything of importance: the coal cellar and the stolen nuts, the horns of the Telkan's riding party, and yes, even the iconic, the inimitable pink peppercorn tree. I have breathed on shadows, as one breathes into a soap bubble, to give it breadth and life. I did it because I had to, because human beings cannot live without history, and I have no history or tradition that is not located in a pale, aggressive body lying in the dirt, or hanging from a tree. How cruel it is to live in a community of two. I used to crouch on the floor, with my bedroom door open a crack so that I could peer out, and watch the lamplight on his motionless shoulders as he read, just to feel that another person was alive. I stole his papers in order to feel that I was not alone. I went through his cabinet. (I found nothing there but pencils, lamp oil, and thread.) I read all his books and tried, in my clumsy way, to debate them with him. What is the difference between a genius and a monster?

The truth is I know nothing. Perhaps he led a completely different life. Perhaps there was even a secret lover (Redis? I ask myself). Our relationship was so distant, barely perceptible except when we were jolted into intimacy by a quarrel or an illness. His tenderness over my toothache, astonishing. He brought me a glass of almond milk. How I struggled not to cry. And when he approved of my translations he'd raise his eyebrows: "Well!" My happiest moments were those in which he was talking to me.

If Ura, the Bloody Imp, was right, and suffering causes lumps to form in the heart, then surely suffering is the geography of the body. I have tried to reconstruct the inner geography of a visionary by imagining how those lumps, those hills, were raised. Dear gods, the powers of children are terrible! A child can conjure a universe from the feel of a worn glove. A child like the one I was, given only a hand-mirror and a cold figure in a black robe, will make a family saga: Ivrom and Tenais.

Such delicate history. Blow on it and it flies away like soot.

It is the second day of Avere, the Month of Rain. On this day, in an earlier time, the Telkan's beard was scented and dyed blue for his meeting with the Master of the Galleries. The Teldaire inspected her ladies-in-waiting, who were expected to exhibit immaculate stockings. The heels were examined with particular care. A dirty or threadbare heel sentenced its wearer to two years in the kitchens. But this is not that story anymore.

This is no story I have ever read. On the paper before me, in turquoise ink:

Dear Tialon,

I suspect you have never heard my name: Lerel of Bain. I am your father's cousin. My mother—Fadroe of Bain, dead now twenty years—was your father's aunt, and used to host him here at our house when he was a boy. I make a point of writing to your father, and to you, every year on the Feast of Lamps, when, as the poet says, all debts are forgiven. I am sorry to say I have never received a reply—though you must know this. I write again now in the hope of receiving some news of you and your father. We are all concerned for your safety—dreadful rumors come from the Isle, and here in the capital there have been attacks on your father's followers. I might as well tell you that we are all old-fashioned devotees of Avalei here, but even Fanlewas admitted that blood flows farther than language! If you

would allow us to receive you, we should be honored! I have always
felt it was wrong for us to be so estranged, not to know each other at
all. Your mother's family, too, wishes to reach you. I am sending their
letter with mine. Like me, they write to you every year . . .

In the second letter:

Dear Tialon,
This is your cousin Bron of Kasanhu I am of the Tetherin branch of
the family. Your mother and mine are cousins. Forgive me if I do not
write well we are not very lettered here certainly not like your mother's
branch in Bain. But perhaps you will remember me from the funeral
of your grandfather. I took you into the barn to look at the cows. I am
writing now to say if you wish to stay with us we will have you. I
think you cannot stay on the Isle anymore . . .

To think that my father kept such letters from reaching me.
For years.
For in a field you have found a hidden treasure.
I searched his papers so often, yet I never found letters like
these. He must have requested that they be destroyed on arrival.
Such cruel, absolute integrity. He would not read a word. He would
not even poison his mind with the address above the seal. And
his daughter was in her bedroom drawing pictures of herself at
tables, in carriages, in cozy rooms, in the garden of an aunt. And
she would have given anything for such a letter. She would have
raised the paper to her face, as she does now, and breathed in its
fugitive scent.
The light is fading. I must work quickly. I crawl around the
floor like a child at a game, cutting a sheet to make a skirt. It is
white, and I have only black thread. I will look terribly strange, like
some deranged ragpicker, but at least it is appropriate for me to put
on mourning. I'll stitch the white skirt over my black and transform myself from a Stone worshiper into—what? The thought of

it makes me wheeze with laughter. I bite my lip to stop the sound, it doesn't seem right, not now when I am surrounded by dangers. Wind shakes the windowpanes; somewhere it's whipping the sea. Perhaps I won't be able to find a boat. Perhaps I'll run into the duke's warships and be struck with a flaming arrow. *The towers are all aflame and I, I skim the air between them, defiant in my feathers of burnt lace.* In the Seventy-Fifth Elegy, Fanleshama's owl remains loyal to Velvalinhu, it refuses to leave the place where its life is turning to ashes, but I will not, I am making myself the costume of a humbler, shrewder creature, a piebald crow. At last I am telling myself to run.

From Our Common History

In the Valley, the peasant revolt is crushed by noblemen on horseback. And Veda of Bain, who never wished to lead, who already seemed an old bachelor at the age of thirty, when the death of his uncle made him Duke of Bain— Veda retakes the Isle. By the time he has regained control of the capital, organized a sea-going force, and traveled to Velvalinhu, the usurping prince is nowhere to be found. The tatters of the rebel army shiver among the palisades. The sea glints like the flat of a sword.

The rebels surrender. Deprived of their leaders, Lady Tavis and Prince Andasya, they shed their plumage of weapons like birds in molt. They are boys, just boys, some from the Valley, others from Kestenya, all of them dazed as if torn out of a dream. The duke speaks with the Kestenyis in their own language. "Spare us, *sud*," they say. The duke's heart swells. All its fences are broken. He remembers riding with boys like these in the hills around Ashenlo: perhaps the fathers of these very boys, these "rebels."

The boys from the Valley kneel and press their foreheads to the ground. "Rise," he says. They tell him they did everything for Avalei. "Well," he tells them, "congratulate yourselves. Olondria belongs to the goddess again. The Cult of the Stone is dead."

Dead. Like its priest, slain by the rebels. Like the duke's brother, Ahadrom II, who hanged himself in the Tower of Lapis Lazuli. "We didn't know what to do," says Vars, a hollow-eyed youth whom the others regard as their leader. "We just cut him down and buried him in the park."

Oh, Andasya, thinks the duke. You have killed your father.

To Vars he says: "Where is the prince?"

"Gone," the man answers. His eyes so bleak. A sob caught in his throat. "They . . . flew."

"What?"

"They flew on an ilok. They're gone . . ."

"An ilok?"

The duke stands stunned. It's like something out of a legend: a saddlebird. Legendary, not because it no longer exists, but because its ancient role has been forgotten for so long it has come to seem preposterous, impossible. He remembers, of course, peering into the bird garden on childhood visits to the Isle, nose buried in the crook of his arm against the stench. Irilas threatened to throw him down there once. "They'd gut you like a hare." He remembers their scaly necks, rubbed raw by the chains.

They flew away eastward, the rebels say. "Over there." Waving exhausted hands toward the Tower of Aloes. Beyond that looms the Tower of Pomegranates, where the Teldaire stays in her rooms, as if her son still kept her a prisoner; and beyond that lies the sea. "We must search for Andasya and Tavis," says the duke's cousin Hinro, incensed (but clean, at least; one of the unlucky ones, he spent a month in the dungeons, and emerged, as he said himself, stewed in his reek like a pheasant in jelly), "and when we find them, they must be publicly hanged."

The duke smiles.

"We must make an example of all these rebels," Hinro insists.

But the duke has already begun to let them go. Those who wish to leave—mostly Kestenyi boys—are setting out on the remaining ships and barges, prows turned eastward. Others stay, and he is grateful: he needs them for the rebuilding effort. He needs carpenters and stonemasons, especially for the ruined libraries. He needs scribes to mend whatever can be salvaged from the wreck. He needs gardeners, blacksmiths, glaziers. He needs nurses.

Peace on the Isle. Peace under Veda of Bain. There is a general cry: *Veda for our king!*

The duke writes to his brother Irilas in his sprawling hand (he has never been good at letters): "For the love of life I did not even want to be duke but if it means a lasting peace of course I am willing and then I'm a better choice than Hinro with his gambling what do you think?"

A woman is brought to see him: the dead priest's daughter. Tall, with a face like beaten bronze. His men apprehended her near the Outer Harbor. She carries only a writing box and umbrella, and wears an ash-streaked cloak and a wrinkled, dull white skirt. Her face is pinched with hunger and something else—excitement or terror. He expects her to ask him for the Stone, and prepares himself to tell her regretfully that she cannot have it, that it has been placed in the shrine called the Girdle of Avalei, deep inside a hill at the edge of the Telkan's deer park. But she does not ask for the Stone. She asks only for passage to Bain. "Of course," he says, surprised. She seems to care nothing for her father's legacy. His assent to her request goes through her like lightning—when he gives her a letter of passage, she seizes it and rushes from the room, her umbrella clacking.

She is right, he thinks, to distance herself from her father's cult. For a true Stone worshiper, Olondria has little to offer. Peace has come to the cities and the libraries no longer burn, but the Valley remains in the grip of a frenzied love for the goddess. Caramel pigs and ostentatious charm jewelry everywhere. People are calling the revolt "Avalei's Revenge." They say the Priest of the Stone called down her wrath. A popular song describes, in gruesome detail, his torments in the afterlife.

Others say the goddess was never threatened by the old raven. They say it is Olondria's destiny to be shattered. Kestenya broken off now, floating, lost. They say: "Remember the War of the Tongues." They call Andasya "the Dreved Prince."

Alone in the room he has commandeered—formerly a scribe's office—Veda puts his head down on the desk. *Why could you not wait?* he asks in his mind. *Dasya, why could you not wait? Where are you? Where are the girls?*

He closes his eyes. He'll rest them for just a moment, he assures himself. He is instantly asleep.

When he wakes, he will have to read reports from Nain, where scattered fighting continues between the loyalists and the few but passionate Nainish separatists. He will have to pay his respects to the queen in the Tower of Pomegranates, where she will stare at him unseeing, the line between her lips dark with milim. For now, he dreams of Kestenya. He is riding in the mountains through clear air, and his heart is light, so light. Then he sees a wagon full of children teetering on a cliff. He rushes to save them. He will be too late.

And far away, to the north and east, where winter clings to the air, a vast shape descends toward the roof of a ruined temple. It lands hard, talons in snow. Two figures slip and fall from its back. One staggers to its feet. The other lies still.

A third figure slides down from the creature's back, more expertly, never letting go of the chain on its long curved neck, and loops the chain around a fallen statue. The great bird shakes itself, then lets loose a deep, mournful, piercing cry.

Both of the standing figures cringe at the sound of that harsh lament. They face one another in the low radiance of an early winter dusk. It is clear that they are siblings: the same emphatic brows, the same skin. Sisters, in another life. Siski and Tav.

One moment. A sob. And Siski throws herself into her sister's arms.

"Hush, hush," says Tav, stroking Siski's hair. "Hush, you'll be all right here. Nobody lives here now. Listen, hush, you'll like this: this is where I went to school."

Siski pulls back, startled. "Here?"

Tav nods.

"But that's awful!" Siski cries, looking about the broad roof in dismay. In places, cracks show under a coating of snow.

"I know," says Tav. And suddenly they are laughing, with a rare and intimate abandon. They laugh the way siblings laugh, or people who have been friends since childhood. "Dear," Tav says to Siski in Kestenyi. *Murye*. She calls her sister her lamp and her little foal. "You won't come with me?"

"No," says Siski. "No. We'll stay here. This is perfect."

They both look down at their cousin, who lies unconscious. His face so pale.

"I'll take care of him," says Siski. "I know how."

Tav presses her lips together and nods briefly. "We'd better get him inside. I'll help you before I go. And you've got to have some sort of fire."

Her sudden withdrawal, her curtness, is born of grief, Siski knows. She does not argue. How wonderful to exist in such effortless harmony. Taking their cousin down into the temple, arranging him on a couch, breaking apart a closet door to use as kindling. Why now? Why so late? Why in such terrible circumstances? It's as if they've never quarreled in their lives. When they have finished, Siski accompanies her sister back up to the roof, where the ilok turns its head toward them with a moan.

"Look at it," Siski says, shivering. "It's like we're living the *Vanathul*. Riding the 'winter beast.' You remember that?"

Tav nods. The moon has risen; its light gilds her face. "I'll tell you the truth. I never thought I'd ride it at all."

She keeps her eyes on the ilok as she speaks. "I wasn't planning to ride it, at first. I simply climbed down there to die. Into the saddlebirds' garden. I thought they'd kill me. It seemed a fitting death. But they didn't. And this one came and rubbed her head against my hand."

She sighs. "Dramatic. Death by saddlebird."

For a moment they both stand looking at the creature. Then Siski says softly: "But now you don't want to die."

"No. I probably never did. It just seemed—it all seemed impossible. The war had failed so badly in Bain, and in the Valley. And Dasya . . . well, I couldn't see how to go on." Tav shrugs. "It was stupid. You could say this ilok gave me my life, but you can't really say I deserve it."

"That's not true," says Siski. "You're the best of us."

She squeezes Tav's gloved hand. Tight, as if she will never let it go.

The time will come for farewells and for the last tears. The time will come for Tav to speak of her lover, a woman of the feredhai, and for Siski to listen. *If only the rain would stop*, goes the old song, *we might speak of these things*. They will have that good fortune: a moment of air and of speech.

Too brief, too brief. It is already so cold, and it will be colder in the sky. For now they stand on the rooftop, silent, holding hands. In the deep chill, they can hardly smell the ilok's stench of decay. They stand. Hearts in unison. Breath lit by the moon.

BOOK THREE

The History of Music

Coming down hard like rain.

You, riding over the fold of the mountain. Coming down hard like rain.

You, riding over.

You, coming down hard.

Coming down hard like rain.

∞

This is the book of song, which means the book of laughter. In Kestenyi, song, *yai*, is related to laughter, *kyai*, which is related to the Olondrian *ke*. Your *limike*: "doves' laughter." I say "your," I say it without meaning to hurt you.

In Kestenyi, for book, we say *Bain*. As we do for everything that comes to us from the west, north, or south. Only that which comes from the east is ours: dragons, iloki, rumors, cruel winds, snow. So, the book of song, that is the Bain, the city of laughter.

Laughing city. Capital of the world.

But in the *che* we have another word for book. We call it *hawan*, lamentation. I don't know why. Perhaps long ago a woman saw someone weeping over a book. Or perhaps it's because we call every long poem *hawan.* Our many *hawayn,* histories of death and mourning. We, we women, we sing them, but we don't compose them. It is said that we don't compose them. We are always too late for the battle, we come behind it, we compose little songs, *yaili,* we don't have time.

So: the book of song. The *hawan* of *kyai,* the lamentation of laughter.

Che, women's language, is also related to *kyai.*

The mourning of laughter, the sob of mirth, the tears of joy, are you finished yet, have you got it all?

How slow you are! How slow!

∞

No. Don't stop.

Look at old Shernai! She pretends to spin, but she's really watching us. Clicking and chewing her lip. She doesn't like to see you writing, Tav, she's superstitious, she thinks it's like making the bone map, a dangerous kind of magic. I don't believe that. I don't think writing is sorcery, something forbidden. I think it's more like a comb, it separates your hair more easily than you could with your fingers. It's like riding a horse to go somewhere instead of walking. You go to the same place, but you can carry more. I think writing is a horse.

Or it might be a knife. An axe.

In the days of the sovoi, they used to stop us with paper. Look, you can't go here, look, it's written. No grazing here. No water. There was writing around the wells. They'd ask for our papers, their eyes innocent, their mouths holding cruel laughter. Why, if you have papers, show them, it will be our mistake then, we'll beg your pardon! And we'd pack up and go, the children crying with disappointment. Little black marks, little red marks on a page you could chew up and swallow, and they were stronger than us.

That's why Shernai curses over her spindle.

∽

You will have noticed that all the great songs are sad. "When Tir rode out from Eilam's halls, he rode to sorrow, oh my brothers!" "Ah, would that I had died before my Sarya, for my life now is a broken desert and a plain of stones." When I was small, when I was learning music, I didn't notice this, I simply sang, it didn't occur to me that there could be happy songs. Not real songs, I mean, not the great ones. Of course there are little ones, songs for dancing. But the great *hawayn* are inseparable from grief. Fathers and brothers fallen, horses slain, bereft women everywhere. Ruined country. Whole lineages snuffed out: this is the greatest horror. The dream of *hawayn* is one in which the world contracts in violence. Everyone dies, their blood flies away like scarlet crows.

> *When Tir rode out from Eilam's halls, he rode to sorrow, oh my*
> *   brothers, oh!*
> *And he was like a reed, and like a field in bloom,*
> *And he was like the moon reflected in a still lake.*
> *Now the horses have gone to drink, the horses have muddied the water,*
> *The moon lies broken, oh bones of Tir on the high crags!*
> *Oh bones of Tir that once, still well-knit, leapt under flesh,*
> *Struck fire from his enemies' bodies, fire from the jaw of Kavinduor.*
> *Kavinduor, slack-jaw, may your lips never meet!*
> *May you speak with toil and eat with agony,*
> *May the Long Pain sit with you at table, sleep in your bed,*
> *May women turn from you and children flee,*
> *May you curse your own name morning and evening,*

May you eat pap like a toothless child!
And when you see us, cry: "Ah, my deliverers!"
We will deliver you, Kavinduor and the sons of Kavinduor!
We will deliver you, sons and brothers,
Male kin as far as the necklace can be reckoned,
Even as far as the smallest bead!
For Tir, Tir, Tir on the mountain, Tir who knelt that night and prayed,
Moon, fill my life with honor as a cup with wine.
Then he turned to Haskon his companion, he of the shattered wrist.
Tomorrow, friend, we nail our stirrups to our boots . . .

Such praise songs. A delirium of honor. When I was younger, I liked nothing better than listening to the *hawayn*. Music makes men immortal. Listening, I saw Tir again, alive, his silver body, and I saw him broken to pieces on the crags. Music so potent you could swoon. A sort of communal fever. People cried out, they sobbed for a man who died a hundred years ago. And music keeps anger sharp: that's why in the *che* we call the guitar *sevret*, a whetstone. Music keeps everything alive.

That passion for *hawayn*—I think that's why, years later, I fell in love with a soldier.

Your shoulders and your swinging walk.

That mark on your face. Not a physical scar but a shade of expression, a cast. The look that said: I have killed and will kill again.

A fierce look, I thought then. Now I think: broken. I think: lost.

And Shernai talks to herself over her spindle. An old woman, she has earned the right. Her hands are stiff, but expert. Her thread seems endless. Brightness called out of the air.

∞

The men are going to war and the women are spinning. The women are spinning and the men are going to war. The men are going to war for the women. The women are singing the men to war. The men's hearts grow hot and sharp as blades from the singing of the women. The women are memory. They are the memory of men, of those who have died. The men sing of the fallen and the women keep their songs and memories alive. The women spin threads that never break. The women are spinning shrouds. All the men and women are singing themselves to death.

∞

You had crossed over. Everyone admired this. The men, who had nothing to lose, admired it easily, almost without effort. For them, it was enough that you rode, hunted, ate raw liver, survived cruel wounds, that you were a veteran of war. It was enough that you were silent and never complained, that you didn't speak the *che*. And of course you were an outsider, no wife or daughter of theirs. For the women, it was more difficult, but they, too, admired you—I know you don't believe it, but they did. They do. Envy is a kind of admiration. Sneers are so often the product of longing. Many women would like to do as you do. Some have begun, in the aftermath of war. They wear their hair loose. They would like to dress like men, to kill like men. To kill.

You say: "No more killing. No more." But you are still a hunter. You bring me the body of a shambus bound to your saddle. Blood for soup, meat grilled over the fire, the pelt for slippers, you joke, to keep my feet from freezing in the cold. This smooth pelt, now, in summer. Tav, I will make you a new vest. I will make you gloves of the shambus you killed for me. "For us," you say. Before you struck it dead, you begged the creature's forgiveness. Something you have never done for men.

At night you whisper: "I wasn't sure I'd killed him. I wasn't sure he was dead . . ."

Fear.

You are afraid of the Brogyars rising from the snow.

You are afraid of the dead in the Valley. The ones who died in the war, your war, the fire that freed Kestenya from the empire. When you entered that war, you believed it would be clean. One swift stroke, a final blow for honor, a farewell to the sword. But the dead in the Valley cling to you, breathing smoke. What you are learning now is not clean war. It is the absence of war.

What you are trying to learn. "No more," you say. And the dead cling. And your hand remembers the sword, its friend. So true. So sweet.

We need new songs, I think.

Tav, I will make you a new vest. Tav, I will bring you nalua flowers, dark as your hair.

∞

Look, there's Kaili, laying out feathers to dry. Gray ones, plucked from a Nainish goose: a traveler, like you. Kaili is twelve years old now. Twelve years old. She'll use the feathers to fringe a shawl. She murmurs to herself, intent.

∞

Tav, I will bring you flowers dark as cloud, dark as your hair, your hair is cloud. My hands are flowers in your hair. Tav, your hair in wind. You, riding over the fold of the mountain, such wild hair we thought you were a boy. You and Fadhian riding over the mountain that first time and into camp. And everyone thought you were a boy. Who is this slight Olondrian boy with hair blown in the wind, ragged in wind? And in every way we were wrong. Wrong about you, the stern boy slipping lightly off his horse, my stern Tav, your shoulders and your swinging walk. Not Olondrian, Fadhian told us, holding in his smile, and not a boy. Lady Tavis of Ashenlo.

You, riding over the fold of the mountain.

And Fadhian gone now. Gone. Dead in your war. Can I say these things together in this way? You riding over the fold of the mountain and flowers for your hair and Fadhian dead. Can I say it? Can you write it?

Yes, you will write it with your rough hand. Your passion now for letters. Something new.

That dark night I told you of Fadhian's death. After you had come back, so strangely, riding on a bird, an ilok, landing hard beside the camp like rain. Like rain, and that death smell. Everyone came to welcome you. By the fire they gave you meat, stedleihe, tea. "Fadhian," you said. Then they avoided your eyes—all except me. You gazed at me, stricken. "Dead," I said.

He fell in the Battle of Bron. The one that gained us all the land between the Tavroun and the Duoronwei. Torn from his horse. Pierced through the throat.

Shall I sing of it? Who was his killer? Shall I sing the name? Should we remember? Should we seek vengeance, even as far as the smallest bead?

I am asking you: What is music?

Tav, so much loss. Fadhian is gone, and Mantia who was your friend. So many gone. If I had the sight of a kalidoh, I'd tell you, I'd be able to see it written in your bones. The kalidai see through flesh, they see the spots where the bones are weak, too starkly curved, missing pieces, full of holes. Every loss creates a gap. This is why the bones of those who live for many years appear to be made of lace.

So many gone. Your sister. Your cousin. Your friends. My father. My mother. Keliar, who loved me. Tosha, who loved me. Haidhas, my brother.

Your father. Your mother. Fled now into the Valley. Your sister, lost. And the beloved cousin who should have been your king.

Haidhas. My brother.

☙

What song can bring him back to me?

Haidhas, my brother, dead twice over. Dead to our house when he ran away, dedicating himself to vengeance. Dead again in the war for Kestenya. They say he died at the gates of Eilam. They brought this news to me as a kindness. Like the song: *Only tell me where he lies.* Knowledge is comfort, they say, even knowledge of death. *Only tell me where to seek his grave.* At the gates of Eilam, they told me. But for me he was already dead, had been dead for years. And I had lived those years in mourning.

It was after he died that I became a singer for hire.

Why not? I couldn't feel myself sing. And we were moving in difficult country. Farming country, full of roads. The lands around Tevlas, which now are free, or what we have come to call free: available to anyone who can defend them. But then it was hard country, you needed papers, or else money; you had to pay the farmers to pitch your tents in their meadows. So some of us went to make money. We went to Tevlas, we sang in the streets, we sang in cafés, collecting coins in an old skin.

Loublai taught me to sing for money. She scrawled black around my eyes, red on my lips and cheeks, she gave me cheap necklaces and bangles of green glass. She taught me to roll my eyes, to wince, to exaggerate all my gestures, to sob while I sang. "You have to forget your training," she advised me. It's true: in order to sing in the towns, to sing at Olondrian houses, you have to forget everything. The delicacy, the restraint. The quality of *chaif*, "absence," which is so highly prized in our music. There is no absence when you sing for money. Everything is there.

I was a good singer. I gave until I was hollow.

Learn to keep the music in your voice. That's what Loublai told me. Don't let it hurt you, don't think about the words, put all the feeling in your face alone.

This painted, twisting face. No restraint. Only distance.

I sang for you, in the garden at Ashenlo. I know you don't like to remember. Or rather, you don't like to remember that you forgot, that you forgot me. A hired girl.

∞

We need new songs, I think.

I will bring you nalua blossoms.

Tav, I will bring you flowers in these two hands.

I will make you gloves, a vest.

Tav, I forgive you.

So much loss. Kaili murmurs, twelve years old. Her father is dead.

Fadhian, her father, died in your war. I say "your," I say it and I mean to hurt you. Don't stop writing. Look how Kaili tucks her plait behind her ear, then scratches her ear, the flesh translucent as a leaf. There's sand there, irritating her. Sand under her nail. Now she flicks the back of her hand against her cheek. This is what we lose when we lose someone. A manner of moving, something no image can capture. The gestures never come back.

∞

I have my mother's eyes. Haidhas had my father's. I love to sing. Haidhas loved to ride. Haidhas loved the morning, he'd get up early and ride out across the plateau. I love the night, when the singing starts. I never want it to end.

Haidhas was quiet, he brooded, he held a grudge. My mother said: "Fire under ashes." He would go days without speaking, if you angered him. Me, I'm all on the surface. I shout, I'll throw sand, I'm ridiculous, too much. I burst in an instant and then I forget everything.

To lose a sibling is to lose the one different from you. There's no one now against whom to say: But I am like this. I am this.

"I'll always be alone," you said. You were frozen and trying to melt, speaking to me of your sister who is gone. She'll never scold you, never laugh at you again. I said: "But maybe—" You said: "No." It was the way she looked at you, you said. The way she clung to you in Nain, on the terrace of an abandoned temple of Avalei, where you left her alone with your cousin. You could tell she was saying good-bye forever.

I think when we love we look for someone against whom to say: But I am like this.

Say something. Speak against me.

∞

Speak against me as I will speak against you.

I'll make you a vest. I'll make you gloves. From the hollowed bones of the shambus: prayer bells for our tent. Bells that sing to the gods all day, on our tent, ours. The two of us here. In the deep night, a small lamp on the floor.

You say it's impossible. It won't be allowed.

But why not, why not? Everyone knows. You're here. You say: "But eventually I'll have to go." I say: "Go if you like, but don't pretend it's because you have to." I say: "Listen, I defended us while you slept."

Yes. While you slept. On that first night. You were exhausted. You had come out of the sky, on an ilok, miraculous. You had left your sister and cousin in distant Nain. Do you remember? I brought you into my tent and you cried yourself to sleep.

Then I went to Amlasith. I said: "Tav is staying with me."

So much loss. I'm finished with it. No more now.

Amlasith sat on her bed, surrounded by women as always, beautiful
as always, dripping with gold, but in white now, in mourning for
Fadhian. Her eyes so deep, and the deep lines under them. Someone grumbled when I spoke: Melya, I think. A click of the tongue.

Amlasith looked at me with her deep eyes. She has seen so many
die from her ausk. So many have gone, never to return. And I said:
"We'll go. Tav and I. We'll go away on our own. We are going to be
together. We have lost and suffered like everyone else."

I shout. I burst.

It's foolish. Tosha told me that. My most distant and difficult lover.
"You little fool." During one of our quarrels, she slapped my face.

But there is a song, our greatest song, the longest. The Song of Lo.
Most think of it as many songs, they say "the songs." But really
it's just one song: prophecy, prayer and map. If you know it, you'll
never get lost on the plateau. You sing. You sing and you walk. The
line for this place, where we are now, is: "I am a fountain and a field
of clay." And if you walk north, to that ridge of hills, the song
becomes: "Clay on my boots, clay in my heart, I am of clay like the
Firstborn."

If you know the Song of Lo you can walk anywhere. It is more
faithful than the stars.

I sang a line of it, there in Amlasith's tent. *I am a fountain and a field of
clay.* I said we'd go, we'd walk, I'd take us away, alone across the sands.

Snorts, disapproval, clicking of tongues. Tosha was there, also in white, her husband dead with Fadhian at Bron.

"We'll go," I said.

Amlasith wept. She held out her hands to me. She gathered me close, in tears. "Seren. My little horse."

∞

Shernai sings. *Ta-ta-di-dai-di.* It doesn't make sense. A woman's song. Just a tongue tapping and a warmth low in the throat. It doesn't mean anything, and so it's open, always available, a bucket being filled up at a dark well. *Ta-ta-di-dai-di.* It tastes like water. Now the wind blows, and Kaili gives a yelp and jumps up to catch the feathers whirling with the sand. She laughs, look, she's laughing, the feathers in sunlight and I don't want them to come down, I just want them to stay up in the air.

∞

In your home, in your cities, I know, the mother and father live together. Your mother and father live together in the same house. You say they're unhappy. You think, you don't know, you haven't been home in so long. But happy or unhappy, they live together. Here it is different. The men and boys follow the cattle, the women keep the children and old ones safe. Father and mother stay in one tent only when he is home: when the season permits it, when there isn't a war. Such a golden atmosphere, when the men and cattle come back to us in the spring. The season of "earth ringing." Ringing bells. A bull slain, meat for all. Lovers in each other's arms again, at last. *Chadhuren,* we call it: "tent heart."

Chadhuren, where everything lives. The place that moves, that sometimes goes dark but can always be revived again, the lamp lit, the rugs shaken out. That's what I told Amlasith and the others while you slept. "Tav is my *chadhurei*," I said. My *chadhuren* dweller.

∞

Let's say this: I who sing am Seren the daughter of Larya of the seventh ausk of the Blue Feredhai of Tosk. I am a singer. I sing and I shout and I love, that's mostly what I do all the time, I don't believe I am complicated. My first love was Keliar. She was just my age. Her plaits were always coming out. She had a chipped tooth and she rolled her sleeves up like a boy. When we played she was Hivnawir and I was Taur. We played that story over and over, she was the boy and I was the girl. At first we just repeated the story, forbidden love, the two cousins, a boy and a girl, we'd hold a scarf between us and giggle and kiss through the cloth, but then we started changing it, in our story the scarf came down, the maids went away for some reason, the lovers opened their shirts. And then one day Keliar's plaits were so tight and her sleeves rolled down to the wrists and she said we were women now, too old for children's games. I didn't see why we should stop. She said: Don't make it complicated. That was all. She got married later that year.

I don't think I'm complicated. I think I'm completely simple and clear. I only want to have all the feathers up in the air.

My second love was Tosha. She had two children, her husband was dead. She was one of those dangerous people who take fire with them everywhere. Everyone wanted to be with her. She was vicious sometimes, she sneered, but her warmth was incredible too, when she smiled little lights would come on under your skin. It happened to everybody, not just me. She wanted a husband, but she was taking her time. When she found one, we quarreled, and Tosha slapped my face. It wasn't our first quarrel, but it was the last. Her second husband is dead now too. Tosha's alone. I think she prefers it.

Then you. Riding over the fold of the mountain. Everybody thought you were a boy. Everybody except me. Your dark hair and dark brows, and that cold look. You were my exact. You were my exactly. What I was looking for. You were perfect.

∞

Waking in the night, you're afraid. I soothe you to sleep again. I sing, *Moon, fill my heart with honor as a cup with wine.*

Moon, fill my cup.

Lost goddess, come.

This is something they say is changing: they say the goddess is coming back. Roun, in her boat. She was never really gone, of course: the gods, we know, will live as long as the world. But she has been buried, forgotten. Her places of worship, the aklidai, destroyed and abandoned. We have learned to think of them as places of haunting and death. Where girls should not go, lest the spirits of the dead kalidai discover them, turn them into birds and roast them over hot coals. This is how we have learned to think of the aklidai. We sing: *She strayed among the stones, and he was waiting there.* I, even I, when I see an aklidoh, I who long for Roun's return, when I see those white domes it chills me to the heart.

Still, they say Roun is coming. Roun, the great patroness of Kestenya. In her boat, alone, without father or mother or lover. Her boat which is the moon. We were told that she was Avalei, and then we were told that she did not exist. How changeable you are, you Olondrians! Every ten years another god. For a time we tried to

worship Avalei, because it was law. I remember my mother speaking of her as the Rose, this we understood, we have always sung
of roses in the highlands, where they bloom so briefly. But the
rest—the pigs, the vultures, the grain—this confused us and left us
numb. Where is our grain? Where do we bury seeds and revive them
in the same place? My mother was vague about this aspect of the
goddess. "She dies and then returns," she explained at last. "Like
spring. Like the moon."

Avalei is untrustworthy. Always in bed with a man. If she is happy,
she will produce a line of kings. When she is sad, she goes to bed
with the Plague, and produces vampires. You laugh at my words,
but I tell you, you're laughing at yourself.

Avalei wanders. Is she alive or dead? You never know.

But Roun rows. In her moon-boat. She lights the lamp, then dims
the flame.

The stars follow her. They are her children, because she loves them.
As I am Amlasith's child, because she loves me.

Roun, fill my cup.

∞

Today there's a heat in the air. A dryness. Summer is almost here.
The end of our year.

How determined you are, my heart. Dear heart.

Your furious scribbling. Nearly as fast as I speak. You miss almost
nothing. Your terrible soldier's hand grasps the pencil like a stan-
dard. You say you'll make copies, leave copies of my words every-

where, under stones, in fences, in Kestenyi and Olondrian, you're an idiot, copies of what?

Copies of this, you say. What is this *this*?

Copies for others to read. Who?

You say: Bildiri fleeing the farms, lost people, anyone. Anyone who thinks the *feredhai* only make one kind of music. Oh, Tav! You are very Olondrian and stupid.

No. Don't stop.

I love you.

Every copy will bear a dedication. To the anonymous reader. Someone who can read.

Give me your hand.

Give me your hand. Give me your hand Tav riding over the fold of the mountains. Give me your hand Tav coming down hard like rain.

But let's say it, let's say what there is to say. Let's get it out, let's write it, let's put it there. You are from everywhere and I am from Kestenya. You are from mansions and palaces and cities and mountains and emptiness and pleasure and I am from the great plateau. Let's say and let's get it out that your grandfather was Uskar of Tevlas who signed the shameful treaty that ended the last, unsuccessful war for independence, that he was a pawn and a dupe and also a traitor who knew very well what he did and a mystic in thrall to a man with ribs like gullies in a drought. Your grandfather prayed with the great Olondrian visionary who made your grandfather sleep on planks that brought out sores on his soft and timid body, and my grandfather slept in a mass grave on the road to Viraloi where he was hung by the heels with seventeen others until they died of thirst. Let's say that. Let's write it. Your grandfather punished his body, my grandfather's body was punished. My grandfather was a freedom fighter, or, to use the Olondrian term, a bandit. One of those whose names became synonymous with horror on the Karafia when little children were dragged from their beds and slain. My grandfather was not there, in Tevlas on the Karafia, he was at Viraloi, part of another branch of the resistance, this resistance so discontinuous and diffuse it resembled the skeleton of an elderly person or a piece of lace. My grandfather was holding Viraloi under siege. While at Tevlas, your grandfather with twenty-seven Kestenyi nobles signed a treaty, and welcomed the Olondrian army, I think they were called a "pacifying force," and they captured my grandfather and hung him by the heels.

Let's say that your grandmother was the sister of the Telkan. She loved birds. She dyed her hair yellow and wore a green scarf and Kestenyi trousers. She was a Lath of the royal line and she loved the desert and at her mansion she entertained the robber barons who were the last dregs of the resistance. But there was no resistance anymore, only theft and parties at your grandfather's house where your grandmother served the thieves Olondrian teiva. They were so broken they drank and danced with her. Let's say that my grandmother was a great singer who died singing of my grandfather.

Let's say that. In her white mourning robe. Her eyes ringed with thick black paint. When she wept the paint melted slowly, like oil in winter. She sang an old *hawan*, a conventional lament, putting in my grandfather's name because he was not important enough to have his own song. Thousands had died and my grandfather was not one of the leaders or from a great princely house so none of the men had composed a song to honor him, so my grandmother sang of him as she could, in the usual way, the way most women sing, putting the name of the lost one among the conventional lines. *My clear one. Horse of the dawn. His breath like snow. His body shattered like ice. I will tear my flesh for him, my flesh will not forget.* My grandmother had scars on the sides of her face where she had torn the skin with her nails. Most old women have these scars, it's normal.

The same songs, over and over. *Horse. Clear one smashed like ice.* It would not have occurred to my grandmother to compose a new song for her dead husband. She sang as she had been taught. She sang like a woman. Always coming behind, picking up the bones that look exactly the same. And she died at the place called the Little Doves, between Suvias and Bron, with my grandfather's name on her lips. While my grandfather slept in a mass grave at Viraloi. All her life she tried to get her daughter, my mother, to convince my father to ride to Viraloi and avenge the dead.

"Tell him to go. Did I give you to him for nothing? . . . He's my son! He married my daughter and now he's my son! . . . If you had brothers, would this have happened? . . . He is your husband, your brother and your blood! . . . Is he a man? . . . Did I give you to a man, or to another woman?"

Over and over, between the laments. This endless, raucous cry. Sometimes in common Kestenyi, sometimes in the *che.* My grandmother was just this woman in white, crying, haranguing, berating, she drove my father away sometimes, or he'd turn and shout at her too. You've heard that shouting. Family quarrels. If it happens outside you go and intervene, if it happens inside a tent you pretend you haven't heard. You can hear it, physically you can hear it perfectly well through the side of the tent, but you pretend you can't, and then you really don't hear it. You can sit on the ground right outside, making butter, and you'll just hear the birds while behind you someone is being accused or beaten or born. It happens like that. It happened like that for us. The terrible voice. The men sing songs about the nagging voices of women. *Your voice is a rain of hot salt.* My grandmother proved them right every day. She loved no one but Haidhas, my brother, her little hope, her dove, her killer-in-waiting, her little stallion as bold as a whip, after shouting she'd take him on her knees and croon to him, kissing him over and over. I hated her.

I hated my grandmother. You were afraid of yours. In her old age your grandmother smelled of bird dung. Feathers clung to her dress.

The eccentricities of royal ladies! She let her eldest sons marry two sisters, a pair of noblewomen from Nain. The whole empire was united now, in blood! The celebrations even reached the desert. Sweets were handed out in little velvet bags. My mother was given one of these bags. She was young, seventeen, the same age as your frightened mother who came to live in Kestenya accompanied by her nurse. My mother ate the sweets handed out by Olondrian soldiers and kept the little green bag. She kept her needles in it, and later my brother's milk teeth. She didn't keep my milk teeth, because I'm a girl. I asked her once what had happened to mine, my baby teeth. "What a question," she said.

The two oldest sons married noble Nainish women. Success. The empire is a success. This success is really you. You and your sister and your cousin. The three of you weaving the strands of the empire together: the Fayaleith and Kestenya and Nain. These three strains are destiny, one people, a single radiant language splintered on the departure of the gods. You, your sister, your cousin, you are paradise. One in the desert now, and the other two in a ruined temple in the north.

The two oldest sons married noble Nainish women, but it's the third son who rules Olondria now. Your Uncle Veda, the Duke of

Bain. He's a good man, you say. Not a natural king. You're sorry for
him. I asked, what's he like, and you said, "Resigned."

A king on the Isle. Avalei's temples thriving again, now that the
Priest of the Stone is dead. It's as if everything wants to go back
to what it was. Everything wants to go back, except Kestenya. *Kestenya Rukebnar.* It wants to go forward, or sideways. Tav, let's never
go back.

Kestenya going, parting from the Valley. Perhaps Nain, someday.

You say, no. The Nains will never rebel. They want to become
Olondrian. They're passionate about it, even though they pretend
to be proud of who they are. You speak of your terrible Aunt
Mardith. "A bloodless woman," you say. She was determined to
be Olondrian, but on her own terms. She wished to rule. She was
working toward it, amassing wealth, arranging marriages, absolutely
cautious and single-minded. Her patience for this game was outra-
geous, twisted, it deformed her. When you speak of her you remind
me of myself talking about my grandmother. You say your Aunt
Mardith wore pearls at her wrist and throat. She would have killed
anyone for money. Of all your family, you say, she was the most
like you.

She is. She's still alive.

Your relatives live for a very long time. Mine do not. Let's say that
too. When my grandfather died he was twenty years old. Let's say
that your people live and my people die because that is so and I am
an orphan, I was an orphan when we met. My father was killed in
Tashuef at a cattle auction, something went wrong, some negotia-
tion and he was stabbed between the ribs one afternoon, and my
brother crept out and avenged him slitting the throat of the one
who had killed him and then he died, my brother, he buried himself

in the mountains, escaping the sovos. The sovos came to the camp looking for my brother and I burned him with my eyes, I wished all kinds of evil on him, blood and scabs and pests. Women, they say, have a propensity for witchcraft, but in my opinion this is not true, it's only another joke they play on us, to laugh. I don't know a single witch. I wish I did. I just looked at the sovos, helpless. Knowing I would not see my brother Haidhas again. The sovos asked us questions and took notes. We were very polite, as always, not causing trouble, that was Fadhian's way. It was important to have a good reputation if you were feredhai, to be known as docile, to give in to paper every time. My heart, Tav, this politeness. I think it's politeness that really went to the heads of the men when they rushed into Bron to set fire and kill. They say the library of Bron went up like the world's most beautiful bonfire. Everywhere it was like the Feast of Lamps. I imagine them leaping and crowing against the flames. They found the sovos of Bron, they forced him to eat all the brass buttons on his jacket. That is the sort of thing my people do while your people are quietly buying land and organizing garden parties. They forced him to swallow the buttons on his coat and then they stood him against the wall and four of them shot him full of arrows. And far away Haidhas died a second time, he died for good in this war you brought us like a garland full of thorns. And Fadhian died and Mantia died and so many others died and we, we women, we were hiding in caves, rehearsing.

The caves. They smell of filth and decay. They sound like children crying. Every night I lay down there I thought I would die.

I could hear women muttering in the dark. Especially the old ones. Practicing. Not my grandmother, though. She was dead by then.

My son. My brother. My silver horse. The same songs, over and over. And children crying. I pressed my hands over my ears. I thought I would die. The songs were all over me like spit, like a caul. I'd lie there gagging. *My horse, my love, his body broken on the high crags.*

My grandmother died. She died of a broken heart. Not because Haidhas was lost to us, but because he had gone without avenging his grandfather. He had avenged his father instead. My grandmother hated her life. My mother died soon after her, of a winter fever.

I was just going in circles then. Spinning.

And in the caves I was spinning. Spinning.

And you were entering Velvalinhu with a sword. Say that. Say that you move with swords in palaces and I lie in my own filth dying and pressing my hands over my ears. Say that you planned death and you ordered death. Look Tav, here it is, your independent Kestenya. More than half the men dead, many others wounded. Tav, they killed Fadhian, they pierced his throat with a spear and the blood came loose.

Fadhian so polite they pierced

who never

and in the Valley the towns on fire, towns that now

and ashes

stinking

they say in places the river

for what? Because you wanted

when you were young

the vultures

where

I don't know if you're still

Tav

Tav

Tav

Tav

↗

Today it's hotter. The birds are still, except for the desert susa. That creaking call.

The pen looks strange in your hand. You're clumsy, everything's smudged. I think it's because I've hurt you. You've hurt yourself. That look I used to think was fierce. You are broken on the high crags.

No. Not that.

New songs, I think.

Your sword-hand writes, a scrawl. You'll make copies, you say, you'll leave them in fences, in villages, under stones. I remember in Tevlas once, a professional reader in the square, his wide-brimmed hat, one brown knee crossed over the other. Reading from a tattered book of tales. Men stood around him, smoking. A woman leaned in a door-way, holding a child. A little girl ran up to the reader and gave him a glass of cider. She waited to take the glass back, listening, eyes wide.

Crrk. Listen, a susa. Making noise.

I am generally happy. Some people are generally sad but I am generally happy. I think that you are more sad than happy. Haidhas was too. And my mother, who kept her son's milk teeth in a little Olondrian bag. She taught me how to sing. She was very strict. You sit up straight, you keep everything tight. You are not dancing or playing the diali, you are singing. You are carrying the scars of the ausk. You sing with this tightness, it makes the *chaif*, the absence, what you won't let go. Don't let go, don't smile but don't cry either, control your breath. You are singing. My mother sang beautifully, in a hard voice like a tree. I have that same hard voice, but I am naturally sloppy, spilling everywhere, it was easy to learn how to sing for money.

Generally I am happy. Even through loss.

I lost my brother and I was spinning. And after you went away I started spinning again. Spinning in the dark and in the cave. But it's not normal for me, I've never had that natural melancholy. I think this is why I can't become a great composer, after the first reason I mean—the fact that I'm a woman. After that first, original reason, which is really enough, there is this problem of not being a serious person. I used to watch the little goats and just laugh. In the spring. They're so comical, and there's this dense light everywhere. When you throw your head back and gaze at the sky it's as if your heart is lifting out of your body, just going up, just going up.

Tav, I will make you something new.

"Did I give you to a man, or to another woman?" My grandmother's jeers, her terrible contempt. This, more than anything,
showed me that the life I imagined was impossible. "Didn't I give
you to a man?" My father went to eat outside the tent, though
the sun was setting right in his eyes. He wouldn't give my grandmother a single word. My grandmother inside shrieking. I went
out too and sat beside him, feeling cold because I was thinking
of Keliar. We were going to meet that night, as usual: we'd sneak
away from the artusa during the dancing. Giggling, knowing that
nobody cared, it was just play. Suddenly the thought that it was
"just play" twisted around itself, making a painful knot inside
my heart.

Play. In the Valley, it's prayer. You told me that. You said love
between women was only possible in a temple of Avalei. In the
aklidai, too, it was possible, in the old days, under those chalk-
white domes, everybody loving as they pleased. Perhaps someday it
will be that way again, when Roun returns in her long boat, when
she begins her stately glide across the sky. But it's not the life for
you. You were born beneath a wooden roof but you're a true wan-
derer: a feredha, like me.

Something new. But what? I spill everywhere, I'm too much. You
can't find a single person in the camp who takes me seriously. Ask
them! I've never been married, I'm a perpetual girl to them, they
indulge me, they'd only laugh if I told them I was composing
music. Music—a serious art! Death and remembrance! The soul
of the ausk! And me, Seren—so messy, only a susa, laughing too
much at everything, holding her ribs and laughing at goats, suddenly angry, shouting at people, forgetting it all in an instant, just
forgetting.

New songs, Tav. New songs, I think.

Something fresh, light, like a breath. You must have noticed that things are different now, with the men so few. Girls herd cattle and even hunt. They're shy, but they like it. Everyone's wondering what will happen in winter. It's in their minds that you have gone to the winter pastures. And other things have come to the surface, revived. I remember when you told me about the False Countess, a woman warrior you read about in a book. You said she was Kestenyi, and I laughed. It seemed impossible, but afterward I saw that it could have been true. I remembered stories that seemed to resemble the story of the False Countess. A tale of a group of women defending themselves and their children in the hills. They fought with knives and stones, one with a tent pole. And there was a robber princess who lived without a home, without an ausk. She was said to be terribly pale and death to the Laths. I remembered these stories. Now it seems to me that they're all tied together, like a web, they seem like a series of gaps rather than a presence but when you lay them out you can see the outline of a skeleton on the ground. The outline of a woman who has died, but who was there. This is the outline of our women now herding cattle on the plain. The outline of your hand remembering how to form letters, how not to use a sword. The outline of our *chadhuren.*

The outline of a group of women riding toward the mountains. A few men among them. Cattle. *Hesensai:* "traveling without women."

Stupid. It doesn't make any sense. *Ta-ta-di-dai-di.* Only a foolish person could come up with something like that.

New songs. Foolish songs. Why not?

And at the same time the boys are so precious—like pearls, like myrrh, because their fathers are dead. You can see it in the way the women touch their heads, even women who aren't their mothers, even me, I feel this adoration for the small boys. An enormous, protective passion, already weeping. *Live. Don't die.* This is what my grandmother felt for my brother Haidhas. *Live, live, don't die, my sweet, my clear one, my bright horse.* And somehow "live, don't die" becomes "Kill, kill, kill."

This is why I say that music should not be for remembrance. We remember too much. We need music to forget. Songs that leave no scars. All these women with scarred faces and the men would say, "She goaded me to kill." It was the common defense in the case of murder, so conventional, like a song, every case of murder seemed to be the same, even long blood feuds among hundreds of people, always the same, it was always a case of honor and there was always a woman who goaded the man to kill. Women like my grandmother, with voices of hot salt. Sometimes at a trial a woman would stand up, screeching. Other women would hold her back. She'd still be screaming for blood. "She goaded me." I always felt that this defense was true, but also false.

True because of the way my grandmother tried to goad my father, to make him kill. False because something else was standing behind my grandmother. A vast and terrible logic. Formulaic, like a song. The closed and shining logic of men and women.

All of us, singing ourselves to death.

Sometimes, yes, sometimes an aching sadness comes to me across the plain. I think of the girls in stories who are set impossible tasks: count every grain in the field, weave a net out of water. Always a girl. She's bent over, counting grain. She doesn't know why. It is her fate. She is the victim of a closed and shining logic. Why does she never stand up? She says: "I have to save the world." Tav, let's never go back. Let's not even remember.

Poor lost bird, you flit from place to place but cannot find your home.

Forget. But the dead cling. You remember your servant Fulmia. Sometimes you wake in the night, suddenly, calling his name in fear. You speak of the day you understood that he hated you. You had fallen and cut yourself, and he was bending to help you up. His hands were tender, but suddenly you knew. Such thick veins in his hands, you told me, they reminded you of rivers. You went to war for this man, to restore his stolen birthright. *Kestenya Rukebnar.* Stolen by you, by your people. You hope he is free, but he might be dead. In your war. So he clings. And when you're riding, if a stone falls, you whirl, ready for violence. Your body remembers war. This body I love. War has shaped the beloved body.

∞

Music for forgetting. What kind of music? What's the point of music that doesn't want to remember? Why sing at all?

We could remember different things, perhaps. The bones of a woman laid out on the ground. Or the men could remember the *che.*

They know it, these small boys. They learn it in their mothers' tents. They drink it like milk. Growing fat and happy on the *che.* But they're not allowed to speak it. The women won't let them, they slap their heads, lightly but seriously, don't talk like that, don't say that, say it like this! You—*slap!*—you're not a girl! They laugh: shrill, blood-tinged laughter. This thing is theirs, the *che.* They're going to keep it safe. "Listen to him!" "Are you a girl?" I used to love it when Haidhas got slapped for answering in the *che*, so happy I wanted to hug myself. I was the good one, I never got slapped for talking. He was an outsider. The *che* inside me like a well of gold. And then I grew up and this gold was worth nothing, nothing. You can't use it anywhere. It's only for fighting with other women, or for crying.

∞

Or could we? Could we compose a song in the *che*? It makes me want to laugh. What kind of song? A song about milking goats? A song about thread? We already have those, scraps of nonsense, *ta-ta-di-dai-di*. And little songs about being abandoned, left behind.

A great song, though. A *hawan*. In the *che*.

What makes a song great?

It has a great subject: war. It's about male kinfolk and the death of men. It always ends in blood and a call for blood. I've said this before. Tav, I'm spinning. Tav, I feel like I'm spinning around.

Spinning and spinning. After I lost my brother.

We sang in cafés. We'd go from door to door. Collecting coins in a bag. Loublai taught me to do it. You have to forget. I sang like an evil dream about singing, someplace you were caught, you couldn't escape. In the dirty town with the dirty sluggish canal. Carriages everywhere. The dust choked us. I don't care if I live, I don't care where I go. I might as well sing for money. I snapped my fingers, rolled my eyes. At some cafés the men tried to talk to us, they wanted to take us home. Loublai got between us and the men and yelled, they said she grated like a susa. Someone splashed stedleihe on her dress. The next day we were walking and someone threw eggs at us from the window of a carriage. I don't know if it was the same men, or different ones.

Spinning. Just spinning in place.

You have to forget, but at the same time you remember. This is how it makes a circle.

You forget, you make faces, you stretch your throat, you sob. It's ridiculous, coarse, you've become a clown. And at the same time the words of the song are tearing your face. The words tear your painted face and your painted heart. *I am calling, where are you?* Every time I remember Haidhas.

You're in the garden, listening, or not listening. You. Tav.

This is our story. The beginning. The part we remember over and over. We can't forget it, and maybe we shouldn't forget. We shouldn't forget that you forgot me. I reminded you later and now we can't forget. I dream of a way of remembering that would not leave a scar. I dream of a way of forgetting that would not mean destruction, burial, loss. A spinning that makes something, that makes a thread, a thread to sew feathers to a shawl, a shawl unfurling in the air.

Feathers. Flying.

I want them to stay up. Even though I wanted you to come down.

You returned on the back of an ilok. The only person I've ever lost who came back. The huge wings, bells ringing on the tents, the thunder. Coming down hard like rain.

∞

It was night. We all came running. You were exhausted. Torchlight. They stopped and I kept running. My knees felt weak, it was like I was running into the ground. My legs dissolving into the ground like water. I was running down underground, I was going to be buried alive, I'd never reach you.

You'd landed in other places too. At Mereves. At Bron. Looking for me, for us. The Blue Feredhai of Tosk.

You came out of the sky. A legend. They have begun to call you *Shast-uen* now. "The Winged." And in Kestenyi the word for "vampire" is *shasladhi*. It means "the flying Lath." You draw a distinction between the Drevedi, whom you call monsters, and the ancient Laths riding on great birds. We do not. All of them come from the sky and all of them kill. I don't want to remember this, winged predators from the Valley, and at the same time I don't want to forget. I dream of a kind of music in which everything would be held together. All the feathers in the air at the same time. Kaili, this girl with plaited hair, and Shernai with her spindle and you on horseback and me singing and all our dead.

∞

Stop, Tav. Kiss me.

This is the lamentation of laughter. This is the only kind of *hawan* I know how to make. When you read it back to me, it makes me laugh. Is this music? All these goats and old women and feathers everywhere.

I will sing of a woman made of lace. She's so old! So old she's almost invisible to us now. Her body lies under the sand, intricate and vast. Do you know how to make the bone map? You do it with the shoulder bone of a calf. You ask the bone a question and throw it down, and it answers you by the way it falls. I don't know anyone who knows how to do it anymore. I want to ask a question of the shoulder blades of my ancient, invisible woman, whose bones are like cobwebs. *What is music?*

Kaili is sewing today. Her feathers have dried.

Shernai spins. A sidelong glance. Her curled lip, tufted with fine hair.

It's hot. We'll have to move soon. I will sing you the Song of Lo. *I am a fountain and a field of clay.* North. *Clay on my boots, clay in my heart, I am of clay like the Firstborn.* East. *With her necklace of glass beads.*

Glass. Bone. Everything smooth. Ornaments. The future.

Prayer bells made of bone on our black tent.

We'll move. You'd like to go north, you say, to see if there's any-thing left of the forest of hetha trees your uncle sold for timber. A forest, you say, protected by the cliffs. In winter there, there was so much snow. You wonder about your old house, but you're also afraid to go back. Imagine we go there. Tents in the yard. We'll dance a sadh in the dusty ballroom, clutching each other's hands, you and I.

Dance with me! Imagine the children peering at us through the doorway. Convulsed with laughter. Let them laugh. Imagine there's laughter everywhere. I'm tired, so tired of lying in caves. Let's go! Write faster! Let's go riding. Throw me onto the back of your saddle like a stolen bride.

Throw me. Steal me. Let's go faster. Fly.

A song without *chaif.* Without restraint.

If music is anything then music is everything. Then music is feath-ers and a field of clay. Then music is played even in the stupidest and most useless of languages.

Ta-ta-di-dai-di.

We'll go north. We'll pass the farm where I went with some of the girls to get onions the other day. The woman there, a bildiri, she was so happy, she gave us a pot of grape preserves. "Take it! Take it!" The war is over.

The war is over. Still, there are rumors carried by the winds. Near Bron, they say, two ausks clashed over the rights to a field of grass. Three killed, two men, a boy. Somewhere near Bron the war is over and they are singing *clear one broken on the crags.*

Broken. I think: broken. I think: lost.

We need new songs. What kind is this?

Brightness called out of the air.

Tav, your shoulders and your swinging walk.

Shernai's spindle and glass beads, so smooth. Their edges when they break.

The bildiri woman reminded me of Loublai. Generous like that. The same harsh voice, the same extravagant gestures. Loublai, my last mother, who taught me to sing for money, who died of a catarrh on the road to Neiv. She complained to me gently that a demon was sitting on her chest. It was so cold, and she kept asking me to take the blanket off. "Take it off, take it off!" When I obeyed at last, shaking and crying, she sighed so deeply, so happily, in the cold tent. A smoking lamp and her smoking breath in the cold. "Thank you, daughter!" Her breasts were flat and loose, a vein moved in her throat. Her great eyes, deep like wells. She said: "You're never going to be happy unless you learn to keep the music in your voice."

Always in your voice. Never in your heart. Her instructions. She was a wise woman. In the morning I told Fadhian she was dead. He nodded, he would do what had to be done. For a moment he put his hand on my cheek. I didn't cry. I thought I was done with that forever.

But if music is everything, then it can't be only in the voice.

You, riding.

And the creak of the susa. The ugliest bird in the world.

If music is everything, then music is even my grandmother's taunting. That ragged note. Then music is even the thunder of my brother's horse. My brother's horse when he rode away. My heart was tied to the back of his horse, beaten on all the rocks, smeared by all the dust. *Learn to keep the music in your voice.* By the time I met you my heart was bruised and swollen and still I thought my perfect my exact. When I saw you. Your cold look. Then music is not only in the voice, then music is under everything like bone.

Tav, I will bring you.

A stolen bride.

Roun in her boat. A guiding lamp.

Tav my Tav I will bring you a feathered shawl.

In our tent you are like a reed and you are like a field in bloom and you are like the moon reflected in my eye.

Roun in her boat. And your rib beneath my fingers is a boat. If music is everything then music is also this rib in a darkened tent. Tav, say something. Speak against me. Tell me I'm foolish, too loud, too much, incomprehensible, spilling everywhere. Speak against me and I'll speak against you, my lips against your rib. *Ta-ta-di-dai-di.*

A tapping tongue, a warmth low in the throat. If music is everything. Screeching women and hoof beats and children crying, the
susa creaking and children crying in the cave. I crawled out covered
with filth, filth in my hair and I was so happy because *I don't want to
die*. I don't want to die! Tav, is this music? What would happen if I
chanted this song, tonight, in the big artusa, in front of everybody?
Tav, this is where you speak. I think they'd laugh. This isn't music.
Now, against me. Right against me. The susa is the ugliest bird.
It's a desert dweller, the symbol of Kestenya, it's also slang for a
feredha girl, for us, noisy, childish, ugly. That harsh, raw voice. And
the spindle spins. *Ta-ta-di-dai-di*. Then music is also this rib and my
hand tight in your hair. Against me now. Over the fold. Coming
down hard like a rain of hot salt. *Di-dai-di* now shatter me like ice.

✺

It was as if I was being buried as I ran. I'd never reach you, but then
I did. You slid from the back of the ilok and landed on the ground.
Hard like rain. Collapsing in torchlight. I thought, I'll never get
there, but I did. I fell. Tav. I was breathing your hair.

Tav, I will bring you flowers like your hair. Nalua flowers. Black like
that.

Brightness called out of the air.

Tav, the men are singing. They are singing, the last men. They are
singing to each other about a flower. The women are singing to the
men. The men are singing to the women. The mothers and fathers
are singing to all the children in the world. The women are singing
to each other, they sing a song about feathers. The children are singing each other a song about the goats. The hills are singing to the
stars, the horses to the rain, the bells to the wind, and the moon is
singing to everybody.

And we are taking the cattle north and east. We are traveling without women. We laugh about it for hours, for days.

Just play. And the susa makes a merry sound: a clicking tongue, dry sticks beaten together, children dancing in spurs.

I who sing this am Seren of the Blue Feredhai of Tosk.

Who will find this script? To you I sing through the pen of my *chadhurei*, Tav.

Give me your hand. Fly.

You, riding over the fold of the mountain.

Give me your hand.

Coming down hard like rain.

by the hand of Tav Lanfirheia Faluidhen
lately of Ashenlo, now of Tosk
known as Shastuen
the Winged

From Our Common History

Slowly, Olondria settles.

Veda of Bain accepts the crown. His brother Irilas, escaped from the newly independent Kestenya, moves into the Ducal Residence. By the end of the year, he will be Duke of Bain. Now he paces the gardens, his beard powdered with cigarette ash.

Upstairs, his wife Firheia sleeps, exhausted. In the corner, her elderly servant—her nurse in childhood, and now her personal maid—places a few belongings in a bag. Her face is serene, as always: she might be sewing, or adding a garnish of fennel to the soup. She leaves her mistress a note propped against the lamp. *Dear lady, I am sorry to leave you. But though you will be happy in Bain, I think I will not. In my old age, as the song says, my marrow longs for the north. Bain is too soft for me; and I must see how my niece is keeping the farm.*

The spice markets open. Ships fill the harbor. The High Priestess of Avalei returns to her temple.

The Brogyars sign a treaty with Olondria. The war is over—a war that has simmered for generations. The Brogyar chieftains seal the oath in their own manner, sipping gaisk and melted fat.

In Nain, the fighting cools. The separatists have lost. Lord Fenya of Faluidhen throws an extravagant ball to celebrate. His mother, Lady Tanthe, wears a stupendous emerald tiara. They are loud, hectic, making it very clear where their loyalties lie. Sometime after midnight, Lord Fenya goes so far as to burn his nephew's portrait in the drawing-room fireplace. He listens to the cheering with a fixed and wintry smile. Under the comforting tick of his pocket watch, his heart pains him: he has lost a fortune in Kestenya.

In her grand, gloomy castle of Rediloth, Lady Mardith of Faluidhen sits at her desk. A lamp with a blue shade burns beside her. The fire is low. The elderly chatelaine wears a rich robe the color of periwinkles.

She dips her pen in the ink. She is writing a letter, though she doesn't know where to send it. She will discover the address in good time. *My dear Siski. I require your presence at Rediloth. Faluidhen has suffered a blow, but we are not quite desperate—*

She sets down the pen. Her reflection regards her from the dark windowpane. The image trembles. This will not do at all. "Stop it!" she hisses. If she should fall to pieces, when the rest of the family lies scattered about the ground like a broken necklace! She crumples the paper, dips her pen in the ink and writes on a fresh sheet:

Siski. You will come to Rediloth. You will not stop in the Valley. You will not pay any visits to "friends" with good cellars and londo tables. You will be prompt and obedient. I am most displeased.

Again she sets down the pen. She flexes her fingers; the knuckles crack. This time, when she glances at the window, she looks beyond her own reflection at the image of the strongbox against the back wall of her study, her Uncle Virdan's strongbox with its gilt edges and magisterial lock.

No one knows of the pleasure she takes when, alone, the maid gone home for the night, she sits at the desk and pretends to busy herself with mundane tasks, feeling behind her the golden, insistent attraction of the strongbox which grows more intense the longer she feigns indifference. Shall I open it, shall I not? Oh, there's really no reason to, tonight. She goes so far as to stand, yawn, and walk to the door. Then, when all seems lost, she turns with an avid brilliance in her eyes and falls upon the lock with her little brass key.

Inside, never mind the notes, she has thousands more with her bankers in Loma. But the deeds she takes out and spreads on the desk beneath the frosted lamp. Those forests, lakes, and wheat fields, some of them tiny estates in the Ethenmanyi that she has acquired without telling anyone. She touches the deeds, their rich red ink. Then, thinking she hears a sound in the hall, although there is not a human being within two miles of the castle, she hurls the papers into the strongbox and locks it, flushed and panting as if she has just escaped from a runaway horse or an amorous embrace.

Oh, how she longed for that box when she was a girl! "I should like to have *that*," she piped, a child of ten, when her uncle asked what gift she would like for the feast. Her tremulous finger pointing at the box with its lead reinforcements and delicious leather strap, for traveling, fastened with iron buckles. Such a cavern it was, a grotto of treasures glowing with greenish magnificence. Her uncle laughed, pinched her cheek and called her his pretty duck. And instead of turning away as he usually did after one of his brief, infrequent caresses, he stood looking down at her with a pleased and curious stare. She dropped her gaze, unable to bear the regard of those splendid dark brown eyes adorned with glittering pupils and regal brows. "Well, you shall have something nice," he said, patting her cheek with a hand as hard as a mallet and overwhelming her senses with the musk of his sleeve.

She does not remember what she received for the feast. She recalls only the flavor, the tone, the special poetry of those days, of the days when her Uncle Virdan was still alive and master of Faluidhen. The air has never recovered the limpid quality it had then. The very dust smells different, as if parched for want of his footstep. Nor do the doors reverberate with the vigorous clang of the past. As for the sound of his stick on the path, not once has another stick been able to duplicate its fierce and unflagging rhythm. Her father was still alive then, though his end was swiftly approaching, but her memories of him scribbling in one of the smaller rooms of the house, of his cough, the bit of flannel about his throat, and his funeral at which it rained so heavily, are less clear to her now than the image of her uncle. As for her mother, surely she never did anything but sit in the drawing room with her feet up, stroking her pug and complaining of the cold. No, it was Uncle Virdan who provided the charm of those distant days, and what Mardith remembers best is related to him. Waking early on winter mornings, reaching out stealthily to find the dress and shoes she had been careful to lay out the night before, washing and dressing in the dark and sitting upright with glowing cheeks to await the sound of his valet's step in the hall. And when the valet began striking at the doors to awaken the sleepers, running downstairs, feeling her way because the staircase was still dark, and bursting into the room where, in the feeble light of a lamp with a yellow shade, her uncle was raising his glass of tea. Showing him her copybook on his visits to the schoolroom and hearing his approving grunt as he closed it. Watching her brother and sister, who always turned pale at his approach, quiveringly hold out their soiled and tattered sums. Oh, what a merry crack his stick would raise from her brother's palms—it made her jump! And little Tanthe, who was considered too frail to be beaten, would sob as he took her peremptorily by the ear and made her sit with her nose against the window for half an hour. It seems the weather was always excellent then, either a ringing frost which the gardener's feet would break with a crunch as he walked by the schoolroom window, or a glorious summer day that dawned on the mountains with a watery brilliance, blue as a columbine and noisy with birds.

On just such a summer day, when she was eighteen, she began to work for her uncle. She remembers the tightness of her new hooked bodice, the curls on her neck, the way her fingers flew when she wrote out the letters he dictated to her and the odor of jam wafting in from the kitchens. And always her awareness of him as he stood at the open window with his hands behind his back, his shoulders square in his brown twill coat, or walked behind her, making the floorboards squeak, or drummed on the table with his hand which wore an enormous emerald ring. And the letters, how she remembers them. Their bold and blustering tone, their scathing irony for some inferior who did not want to pay his debts. Sometimes while her uncle spoke his eyes would bulge and he would pick up a pencil and break it to relieve his pent-up rage. But she was never afraid of him, not even on the moonless night when he called her to help with the corpse of a man he had beaten to death. How could she be afraid of him? His face was as gray as his mustache when he said: "Mardith, come out, I've done something dreadful Mardith!"

No, she was not afraid. She held the lamp with the shutter almost closed while he buried the corpse in the wood, and she washed his clothes and wrung them out, and the shirtfront which would not come clean she quickly replaced with one she sewed herself the next afternoon, before the servants had noticed its absence. And she never asked him about the corpse, not once. He flexed his hand which he claimed to have bruised when his carriage rolled into a ditch, and said to her: "A hot temper is a terrible thing my dear. But there, he won't be missed. And now I can turn that water into the bean field."

That was the willfulness, the spirit that changed the fortunes of Faluidhen, transforming it from the musty seat of an intellectual family into the frosty, formidable estate, respected throughout the empire, from which Mardith would negotiate her nieces' brilliant marriages. Uncle Virdan attempted such a move: he sent his nephew Brola to Velvalinhu, bullied him into befriending the young Prince Eirlo, and tried to secure Princess Beilan for him. But the war in Kestenya was too recent, and the princess married Uskar of Tevlas. Alas, Uncle Virdan did not live to see the fulfillment of his hopes. When Mardith was thirty and he only fifty-five, a fit of apoplexy struck him on his way to the mill, and he died in the house of a peasant where he had gone to beg for a cup of water. "First he was red and then he went yellow," the peasant woman said, gazing down in awe at the master stretched out across her kitchen floor. Mardith fought her first battle with her mother over the funeral, which she knew that her uncle would have liked to keep simple and inexpensive. A battle she won. Her mother retired upstairs with a slam of her door, and the boxes of lilies, the hideous garlands of sentimental chrysanthemums, were returned to Eiloki posthaste. The niece was accused of not having loved her uncle, and smiled for the first time her signature distant smile.

But perhaps the smile was more bitter in those days, when she wore it with a fresh pain unseasoned by the philosophy of the years. No one, no one knows what she suffered during that dark, vertiginous time when chasms opened beneath each step of her undyed cotton slippers. And she has never spoken of it to a single soul. That is pride. Not for her the shut door, the consultations with doctors, the hysterical displays which, when she thinks of her mother's final years, still rise in her memory to fill her mouth with gall. No. For there was the lawsuit with the Arheni to be settled, there was the wet nurse to be found for her sister's second child, the rents to be collected, a drunken groom to be delivered to prison, the menus to be written for every meal. And so her mourning consisted only in giving up balls and brightly colored gowns, which had never been much to her taste in any case, and in weeping with both hands pressed tightly over her mouth to stifle sound in the dim and somber privacy of her bedroom. Her smile, which no one can look upon without a creeping awe, has been carved from her face by a cataract of tears. Her face was never to be the same. It would never inspire a sensual love, though people continued to call it beautiful. For years it remained as lifeless as a plate. And it only softened when her goal was achieved: when her niece Firvaud was seated on the throne, her niece Firheia a duchess, and her great-nephew and great-niece poised to seize the throne for the House of Faluidhen.

But oh, these children—careless—spoilt! Andasya, she supposes, will have to be hanged—he who would have been the first Nainish Telkan. The thought of him is like ground glass in her heart. Tavis will be hanged as well, like the soldier she is—a loss that is easier to bear. And then there is Siski, the eldest daughter of Faluidhen, by all accounts a stupid flirt, who might have been the next Teldaire, who might yet be persuaded to marry well. Lady Mardith takes up her pen again. *My dear Siski. The lives of women are very hard.*

My dear Siski. You are no doubt as shocked as I am by recent developments. We must pull together, my child, if we are to keep Faluidhen afloat!

My dear Siski. Where have I failed?

Siski. I write to you because you appear to be the least hopeless of a generation of fools.

A pool of crushed paper gathers about her feet.

Siski. I am ashamed of you all!

My dear Siski. Imagine the life of an artist. Imagine she works on a single painting for half a century. And now imagine a child tears it with a razor.

Something strikes the window: a soft blow like a gloved hand. Mardith looks up. She is startled by her own face in the pane. It's nothing, she thinks. An owl has brushed the shutters. She dips her pen in the ink. *Faluidhen Faluidhen* echoes in her heart. There is war in Kestenya: her niece Firheia, that fresh little girl with the laughing eyes, may be dead. Firvaud is addicted to milim, Andasya and Tavis lost. She presses her elegant pen down hard, her fingertips almost white. *Siski you will not defy me you will come.*

A tear on her knuckle.

How do we know? Why, because we were at the window, peering through the slit between the shutters.

Siski you children are all the same. Siski your duty. Siski your failure.

Siski the lives of women.

Dear Siski. Forgive me.

# BOOK FOUR

The History of Flight

My heart is white with love.

I. The Land of Bells

The young woman arrives in the town at the time called "the tip of winter's beard." The air is raw, the streets piled with dirty snow. She is not the only one to arrive. Others have been coming for nearly four months, driven or frightened out of their homes to the north and east. They still come, but not so many, and the townspeople say this is a blessing. They say: "The war is over." They say: "The new Telkan will set all to rights." The young woman arrives as part of the last, small wave of refugees that the people of the town would like to see quickly swept away.

The refugees congregate in the square, underneath the new sign that forbids loitering. Some pace in circles, others sit down on the temple steps. They muddy the fountain. The women call for their children, they walk about clutching their hair in both hands. No one knows where to go.

The young woman goes to the square with the others.

She wants to find work. She thinks she could work as a governess. She knows how to write and sing.

No one knows how to find that kind of work.

She leaves the square. She follows the smell of coffee to the back of a café. She hopes for a strip of kebma, a bone with some meat still on it, but she sees at once that she has no chance: there are too many others there.

She walks through the town. She walks and walks. It's a quiet Nainish town by the sea, and the odor of herring hangs everywhere. The town's good fortune is its fishing industry, its ill fortune is its position here, at the edge of the land, where the refugees stop because they can go no farther.

The young woman passes a lamplighter armed against night with his ladder and light.

She sees a young woman about her age leaving the back door of a house. She follows her without knowing why: because the stranger has a kind, nervous face, because she walks purposefully, because of hunger, because of the cold.

The young Nainish woman stops. She tells the refugee woman that she works as a filler of mattresses. She's not from the town, she's from a village three miles away. She takes pity on the refugee. She gives her a stick of raush and the address of a place she should go tomorrow morning.

The refugee woman thanks her.

The two part ways. The Nainish woman is going home to her village. The other young woman is not going home. She leaves the town, she walks northward through the snow, up into the hills. On the way she eats half of the stick of raush.

She walks so far, making her way by starlight. When the way grows steep, she crawls.

At last she arrives at the great stone edifice. Long ago it was a temple, then for a time it was a barracks, now it stands empty. Almost empty. She goes inside.

He is lying where she left him, wrapped in his cloak. The fire has sunk and she builds it up again, adding sticks from her store against the wall. Dear small warmth. The light plays on his face. She crouches down beside his makeshift bed and gives him the piece of raush.

He eats. It's hard for him to chew. He weeps. He says: "You shouldn't have come back."

The young woman is silent. She holds her hands to the fire. Her hands throb painfully, and through the pain and through the brilliance of the firelight she can see her former life.

☾

Into the distance, into Kestenya, into the land of bells.

When they were small they used to go to Sarenha every autumn. The nights came swiftly, filled with shooting stars. Each well had its own particular taste. The well at Sarenha is known as the Well of the Black Ewe. It lies in the garden among the vines, visible from the terrace. The feredhai come up the path with their skin buckets, they are noontide people, sundark and mapless, singing the Song of Lo. The buckets sing too, going down into the well. When they rise again the note is lower, replete, a round and delightful music. She leans on the balustrade watching them through the trees. We'll go with them someday, we'll walk in the desert, wearing out our shoes. It will be easy. Look at them, they just go down the path and through the gate. Then they keep going on from there. They walk as far as Eilam, as far as Bron, as far as the mountains where they hide their cattle in gorges filled with mist. And we'll go too. Yes, but now there are noises from the kitchen and the odor of smoke, and Nenya dishing out platters of sticky rice. Each with its knob of onions, meat, and sauce. It's called the topknot. Siski seizes it in her fingers, dripping oil.

Dasya hides his mouth in his sleeve, his eyes moist with laughter. Tiny bells adorn his plaited hair. Let's go up on the roof. Let's go up to the old observatory. Let's climb the trees in the orchard. Let's hunt owls. Silence and mystery of the rooftop at night beneath an autumn moon, breathless immobility of the orchard. She dances among the fallen leaves, churning them with her boots. From the branches comes her sister's fierce owl call.

It's no use, Siski has frightened the owls away. Let's go in, it's getting cold. The lamp is as tall as an effigy for the Feast of Angels. Placed on the floor it illuminates the whole room. Dasya sits cross-legged, his head bent slightly, tuning the limike. Tav lies on her back and drums her feet against the wall beneath the painting *Night at the Inn of the Heartless Dove*. Siski turns a page of her book. She raises her head when the notes come softly, softly, like a wing against the window. Dasya's fingers are bright in the light of the lamp and she can see the scar where he gashed his hand on a tree playing rings-and-arrows. He is not singing but when Siski sings he glances up and smiles. *O illustrious city, opal of the sands.* She sings of the white stone streets and beautiful horses though she knows that Tevlas is really a city of smoke-stained walls and trees choked by the dust. For a moment the other Tevlas, the Tevlas of song, is called up by the music and opens its quivering doorways in the air.

The house is old, neglected, full of decrepit pieces of furniture and paintings rejected by even the humblest members of the family. The children blow the dust from the portrait of Hafyan of Bron in the formal parlor, revealing colors that owe their freshness to an austere climate. Hafyan exhibits the firm tanned cheeks of a sportsman, an epicure's paunch, and the lazy, smiling eyes of the recently ennobled. It was he who built this house at the edge of the sands when he was made a baron by Vaud the Dreamer for his services to the Olondrian Empire. And merry, glittering kebma parties were held in this great dark room, the ladies wearing fronds of the sabior plant in their hair. Hafyan terrified them with tales of feredha witchcraft, of which he had made a long study, his teeth clenching the stem of his olive-wood pipe. It is said that he bathed in warm mint tea to soothe a troubled liver and that he could not bear to look at a man whose mustache was not trimmed well. A lifelong bachelor, he was devoted to his bildiri hunting master, and died with him in an avalanche in the Tavroun.

Once his angel appeared to Dasya here in the formal parlor: Dasya said he looked like a shadow filled with moonlight. "Uncle Hafyan!" Dasya cried, and the angel nodded sadly twice before disappearing, leaving behind an odor of caramelized onions. Thinking that his grave must be untidy, Dasya asked Nenya where it was. "Him!" said Nenya. "His bones are mixed with those of his horse." And that was how the children learned of the avalanche that had swept Uncle Hafyan's hunting party down the side of Spring Mountain.

A distant rumble as of thunder out of the hard blue sky. A ptarmigan shoots suddenly over the cliff. Uncle Hafyan looks up, and then the light banter, the goose-feather hats, the insouciance are snuffed out by the snow. A moment later a dreadful silence reigns. And down at Sarenha the overstuffed chairs, as if knowing they are soon to be abandoned, split their seams for grief, and the mirrors give back images in a tumbling disorder, panicked by a rumor of death.

Even now the big parlor seems distressed. A hundred years have not sufficed to erase the memory of grander days, and the children prefer the informal parlor upstairs, the "Kestenyi parlor" which, never having known opulence, seems undisturbed by the passage of time. Here embroidered cushions line the walls, perfect for collapsing on after a day of riding on the plateau, and the shelves are stacked with curious old books, including some big illustrated ones on the geography and plant life of the desert. Siski lies on her stomach and reads about the karhula flower "whose whiteness fills the traveler with melancholy thoughts." The watercolor plates are faded, and when she turns the page a pair of silverfish go scuttling toward the dark.

"I want to stay here forever," says Tav. "Don't be silly," Siski tells her, "you'd miss Mother." But Siski too would like to stay in that crumbling palace, to play for the rest of her life in the spacious avla where light and leaves and birds come through the broken panes in the colored dome. Forever would not be long enough to live at Sarenha Haladli, to trap the owls and desert hares that come to hide in the orchard, to ride out onto the chalk plateau and sleep in the big old upper rooms where the shutters creak and the beds are covered with furs.

In the evening, after her bath, Siski wants to see Tuik. She goes outside in her slippers and runs along the little path to the stable. She can hear the horses moving in the dark. Tuikye. Darling Tuik. His breath in her face with its odor of new snow.

∞

Tuik in daylight.

He is the color of day and of the desert. He has no equal between Ashenlo and Bron. She thinks he has no equal anywhere. His eyes, his elegant foot, his powerful shoulders, the way he holds his head. He moves as lightly and gracefully as a hawk and he is strong for their long rides and has no fear of waterless places. His trust in her is absolute and this is where he shows his worth, in his perfect docility, faithfulness, and courage. He loves the plateau because his mistress loves it, though in dreams his heart may linger in gardens burgeoning with fruit. Horses have dreams, for they are the only animals to possess souls, and this is why they are buried in cemeteries like men. She thinks that someday she will be buried in the same grave as Tuik, like the prince who owned the great horse Unsaur the Wind. She has told Tav and Dasya, so that if anything should happen to her, they will tell her parents how it should be done.

Wind, silence, the openness of the desert. Sometimes she lets the others ride Tuik, and whoever rides him wins the race. Then, astride the restive Na Faso or the pony Nusha, she is overcome by jealousy and rage. "Get down!" she snaps. And Tav, riding the horse in circles, whooping with triumph, senses her irritation and grins at her. When Tav has dismounted, Tuik comes trotting toward Siski over the sand, contrite, and pushes her gently with his nose. Still he cannot forget his victory, and his eye, reflecting the dancing light, seems to say proudly: I could not lose, even for you. She flings her arms about his neck. Astride him she feels she is riding through the sky. She sings him all the songs the feredhai sing to horses. *Love, swift dancer, companion of my heart, I bring thee water carried for twenty thousand miles in these two hands. Beloved the color of almonds. When the dew is on the mountains. Ah, would that I had died before my Sarya.*

Beloved the color of almonds. When they ride on the great plateau they pass feredhai who always stop to look at Tuik. Siski keeps her head high like a feredha girl while her heart beats faster. Coming abreast of the strangers she turns her head. The men nod and she nods. Once she grows frightened and clutches at Tuik's mane, for one of the men wears a mantle dyed red and printed with dark green leaves. She remembers that the man who sold them Tuik wore such a mantle, two years ago in the horse and camel market of Tevlas. Yes, a red mantle with green leaves. A tangled beard, tin rings on his fingers, exhaustion in his strange light-colored eyes. Tired, oppressed by the noise and smells of the market, she stands beside her father with her arms crossed and stares at the muddy ground.

"Siski, what do you think of that horse?"

"He's beautiful," she answers, gazing up at the marvelous golden creature cloaked in a dirty blanket. The young horse moving restlessly, worn out by the noise and ceaseless crowds, like her. His master has not even combed the tras-seeds from his tail. She looks away, yawns, wishes she was at home with her mother. Not to go back to the chill and the boredom of the Ducal Residence. Silent meals with her father, the strain of being alone with him, and then the ghastly bedroom crammed with satin flowers. Suddenly money changes hands and her father says: "He's yours." She stands with her mouth open, gripping the halter in numb fingers. The incomprehensible actions of her father. "Well," says the man in the scarlet mantle, regarding her bitterly. "Thank him, little princess."

Sometimes she dreams that the man in red comes back to claim his horse and she wakes sweating in a crimson universe strangled by huge vines. "What's the matter?" says Dasya as they ride down toward the road. "Nothing, nothing," she tells him breathlessly. "Keep riding." And only when they are on the road with nothing in sight but the lights beginning to flicker in the bildiri villages, only then does she confess her fear of the man in the scarlet cloak. "I've never heard anything so mardh," says Dasya. His ringing laugh on the empty road. "But I was afraid of him," she says, beginning to smile in spite of herself. Tav is shaking her head in disgust and Dasya goes on laughing, trotting on Na Faso, upright in his black coat. "Look where you've brought us to," he crows with a broad sweep of his hand. "Running away from a man because he was wearing red." She laughs, looks about her, exclaims: "Yes, and it's getting dark." They can smell kitchen fires on the fading bluish air.

No time to go back to Sarenha. "Let's go to Uncle Veda's," Siski says. All the way she is happy and even warm in the twilight. The intimate jingle of harness, Dasya riding close to her over the bridge. And at last the yellow windows of Valedhara.

Years later, at a ball, she will speak of her Uncle Veda's house. It seemed enormous to us when we were children. There were so many people coming and going all the time, the strangest people, herdboys and merchants and feredhai. Sometimes there were black tents in the courtyard and children playing around the well, or there would be goats destroying the garden. And the neighbors' bildiri servants used to hide there when they were drunk or got into trouble, and there would be terrible fights about it. Someone even tried to shoot my uncle once, I think, over a maidservant who had been accused of theft. But no one ever stayed angry with him and everyone used to come when there were parties or country dances at Valedhara. No, not proper balls of course, but wonderful dances all the same. They were held in a barn that was never used for anything else. It didn't seem strange to me when I was a child. I used to go with my mother, and later I went with my sister or even alone. Imagine: a barn full of people, with hardly enough room for the orchestra, and everyone stamping and clapping and making noise. You would see landowners dancing beside their servants, and no one cared. It was as if, in that barn, it was always Tanbrivaud Night . . . There was a dance called the sadh that we used to do—oh, I can't do it anymore, but it was a real Kestenyi dance, a feredha dance. To do it you had to keep your chin high, like this, and look very arrogant and severe. It didn't matter so much what you did with your hands and feet. We used to laugh at Olondrians—pardon me, but we used to laugh when Olondrians tried it, because they would concentrate so hard on getting the steps, and their heads would just hang down and make them look so awkward and funny. My uncle used to say, "Your eyes should be like a pair of arrows." He was wonderful at the sadh himself. I used to feel almost afraid of him when he danced, he looked so magnificent, so proud. And really, you know, he was just a sweet and scatterbrained kind of man, who already seemed elderly when I was a little girl.

Once we found ourselves on the road after dark, and we went to Valedhara without having warned Uncle Veda that we were coming. We found him in the front room—a cramped little parlor with a green carpet and smoke-stained walls—tying up a dog's injured paw. The whole place smelled of dog. There were a few other visitors there, as always, a few old men and a herdboy with a fever. And Uncle Veda jumped up and kissed us and squeezed the breath out of us, so happy to see us, you could see that he was delighted. Right away he began to turn the house upside down to find things for us to eat. He had a servant, a sort of high chamberlain if you will—steward and valet and butler all at once. A lot of Kestenyi gentlemen live that way, dependent on just one servant. This steward of his was a very capable organized sort of man and Uncle Veda used to praise him to everyone, and really it was probably true that he kept my uncle from losing his lands, Uncle Veda was so softhearted and hopeless at business. Of course the steward was always at his wits' end—I still remember his pained expression and how we children used to mimic it. But he was devoted to my uncle, despite the difficulties, and when my uncle moved to Bain, he left Valedhara to his steward.

That night, the night I was telling you about, Uncle Veda patted him on the shoulder and said, There, there, I leave everything to your intelligence. And the steward created a wonderful supper, nuts and cheese on toast and an egg pudding, and we spread out an oilcloth and ate on the parlor floor. You see it was the only room with a fire. And when we had finished Uncle Veda gave us each a tiny glass of Eilami brandy. I was only thirteen or so, it was terribly special to be allowed to drink brandy. It made me feel so warm on that cold night . . . But it wasn't enough for Uncle Veda to feed us, he began frowning and fidgeting and snapping his fingers, and finally he stood up and exclaimed, No, it's too dull for young people, we must have a dance! It was already very late, but he knew everyone and he sent to the village for several of the young men who could play the diali and the guitar, and he ordered in all the servants, even the herdboys and the gardener and the grooms, and the girls who used to come up and clean the house on feast days. There were twenty or thirty of them. And they rolled the carpet back, and the musicians, winking at each other and looking very amused, began to play so vigorously that you felt like dancing at once. Even the girls, who were terribly shy, took off their shoes . . .

She is quite drunk when she tells this story but not so drunk that she does not know when to stop. Her listeners have lost interest. She raises the glass to her lips. Looking at the windows white with steam where, among the floating lights, dancers turn like the bodies of the drowned.

The morning after her uncle's dance she slips downstairs in her stockings, into the rustling, sighing sound of communal sleep. She peeps into the parlor where, among the herdboys stretched out on the carpet, dogs lie snuffling against their tails. Some of the dogs have already gone into the kitchen, to be near the stove. A pearly glow falls through the oiled paper pasted over the windows. Uncle Veda turns, holding the handle of the coffeepot. "Ah, my dear. I knew you'd be up before the others."

"What time is it?" she asks.

He glances at the windows. "Nearly noon. Now try this." Pouring coffee into a blue tin cup. "That's fresh milk from our Sinoud."

She laughs, sitting down at the table. "Surely you haven't been milking already."

"And why not?" he cries, as he seats himself before his own battered cup. "She wasn't dancing all night, poor beast. Why should she suffer? Ah, you see, there's nothing like fresh milk. Now, what to have for breakfast?" He frowns, smoothing the few sparse hairs on his ruddy head.

Dear Uncle Veda. No one can help being happy in his presence. Even the smoky and cluttered kitchen seems cheerful when he is beside the stove, in his brown work shirt and a blue scarf fastened about his neck with a pin. His pipe diffuses the comfortable smell of rooms where people have come in from hunting. When Tav and Dasya come down he pours them coffee and hands out sticks of raush. Just to hear him exclaim in triumph when he discovers a cheese in the pantry, to see him put on his vast green hat, is enough to make one laugh out loud. He waves to them from the porch for a long time.

> *By the red field,*
> *by the black field.*
> *Oh, the impossible distance.*
> *There is no rest, no rest on the road*
> *that leads to Harmavyedh.*

> *By the red field,*
> *by the black field.*
> *Great fields of singing wheat,*
> *pity me where I walk in the silence and bitter solitude*
> *of the tras.*

Songs of her heart, Kestenyi songs. Songs of Bron and Tevlas, of the hills. They sing as they ride, following the rhythm of the hoof beats. One night when they hear music they creep out and crawl on their stomachs up the rise to where the feredhai are camped on a plain of stones. Fires in the night. Shadows move to and fro, shadows of women and of horses being led to the big artusa. Shadows of hands clapping. And the tents lit by the lamps inside, taking on the color of the human body. She watches, her eyes as huge as the stars above, hardly breathing, desperate to memorize each line of song as it pierces the cold air. Knowing that she may never hear this song sung in this way again, that the feredhai will carry it away with them into the desert. As they will carry their knowledge, all the secrets of survival in a wilderness of sunlight, wind, and chalk. The map of the wells, the taste of mare's milk. She seizes the song and draws it into her as she would draw that nourishment, that knowledge. She drinks two songs, three songs, entranced. When the camp is silent at last and she and her sister and cousin slip back to the house, she will not speak to them, she can only hum and mutter to herself, helpless as if in the talons of a fever. And lie on her bed with her eyes wide open, lightly touching her fingers together, singing. Perhaps she even sings in her sleep. At dawn she is rewarded by the music she still remembers, notes that have not deserted her in the night.

The windows are pale, the room very cold. She reaches out with her mind, as if groping to lay her hand on a book in the darkness, and is sad because she cannot remember the tune of one of the songs although she tries it with a number of variations. The words, too, some of the words are missing, as if the gold leaf has begun to crumble from an illumination, and the more she struggles with it the more her efforts rub away at the delicate surface, inflicting further destruction. But she is happy with the songs she has and she sings them over and over as she puts on her mantle and slippers and pads downstairs, and as she enters the kitchen where Nenya is already boiling milk for the coffee and Tav is washing her hair beside the stove.

> *It is not fair, it is not right.*
> *Four gold moons on a branch,*
> *four gold moons.*
> *Oh unhappy spirit,*
> *drink at another well.*

"Don't sing that in the morning, it's bad luck. You should sing happy songs."

"But the feredhai don't have any happy songs."

"Then don't sing feredha songs," says Nenya, pouring the thick hot coffee into a glass. Siski takes it outside to drink on the empty terrace. Her breath is white and frost hangs on the trees. She does not believe that feredha songs can ever cause bad luck, not in this place where the words and music seem to be a part of the air, the shadows of the mountains, and the sky. *He lay with his face alight, alight. And his hands in the light alight, alight. Alight, alas, and the color of molten silver.* In the music she sees the boy struck down and wrapped in his mantle on the sand with an oil lamp burning beside him through the night. Killed in one of the feuds that sweep through the desert, setting everything ablaze. His soul goes walking over the mountains into Oud. *Shall we ever see that place, shall we ever find him, our winged stallion?* She watches sunlight color the trees.

"*I follow you, Iselda.*" She turns with a cry of delight to see her cousin walking toward her, rubbing his eyes.

"Do you remember all the words?"

"What are we doing up so early?" he says, squinting into the brightening orchard.

"Never mind that, do you know the words?"

He grins, sets his coffee glass on the balustrade, theatrically clears his throat. Then his voice, sad and true, darkens his eyes, which can never retain their mocking light once he has begun to sing.

> *I follow you, Iselda.*
> *My arms are bleak with love.*
> *Oh silver brooch, clear spring,*
> *wind that brings the rain from the mountains.*

> *I dream of you, Iselda.*
> *My eyes are ringed with love.*
> *Come lift the door of my tent*
> *at the hour of confidences and lamps.*

I torment you, Iselda.
My heart is white with love,
and you spit at my shadow as if at an evil thing.

It's growing colder and soon Dasya must go back over the mountains, back to his home on the Isle before the first snow. Tav scratches at the stove with the tip of her Amafeini dagger, unhappy because the autumn is almost over. Because at Ashenlo their tutor awaits with his dreary diagrams, maps of the empire penciled on rough paper. Dinners with seven courses, riding the horses round and round the little yard. And wet woolen stockings. And their father.

"Don't think about it," Siski says, tweaking one of her sister's plaits. The hot stove makes her glow all through her clothes. And Dasya comes in yawning, looking strangely tall from where she sits on the floor. He wears a white tunic with short sleeves.

"Aren't you cold?" she asks him.

"No."

He leans back, propping one heel against the wall. "Where are we going to ride today?"

That's it, she thinks. He doesn't think about it, I try not to think about it but he, he really doesn't think about it.

"Maybe into the village again or around the edge of the Kesuen lands," she says. "Maybe as far as the Well of the Hornets."

"Yes, to the well." By his smiling eyes she knows that it is true, that he is turned toward the future, shining, without regrets.

That night, even Tav and Siski forget their sadness, climbing a rickety footman's ladder to light the lamps in the avla. The old lamps sputtering, black with filth. Above them hangs the ornamental dome, colorless now, showing stars where panes are missing. The children's slippers glide across the floor, their shadows haunt the walls. They are playing londo with bits of broken marble. *Flutes. Eight. The South.* The sound of the makeshift pieces striking the mosaic floor sends echoes toward the night.

"I don't think I could do it," says Tav.

"You would if you had to," says Dasya.

He casts the West and moves his marble chip forward with his toe. Tav stands with her hands on her hips, sucking her lower lip, observing the floor. "No," she says. "I'd rather starve."

"You don't know, you've never starved," says Siski. She casts a Nine.

"No, but I've been hungry," her sister argues. "You remember when I got lost in the Abravei for a whole day. I was hungry but I'd never have eaten my horse."

Tav squats and casts. Seven. She moves her chip to a square of jasper. Then Dasya casts, his wrist supple in the grimy light of the lamps. He looks up and swears and the sisters glance at one another and giggle. "We ought to make you put your tongue on the stove," says Siski.

"Try it," says Dasya, smiling. And because of the arrogant tilt to his chin the girls chase him, sliding and losing their footing on the floor, and the avla rings with shouts and with a high wild squeal as Siski slips on a londo piece and falls hard on the tiles. "That was mine, you shedyun," her sister shouts. "I was winning!" Dasya is laughing, holding his stomach, leaning against the wall. Siski scrambles up and throws herself toward him, snatching at his belt as he twists away, locking her fingers under the leather.

"Get him, get him!" she gasps at Tav, her arm jerked forward as Dasya whirls about, trying to yank himself out of her grip. He seems to be dancing, the lights spinning about him. Then he falls backward on the hurtling, compact body of Tav, who has seized him about the neck. Siski falls on top of them with a scream and pulls her fingers free of the belt. "Who am I?" she says, her arm on Dasya's throat. He arches his back but Tav has pinned his arms from beneath and he soon lies still. "I don't know," he says in a choked voice.

"Who am I?"

"A twenty-year-old mare."

"Who am I?"

"I don't know."

"Say it."

"A shoemaker."

"Ugh, get up," groans Tav.

Delicately, severely, Siski presses on Dasya's neck. His eyes are bright, his cheeks turning red.

"Say it," she warns.

"No," he laughs.

"Say it or I'll never get up."

He closes his eyes and tries to shake himself free of her hair, which is falling onto his face.

Then he opens his eyes again. "You beshadun," he grins, panting. "All right. You're the Queen of the White Desert."

2. And All the Windows Fade

The refugee woman stands in front of the house. She has arrived early. She blows on her fingers and stamps in the pale gold light. At last she sees her Nainish friend coming briskly down the street with two others. The refugee already thinks of this stranger as her friend.

They go around to the back door, and the quick-mannered Nainish woman knocks. A small boy opens the door and lets them into the kitchen. After a moment a footman arrives with half an apple in his mouth. At the sight of this apple, saliva floods the refugee's mouth with sweetness.

The footman leads them into a huge, cold storeroom. Mattresses lie tumbled at one end and there are piles of cotton and down and dry leaves everywhere. The refugee's new friend rolls up her sleeves, and one of the others, a tall, plump girl, takes a spool of white thread from between her breasts.

The new friend is called Dai Norla. The tall girl is Dai Kouranu, and the third is Dai Gersina. The refugee gives her name as Dai Fanlei. It is the first thing to come into her head, because of the apple in the footman's mouth. She has named herself after apples, after high summer.

Her new friends are professional menders and turners of mattresses and pillows, they upholster chairs, they hang curtains and lay carpets. Their eyelids are slightly swollen, they all have the same dry cough; up close they smell faintly of red onions and bread. They want to know everything about Dai Fanlei: where she's from, how many brothers and sisters she has, what she puts on her hair to make it grow. They laugh because Dai Kouranu once put egg on

253

her hair and rinsed it with hot water, and then her hair was full of cooked egg!

"An omelet!" she exclaims, shaking the end of her plait with one hand.

Dai Fanlei laughs: a brittle sound. The others exchange glances.

She tells them that she is a schoolmaster's daughter from Barbilnes. When the war came there, the schoolhouse was burnt down and her parents killed.

The others say: "Bastards, bastards." They pat her shoulders and stroke her arms. They say it's all right now, there's a new Telkan on the throne. They ask where she's staying; she says with an aunt, in the country. No, she tells them, it's not too far to walk.

When the mattress is turned and dropped it falls with a thud and dust flies sparkling into the air.

Dai Fanlei helps turn the mattress. She's stronger than she looks. The others approve of this. She makes nice stitches, too. When she pricks her fingers, she sucks them. She doesn't get any blood on the cloth.

Dai Fanlei coughs. She is cold and dizzy. At noon Dai Norla gives her a heel of bread with a scrap of onion pressed into the center. And at the end of the day, after the housekeeper comes and inspects the mattresses, each of the young women is given seven droi.

The streets are dark and frozen. Dai Fanlei bids the others good-bye. She stops at the edge of the town to buy currant buns and raush. She has no bag, so she puts the raush in her stockings and carries the warm bread in her arms, as if nursing a calm, sweet-smelling child.

All the way up the hill, she weeps. The bread will taste of salt.

She is thinking of how her new friends cursed the name of Prince Andasya of Faluidhen. Already, they told her, young children are threatened that if they don't go to bed, Green Dashye will come up the road in his coach of bone and catch them.

∞

Look, there it is: Faluidhen.

That spring they went there together, all three children, but Siski had already been there several times before. She had even been there alone and she knew the inn where they stayed at Noi and how it was proper to leave, on the springy white pillow, a coin or two for the maid. From Noi it is not at all far, it seems so fast when you come down out of the hills and begin to see the orderly Nainish farms and the walls of the gardens, the great black fields where the gusts of wind come wetly bringing a smell of milk and the straight roads crossing each other, bordered by cornflowers. The villages are laid out like games of cards. Passing the Neidhvian you can see the keeper riding in his red cap. Then a gentle curve in the road and look, that gray roof, that's the house. Light gleams in the windows of Grandmother's hothouse.

In the antechamber one always eats bread and salt beneath the portrait of Uncle Virdan, and endures Aunt Karalei's kisses and endearments. Dasya crunches the hard Nainish bread, wipes away the crumbs, and then shakes his handkerchief surreptitiously under the table.

Aunt Karalei advances with painted eyes. "My darling niece." She has thick fingernails, rheumatism, a long necklace of greasy beryls, and heavy hair that keeps its blackness through the arts of a coiffeur who comes from Eiloki once a month, her only extravagance. Her round lips tremble, her fingers are red from being pricked with a needle. She leads Siski upstairs with a handsome silver lamp. Everywhere there are paintings, faetha, chairs ruminating in corners and unnecessary shelves where snuffboxes gleam like beetles. This is Faluidhen, all these cupboards and vases, these high doors. After her bath, wrapped up in a cream-colored towel, Siski unpacks the dressing gown that has come from Ashenlo without being used, folded in muslin and scented with orange water. For Aunt Mardith will certainly come in. And indeed, as Siski stands at the window in antique lace there is a soft knock at the door, and before she has spoken the tall old lady glides forward, reflecting the lilac light of dusk with her silks, her perfect teeth, and her spun-cotton hair.

"So lovely to have you with us my dear." Her kiss delicate, a snowflake's touch. Smoothly she closes the shutters and hides the view of the fields. "Once the lamps are lit one should always have the shutters closed." She touches Siski's hair, her shoulder. "Welcome home."

For this, this great gray house, is home. "The home of your blood," Aunt Mardith says, turning down the lamp. "You don't need so much light to undress. Yes, the home of your blood," she repeats, her figure copper-colored in the mirror that hangs on the door of the tall wardrobe. Her voice is very soft, almost melancholy. "Alas, we women are so seldom granted the joy of living at home. Unless we are very lucky, marriage takes us away, it scatters us. Why, just look what her marriage has done to your mother."

She smiles, her lips pressed tight. "But I don't want to be so grave on your first night." She raises her hand, attempting a light and frivolous gesture. And her six pearl bracelets, fiercely white as if lying in their box and not against flesh, gleam with an almost martial elegance.

Grass in the garden already, transparent buds on the apple trees. And the crocuses, upright and golden, piercing the earth, give off a heat that melts the last of the snow. The wind is fresh and wet clouds race one another across the polished sky. Dasya leans against a tree, grasping a low bough with one hand. His shadow, falling across Siski's red dress, is distinct from the shadows of bud and branch, separate, with its own character and weight. He holds up the book, his thumb across the fluttering page. *Emerald skies and a storm in which your name strives for existence, far from the earth, here at the fountainhead of the clouds.* That spring they read so much poetry. Tamundien, Karanis of Loi, Damios Beshaidi, verses out of the *Vanathul*. Dasya has come with books from his father's library on the Isle, Siski with books she ordered from Ur-Amakir. *O small bird, the spring rain presses hard on the kernel of your mouth/ and brings forth pastures of lavender, blue with song.* It rains. She lies on her back on a white wicker bench in the conservatory. His voice moves under the cadences of the patter on the glass roof, as he sits on the floor near her head, beneath the potted oleander whose pink blooms have the artificial shimmer of satin. Reading to her. Instead of his face she sees the gray glass above her splashed with rain, instead of his mouth pale crimson flowers. Only the drunken gardener, clashing shears and murmuring out of sight, disturbs the perfection of their solitude. *For I am unhappy without you, lakes are dimmed by the absence of your eyes.* An old poem, clumsy in rhythm, harsh with longing. She sees the stern poet sitting beside the lake in which a stone, when he throws it, sinks like a man whose beloved has gone away. That's the way I'll feel, she thinks. She says: "That's the way I'll feel when we leave." She turns on her side to look at him, and his eye, unexpectedly close to hers, meets her with its darkness in which her face is reflected as in an obsidian mirror.

In the evenings, when the weather is fine, they walk down to the edge of the lake. Moving through the infinite variations of the twilight, at the maddeningly slow pace dictated by her grandmother's frailty and good breeding, she feels herself part of a holiday procession. Sometimes, across the deep blue sky, a flock of swans is flung like droplets of milk. About the crimson lantern carried by Grandmother's footman, myriad fascinated country moths stumble against each other, singeing their wings when they get inside the glass. The moon gleams high and faint: a tender moon, unlike the hard moon of the desert. Someday Siski will own this house, and she and Tav and Dasya will all come here in the spring when it is too dusty to be comfortable in their true home, Sarenha Haladli. Tav will sell Aunt Mardith's castle of Rediloth when she inherits it and spend the money on horses, weapons, and dogs. "Let's always keep these bushes." Siski spreads her arms and presses herself deep in the dew-laden branches of the honeysuckle. She feels the silk of her frock being stained by moisture, feels the delicate sprays of candle-colored blossoms showering her with their dense perfume. Inside the house again she wears her shawl to cover the marks on her dress, and is seated on the couch with a glass of tea, when Dasya leans and plucks a leaf from her hair, bringing into the lamplight the bitter, humid luxuriance of the garden.

Dear old Nain. Suddenly there are harp notes from the corner where Aunt Karalei plucks the strings with her curved hands. Uncle Fenya, half asleep, grunts and taps his knee with his pipe. A threadbare hound rises and shuffles across the room. The tune is very simple. Grandmother nods her head and motions for the footman to bring her another tiny glass of los. Dasya stands and begins to sing. Siski did not know that he knew any Nainish songs. She does not know the song herself.

> *Aragu med hauven, hauven*
> *ande linde o.*

A song, she thinks, about mist, black geese, and firelight. A song about the smoke that rises from the little thatched houses buried up to the eaves in snow, where peasants are drinking. But no, when she asks Aunt Karalei, she learns that the song is about the musk deer that come to nibble the last of the cabbages in the winter gardens. The young girls set out milk for them in bowls. But one of the girls, as she stands at the window, sees a young man take the bowl of milk from her step and drink. *Aragu med hauven, hauven/ ande linde o. Would you steal my milk, my milk/ and leave my deer to starve?* The young girl scolds the stranger, but he doesn't answer her, he only stares at her with eyes the color of wheat. And when she runs out to chase him away, he springs off toward the forest, leaving beautiful small hoof prints in the snow.

To bed, everyone must go to bed—for tomorrow is the ball.

"I'll never get to sleep," Siski whispers.

"I know," says Dasya.

They stand in a drafty space between two staircases. Murky portraits glower from the wall.

"It's nothing," Dasya says. "It's just a party."

"It's not, it's a real ball, it's my first ball."

"But I'll be there. I'll take you for the first two dances."

"Will you?"

"Three if you don't mind."

"But why should I mind?" she laughs.

The thought of dancing with Dasya carries her through the hours of preparation, the face painter coming to draw an orange rose on her brow, the battle with the hooks of her gown of apricot-colored silk, the crush in the doorway of the great ballroom of Faluidhen. The orchestra plays soft music; all the walls are hung with flowers. "Congratulations, my dear," says Uncle Fenya, kissing her cheek. Her hand in his is limp and numb as if broken, and she forgets to return the congratulations although it is his birthday. Everything makes her start: a sudden burst of laughter behind her, from across the room the popping of a cork. Every time she moves, her arm brushes against the bouquet of starry clematis fastened in her sash.

Suddenly everyone is bustling, getting into line.

"Where's your partner?" asks a dark-browed older lady.

"There, in red."

"Don't point, my dear. Come now, you're on my left."

Music, bold and lively, fills the room.

Her eyes are foggy with tears of excitement; she can barely make out his scarlet coat and the long gleam of his scabbard. Trying to move in step, she finds with horror that she has grown clumsy during the night. At last she grasps the spar of his hand.

"It's just like Uncle Veda's," he says, smiling.

"No it isn't, how can you say so? Watch my flowers!" she hisses, turning toward the wall. The measure changes smoothly, becoming more vigorous, and as she whirls her body remembers the steps, permitting her to forget them. She begins to look around her, taking pleasure in the music. By the arilantha she hopes it will never end. And during the klugh, when she opens her little fan with the gold tassel, she feels pleasantly dizzy, light-footed, walking on mist. She laughs. There is another girl with a painted rose on her brow and Siski embraces and kisses her, a complete stranger. Everyone must be happy, everyone. It is a ball. Behind the open windows, the tapestry of night.

"Come over here for a moment my child, sit down. Didn't you hear me call? I want to introduce you to our neighbor, Lord Valmion."

A small crimped face, fingers with swollen veins, a beard that looks dirty because of the threads of black remaining in its white.

"This is Firheia's daughter."

Siski squeezes the old gentleman's hand, gazing on him with pity and affection. Everyone must be happy, even this relic in the shiny coat whose face expresses chronic ill-temper and pride. "Yes, it's a sad thing to give up one's daughters," Grandmother sighs, dropping her eyes to conceal their triumphant glitter. "But there! My poor girls married well! It has nothing to do with me anymore, I'm just an old doll to be set up on a shelf."

Slender, erect, dressed in mauve, with recently slaughtered rare orchids in her hair and tiny beads on the hem of her gown, Grandmother is as fresh as a girl of sixteen. Success has kept her that way, her callous spirit, the arrogance of her blood. Every one of the highly bred ladies who snubbed her in her youth now sends her a basket of flowers and fruit on the Feast of Plenty. Each day a heavy plateful of letters, cards, and little presents is carried in to her by a staggering lady-in-waiting. Utterly lazy, devoid of interests, she is never bored. She spends her days in the composition of notes that drip with sweetness and malice, and in the pursuit of the physical pleasure afforded her by heated baths, new varieties of perfume, and elegant clothes. Nothing has disturbed the shallow existence in which she splashes like a duck since her brief marriage, years

ago, to a lord who conveniently died of a fever. The lacquer of her
prettiness, unmarked by self-reflection, conceals as soul as shrewd
as a jackdaw and as rapacious as a caiman.

"May I introduce you to my son?" rasps Lord Valmion. Siski
looks up to see a tall man breathing through dilated nostrils. She
already knows him; she's seen him at her uncle's hunting parties.
Red Guldo of Dhon, a notorious brawler and breaker of furniture.

She rises, flustered, fighting the urge to giggle. He dances badly,
hiding his awkwardness under stamps and misplaced shouts, and
overwhelming her with the avid brilliance of his close-set eyes and
the powerful, heated gusts of his winey breath. Spinning, she sees
Dasya in the clutches of a strikingly tall and slender lady with
clumps of powder in her hair. "Table," he yells when she passes him
again, and she laughs at the desperate strength with which he whips
his partner in circles.

They meet at the table with their partners, under the potted
orange trees. Wine overflows, staining the tablecloth pink. She
laughs up into her partner's face, pretending to be interested in the
Bainish tam he has ordered for going to parties.

"Just for balls," he says. "I'll never use her for anything else."

"Oh, how fine."

"She'll have red wheels and gold knobs all along the roof."

"Oh, gold knobs! Did you hear that, Dasya? Gold knobs on
the roof!"

"By my heart," says Dasya, "gold knobs on the roof."

Having got rid of Red Guldo, she falls laughing against her
cousin's shirt. Stars are falling, lights hang in her hair. People are
talking loudly all around them as he takes her hand. "Come," he
says. The second arilantha.

How beautiful everything is! It will gleam in her memory afterward, this night, like a pendant flashing at the end of a long chain,
after a subtle poison has seeped into everything, a creeping weakness and fog she will recognize, many years later, as shame. Shame
seeps into her bones, chilling her limbs, when Aunt Mardith takes

her aside at the beginning of summer, in the gray parlor at Faluid-hen where priceless porcelain statuettes stand solemn as generals along the mantelpiece. Siski perches on an armchair stuffed so full it seems to be holding its breath. Red plum trees shower scent through the open window. Aunt Mardith, seated upright on a bredis, touches her handkerchief to her lip. "A pleasant spring," she says.

"Oh yes," says Siski.

"I believe you particularly enjoyed the ball."

"Oh, yes!"

Again Aunt Mardith pats her mouth with the handkerchief. Siski swings her foot, then stops. Aunt Mardith clears her throat. Her eyes are bright, unreadable. When she speaks again, her voice vibrates.

"You know, my child, that I have no gift for idle chatter. I am on firmer footing with the essentials. Let us turn to the essentials, then. I have observed—we have all observed, your grandmother, your uncle, and I—your great affection for your cousin."

The room grows quiet. The figures on the mantel seem to be listening.

"Now," says Aunt Mardith, with a chilly attempt at a laugh, "don't look so alarmed, my child! I haven't brought you in here in the middle of the day to give you a scolding—quite the opposite!"

She tucks her hands under the bredis and, with a series of small jerks, draws it closer to Siski's chair. She reaches out to pat Siski's knee—a gesture so out of character that Siski freezes, nails digging into her chair.

"I don't intend to scold you, but to encourage you," her aunt breathes. "You have had a decent enough education—you know that the marriage of first cousins is frowned upon—but you may not be properly familiar with the genealogy of the Telkans! I am sure you know how to recite *Hernas the Shepherd, Beloved of Love*, but the family tree of the Royal House is more tangled than that, I assure you! Rava, the Opaline Princess, married her cousin—did you know? And so did Thul the Heretic—the one the Laths are always bragging about! His first wife was his cousin through both

Houses—exactly the way Andasya is with you. Her name was Arinoe. She died in childbirth, poor creature, and the infant too . . . but that need not concern us."

Aunt Mardith touches Siski's knee again. She leaves her fingers there. The spot grows colder and colder as she speaks.

"So there is nothing, nothing at all, to prevent you from marrying your cousin. And what it would mean to us—well, a clever girl like you must see that, surely! A Nainish family on the throne! Not for one generation—which is what will happen if they manage to marry some Lath to your cousin—but for untold years."

Siski's heart slows, then speeds up again.

"The dynasty of Faluidhen," her aunt says in a whisper. "Our House bound up with the future of the empire. And you can do it quite simply, quite simply. Without even trying. He's enamored with you, anyone can—"

"Aunt, please stop."

Aunt Mardith removes her hand from Siski's knee. She laughs. "Come, my child, no false modesty! Let us be candid. We women have special burdens, and we must share them. You are fifteen years old; you cannot be married with propriety before seventeen. These next two years, then, are of particular—"

"Aunt, please!"

Siski stands, her breathing difficult and fast. "You're mistaken. I don't know what you're talking about."

"Dear me," Aunt Mardith says. Her eyes are mild, appraising, watchful. "We are very nervous today. Sit down."

Siski obeys.

In the long silence that follows, it is difficult to tell if Aunt Mardith is breathing. Such wonderful, appalling stillness. At last her lips part. She clears her throat. While outside the window the plum tree waves in the breeze, sometimes caressing the windowsill.

"Freshness," Aunt Mardith says, "is a quality much to be desired. The freshness of happy young things. There is no substitute for it; no cream or paint can achieve it. It is a quality more spiritual than physical, yet it overflows the spirit, as it were, and lends its glow to the flesh."

She smiles. "I do not have it, of course. Perhaps I never did. I have always been called too serious, too old. Mature, people used to say. Not an attractive word to a girl, but in time I learned to turn it to my advantage. You, however," she continues, smoothing her skirt over her knee, "you possess that quality of freshness. Your mother did too, as a girl. A kind of interior brightness. It made her very appealing to gentlemen. To arrange her match with your father was really almost too simple—something of a bore! He wanted to marry her when she was only sixteen. He asked for her hand in this very room. I made him wait a year. Irilas of the Hiluen, fruit of a royal House."

Again the smile. The teeth perfectly arranged. The plum tree performs its perfumed dance. Siski's skin tingles. Her face is too warm.

"Firvaud was different," Aunt Mardith says with a sigh. "More like me, perhaps, though less disciplined. Certainly she had ambition. Even when she was very small she had to win every game. She always insisted on taking the largest honith, the prettiest of the apples. A tyrant, even to Fenya, though he was older than she. Now, one would think that such a girl would easily get whatever she wanted, and that Firheia, who was more easily contented, would lag behind her in all things. And I believe this is how matters appear to most people. After all, Firvaud married a king, and your mother married the lord of a miserable highland town; Firvaud dwells among princes and your mother among goats. But this view is too simplistic. Firvaud had to work to get the Telkan. It took effort and patience. While Irilas fell into your mother's lap."

She watches Siski, as if to gauge the effect of her words.

"I don't understand why you're—"

"Of course not. Of course not. That is precisely the point. You do not understand, you do not think. You live, and dance, and laugh, while others understand and think on your behalf. That is the way you have lived until now, and it has been quite successful.

Like your mother before you, you are greatly admired. You have grown up without the slightest insecurity or worry, and this has given you a bloom of charming innocence. Very good. I applaud you. I applaud myself. But no woman can afford to keep her innocence forever. We are the doors of the House: we control its borders. We protect. At some point, we all learn how to work a hinge.

"Come now. Why this expression of distaste? I am telling you, you have done well. You have bewitched your cousin, as I hoped. It is only necessary to take care, now that you have begun to go into society, not to encourage another suitor too much. You will have many, despite your mixed blood—dear me!" She laughs. "How easily offended we are! Perfectly crimson! Really, my child, be sensible! Of course your mixed blood is a disadvantage—especially the Kestenyi strain—one wishes it were possible to hide it, as so many others have done—my heart, yes, you'd be surprised what's not written in the *Hath*, all sorts of brilliant deceptions have been practiced on unsuspecting princes. They say the Duchess of Ethendria has Panji blood. Just imagine! But you, of course, can hide nothing, being the empire's most illustrious mongrel. This will make some people reluctant to associate with you; but not all of them, not by any means. That is why the next two years will be so delicate. You must avoid any sort of attachment that will give a man a claim on you, but you must not reveal that you plan to marry Andasya . . ."

Siski forces her hands to relax, to release the plush of her chair. A tiny movement. She doesn't want her aunt to notice. She understands now that her body speaks a language of which she is unaware and the thought makes her feel exposed, stripped down to nothing. Aunt Mardith is speaking of parties, of feasts, of balls, she is breaking them down so that they become, not music, not laughter, not the sweet energy of the dance, but functions as carefully organized as military campaigns. She stresses how important it is that Siski keep her love secret. Their enemies—oh yes, they have many enemies!—must not be given the chance to organize themselves in opposition to the match. She says it must be a surprise attack. She says *love* when Siski has never said it herself. The word seems to cringe, revealed in harsh light.

Afterward Siski will go to her room and curl up on the windowseat. The afternoon outside still pulsing with color. She will pick up the anthology of poetry she has been reading with her cousin and let it fall open on her knee. A poem by Arduen of Suoveni, known as the Gray Lady. Not a poet who has ever interested them. Dull, says Dasya, and Siski agrees. When she reads the Gray Lady's poems she has always felt vaguely tired, prone to distraction, as if listening to a pair of scissors. Hardly surprising, as the Gray Lady never left the estate of Suoveni and wrote about nothing except her singularly routine and eventless life. She was, states the brief introduction in the anthology, "the poet of the cushion and the comb." But now Siski reads her poems, and the words stand out in lonely beauty. *Nine crows on a branch*, she reads, *and seven will not fly*. She sees the Gray Lady closing a door, correct, irreproachable, desperate. *Twilight has fallen, and all the windows fade.*

A fog over everything. At dinner she cannot raise her head. She cannot look at Dasya without blushing. And while the feeling will lessen, becoming bearable, even ordinary, habitual, it will never go away.

The night of the ball is detached from that fog of shame, and so it shines forth even now, when the world is utterly changed and Ashenlo is lost. The way she turns in Dasya's arms, in his odor of cut grass and healthy sweat. Stepping away from him, spinning, arms above her head. Grandmother nodding in the corner, exchanging a roguish look with Uncle Fenya. The best of Nainish society drifting in bright silks. The lights so hot.

She turns to face him again, lowering her arms.

"Do I look all right?" she whispers.

"You," he says.

3. Beloved the Color of Almonds

Every day, Dai Fanlei meets the others. Every day she turns mattresses, rips out threads, beats, stuffs, sews. Her fingers grow small transparent calluses. Her gums bleed. She does not have the same body anymore.

She is tired. She grows ill. She coughs and spits a pallid sputum on the road. There are flecks of down in it; they blend with the melting snow.

Her feet are bruised, the nails black. Dai Norla teaches her to wrap them in cast-off strips of cloth, to keep them warm and dry.

Every night Dai Fanlei walks up to the abandoned temple. In her mind, she has begun to call it home.

She cares for him. She gathers wood in the forest and builds up the fire. She brings him a drink of snow in her cupped hands. She tears the bread very small in order to push it between his lips, while he gazes at her with his angel eyes.

"Leave me," he says. His voice slurred.

She lays her hand across his eyes. "Sleep now. Sleep."

And when he sleeps, she quietly opens the book. The only book they have, the one they brought because he had hidden it in his shirt, close to his heart, against the skin. A very old copy, rare, adorned with the somber woodcuts of the past. The gilt looks fresh, undisturbed by human touch. The heavy pages give off the sour and melancholy scent of volumes that no one has thought to open for many years. It is a book kept only for show. She can't tell whether even Dasya read it, or whether he merely carried it like an amulet. She holds it tilted toward the fire, the light on the page a pattern of rippling color, harsh in her eyes and red as veins.

712. *Three children and one woman forty-five years of age disappeared in the village of Feirhu. A rough man, without horns, and exhibiting wings too small for flight, was netted and beaten to death in the neighboring woods.*

713. *A pair of twins born with horns near Sinidre. Executed.*

725. *A cocoon was discovered in a wind tower in the city of Deinivel. The guard lay in wait for the creature, and three died valiantly before it was captured and drowned in a bucket of wax.*

726. *A knocking was reported in the cellar of the Temple of Heth Kuidva outside Breim. The area was excavated, and a Dreved preparing for its cocoon stage, fortunately very weak, was discovered and destroyed with fire.*

727. *A woman with black feathers protruding from the flesh of her back was discovered and drowned in melted wax in the Hadmanyi.*

731. *A child of five years began to show horns in the city of Asarma. Executed by hot wax.*

732. *A woman with one wing discovered in the Tavroun. Drowned and then burned.*

733. *A child with no whites to his eyes executed at Elueth.*

735. *Eiloki. A female reaper, seventeen years old, complained of a headache. Horns developed, and she was executed by fire.*

735. *An infant with wing marks executed at Yenith.*

736. *Ur-Fanlei. A child born with blue flesh. Executed.*

Tuik died in the autumn. It was cold, too cold to sleep out on the plateau. The chill seeped down from the empty spaces between the stars. The chill of the void, deadening, indomitable. When she wakes the distant hills are black against a ruddy sky.

"Tuik," she calls.

The horse has strayed. It is Siski's fault: she must not have locked the stable door. She sits behind Dasya on Na Faso, Tav following on her pony. "*Tuik!*" A feathery whiteness leaves her lips and disappears at once in the cold dry air.

"He came down here," says Dasya.

Tav rides silent beside them, her face sinister and strange in the early light. Following the horse's tracks, they descend the ridge and discover, in the rising light, a valley of misar plants.

"No," says Siski.

She slips from the back of the horse. The others sit motionless. She runs. The spines of the misar slash her trousers, cutting her legs. The light becomes harsher, white. Tuik stands very still with his belly bleeding and curving spines protruding from his lips. His gums and eyelids already dark. He looks at her with the same confidence as ever and her heart cracks like a glass held over a flame. Beloved the color of almonds. "When the dew is on the mountains," she sings to him, taking the halter.

A chant of sobs. In the stable at Sarenha he lies down quietly on the floor. Nenya stands in the doorway shaking her head. Carefully Siski pulls the spines from the tender belly and mouth of her darling and rubs him gently and covers him with a blanket. He will not eat or drink. His breath comes jerkily now, in spasms, and it no longer smells of mornings and of the first snows. She lies beside him, her cheek on the floor, and looks toward the others who squat in the doorway. "You've got to come in," says Tav. "It's too cold."

But she is not coming in, not now, not ever. The others go out, leaving the lantern on the floor, and Dasya returns with furs and blankets. He covers her and sits by the wall with a shambus pelt draped over his knees, silent. Outside the doorway the night is blue.

"I don't want you to look at me," she tells him.

"It's not your fault."

"It is my fault, it is."

"Don't say that."

"Stop looking at me."

He looks away. In the morning the grayish discoloration has covered the horse's head and neck and is creeping toward the heart. She looks at Tuik. She weeps. "I dreamt that none of it was true, that it hadn't happened." Shadows of trees are playing outside. She covers the horse's face with her hair, kisses his nose and then recoils from the bloated skin with its repellent hardness. Only his eye recognizable. He has begun to tremble and looks at her as if to beg her pardon for the indiscretion. She feels that she cannot bear this nobility in him but she bears it all that day because the alternative is unthinkable. Her forehead against his neck, her eyes closed. Night falls, the second night. Again her cousin sits silently by the wall. The two of them and the horse awake in the small light of the lantern. Then Dasya says: "You can't go on like this."

"And what do you know about it?" she cries, savage. "You don't love him."

But she knows he is right. She remembers Mun Vidara's mare that took almost two weeks to die of misar poisoning, lying in the yard. And Mun Vidara came to the house and told the story, sniffing into her handkerchief, and there was an immense silence at the table. And at last Uncle Veda said, his voice thick with emotion: "Forgive me, my lady—you have acted monstrously."

"All right," she says. "Quick."

His Amafeini dagger is very sharp. Ah, would that I had died before my Sarya. Would that I were with her again on the wide plateau, on the wide plateau, in the sweet south wind, beneath a flowered sky.

"No, I'll do it," she says.

She takes the knife. She has hunted shambusna on the plains, she knows where to find the heart. But she is not strong enough, and Dasya helps her. His hands closing over hers, the sudden pressure, the black blood soaking her knees. Even now, not a sound from the horse. Only an increase in his trembling, which gradually subsides with his surging blood. She keeps her eyes open until the end. It comes very soon, in the light of the lantern, there in the stable at Sarenha Haladli.

In the morning she learns of the universe without Tuik. And the ringing silence without Tuik. News of their coming has gone before them, carried by herdboys, and her mother comes into the courtyard to meet them, wearing her yellow dress and with anxious eyes.

"Tuik's dead," Siski says. "He got into some misar."

She holds her mother close, prolonging the embrace so as not to see the compassion and sadness clouding the clear brown eyes. She cannot bear to make her mother unhappy, it makes her want to die even if it is unavoidable, not her fault. And this time it is her fault.

"I'm so sorry," her mother says.

"I'm all right," says Siski, drawing back. At the side of the house, in the sand court, girls from the farm are pounding grain in big stone mortars, singing a nonsense song.

"We're late," her mother says, following the direction of her gaze. Her smile makes a weak light in the exhaustion of her face. The preserving is behind as well. A smell of jam hangs about the house, as if spring has come to the autumn.

Later, in the evening, Siski's father enters the drawing room in his scarlet dressing jacket and frayed trousers. A certain elegance in the way he lights his cheroot at a candle. "That horse cost seven thousand droi," he says.

Home. The hook where she hangs her cloak, the threadbare rug in the hall. Light from an inner room, translated light. It is the glow of the library fire reflected in a mirror and flung out here, to this hall with the flaking walls. Walking past, she drags her fingernail along the plaster and a white chip drops. A little bit each day. She does this absently, as she touches the head of the figure of sorrowing Leilin that stands outside her mother's morning room.

Inside, her mother. A cheerful blaze on the hearth, a vast white bearskin on the floor. All the curtains drawn back to admit the morning light. Her mother is seated at the big rosewood desk that came with her from Faluidhen. She sets aside her pen, her cheeks flushed slightly with pleasure.

"Siski. Siskiye. Have you been out already, so early?"

Her gentle, fragrant kiss. "There's coffee in the pot."

Siski pours a glass and sits on the leather stool in front of the fire, crooking a finger inside the heel of each slipper to pull it off.

The fur of the rug so deep. "Are they still harvesting?" she asks. And receives that gift, her mother's half-laughing, half-despairing gesture, the optimism that never seems to desert her, that gives even her most dreadful and disappointing stories a piquant flavor.

"My dear, you wouldn't believe it if I told you." She goes on talking in her easy, simple, inimitable way, telling of stolen oxen, storm-damaged trees, a fence that can't be mended until she finds money to buy posts. As she speaks her hand hovers over the notebook in which she keeps the accounts. It is covered in baize and held together with string. She is not good at sums and always works them out two or three times on the backs of old menus before she enters them in the book.

"Sometimes I'm afraid to open it," she confesses, laughing and wiping her eyes. Tears shed between amusement and grief. Her delicate skin, scrubbed by the air of the desert, shines beneath the dark wing of her hair where a few pale threads are sparkling. And Siski knows by her resolute smile that despite the catalogue of disasters there will be gifts and a ball again this year on the Feast of Lamps. This is not one of those moments of crisis, occurring two or three times a year, when her mother paces the rug, muttering and counting on her fingers.

During those times the house grows dark; they are ordered to save the oil. Nenya goes about with a fierce stiff face, carries trays to the morning room and makes certain grim allusions which the children are too frightened to examine. At night there are strange bumps and scrapings: their mother, in her dressing gown, is emptying cupboards, looking for things to sell. Worst of all are the Tolie mornings in the huntsmen's room when she explains to the servants that she can give them only half their wages. The rough hands, clad in gloves if it is winter, close about the coins, and the herdboys shuffle silently toward the door. Afterward her mother returns to the morning room. Her uncombed hair is fastened with pins, her arms hang by her sides. The children crouch at the edge of the door she has forgotten to close and watch her gesturing, animated by desperation. She insists that their tutor go over her sums. "We must think of something!" she cries. "You will surely see something I have missed."

She makes him sit in the chair and kneels beside him. And the tutor snatches off his skullcap and throws it on the floor, a habit which is comical in the schoolroom but not here, not here. "I am not a steward!" he cries. "You ought to have a steward."

He fumes, kicks at his fallen cap, sometimes even weeps. Their mother rises at last and goes to the window. A strange half-smile on her lips, she rests her forehead against the glass and gazes out at the desolate countryside.

But today, no, today there is no despair, only the usual struggles, and fires burn in the library and the little family parlor. Siski goes into this parlor, where skins cushion the floor and a pair of Savrahili sabers hangs on the wall. There are no flowers now, and the parlor looks plain, even austere, but it is still one of her favorite rooms. Only, in the air, she can detect the chill that follows wherever her father, that stranger, that interloper, has passed.

All morning he sleeps. Siski and Tav and their cousin wander through the south wing of the house, they look at the books in the library in silence. They are examining pieces of armor in their dead grandmother's audience hall when a shield slides off the table and falls with a clang.

They look up, frozen in the light from the window. Slowly the clamor dies away and they hear the beating of three hearts. But there is no other sound until noon, when a creak on the stairs admonishes them to seek the amadesh, the orchard, the hills. Usually they go riding at this hour, but Siski will not ride without Tuik, and the others walk with her under the apricot trees. Dragging branches through the fallen leaves. The house stands over them, aloof, pierced with windows like broken mirrors. The house in which he walks, drinks his coffee, sits in the library alone. They stay away, running wild in the orchard and on the farm, eating raush from their pockets and drinking milk behind sheds where goats are being slaughtered. They run filthy, half-frozen, harassed by dogs.

Dasya looks up at the purple sky. "It's kebma time," he says.

Slowly they return to the darkened house. Certain formalities are preserved. They bathe, they dress for kebma. Siski wears a pair of agate pins in her hair. In the drawing room she stands near the fire, holding her plate, chewing. She does not know or think about what she eats. And all of them stand like that, just eating, silent, unless her mother clears her throat and begins a tentative conversation.

Then all the children help her. "Oh, did you know?" "I think." "I saw him too." Her father stands by the window with crossed arms. His smile is taut, derisive, false. "Is that what you think?" he says. The silence closes. No one looks at him. They eat.

Evenings of candlelight and dread, without innocence, without pleasure. Her high lace collar scratches the back of her neck. In the dining room the candles stand on the table in pallid rows while on the walls the portraits kindle their abstract smiles. Her father eats doggedly, attacking his meat. He mutters: "The meat is tough."

"I'm sorry," her mother says softly. "It was roasting all afternoon."

"That's why it's tough, you let them overcook it."

He beckons and Fodok steps from the shadows with a bottle of dark wine. The liquid curls in the glass with a tinny music. Outside moonlight covers the fields, roads, and canals with a mantle of chalk. Hired men and girls are going home along the roads, singing, stepping vigorously in their rawhide boots. A few herds of cattle and sheep are on the roads as well, being driven home in the dark. The herdboys sing their peculiar *oh-ee, oh-ee* notes. Light shines from a kitchen with a waxed floor. At the Three Falcons, Durs is easing out corks with his heavy tufted hands. Men sit everywhere, on the steps, at the table under the fig tree, reaching for bottles, coughing, pulling off their gloves. Young Osenor, who plays music in exchange for drinks, sits in his special chair and plucks the diali. *With a comb in her hair.*

Children run through the yards, chasing each other. Dogs are snapping at bones. And we sit here, immobilized by silence. The house is hushed and empty, it seems as if even the servants have gone away, taking with them all naturalness, light, and color. Life, real life, is banished to the golden, bread-smelling amadesh, where a little window is open to let out the heat, where the cook sits with her feet soaking in a basin and Nenya takes off her kerchief to let the servants' children plait her hair. Life is in the morning room, peeping from under the bearskin rug. It is in the little parlor where, on the day before Tanbrivaud, Siski and Tav and their mother will hang up ribbons and evergreen branches, bursting with laughter, standing on the hard leather chairs. The children cover their mouths when they laugh, they hide behind the curtains. Their mother is purposeful, lively, like anyone's mother. She scolds them, chases them with the branches. Then suddenly she raises her hand. "Shh." On her cheek a pale mark like a star.

In the dining room, the stranger raises his glass. He stares before him at the candles. He is the author of this enervating silence. For them, for his family, silence and contempt. It is for others that he unpacks the jewels of his intellect and charm. She has seen him hold a room full of visitors spellbound with his talk, convulse the most sober listener with his wit. From the old conservatory where he spends his evenings alone or with the doctor, she has often heard his shouts of unnatural laughter. Yes, he laughs until he chokes, he cackles, he pounds on the table. But not here. Here he sets his glass down by his plate. He says something, she doesn't know what, something that makes her mother tilt her head, a public smile crystallizing on her lips.

"Perhaps not necessary," her mother murmurs.

He goes on talking, he is talking now about money, lamp oil, wood. "The earlier you rise, the more wood you consume. You sit in that parlor of yours, a huge room, and heat the whole place for seven hours."

Her mother laughs, a little frown of pain denting her brow. "Oh, never seven hours. Never that long."

Siski looks at the window but she can only see their reflections now, the night is too dark, the dining room too bright. She sees her mother's image motion for Fodok, order more apples, the servants mustn't hear them argue, it wouldn't do.

A familiar despair, as easily recognizable as home itself, comes in from the night and the desert, from all directions. Don't say anything, don't look. For evil is here, among the plates. Afterward everyone will rise, fleeing that high cold room. The children will go to the parlor, running, bumping into the walls, shoving each other, giggling, behaving as they think other children do. In the parlor Dasya will throw himself on the floor in front of the fire. "Alas my heart, I've eaten enough for fifty men." Tav will string the little bow she carved that afternoon and pursue them until bedtime with her toy arrows. "Stop it!" Siski shrieks, flinging herself behind the couch. "I don't want to play, I mean it, kad shedyamud." But she does want to play. The restlessness, the need for movement and light, is terrible. She rolls on the skin rug, laughing, clutching her ribs.

Sing more, play more, make more noise. Father is in the conservatory cutting up cakes of bolma, he won't hear. Subdued at last, exhausted, they go upstairs where they can hear their mother playing the limike in her dressing room.

Oh joyful the morning, the fairest is walking
on field and on hillside her blossoms to shed.

Every night the same tune, a very beautiful tune by Hailar the Blind, that master of rhythm, harmony, and mathematics. She plays it every night, again and again. Sometimes she sings. The children fall asleep to those complex and ordered tones. She is not talented; music is difficult for her, she makes mistakes, goes back to repeat the most intricate measures. She plays it quickly, as if she would feel how fast her fingers are able to move, and then slowly as if to drain each note of its essence. Sitting cross-legged on the low flat couch, not looking in the mirror. About her the light of the porcelain Nainish lamp. She plays. On the wall hangs a portrait of her father in an ebony frame, below it a painting of Faluidhen she made herself, long ago.

Dim gray walls relieved by clusters of roses. No one knows why she plays the same air every night, that song and no other. Perhaps, on the wave of music, she returns to the fresh, cold climate of the north, to the vast pink orchards, to the pines. Or perhaps the challenge of Hailar's composition enables her to forget, for an hour, the relentlessness of her life. Or perhaps the music she loves so dearly compensates her for the hardships, the losses coming one after the other. The struggle to maintain the house, to keep from having to sell the carriage, give up the tutor for the children, cut down the woods. For the battle to keep dishonor at bay, the necessity to smile, to lie, every day. And for her husband, always for him. Yes, perhaps those liquid notes and the pleasure of creating them each night is a recompense for his disappearances to Tevlas, for the money he spends which he will never explain. For her suspicions, her secret tears, the sobs she smothers with her pillow. For the humiliation she suffers when one of the servants knocks at her door because the master is lying unconscious in a hallway, and she must give permission for him to be carried upstairs, undressed, rolled into bed, so that the children will not discover him in the morning. For the night she glanced from the window, having heard a noise below, and saw him urinating drunkenly in the garden. For his coldness, his rebuffs. The way he mocks her for praying, calls her a fool, sneers at all her interests and amusements. And the way that the children, as an extension of her, meet with the same repulsion and scorn. The way they shrink from him with their huge despairing eyes—her children who are so eager to please, so sensitive that the least unpleasant word brings out great bruises on their hearts. For the way that the house has become a place of sighs, a trackless wasteland in which happiness is kept hidden like a crime. On holidays the children cluster whispering in her dressing room, unwrapping their little presents with cold fingers.

And then there are the sudden changes, his violence, his caprices. The gifts that overwhelm with their strange brilliance. The Bainish gown he purchased for her, its skirt encrusted with Nissian rubies, or, for Siski, an astonishing, princely horse. And the outings, abruptly decided upon, the excursions to Solfian in an open wagon. The wind pulls furiously at the children's flying hair. Seated on bales of straw, frightened, disheveled, they cling to one another, jolting over the roads in an ashen twilight. It takes too long to get to the wood; they are hungry, thirsty, desperate. Their father's face grows harder as it becomes clear his plan has failed. By the time the little rush lights are lit, those lights which are meant to give them so much pleasure, Siski is weeping softly and Tav has fallen asleep.

> *Oh joyful the morning, the fairest is walking*
> *on field and on hillside her blossoms to shed.*

Siski looks at her father. She looks at him. She hears his voice. "I'm only trying to make a bit of conversation." A flash of movement, the quiver of a whip. He has thrown his napkin down. "That's what you wanted, isn't it? Conversation over dinner."

He reaches for a candle, and the light drawn close picks out the gray in his beard and illuminates his handsome, hawk-like, deep-lined face. A face that seems almost petrified, except for the roving and fiery eyes. He lights his cheroot, dripping wax on the tablecloth.

"Careful," her mother says, very quickly, not thinking.

"What did you say to me?"

He stares.

Her mother's eyes are downcast, her fingers fluttering. "It's nothing, it's only—the tablecloth, you're dripping—"

"And isn't this my own house? And can't I spill whatever I like on the tablecloth?"

The same, every night, the same weariness and oppression. No one eats.

Siski looks at him, the world about her beginning to dissolve. No, it is not the same every night. Tonight it is not the same.

"It's because Mother has to clean the linen," she says.

Silence. He looks at her in stupefaction before the eyes with their discolored whites and scarlet veins begin to gather their fury. She hurries, afraid she won't be able to finish.

"It's because she has to clean the tablecloths, that's why she doesn't like them to get stained."

Already her eyes are full of tears. He sits back in his chair, cold, sarcastic. "I suppose she doesn't have servants to wash the table-cloths. Or perhaps she makes you wash them, is that it?"

She hears herself stammering. "She. She has to ask Nenya. It makes extra work, she doesn't like it— "

And with shame, rage, loathing, she feels herself beginning to sob, because it's horrible, this existence, ignoble, demeaning. And because, by weeping, she has already lost.

"You dare to open your mouth. You killed that horse. You've cost me more money than your mother with her firewood."

She cannot see him anymore; the table slips and blends with the wall, swirling about her, melting in the light. She imagines the others staring at her in horror, at this violent display, this scene. But she has gone too far to stop. "Mother gets up early in the morning to do the accounts," she cries, weeping and shaking, her hands clenched on the table. "She needs the wood, she needs it. She always saves, she never wastes anything. Let her have the firewood from my bedroom, I don't want it."

"Siski," her mother says.

"No," her father interrupts, his smile malicious and triumphant. "She says she doesn't want it. Very well, you won't have a fire, but you won't give the wood to your mother because it is not yours to give. It is mine."

Pressing. Pressing. "Pressing and pressing," she sobs. "Pressing on everything all the time." She kneels at the edge of the sunken garden, her face on the low stone wall that is dusted with snow. She turns her head, rubbing her cheeks and forehead on the rugged stone. Her hand tight over her heart where she feels it pressing. Why is it? Why? Why all the time? Stars burst and glitter behind her eyes, the steadying pain of her forehead stung by snow. Still it keeps pressing and it is possible to die here in the dark, deserted garden.

To die of it. To die. She shivers, snow is on her neck, her knees are wet, her feet numb in the embroidered slippers. She turns her head again. Snow on her eyelids. Someone comes and stands beside her and she feels that it is Dasya.

He does not speak. She raises her head. Lights in the house behind him and she knows that he can see her upturned face. She cannot speak of it, she would rather die. "Tuik is dead," she chokes. "I killed him. And you're not happy here anymore."

He crouches beside her, jacketless in the cold. "I am happy."

She shakes her head. "You're not."

She wonders if Aunt Mardith took him aside at Faluidhen. If he, too, is under the fog of shame. Is that why he is so strange with her, so distant?

"Siski," he says. "Look, stand up. You can't stay there."

He pulls her up. Suddenly she feels quiet, remote. As if all the world has fallen away from them. He holds her hand as they walk to the end of the garden and stand looking out at the snow-dark night. Two figures in a shapeless landscape.

All winter her room remains cold. She tells herself she'll grow used to it. Nenya brings her heated bricks in secret. "Here, sudaidi." Her guilty face, the bricks wrapped in a sheet, her glance down the corridor as she thrusts the bundle into Siski's arms. And before there is time to thank her she has hurried off toward the stairs, her kerchief shining in the dark and then winking out. Silence. The lamp on the desk seems smaller, pale. And Siski understands that it was really the glow of the fire that lit the room in the past.

It takes a long time for the bricks to heat the bed. Her book shakes in her hands. She tells herself that everything is the same, just the same. But she cannot read the beloved words. The forget-me-nots in the margins quiver and turn to clouds in the dazzle of her tears. She wipes her eyes on her wrist and tries again. The green green wood. She bites her lip. At last she lays down the book and sobs in her crossed arms. But in the morning she is pale, defiant. No one must speak of it. She snaps when her mother tries to comfort her.

And very soon no one speaks of it, as if nothing ever happened. In that cheerless chamber she goes to bed each night. Here she retires to be alone, to weep, to nurse her flayed heart when she learns that Uncle Fenya has bought all but a tiny strip of the farm. Lying under the blankets in the dark. Once, in the little parlor, her father himself attempts to speak to her. "How was your night?" he asks gruffly. "Fine," she says, and leaves the room. That night his hard eyes flash as he mocks her across the table.

But still there are the conventional gestures, the meals, the celebrations, at the end of the year the colored lights in the avla. She stands at the window, behind her the scraping of the Tevlasi orchestra,

the stamping of spurred and booted feet. Someone takes her arm
and she turns, the lamplight in her eyes. Mun Vidara wears black
and has black eyebrows. Her face is tense and eager and her creaking
dress smells sharply of ammonia, dried sweat, and eau de cologne.
She drags a young man forward by the elbow. "It's our Tadi!" she
shrieks, beaming with her long dun-colored teeth. "You'd never
have known him, would you?"

Siski smiles and shakes her head, regarding the tall soft-bodied
youth with the curling hair. Behind him a blur of dancers, colored
skirts unfurling in light. She hears her father's wheezing, delighted
laugh, his special laugh for responding to flattery, and sees him
leaning heavily on Em Makov's shoulder. "That's it!" he shouts.
"Exactly what he said. And I said to him, we'll have another bottle,
these ladies are still thirsty!" Evergreen boughs hang limply on the
walls. It is the Feast of Lamps, the annual holiday ball at Ashenlo.

Tadi does not dance badly. He talks of Eilam, the shops, the
carriages, "*Vai,* it makes our Tevlas look like a 'Rouni farm." She
answers vaguely, looking over his shoulder. She sees her mother
beside the table of drinks, discussing something with Nenya. Nenya
wears a small crown of satin flowers for the occasion and an apron
embroidered with heraldic greyhounds. Her mother wears the same
gown she wore last year, a crimson silk refurbished with black lace
borders at neck and hem.

Someone is laughing loudly: it is the darwad, already drunk.
His pigtail bobs behind him, thick with grease like the tail of a
shambus. The orchestra plays as if they will never stop, thrashing
their feet to ring the clusters of bells about their booted ankles.
There are no bouquets. Only Mun Miraleth wears some lank lilies
in the powdered confection of her hair, touching them every few
minutes. She has coaxed them to stay alive in her conservatory,
warmed by pots of hot coals.

Instead of flowers, Siski wears a great diamond and ruby brooch
pinned to her shoulder. Tadi ogles it. "Are those imperial jewels?"

"Yes, it was my grandmother's brooch."

"My heart, they're as big as cherries." His hand, slick with perspiration, tightens on hers.

Suddenly tired and sad, she looks for Dasya and sees him dancing with Mun Miraleth. He too looks unhappy. His coat is loose about his thin flanks, his hair pulled back, and his face in the lamplight looks so drawn and strange that she is afraid.

Earlier in the evening they set lights to float on the Oun; they had to break the ice. "Are you quite well?" says Tadi anxiously. "You seem a little—"

"Oh, I'm fine," she laughs, but still the young man takes her arm and leads her to the table. She wants to drink wine but her mother is watching and so she has tea instead. "Mm," she says, nodding at her partner. Hairs rise on her skin: her father is near. She sees him take a glass of wine, holding it loosely near the base. Despite the noise she hears him say to her mother as he passes her: "Humiliating. You look like a schoolteacher's wife." He turns away abruptly, welcoming someone in loud, genial tones. Her mother's hand taps jerkily on her knee.

The air of the avla is murky and golden, obscured by a haze near the ceiling, where the windows are beaded with moisture like chilled tears. It is a place of bitterness, inconsolable. The orchestra shatters one's thoughts with the clamor of its unending lamentations. A crowd has gathered about her father, who dances now with Mun Miraleth, his small beard pointing, one broad arm flung out. His face glistens with heat, its expression set. He dances flamboyantly, with such fierce energy that she is afraid he will fall. Every few moments, an outburst of applause. She looks for Dasya and sees him standing near the entryway with Tav. "Dance with me." He gazes over her shoulder, never into her eyes, as they turn together, far away from the group that surrounds her father.

Here the floor seems empty, as if the ball is already over.

"Why do you want to break my heart?" she says.

He does not answer. His hand on the small of her back. She hides her face against his shoulder. "Why, why won't you tell me what's wrong?"

The music races ahead of them; they are not moving in time. When the dance is over she dries her eyes on her handkerchief. "I must look a fright."

"No," he says in a harsh and alien voice that leaves her stunned. He turns his back on her and walks away.

Em Makov appears with his officer's moustache and cranberry-colored hair. "Oh no," she laughs, "it's only the smoke from the lamps." They dance, she laughs at a story about his vineyard, afterward she asks him to bring her a glass of Karsavi from the table. She drinks it sitting on a bench by the wall and later she drinks another glass at the table, careful not to look in her mother's direction. She hears her own bright laughter. Tadi tells a humorous story and then Em Makov is there again with his wry and mournful horse's profile. Mun Vidara admires Siski's dress and Siski straightens her shoulders, her brooch catching the light. Someone beside her says: "A real Kestenyi beauty." The lamps are dim, the musicians are cooling their fingers on lumps of snow. In the silence a succession of terrible echoes.

"A thousand blessings." "Good night." "Good night." The guests go out to the hall to collect their furs. She takes a candle and walks along a narrow passage, finding her way to the stairs, touching the wall unsteadily with one hand. Suddenly Dasya steps from a darkened room.

He steps out straight in front of her, his hand on her wrist to keep her from dropping the candle. "Come with me to the hills tomorrow. Come alone. We'll meet at the north door, without Tav."

"Why?" She tries to pull out of his grip and wax drips on his knuckles.

He does not flinch, but stares as if fascinated at the hardening drops. Then his eyes, raised slowly, dark, searching, unfathomable.

"Please," he says.

"You're hurting me," she hisses, and he releases her wrist. Footsteps and voices are coming down the hall.

"All right, I'll come," she whispers hurriedly. He steps away from her, backward into the chasm of the doorway. Upstairs in the piercing cold of her room, trying to warm her hands at the lamp, she falls asleep with her head on the writing table.

4. The Clearing

A calm descends. Dai Fanlei is quiet. The world is waking up, the snow dissolving, but Dai Fanlei is going to sleep.

She works without pause, slowly. Just motion, arms going up and down. A small smile hangs a finger's breadth in front of her face. She hears them talk, Dai Norla, Dai Kouranu, and Dai Gersina. They say "in the Valley." They say "the Duke of Bain." In this way Dai Fanlei learns that Veda of Bain, called "Uncle Veda" in another life, is to be Telkan of Olondria. And the old Telkan, once called "Telkan Uncle," is dead. His body, first interred in a park, has been exhumed and placed in the graveyard of the kings.

Dai Fanlei's smile hovers. It never fades.

The streets are clearer now. The temples have opened their doors to the refugees. Charities have sprung up: you can see country noblemen, even the darwad and his daughters, serving soup and distributing bales of cloth. They are so happy to have escaped the chaos with their possessions intact that they give with both hands, laughing, full of love. A holiday air reigns in the town square where a wealthy old landowner, famous as a cruel taskmaster, dispenses orange cake from the back of his horse.

Nothing has changed, except that Kestenya is lawless now, broken off from the empire. All the good families there have fled into the Valley. Dai Fanlei does not ask about Lord Irilas, Duke of Tevlas, and Lady Firheia of Ashenlo. She will not.

Wet earth everywhere blackening. She walks through mud now, mud instead of snow. Sometimes storms come, streaking swiftly over the hills, soaking her clothes, chilling her as she walks, until her skin reaches the exact temperature of the rain.

In the abandoned temple, a small red light.

She has had to move his couch away from the fire. He suffers from the light and warmth. He suffers. He no longer eats. He can hardly open his mouth. He winces when she dribbles water over his lips.

His voice, crushed. He grunts and groans. He forms her name: a sound like branches breaking. He says it again, again, again. She thinks he is trying to warn her, perhaps, to urge her to desperate action. She thinks that he is trying to tell her: *Now.*

She shakes her head. She wants to hold him, to comfort him, but it would give him too much pain.

Deep night again, and she opens the book. She reads: *Their beauty, designed to inspire pity in their victims.* She reads: *In seven days it will be too late.*

∽

At that time of year the world was breathless, immaculate, immobile, the standing trees decked with garlands of snow. The sky dark gray above the hills, drifting into twilight. A crow flying across it: the center of movement and life. The crow draws away, diminishes and is lost. She sees Dasya walking from the orchard, his hands in the pockets of his coat. He has been out, perhaps for hours. His face is pale to the lips. He meets her under the dripping eaves. "Let's go."

She walks. She follows him to the back gate and out onto the snowy horse-track. Stolid crunch of footsteps breaking the frost. Her head lowered, she watches her boots and in front of her, his boots. She moves with some difficulty, avoiding his footprints.

They go on walking. The track leads upward. They pass the shepherds' hut, its roof caved in, charred marks on the earth around the door. A preternatural silence haunts the wood. She hears her breath, so loud. The snow creates a radiance under the trees.

After an hour she begins to lag behind. "Wait," she says.

He turns to her with a face transformed beneath the darkness of his hood, a face so thin, so haggard, so much older that she cannot speak. She stands with her mouth open.

"What is it?" he says.

"I—I'm getting tired."

He looks away, then looks at her again. "Let's go a little farther. To the clearing."

When she does not answer, he says: "I can't breathe here."

She nods and follows him again, cold, stumbling in the snow.

A brightness through the trees. As if a blue lamp shines among them. The branches are growing thin. It is the clearing. She pauses, panting, clinging to a sapling with one hand. The darkening sky is visible now, the peaks. Everything lit as if from behind by a somber, wintry glow. She looks at Dasya, her cousin, her beloved. He stands almost in the center of the clearing and raises his eyes to meet her gaze. She says: "Are you going to tell me?"

"Yes."

He says it, he says, "Yes." He almost smiles. A look so pitiful she cries out in spite of herself: "Oh, what is it?"

He looks away. The smile grows rigid on his lips, unnatural. "Siski—do you think a person can be cursed?"

"Cursed?" she says. "Well. I suppose so. Some people ought to be, certainly."

"Don't laugh." His fists are clenched, the knuckles blue.

"I don't mean to laugh, but you're not making sense. What do you mean, cursed? Is it Tuik? Because that was an accident, that was—"

"No."

He stands. His face so still. He's smiling again, but the smile is otherworldly, distant. His lips move. "I'm so tired."

He sinks to his knees. When she sits beside him he lies down with his head in her lap. The snow falls thickly. Darkness over the trees.

Trembling she strokes his face, his snow-damp hair. She weeps. "What is it?"

"Don't make me move," he protests sluggishly. "I want to go to sleep."

"You can't go to sleep. You'll freeze."

"Siski, I'm happy." His eyes are closed. "I'm happy here. Please don't make me get up. Not yet."

She lets him lie there, motionless. His legs stretched out in the snow. He sighs, she feels his breath go into the dark. The warmth of his body. She cradles him, rocks him. "I think I'm under a curse," he says. "Because of my father. Because of his work with the Stone."

"That's ridiculous."

"I've thought about it," he murmurs. "Perhaps Avalei is cursing him through me. Perhaps I should dedicate myself to her. Or perhaps I should run even farther from her, toward the Stone . . . I have to do something. I'll only be able to hide it for a few years."

"To hide? Hide what?"

He reaches for her hand, grips it. His fingers strangely warm. "I'm frightened," he whispers.

She bows over him, hiding him in her cloak, making a circle heated by their breath. A little tent.

"Don't be frightened. Let me help you. Tell me what's wrong."

Silence. He has begun to shiver.

Then he sits up and slowly gets to his feet. She stands too. A stretch of muddy snow between them. She begs him to tell her, she says she doesn't care if he's cursed, she'll never abandon him. She believes it is the truth.

"Now," he murmurs.

She nods.

His face is bloodless, drained of color. In that unearthly surface, the dark orbs of his eyes. He lifts his hands, he pushes back his hood. The snow falls on his hair. He unbuttons his coat. He is not trembling now. No, it is in a new tranquility and a poignant solitude that he moves toward this, the dreaded, the longed-for moment. His coat drops on the snow, his leather jerkin. His hands are in the strings of his shirt, its whiteness a lamp against his flesh. Then the shirt, too, falls to the ground. It catches the air for a moment, billows, sinks. He turns, a boy in snow. His body glowing in the blue of the twilight is more beautiful than a statue. It is the end of everything.

He stands with his back to her, his arms spread wide.

His arms, as lovely as two flames.

His back, half-veiled by the glittering sequins of the snow.

She sees. She puts her hand to her lips but cannot stifle her sudden cry.

It is the end of everything that has been.

On his shoulder blades, two ridges: the dark forms of incipient wings.

They look hard, reddish, like scars where infection has set in. He turns and gazes at her over his shoulder, in the pose of one of the monsters in the *Dreved Histories*.

For a moment she stares. Then she starts as if burned. She staggers backward.

"Siski," he says. His arm outstretched.

The sound, her name, is the last word she hears him say. She turns and runs. She crashes among the trees, sliding on the snowy path, branches tearing her clothes and hair. The moon lights her way on the terrible descent. She reaches Ashenlo with bleeding cheeks, her clothes in disarray. Unable to speak of anything. She pounds at the door of the amadesh and falls on the warm swept floor in front of the fire. Shaking uncontrollably, with a frozen and staring face. She does not understand what people are saying to her. They set her on a stool and rub her hands and feet with teiva. The doctor is sent for; he orders a lukewarm bath. All the time she makes no response to the questions of those around her. Only when she hears them mention her cousin's name, when they ask her where he is, does a feeble ray shine from her eyes, a spark of terror that makes them hush one another with meaningful glances. This reaction to his name, her stubborn or helpless refusal to tell what has happened, the disordered condition of her clothes and hair, are taken as evidence of guilt, as proof that a premature and shameful union has taken place among the young people in the woods. Dasya is sent away at once: he finds his belongings packed and a coach awaiting him when he comes down from the hills. It is considered too dangerous to wait until the dawn for his removal from the presence of his cousin.

They wash her face, her hair, they bandage her cheeks. They dress her as if she were a child. She remains docile until they lead her into her room. Then, when they try to start a fire in the grate, she becomes violent, swearing that she would rather die than have a fire in her bedroom again. "Take her into my room," her mother orders hurriedly. They make a bed for her on the big soft couch the color of beeswax. Firelight dances in her eyes. She is warm, safe, beneath a quilted coverlet with white tassels, in the fragrance of her mother.

She closes her eyes. Such warmth, such comfort, and yet she cannot sleep. A memory comes to her, vivid as a dream. She remembers waking in the stable at Sarenha with the dying Tuik, toward morning when all was very dark and still. Only a spark in the failing lantern. "No, don't move," her cousin said. It was the stinging sensation that had awakened her. Dasya had rolled her trousers up to the thigh and he was washing the misar cuts on her legs with water from a jar.

5. Seven Years in the West

Here is what will happen.

He will grow more and more sensitive. It will become impossible for him to wear clothes. He will grow thin, his body hot to the touch. The unnatural heat will be most intense in his back, where the wings are sprouting.

He will have to lie on his stomach because of the pain.

This is when he is at his most vulnerable. It might even be possible to kill him with hot wax. "During this phase, which is known as *skadri*," the book advises, "the hot wax method ought to be attempted, if at all possible."

Kernis writes: "The wax melted the flesh as if it had been fat upon the fire; in an instant we saw the creature's bones."

She further advises that those who administer wax should wear some sort of protection, perhaps armor, to guard against the creature's saliva. "For the monster writhed most hideously, and spat great gobs of the thickened spittle called *urum*, which is produced in preparation for the state of *thaus*. This heavy white stuff, of the consistency of heated gum, fell upon the leg of our scribe Eivani, who broke out in painful pustules."

More and more *urum* will fill his mouth. His lips will be gummed shut. They will turn dark blue. The state of *skadri* lasts seven days.

Then comes *thaus*, "cocoon" in the ancient tongue. He will be able to open his mouth again, in order to pour forth *urum*.

"Thus, like the silk moth, the creature prepares its nest."

After *thaus* he will be a full Dreved. His wings will burst the cocoon, indigo-dark, almost black. His eyes will be dark, without whites. "Nevertheless the creature's expression is one of abominable pathos."

A Dreved. He will no longer have teeth. Instead, his open mouth will reveal long vertical lines of blue, like the baleen of a whale. These are called *surudin*. Pressed against flesh, they cause the blood to flow with a marvelous and fatal copiousness.

"The Dreved's first victim is usually the first human being in sight."

He lies on his stomach. He can no longer speak. He weeps. His own tears cause him pain, they scald his flesh. He is an angel pinned to his couch and weeping.

"Hush," she tells him. "Hush."

She still can't think about the future: this terror soaring toward her on dark wings.

Instead she descends in memory. All that time, and so much of it wasted!

Time, she thinks. And the mysteries of the body.

∞

Winter in the Balinfeil. The carriage moves at a crawl on the snowy road. At Noi, it is necessary to change from a wheeled coach to a sleigh. The coachman lifts Siski's trunk into the back. "A rough time of year for travel, my lady." He sings as they glide down the road, his voice muffled in his scarf.

> *We got lost seven times on the way to Noi.*
> *The icy winter was combing its beard.*
> *We asked the way at an old footbridge,*
> *and the drunk said, "Stars are falling."*

> *Stars are falling along the road*
> *that leads seventy times to Noi.*
> *Alas my heart, it's snowing in Mendas,*
> *great flakes of silver droi.*

The carriage creaks as it goes down into the fog. It rumbles past Faluidhen and continues to the great, gloomy castle of Rediloth. This is Aunt Mardith's private house. One day it will be Siski's. Rooks skim the towers in the wintry air.

She has come here for her health, everyone says.

The coachman gets out to unlatch the gate. Icicles burst as it opens. In the courtyard, he takes down the trunk. "Come now!" he cries, glancing at Siski, who shivers by the door. "You're young, my lady. It can't be as bad as all that."

The little maidservant opens the door, her worn hands red and dripping from wringing out sheets. Straining, she maneuvers Siski's trunk into the hall. Weeping stones, an odor of soured potatoes, on the wall a single taper glowering in an iron bracket. The cold is elemental, penetrating, persistent as a curse. And here is Aunt Mardith, gliding out of the darkness in pale gray. Pearls on her fingers and at her throat, a pearly radiance in her hair. Her face quiescent, timeless, beyond age.

"Welcome, my dear."

She leads the way to the central hall, which she calls her parlor. Untenanted chairs face one another in the dark. The exertions of the maid raise a blaze on the massive, blackened hearth, calling four soft-padding dogs out of the corners. Aunt Mardith keeps dogs because they eat leftover food, and she does not like spoiling her servants. And so these imprisoned greyhounds, these Nualeithi hunters, serve no purpose but to prevent little Anilon with her bark-shod feet from taking home a gnawed joint in her pinafore.

"Thank you, Anilon, that is all. Siski, give her your cloak." But Siski shakes her head, refusing to give up her mantle. The maidservant scurries out, and Siski and her aunt sit on two of the straight-backed chairs before the fire.

"You're shivering, dear. You may draw closer."

But even if she hurls herself into the blazing logs it will not warm her; she will burn alive before she finds any comfort in this house. Already her cheeks are scorched by the heat but her bones are cold, cold, her teeth chattering, while Aunt Mardith sits in a

portrait-like repose. Her pearls reflect the firelight. "It's your Kestenyi blood," she says. "I'm sure you'll grow accustomed to Nainish
weather in time." In the darkness of the invisible walls the bolted
shutters emit soft groans beneath the incessant punishment of the
wind.

When tea is brought in they move to the table. The porcelain
lamp is lit. Siski resists the urge to warm her hands at its glow. Aunt
Mardith does not speak until the servant is gone and the great
doors have boomed shut. Then she says: "You may pour."

The cinnamon-colored tea trembles in the glasses. There are
diced hazelnuts and miserly biscuits dusted with icing sugar. "I
have lived for this House," Aunt Mardith says. "I have been vigilant
and tireless on its behalf. How have I failed?

"The fact that you do not answer," she continues after a
moment, "means, I suppose, that you are not unaware of my meaning. You know that your sister is lost to us. Lost. Her name has been
published in the newspapers. To us, she is in the tomb."

She lifts a biscuit to her lips and sets it down again without
taking a bite. Her expression is so mild, so controlled, that Siski
thinks she must have imagined the quivering of her fingertips. "In
your place I should be thinking of the future. There is no need to
sneer—yes, I can read your face quite easily. Perhaps you see what
Tavis has done as a sort of prank, a game. You think it will all be
forgotten in a year or two. You are wrong. It will affect you terribly.
You will carry this scandal about with you like an anvil on your
back."

"Why are you telling me this?"

"Because of the rebellious spirit that provokes you to ask that
question, my dear niece."

Aunt Mardith smiles, stirring her tea, which she drinks black
and unsweetened, with a silver teaspoon embossed with greyhounds.
"Because you are young and frivolous, you do not have a serious
nature. Your mother was much more serious as a girl. Though she,
alas, was not saved from making a most disastrous marriage." She

raises her glass to her lips, shaking her head. "I pray that better things are in store for you—you through whom the dignity of our House may one day be restored. Because, make no mistake, that dignity has suffered a dreadful blow. You stare—perhaps you don't understand my meaning."

Her small fist on the tablecloth, her black and motionless eyes. "You don't understand what it means for the heirs of this House to degrade themselves. To throw away the efforts of their predecessors. To expose themselves to pity and scorn, after everything that has been done to advance our position. No. You don't understand. What it means for a woman like the Duchess of Duema, a nobody whose great-grandfather traded in tea and spices, to be able to shower us with her disgusting compassion. She wrote to me. I will show you the letter. Perhaps then you will know what I mean."

"I don't want to read your letters."

"Look at me," says Aunt Mardith.

Siski lifts her head. Her face throbs with heat in the lamplight.

"We are Nains," Aunt Mardith says. "You take your position for granted, you and your sister. You think it was easy to forge a link with the royal House. Your cousin was born at Velvalinhu!" She opens one frail hand in the air, incredulous. "Nainish blood has been mingled with that of the Telkans! But it doesn't mean anything to you. You care for nothing but riding, parties, and defiance."

"You don't know me," Siski says.

"Apparently not. But I intend to."

Aunt Mardith raises a wand and strikes the little copper gong on the table.

"Anilon will show you your room. I have given you the white room, upstairs. In the afternoon it receives some natural light."

White, the color of mourning. White settees and footstools of hetha wood. A high bed with white curtains like a bier. Oh narrow casement, show me a village square. But there are only the gardens of Rediloth, neglected at any season, now covered with snow. Only a woman who never looks out of the window, or who draws some satisfaction from the destruction of harmless things, could leave the little fountain in such a state: the stone nymph broken and her head lying upside down against her plinth. Under a growing burden of snow this nymph becomes ever more shapeless and unreal. Soon she will be unrecognizable, and stand isolated, deprived of all significance, in that frozen waste where the evening deepens her almost unbearable solitude. The wall is too high to see over; its crenellations outreach the pines. And what would one see there? Nothing but snow and mist, the occasional tree. Perhaps, for a moment, the footprints of Anilon where she trudged home after serving kebma. And in the distance the white-capped ruin of the Garahu.

But when storms come even Gara's fortress disappears in the howling snow that batters the shutters and strains at the latch with hands of ice. Siski lies with the door of the high bed open, the long funereal curtains tied back to admit the firelight, and listens to the wind. Its sound as it screams about the ramparts is terrible, and she wakes toward morning jerked from sleep by an avalanche of hail. But almost more dreadful than the noise is the absolute silence that follows, a watchful stillness tinted blue by the snow. In that strange, unearthly light she feels herself in the kingdom of Aunt Mardith. Not, as at Faluidhen, in the empire she controls, but in her original home, a glacial haven of perpetual night where she retires like a she-wolf to its den. Aunt Mardith was born at Faluidhen. But here at Rediloth, which she inherited from her aunt the Princess Ailmali, in this cavernous fortress which had stood abandoned for fifty years, here she has made her true, her immutable home. At Rediloth, which in the Nainish tongue is the Castle of Giants. What giants lived here Siski does not know. But somewhere in one of these rooms Aunt Mardith, as powerful as any giantess, restores the white architecture of her hair. Somewhere she raises her fingers to the lobes of her slender ears, leaving in each a pearl as fair as a narwhal's tusk. The little maid fastens the hooks of her gown. As Aunt Mardith rises, her bones, more sensitive than her ivory heart, utter a creak like a sigh of distress. Siski imagines with superstitious dread the lace-edged nightgown the maid puts away in a cabinet under the bed. No, Aunt Mardith must never undress, for under her gleaming clothes there can be nothing but whalebone, plaster dust, and string. No, she must never undress and never sleep. In the morning she has only to wind the little key cleverly concealed beneath her arm. And here she comes down the hall, the impeccable chatelaine of Rediloth and the monstrous puppet of her own desire.

"Go out for a walk, my dear," Aunt Mardith says. And Siski wanders among the morning-glory vines embalmed in frost. Why is it impossible to see beyond this whiteness, into life? Into the dawn of another life. She walks in the gardens, muffled in furs. Her lashes emerge from the softness, starred with cold or tears. Her footprints follow her everywhere she goes. Down the path between the lilac bushes, past the decimated tulip garden. To the high wall. To the wall. She cannot even reach it because of the snowdrifts, could never climb it. Perhaps, on the other side, life begins. A life that would allow her to abandon the past, as her sister has abandoned hers, running away to the north. Tav with her toy arrows. And Dasya with his. Dasya with. Her mind stops at him, like the heart of that dead robin in the snow. Two months have passed since that day in the hills and still she cannot cross the line he flung across her vision like a bolt across the sky. Instead she walks, for her health. She must grow stronger, Aunt Mardith says. She must not let herself down; too much depends on her body, on her womb. Aunt Mardith is not coarse enough to speak this way. Instead she says: "Society. You must prepare yourself to go back into society." The idea, of course, is to marry well. Siski bends and scoops up a handful of snow. She touches it with her tongue. She rubs it into her cheeks. The chill, the taste of death. Later, when she enters the house, Aunt Mardith will comment approvingly on her glowing skin.

For this is fate, this flesh. Spring comes, even to Rediloth. One morning Siski finds a stack of magazines beside her plate. The *Starling*, the *Watcher*, the *Waxing Moon*. Aunt Mardith smiles at her across the table. "Open them, dear. It doesn't do to be out of touch." Sunlight on the coffeepot, on a plate a smear of jelly. Siski turns the pages. She hears Aunt Mardith talking with the maid. Racing stories, fashion designs. And then his name, *Andasya Lanfirvaud Faluidhen*. Dasya, in letters of lightning.

Her hand tightens on the magazine. His name appears twice, three times, then everywhere. He is staying with their uncle the Duke of Bain. He travels in his own carriage. At the theater he wore green. He spoke with Aunt Sini, with their cousin Afiana. She goes on reading, without hope. She knows she will read the whole page. He rode on the Ban Vanai; he has "the weightless carriage of a nymph." He wears Amafeini boots with scarlet heels. They are new boots, she has never seen them. Nor has she seen the "summer jacket of pale tussore." Her fingers ache, she is crushing the page. To think that he is elsewhere, without her. She did not know it would be like this. This pain, this horror, the fear that his condition will be discovered, and then the rage, for she has been ill while he goes riding in the park! She reads the page, then reads it again more closely, determined to suffer and not to yield. His name has a power that never weakens. Every time she reads it the same jolt of anguish shocks her heart, undiminished by repetition.

When she looks up, the maid has gone. Only Aunt Mardith's calm dark eyes. She knew, of course. Siski hears the click of that ivory heart. Aunt Mardith touches her napkin to the corners of her lips. "You will spend the summer at Faluidhen," she says.

Siski's cousin Latha, Uncle Fenya's daughter, has come from Nauve, in the Valley, where she lives with her new husband. She has not brought her husband, however; he is tied up with the estate, some sort of lawsuit, so boring, Latha laughs, it's not worth trying to understand it. She would rather stay at Faluidhen for the season. She is accompanied by a group of merry young people, all of noble Valley families, insouciant ladies and gentlemen who travel with servants and heavy trunks and take pleasure in calling themselves "old-fashioned types." This attempt to appear old-fashioned, the newest fashion in certain circles, involves a laughing disdain for intellectual pursuits, an emphasis on the healthful benefits of riding, dancing, and wine, and a cavalier attitude toward money matters. Lady Latha's friends are all in debt, and she herself, early one morning in the small blue parlor adjoining the breakfast room, begs her mother, Siski's Aunt Karalei, for six thousand droi: "Just six thousand. You can spare it easily, you'll make that much from the little vineyard alone!"

Coming in from the garden Siski passes the open door and sees Aunt Karalei's normally tawny face disfigured by sudden pallor. "I'll have to ask your Aunt Mardith," she says faintly. "I don't know if we have that much—such an amount—here in the house."

"Ask her then, if you have to get her permission," says Latha. Turning, she notices Siski in the hall, but far from being angry she gives a roguish little smile as she pushes the door closed with her fingertips.

Latha is beautiful in a hard, expensive way, and popular, especially with the gentlemen of the party, but the obvious favorite is her husband's young cousin, Kethina, who, though only Siski's age, has been to seven balls and is well known in society. Lady Kethina has golden-brown eyes that sparkle as if the sun is shining in them. They are close-set and ringed with faint blue shadows, but rather than destroying their charm these flaws increase their attraction by making them seem more intense, intelligent, and sly. She has the sublime, polished, sun-touched skin of Valley women, and already she guards it carefully with unguents and heavy creams. Her talent in matters of dress, astonishing in one so young, has made her the darling of journalists from Duema to Yenith. On her first night she dashes up to Siski. "There you are! I've been dying to meet you. You must protect me," she goes on, leaning close and whispering: "Lord Feren won't stop following me and I cannot, I simply *cannot* bear his cow eyes any longer! Come have a drink."

It happens like that: so easily. Kethina keeps Siski up late, scolds her, fixes her hair, tells her she's very pretty, she mustn't be so shy. She rubs expensive cream into Siski's cheeks with her bony fingers, makes her go to bed with her head wrapped in waxed paper. New styles of make-up are tried out at Kethina's dressing table. Kethina stands back, frowning critically at her subject, her head on one side. "No," she announces, "blue is wrong for you, we'll have to try pink." She dabs her brush in a jar of antimony with quick, expert little jabs.

Afterward, in defiance of Aunt Karalei, they smoke cigarettes on the balcony. Curls of smoke drift slowly toward the moon. They sit with their knees drawn up in the pale balloons of their long nightgowns, looking over the garden, the hedges, and the fields. Siski throws herself into the brilliance exuded by her new friend, the atmosphere of intrigue and whispering closeness. She will not stop to think. She will live, as others live, as Tav is living, and even Dasya, far away.

Faluidhen begins to seem like a house in a novel: a thin romance full of elegant heartache and jasmine perfume. At dinner Siski drinks wine and Uncle Fenya asks her seriously if anyone in Tevlas is selling old porcelain. "I don't know," she says with a laugh, and whispers to Kethina: "How should I?" In her hair she wears a great fleshy lily from the conservatory. Her dress, pale pink, seems to be breathing heavily, having just escaped with its life in the afternoon when she and Kethina tore off its sleeves. Surreptitiously she smells the wine: its bouquet is light and sweet, buoyant, they call it the Wine of the White Bees. Wearing borrowed pearls and her amethyst ring, she begins to feel warm, then incandescent, drinking in light and heat.

A house in a novel. Morhon is seated across from her, his beard and spectacles wreathed in a sparkling fog of adoration. Beside her sits Halor of Ur-Amakir, and farther down the table Ermali of Eilam: Kestenyi gentlemen invited for her sake. "We thought we ought to have some more eastern influence," Grandmother bubbled at kebma, introducing them over a plate of lamb jelly. And at first Siski was nervous, unsmiling, almost unwilling to talk to them, afraid of what they might know about her family. The debts, the land sold, and then the humiliating new scandal—her sister's running off to join the army. But later, flushed with wine, she hears herself laughing about these very troubles, and everyone laughs with her, full of admiration. "This fiery Kestenyi," they say as she speaks callously of everyone she loves. She beckons for more wine, ignoring her grandmother's frown. "A desert thorn," they say. And she knows by the looks of the men in the room that she could not have planned better had she intended from the beginning to seduce them.

Seduce. Certain that she has done well, rejoicing in her success, she feels the death of something inside her radiant body, a death at which she rejoices further, lifting her glass, watching through the window the shadows deepening in the garden. Death, this death, is sweet. Her cutlery glitters in her hands, the anxious breath of the footman warms the back of her neck. She feels the opening of a thousand doors, laughs, touches a young man's fingers as he hands her a plate of olives. Quick language of the eye. His face a blur, it does not matter who he is. She and Kethina, seated at opposite ends of the table, keep up a scintillating flow of chatter. After dinner, everyone runs out into the garden.

Night, moonlight, distance, nightingales, everywhere this tremor in the darkness. And they follow the nightingales, laughing from tree to tree. Over the wall now, stumbling. Someone shrieks, it must be Latha, she is frightened of the ram with the yellow face. "He's somewhere here," she cries. Ermali of Eilam carries the lantern for a joke, because he comes from the city of lamps. But where is the ram? "There," says Ermali, holding Siski's elbow. And she pretends not to see the gleam on the slope of the hill. Because it is pleasant to feel herself alone in the darkness with an unknown youth, she turns, she asks him, "Where?" Her cheek strikes gently against his shoulder, against the delightful creamy cotton shirt, subtly heated by his skin.

Ermali, Ermali of Eilam, the Lamplit City. A younger son, without prospects, spoilt, indolent, in debt with every shopkeeper in Nauve. Proud of his horses, his skill as a rider, his boots stamped with the maker's name, the breadth of his shoulders, the insolence of his wit. Surely beneath his brash demeanor some marvelous creature slumbers: when he raises the lamp it brings out a mineral glow in the depths of his eyes. Then he lowers the lamp and takes her arm. The light abandons his eyes, leaving them blank as the beads on a curtain. Then the kiss.

He sets down the lamp: it's a signal, she thinks wildly, someone will see them. Oh, if only Kethina would see them, how amusing it would be! These are the thoughts she entertains while a pair of hands with eager fingers wanders over the pink terrain of her bodice. At last he surfaces, tormented by the intricacy of the hooks. "Let's go to the summer house, it's just behind those trees." And she feels herself becoming, with triumph, with glee, with a kind of delirium, the dangerous girl of a novel, the one who loves no one.

Certainly he adores her. And then it's warm, there's so much light from the moon and stars, she feels so pretty in her pink gown. At the summer house—a phrase, like "midnight supper," that breathes romance—she finds it delightful that he has to force the latch.

"Shh," she hisses, glancing about as the old wood cracks like fireworks, "someone will hear you, do you want to cause a scandal?" A breath of leaf mold, dust, the door ajar. Stepping inside they stumble over the scattered limbs of dismembered chairs.

He catches her wrist. But now she does not laugh. In the old round building there is a coolness, a mysterious distillation of the past, that pricks the hairs on the back of her neck. They have lost the lantern, but the moonlight is so bright she can make out the lichen on the windows. "No, I don't want to sit down," she says. Her body tingles with gooseflesh. Surely now he should speak, should tell her mellifluously of herself. No, he removes his coat, he throws it over the torn cretonne of the bench, he turns and helps her through the mess on the floor. A moment so charged with misery that she hurries to get it over with, embracing him, seeking the mushroom flavor of flesh. Oh love, love, happiness. And the clanging of an inaudible bell. And now the struggle, the irritation, the fatigue.

Seven years, seven years in the west. She remembers them now, in the ruined temple, with the *Dreved Histories* open on her knee. It began that summer at Faluidhen and it lasted seven years and she never saw Dasya, she never met him even once. She never went back to Faluidhen either, she spent all her time in the Valley, despite Aunt Mardith's letters that followed her everywhere smelling of lilac powder, letters hinting that this or that lordship was coming to stay at Faluidhen and wouldn't Siski like to visit her grandmother? No, she would not go back. She drowned herself in the homes of the west. The sumptuous fragrances, the exotic flowers, the wines. Gambling at omi to buy new clothes and borrowing when she lost and selling her jewelry and replacing it with stylish baubles of glass. Always afraid that the secret would be discovered, that someone would whisper, "Her jewels are paste." Entering ballrooms brazenly, smiling in worthless gems. And promising herself, next time I win I'll buy the emeralds back, but she never bought them and now they are gone forever. The gowns too, and the beautiful shoes, all sold to pay her debts, for she was always in debt despite the generosity of her lovers, the one who introduced her to bolma and bought it for her in pearl-edged boxes, the one who acquired a suite for her at the Jonquil. Remember those lovers, the one who ate bolma, she thinks of him, remembers him, he was from the south, she met him on holiday after she left Berevias, in the city of Ur-Brome where the glazed canals lapped at the steps with a sensuous lassitude and the bridges were cloaked in mist. They danced every night, the music was wonderful, she and Kethina drank teiva in pineapple juice, afterward they almost fell asleep going home in the boat, in the slow, sweet, soundless, miraculous movement of the boat on the lamplit canal, they could still hear music for the Evmeni never sleep. Never, never. And she tried never to sleep, except in the long afternoons. And she had gowns made from the bright pink and orange fabrics of the south. And as if to complete the experience of that charming sojourn she kissed the Evmeni prince with the shapely, close-cropped head and soft-gazing bloodshot eyes. And really, he was so kind. He called her *waloe*, a funny-sounding word; it meant sweetheart. At his mother's house when she went to explore the library he called her gently, "*Waloe*," and coming back to the parlor she heard the old lady say testily: "Doesn't she have a name?" That was the sort of thing she would laugh over later with Kethina and with her cousin Afiana who had also come down for the winter, the three of them at a café with wine and cigarettes and egg sandwiches and the endless coffee they drank to keep up their strength. Afiana dark-cheeked and splendid in a gown of white taffeta with dots of black velvet; she made everyone look at them. She too had a trophy, he drove a fine carriage and wore a silk cravat and they traded salacious stories of the bedroom. Kethina's brittle laugh. She was faithful to her fiancé, afraid of losing him, and pretended to amuse herself with the study of architecture. "Your oily prince," she said, crinkling her nose. And that was unkind of her, for he treated her graciously and sent bolma wrapped in banana leaves to her hotel. Bolma, the whole city smelled of it, the old men in the cafés used to put a few grains of it in their tobacco and the pink smoke would drift over the water, redolent of coastal flowers, of sweat, of the prince's estate where Siski gazed through the wrought-iron fence at the distant forest. That was where it began to end, that trip to his country estate: the place was neglected, overgrown, he hadn't told her there was no plumbing. No servants either, and they were alone. There was one half-wild horse which he tried to ride to impress her, jerking the reins and trampling the long grass.

He waxed sentimental about the crumbling house, the home of his people, he said, it was stupid, he wanted to marry her and she almost laughed out loud. She promised to write but she never did and his letter stamped with gilt dolphins made her giggle when she read it in Bain, in bed with another man.

In Bain, yes, for Dasya had gone to the Lelevai and that left the city open to her with its theaters, shops, gardens, and promenades. And how grand it was, almost overwhelming, everything of the highest quality, clothes, carriages, music, even the conversation at dinner. And so expensive, it made her feel faint when she bought her first gown and shawl. And Lord Danros was friendly, good-humored, and drove a smart tam with a roof of fox-colored leather. In his circle he was the dependable one, he arranged all the parties and races, he had a charming laugh, she envied another girl who was dancing with him. And then, he was staying for only three weeks, what harm was there in a brief romance?—but he didn't travel as planned to join his friends at Sinidre, he stayed, she lived with him at his hotel, when her aunts visited she pretended she lived there alone, she hid his clothes and shaving things at the back of the wardrobe. A rainy winter, and tears. And Kethina said with a patronizing air, "We're no longer young, you'd do better to make it official." For she herself was married now, to a peaked young man with seventy thousand droi whom she bullied into wearing fashionable clothes. To make it official, to marry him. Why not, thought Siski, lying on the enormous couch upholstered in mink in the style of Farnus the Bold. They were a public couple, everyone thought they looked charming together, she so slender, he broad-shouldered, short and stocky as a quarryman. It was said the family had Kalak blood. But it was a very old family, very distinguished, the mother wore jewels that dated back to Ideiri times. In their mansion near the Kelevain this grand lady moved through the faded galleries, walking stiffly with her rheumatic hip. "I'd like to introduce you to her," Danros told Siski firmly, almost trembling because of the terror that filled him at the thought of his family. When it came to the family name, the estate, he lost all his lightheartedness, became craven, serious, combing his hair at the mirror. "What are you doing?" she laughed. For he always left his hair in curls. And he snapped, "For the love of peace get dressed, we're going to be late." The evening was not a success, though he had inspected her costume, removed her big lily, insisted she change into a more modest gown. The house was full of people, everyone knew each other, she stood in a corner and watched them brush past, glancing at her and exchanging knowing grimaces. None of the ladies spoke to her. She met her hostess for just a moment and suffered, her head upright, the intolerable scorn of those black eyes. "You will excuse me my dear," the pale old lady said sarcastically, "I find it very taxing to meet new people." She was eating a sugared biscuit and there was powdered sugar caked on her lips and scattered in the generous folds of her gown. Afterward in the carriage Siski's lover wore a false smile and patted her hand. "I thought you did very well, you managed Mother beautifully. She doesn't see many people," he went on, laughing nervously, "especially foreigners, it was strange to her to have a Nain in the house." To make it official, to marry him. His racing papers, his caution, his mediocrity. All the old Valley families whose snobbery was almost inconceivable, who considered her grandparents' marriage the greatest catastrophe since the marriage of Princess Talomi to a Brogyar, welcomed her for his sake. She was not comfortable in those great old houses full of gilt ornaments and mirrors, but she was proud. She thought: I am here, even I. Spreading her skirts on some knobbed, contorted, extremely precious couch, fanning an air that smelled of roses and old lace. And smiling, always smiling. For she had forgotten how to discover what she felt. It was enough to sit in these rooms, talk to old ladies, in the evening to stand on a terrace so ancient the tiles were cracking and then to dance, to dance with her lover in a ballroom. For he danced well, and they looked very well together. And when it grew too much, this life, there was music and wine and cards being played in a back parlor. She always presumed on her beauty, her wit, the fact that he must be delighted to possess her, a man so ordinary despite his glorious name. And when she had drunk enough she would think with a quiver of energy, a flick of her fan, why I can do anything I like. But their quarrels were dreadful. They quarreled in antechambers, in the carriage, all over their hotel suite. He said that people were laughing at him. He was proud, it was his weakness, it made him cringe when people sneered at her because of her mixed blood. And when she would not behave herself, as he put it, when she gambled, he became incensed, livid, he swore, he was an entirely different man. In the Garden of Plums he said: "Perhaps we should stop." He said it to frighten her and she suddenly saw with great clarity the birds, the trees, the sky. "Yes," she said. And afterward she went out to the Isle of Ban where the trees were putting out sticky reddish buds like watermelon sweets. How delightful to walk alone in the park in spring, to feel the soft fluttering of her scarf, the whispering undulations of her organza frock. She wore a little jacket of lavender tweed, it was still cool, she nodded gracefully to acquaintances beneath the acacia trees. Open to everything: breezes, perfumes, desire. The lure of the possible. She met an acquaintance at the gate of the park and he took her to a café. When he mentioned Lord Danros she couldn't resist, she murmured: "I'm afraid that's over." And saw the tropical green of his eyes.

That was how they came, one after the other. And how she loved the beginning, the overture, the rustling moment before the curtain rose. For one never knew what was coming next, she might fall in love after all, it had happened to others. She woke with a sigh, she had been smiling in her sleep. Moving toward the mirror in green light. She would not summon the maid, not yet. To be alone with this hazy, dim, still-drowsy wonder, this shape in the mirror, herself. And then to dress, the exquisite and sensuous touch of gauze against her skin, the way her flesh breathed against her imitation pearls. With her last, tenderest lover she walked in the square, and when they came to the fountain they walked straight through the great basin in their shoes. Leaving wet footprints on the stones, her heels slipping in her sandals. She would be happy, live very simply, never tell lies. She allowed him to say he loved her, thanked him, walked with him on the Grand Promenade, counted the stars from the deck of a pleasure boat. He wanted to take her everywhere, to every opening night at the Royal Theater, to eat oysters in the quarter of the spice markets, he waited for her while she shopped for books behind the university, admired her, scandalized her Aunt Sini by sending bouquets every day. Every day fresh flowers, fresh delights. Even her sadness was pleasurable when she looked at him and felt that she would never love him. But Kethina was sharp with her, looked at him critically with cold tea-colored eyes, said he was dull, provincial, not our sort. Kethina bristling with sapphires, the choker from her wealthy husband. She wore black velvet, it's proper for married ladies. Now she squinted slightly, affected nearsight-edness when she met Siski's lover at a ball, at last said, "Oh, it's you," with a formal smile. And Siski felt cast adrift, abandoned, as if in a foreign city. The strangeness of the white towers and the parks. Her lover took her to Hama, to his estate, he had inherited it already, his uncle dead at fifty of a cancer. And everyone was so kind, only his younger sister snickered when Siski fell ill because she had drunk too much at dinner. "Let me take you to Miravel," begged her lover. "We took our holidays there as children, you can be quiet there and rest." At Miravel, a landscape of pale lakes and forests of beech trees, the season was already over, for it was autumn. There she could be away from the parties that tired her, he would take care of her, she would read—for he did not read him-self but respected her passion for it. So much so that he sometimes grew worried, asking if she had had time to read that morning. And he would coax her to eat an egg, lie down after luncheon. He loved her. And in the carriage going to Miravel she could only look out of the window and weep, recalling the words of the summer's most popular song. *Remember me, my darling. When you are free, my dar-ling* . . . It was beautiful, silent, all the houses painted white. They walked, met deer in the forests, on an old wooden lookout tower he carved their names. And wearing thick woolen coats they watched a squall over the lake. *I see you sinking gently, and all my days are empty.* There was marvelous coffee, the cheerful landlady thickened it with fresh cream. Siski sat huddled in her coat while her lover rowed on the lake, there were leaves on the water and the sunset created an incandescent sky. "I love you," she said, the first time she had ever lied to him. That night, reading Princess Mia's new book, she came across the words: *For the lover, according to nature, is always nobler and less happy than the beloved.* "Do you think that's true?" she asked, quoting it to him. He laughed. He always made jokes when she asked such questions, he was shy, afraid to make a fool of himself, he knew he was no philosopher. But looking at him where he lay on the couch pretending to whittle something and watching her read she knew that his happiness was as remote from her as childhood. At last they returned to the city. And it was over, she knew it was over as soon as she saw the enchanted streetlamps through the rain. He did not understand why she grew sadder every day, she seemed to have no strength, wept over dead leaves, playbills, ridiculous songs. *Please let me see you in the winter.* He bought her a box of emerald-colored candy tied with ribbon, his last attempt. She sat looking down at it, struck to the heart. The gulf between them. At once she left him to go back to the highlands, back to Kestenya, home.

And there, at Ashenlo, to walk in the hills again, to breathe the scent of mountain pines, to feel the air, was almost too much. She breathes in sharply, here in the ruined temple, and tastes the brusque, invigorating air of the great plateau. She sees herself walking again in the Abravei, a strange figure in a peasant dress and heavy boots and the smart little pumpkin-colored coat. Now she reaches the place where the trees draw apart and enters the clearing where, long ago, Dasya showed her his budding back. And look, a change, a surprise, for the clearing is full of delicate saplings striped with gold by the sun. The sky is the solemn, deep gray-blue of autumn. A garden has bloomed in the desert. She touches the plants with trembling fingers. Here, here is where he lay down in the snow. Here he threw down his shirt. She kneels, snagging her coat on branches, to touch the earth. Here he lay down and put his dear head in her lap. Here he sat up and called her name. With eagerness, with anguish, with rapture, she surrenders to the past. Her body feels hollow, her brow glows like a lamp. I must have come up the path too quickly, thinks that part of her which retains its grasp of logic. It's the altitude that makes me feel so strange. She closes her eyes on a wave of sickness and euphoria, the curse of the high plateau. And opens them, dazzled, crushed, reduced to nothing by this passion of grief that has lain over her whole life like a stain on glass, coloring everything, darkening her perceptions, and that now, with the sun behind it, pierces her with its invincible splendor. At times, usually at the moment when she was on the point of leaving one of her lovers, the flame of a candle would seem to illuminate its design. But always the night came, clouds, all of her daily life obscuring it so that she was aware of it only as a dullness over the world. A tired, faded quality, a fatigue that made her feel as if she could not lift her earring when she was dressing for a ball. But now in the light of this terrible glade her sorrow is clear, magnificent, profound. "Dasya," she sobs in the stillness. "Dasya."

6. The Prince of Snows

Dai Fanlei. Dai Fanlei is a lie. Everything now is a lie. Only what is coming is true.

Horrible, horrible sympathy of the body. In the quick firelight he pulses and snaps. He draws up into himself, then stretches out, pulled taut. A snake, if you strike its head against a tree, stretches out like that at the moment of death, rigid in death, a stick. Everything in the body undone, rushing to the edge. He falls on the floor. Now he is gathered together, curled up in a knot. On hands and knees he heaves. And it pours out of his mouth, white and thick, a river of silk. It pools about his hands.

And she, where is she? Running about the edge of the room, clutching her hair, an immemorial gesture now become a refuge. Gesture of women whose homes are on fire. She has no breath to scream, she babbles and whimpers, crashes against the walls, poor moth caught in a lamp. Drawn to the light and singed. She rushes toward him and then away. He crouches in whiteness, his hands invisible, plunged in cloud. The cloud is rising. It covers his wrists, his feet, he is disappearing in fog, he is weaving a bed of winter and of mist.

It goes on and on. So much. So much. A sea. A sea of milk.

His body falls into rhythm. The ribs, so narrow, rippling, whip-like. An almost impossible movement, exaggerated, like a dance. Punishing dance of whiteness. Up and up it comes.

She sinks to the floor. She heaves. Two dancers now.

But only one is buried.

She leaves a poor spatter on the marble floor.

313

But he: he is far beyond her. Slowly it gathers him. He turns, eyes closed, he sinks in it, submerged. The prince of snows.

Afterward she sits on the floor with her back against the wall.

The room is dark, freezing. She crawls to the pile of wood. Her hands almost useless with horror and cold, she bats the wood toward the fire, shoves the pile together, leans down and blows into it. The spark in the center glows. The fire crackles. She kneels, dizzy with breathing out, until her face tightens in the heat. Then sits back on her heels. And sees in the light the great white bulge against the wall, gleaming dully like an egg.

Threads of dried *ulum* hold it fast, clinging to wall and floor. They glisten like glass, but are as strong as tempered steel. "Once the cocoon has dried," she has read, "it becomes utterly impervious to violence. Only dragon fire has not been tried."

Now is the time of waiting.

"And they rolled the cocoon down the hill to the sea. And the waves bore it away like a chunk of ice. And in twenty days the Dreved Oline came winging across the water, her jaws turned upward in a mocking smile."

Oline. The Dreved of Dolomesse. She remembers playing that Dreved herself, with her sister and cousin in the woods at home. With Dasya and with Tav. To be a Dreved you spread your arms like wings and grunt through your teeth. Sometimes she would put twigs in her hair to make horns. The atmosphere was one of relief, of violence and heady joy. On the day her grandmother Beilan was buried in the park behind Ashenlo, and the house was unbearably sad, all draped in white, they played Drevedi in the Orsan wood, and in the heat of the game they tried to fly over a gorge. Of course, she has always thought, they knew that they could not really fly. They were frightened and unhappy, because of the funeral. There was a self-destructive quality to the game, a desire to tear down everything. This is what she has always told herself. Or—as she has sometimes thought—there was simply a desire for bruises, for the uncomplicated sensation of physical pain, for a pain that could be solved, unlike the suffering in the house, the servants whispering, her father sitting with his face in his hands. And so they ran to the edge of the hill and crashed over, fierce and reckless. But now she wonders if, in fact, they believed that they could fly. They held hands, screaming, until they hit the slope and were jolted apart. The sky seemed to burst above her like a crystal lamp. For a moment she lay in the brambles with her heart knocking at her ribs. Then she sat up groggily. Tav crouched nearby, her knee gushing blood. "Dinner!" cried Siski at the sight of the cut, smacking her lips, still in the character of a Dreved. Far from the house, in Orsanie, in the wood.

Oh, Tav.

She remembers her last days on the Isle. She had gone to her Teldaire Aunt's party on the Feast of Lamps. She did not think that Dasya would be there; if he was, she told herself, she would face him, she would speak with him at last. But she was late to the ball. She stood at the mirror, unrecognizable to herself: the narrow face, the great dark chambers of the eyes. A subtle greenness in the skin, as if it were copper exposed to the weather. The worn filigree of the lace on her expensive, overwashed gown. *A torn shift clings to the fence in the little field.* Arduen of Suoveni, the Gray Lady. *And all the windows fade.* The scene etched in the bowl of the lamp—Felhami of Beal, lying in the tomb—was reproduced in shadow on the side of her bodice. Is this my life? Is it? The heroine of *The Romance of the Valley*, perhaps the most celebrated character in all of Olondrian literature, lying on her back on a stone slab. A lily in her hands. Her image thrown across Siski's ribs, stirring with every breath.

She stood at the mirror too long. In the hall, the thudding of footsteps. A cry.

She ran to open the door, then hesitated and turned the lock instead. She pressed her ear against the wood. She listened for a moment and then hurried to the lamp and blew it out.

A time of flame and darkness. At Ashenlo, when she was a child, they had had to hide during a minor uprising of the feredhai. A shuttered lamp in the hall, her mother standing at the foot of the stairs in her cloak, directing the servants in a whisper. Footmen rushed about with blankets and chests. Siski jumped up and down and laughed because she was wearing her best beaded frock on top of her nightdress. Everyone hushed her at once and they went down to hide in the pantry in the dark among the big cool jars of olive oil. Crouching in the dark. When Fulmia passed with a lantern up in the amadesh, the light stole under the pantry door and then faded out. The feredhai circled the house, once, again, galloping wildly like wild horses in the dark outside the walls.

At Velvalinhu, those days came back to her. The sense of danger. She put on her traveling clothes and cloak. No jewelry, not even a ring. With her pretty, curved, ivory-handled nail file, a gift from her grandmother, she pried the intaglio heels from her boots. When hunger forced her out of the room, she darted through the halls, low to the ground. She found a group of chambermaids drinking wine in a music room. She told them she was a governess, and they told her what had happened. One gave her a piece of chocolate wrapped in stale kebma.

Ashes blew and settled like her thoughts in the strange gray light. In the ravaged gardens she dug up the bulbs of the asphodels. At last, one night, she went out with a stump of candle and faced a drunken soldier swathed in a figured bed sheet.

"I am Siski of Ashenlo. Take me to the captain."

And Tav, the captain, sat on a rooftop. A brazier beside her hissing in the rain. Nearby, under a makeshift canopy, Dasya lay stretched out on the stones.

"You," said Tav. "You're here."

Siski knelt, and they were in each other's arms, there at Velvalinhu, at the end.

"I don't know what to do," said Tav. "I don't know what's wrong with Dasya, he won't wake up, I've had a letter from Uncle

Veda, he says he's coming, he says everything is finished, we have to surrender, he's coming soon and I don't know . . ."

Oh, Tav. Oh, Tav.

Tav in the rain. Tav in her room, the summer they spent at Ashenlo together. Tav on a pillow, recovering from her wound. That cold Tav with her bitterness and her cane. And the earlier Tav, the child, wrestling, running, laughing, falling, bleeding. "Poor Taviye!" said Siski that day in the gorge, dropping her Dreved mask. "Poor knee!" She took off her linen sash and bound up the wound. Dusk was falling and it was, it was paradise. She and Dasya limping with Tav between them, all the way back to the house.

"The end is coming, dark butterfly."

The final, mysterious words of Oulef, one of the last contributors to the *Dreved Histories*. Oulef of Weile, who wrote with such careful detail of the stages of Dreved life and died, it is thought, in the clutches of the Dreved of Ur-Brome. Her body was never discovered. "We must assume that even her bones were devoured—though this is not usual with the Drevedi—or burnt upon a fire." Those pages of scientific discourse and then this sentence opening like a door. "The end is coming, dark butterfly."

This is not the end. Not yet.

Dai Fanlei still goes in to town to meet the others. But she is becoming more remote. The others look at her sadly. They ask her questions, is she all right, they pressure her gently for several days. Then they stop.

One day, in a tall house at the edge of town, Dai Fanlei sits in a streak of light. And suddenly she is breaking. It might be the way the light falls between the high shutters, the brown brocade in her hands, the dust, she doesn't know, but she comes apart. Shaking, her head knocking back against the wall. Tears everywhere. The others get up, they seize her, Dai Kouranu keeps a housemaid from coming in. When Dai Fanlei can see again, she finds herself encircled. Dai Norla is weeping. Beautiful sympathy of the body.

They murmur. They stroke her hands. They say: "I know."

She wants to say no. She wants to say, you don't know, you don't know us. She wants to say: my sister and cousin made this war. You don't know how we have harnessed you and murdered you and made you refugees. She thinks: *For this the gods cursed you with monsters.*

These women should strip her and take her apart like an old piece of furniture. Throw her down, slice her open with Dai Kouranu's curved knife. Tear out everything inside. She begs them in her mind: *Make me new.* But they are not her servants.

So she succumbs. She allows herself to be led. In the kitchen, they make her tea.

Afterward she walks up the dark hill alone. Dragging herself through the mud toward the temple where the great white shadow sleeps. She sings through numb lips: *My heart is white with love.*

At the temple she sits in the glow of the fire and takes a letter from between the pages of the *Dreved Histories.* The letter Tav gave her at Velvalinhu, on the roof, because she had sworn to deliver it. The letter from Dasya.

His hand. The shape of the letters, instantly recognizable. The way the ink thickens at the top of certain strokes. Her chest throbs painfully at the sight of these blobs of ink, although she has read the letter many times.

> *I give you no greeting. I will not write your name. When you receive this I shall be dead, I hope, and everything discovered. I suppose I shall be hanged——the traitor's death. Or, if they cannot hang me, they will drown me in hot wax.*
>
> *A bath of wax. There's something elegant about that. As if one were being prepared for a particularly arcane and taxing ceremony.*

To be made into a statue, perhaps. The idea doesn't repulse me. I find it pleasing. After all I have been a statue for many years.

If they do hang me, I hope it works. I confess to you—not because you're worthy of it, but because I can't help it—that I have night- mares about failed hangings. I see myself writhing on the gallows. For hours. For days. Unable to live. Unable to die.

A perfect image of what I have endured for the past decade. Terrifying.

Does this strike you as self-pitying? A bit maudlin? Where are you? The last I heard, you were at Ashenlo, but I doubt you're still there, as Kestenya has shaken herself awake at last. I, yes, I have ripped the highlands out from beneath your feet like a carpet; you will trample it no more. I imagine you have fled to your friends in the Valley, or to Nain. Perhaps to Aunt Mardith's—how fitting that would be! Yes, you're at Rediloth, licking your wounds, and everyone's lament- ing, the soldiers are coming down from the mountains, the separatists are burning the barns, and you're reading this letter and frowning, tightening your lips (dear gods, they haunt me still) and thinking: "How unlike Dasya—this whining, self-pitying tone!" And I curse you for daring to think it, Siski, I curse you. I said I would not write your name but I will write it in a curse. Oh, Siski. May Leilin smite you, may Avalei turn your veins to fire, as she has mine, for daring to begrudge me my self-pity! May all the gods scourge you for leaving me alone. Without one word. For years. When you were the only one in the world I trusted. Would it have killed you, would it have been too much for your delicate sensibilities, to write me a single word in all those years? One word, to let me know that there was, somewhere, a human being who knew what I was and did not want me dead. Can you imagine what it would have meant? But you would not. You would not pity me; don't dare to blame me for pitying myself.

I am tired. I sleep for the better part of every day. It's not an ordinary sleep. It's like a trance. Sometimes I fall from the trance into a real sleep, the kind with nightmares. I'm hot. I'm sick. I am prepar- ing for the end.

Our uncle will save me. Dear Uncle Veda! He'll have me executed. I won't have mercy on him, I won't kill myself, why should
I? I'll make him give the order. He'll watch the execution, too. His
principles will demand it. Are you disgusted? Good.

At any rate, I have been king! And so Aunt Mardith has what
she wanted, if not precisely in the way she wanted it! Tell her she's
welcome to come to my execution. I'll give her my hair to make a wig;
she can wear it at the next Tanbrivaud.

(I often thought of writing to ask you for a lock of hair.)

Do not think that I am proud of what I have done. What have I
to be proud of? I am a coward. I would have done anything to save
myself, bowed down before any god. I tried them all, I think, before the
end. I studied with the Priest of the Stone and the Priestess of Avalei,
I tried the taubel, geomancy, milim, fasting, books, and at last this
war, a final blow for the goddess, to crush her enemies, in the hope that
she would give me back my life. I am not like Tav. Tav truly fought
for Kestenya, while I have fought for nothing and no one but myself.
Perhaps for this reason, Avalei has not seen fit to remove my curse,
though for her sake I have steeped Olondria in blood.

Blood. In this land of almonds. This land where ladies like you
put up their hair and gentlemen bow to them in the arilantha. The
most beloved book in Olondria is The Romance of the Valley,
because Olondria is the servant of romance. Sweet, sweet land, like
honey with bees still in it! I hope I have made them feel the sting of
it—Aunt Mardith and Uncle Fenya and the rest! I hope I have made
you weep. I hope I have made you think of me for one moment. Just
one moment. I dream sometimes of your wrist. Your shoe.

"Like blue leaves of a murderous autumn," Hailoth says.

Siski I am so afraid.

The world is growing smaller. There is so little time. I struggle
to lift my eyelids. It's like peering from under an awning, into bright
sun. Small people are moving far away.

So little time, and in the short time we had we lost everything. You
took it from us. Your cloak disappearing between the trees. Why, Siski?

*By all the gods, had you turned into a dragon in front of me, I would
have perished in fire before I ran away.*

*Your cloak disappearing between the trees. So swift. And the sky
darkening. And the snow.*

*I take some comfort in Kestenya's independence. The only real
success of this war. Everything else is ashes. Your wretched, outworn,
unfashionable gray cloak.*

*Oh Siski. To see you once more, if only to curse you to your face.
I'm half asleep. We are such frail creatures, we—I still can't
write the word. How did we conquer anyone? How did we terrorize
the world? We, with our burdens. Our pain. Our fear. Our woe.
Our wings.*

She folds the letter and slips it between the pages of the book.
She takes a stolen stub of pencil from the pocket of her dress. Then
she tears out the pages at the end of the *Dreved Histories*, inches close
to the fire to catch the light, and writes.

Dasya. My dear.

I have read the Dreved Histories *and I know that when you wake
again you will not be able to speak. But I think you may be able to
read. So I'm leaving you this, in case. I don't know if I'll get the chance
to speak to you myself.*

*I know you didn't want me to stay. I stayed because I love you
and because*

She stops. Then she begins again.

*I've been thinking about what's happened to you. I know what you
think—at least, I know what you told me that day in the clearing.
You thought that perhaps your father had angered Avalei, and that you
must find a way to placate her, or defeat her. I used to think this was
true. That you were cursed, and that I was cursed through my love for
you. I believed it for a long time, and I lived as if I were dead. Truly,*

as if I were dead. And I fooled everyone, you know. I was so lively, they nicknamed me "the Diali."

I don't believe it now. I don't believe that Avalei was angry with anybody or that you were her instrument to kill the Priest of the Stone, which is what they say, what some people say, or that the gods sent you to break up the empire the way the first Drevedi almost did, which is also what they say. If the gods send us signs—and perhaps they do—I do not believe that we can read them. For, as it is said, the gods do not speak as we speak. Interpretation seems worthless to me. Perhaps I say that because I'm afraid—but not even the Priest of the Stone could translate the language of paradise.

When I went back to Ashenlo last year, I walked to the clearing and I prayed. You know I have never been particularly devout. I couldn't even remember any prayers. I was saying your name, again and again, and then I realized I was praying. I called upon Avalei because my life was a plain of stones and I could not see any way out of what was coming: a marriage to some nobleman, a house, children, feast days, jewelry, gowns, and you lost, and Tav lost, and our autumns lost. Those autumns at Sarenha Haladli, the only times in my life I have been alive. I prayed to Avalei to save me, to set me free. I prayed for a door, and I saw that the door was open. It had been open all along. I only needed to step through.

Not easy, no. But simple. And so I am not sorry for anything that has happened, except that I have wasted so much time. I think of all those years and how you didn't tell anyone and you were alone. And I had run away from you. For that I am so sorry, Dasya. You trusted me and I betrayed your trust. I have not been a person who can be trusted. So many nights I dream of the stable door at Sarenha Haladli, and it's unlocked, and Tuik is in the misar.

If only I could go back. But I can't. I can't.

Time, they say, is a stream. Do you remember where it has its source? You studied with the Priest of the Stone; he must have made you read about Nieb, who created Time and all the gods. I missed all of that; I had a very different sort of education. I've had to go back on *my own and fill in the gaps. So many gaps still, Dasya! Why is Nieb a group of gods and also a single goddess, the mother and bride of Time? And if Nieb's daughter Heth created the world, and Time was before Heth—why did Time not enter the world from the beginning? For there was no Time, at first—there was what the Book calls "the Time before Time." There was paradise.*

Then the Dead King trapped Avalei and turned her into a deer, and there were seasons on earth, and it was the Time of Time. That's where we live. With time and death and betrayal and disease and in the forest, as you know, the Drevedi.

How I wish we could speak together of these things.

But the Drevedi don't speak. Only people barely touched by their influence can talk. That's what I read in the Histories, *anyway. In all those thousands of pages, there's only one recorded line by a Dreved. He said: "I am a Lath."*

What would they say, if they could speak?

Do they speak?

These are the things I ask myself now. We are told that the Drevedi are portents. Bream goes so far as to call them "absolute language." But to themselves, surely, they are something other than words.

Where are the Dreved books, and what is written in them? Dasya, I want to read the true Dreved Histories.

And then I think that the Drevedi have no history, because they belong to the Time before Time. Perhaps, in some terrifying, mysterious way, our most fearsome dreams belong to paradise.

For me, paradise was reading with you at Faluidhen. The words between us. Even the shadows were luminous. Do you remember? The way those words, those signs, seemed to burn through everything, the leaves, the lace at your collar, the light, the book itself. The book and the heavy, humid air and the spray from the gardener's hose and the little bone buttons on the cushions of the couch, and the carpets hanging outside to dry and the faetha in the hall and Grandmother's silver tea service and Faluidhen, and Faluidhen. Grandfather's medal on the wall in the parlor they called the gray room, and the scrollwork on the dining room chairs—all gone. Everything transmuted into fire. History is useless to me, Dasya. I'm living on memory instead.

(And I remember everything and I have been remembering it for years. Do you think I never wished for a lock of your hair? Is that what you think? How dare you. When you were at war in the Lelevai, I almost asked my sister to steal your shirt. I would have done it, only I couldn't think of a way that would not sound strange. "One of his shirts, recently worn, not washed." The stupidity of longing. And what would your shirt have done for me? I see myself wrapped in it, biting it, suffocating, undone.)

Do you remember what Oulef wrote? That the Drevedi exist in the same relation to human beings as the future.

I am ready for the future. I am saying yes. Dasya, let's go through the door. Let's go together.

I remember when Tav landed on the rooftop with her ilok. I was sitting beside you, and you were asleep, as you had been for days. How terrifying it was—those great dark wings, the smell of death, and Tav's face, refusing to weep, more frightening than anything else. I thought we would die, we'd fall, and I did not care, or rather I felt happy at the thought: to die with you and Tav. To die in flight, with you and my sister, the hero—it seemed marvelous. But of course Tav would never let us fall. You didn't wake when we tied you fast, and you didn't wake when we landed here, at this temple, because I told Tav we must find a place to hide, we couldn't go with her to Kestenya, as she wanted. We can't go, I told her, that's all. I couldn't bear to tell her why. You didn't wake when she said good-bye, when she kissed your hands and face. It was only when she had gone that you opened your eyes. No, you said, the moment you saw me. No. Siski, no.

Dasya, the next time you open your eyes—say yes.

7. Dark Butterfly

It is happening now dark butterfly sweet butterfly.

A morning in springtime. Everything green. For the first time, real green between the pillars of the ruined temple. She is ready to walk down to town again, her hair rolled in a knot, her old boots tied, and then there's a sound from the back of the room.

She turns.

For several days she has almost forgotten to look there, at that vast pale form. The curve of it, the slight sheen, like the luster of spun sugar. But now, she looks. There's a sound. A scraping. A knock. She stands poised as if for flight, as if she could still save herself. Somebody's there.

By the time the first stirrings are heard, it will be too late.

Too late. Too late. She thanks Avalei for this lateness, this absolute lack of choice. Thank you, bless you, Ripener of the Grain! She could weep for this blessing, this gift. She does not trust her body not to run.

There is no time to run. Only time to think: If I hadn't been here. If I'd been away. What would have happened to him, where would he have gone? A spark, a momentary burst of gratitude for this: that she is here. Because they have had so little time.

A scrape, a knock, a crack, the white curve bursting, a great dark wing flung up, the two halves of the shell falling back, falling empty, empty on the floor, a second wing unfolding and Dasya standing, Dasya there, alive: Dasya Dasya Dasya in green light.

A sob breaks from her throat.

He looks at her. Black eyes. All black. His expression like that of the faces carved in the temple wall. An expression not human, not animal. Midnight gaze, depthless, unreadable. Small horns on his brow, dark with a delicate fur, like willow buds.

His hair falls on his shoulders. Exactly the same as before. Heartbreak.

She speaks the only word she has. Quickly—so little time! Her hands on the buttons of her worn dress, fighting the buttons, slipping, then tearing, the dress torn away, her breasts now in green light. She drops the dress and steps away. She stands in her underskirt and boots. Somewhere, perhaps, his memory is alive. This is her hope: that he will understand the language of gesture, this word pulled out of memory, this sign.

In the desert there are empty places. Places of utter stillness, utter silence. The sky meets the rim of the world with no window, no escape. There is only sunlight, desolation, wind. The heart grows brittle. These are the regions known as *the fires*, or *the seas of glass*.

He folds his wings behind him. His elegant symmetry makes her gasp. Now he moves toward her, lightly, barefoot on the floor. His body strong again, flawless, cloaked in night, he is like a rich woman in an opera cloak, in opulence, in gems. Eyes of jet and the lips dark blue like ribbon. His sex an ornament of amethyst, his body all of silk. She turns. She turns her back to him, repeating his gesture of long ago, in the clearing, when he showed her the marks of wings.

Now it is happening sweet butterfly. Sweet.

Between the pillars, she sees the green hill. She will die like this, she thinks, with her eyes on the green of spring. Like this she will feel the *surudin* strike where her shoulder meets her neck. *The mouth sticks fast to the flesh and the monster drinks until satisfied.* It will happen like this, if she is to die. He is moving behind her now, unfurling his wings, she can tell by the sudden gust, the wind that lifts her hair. His letter, and hers to him, all those sheets of paper, fly out between the pillars, taking wing over the grass.

Then a sound, unexpected. Snapping twigs. Two syllables. "Siski."

He is saying her name in his broken Dreved's voice.

He has not bitten her. He has not touched her at all. "Siski. Siski."
Repeating her name through the *surudin*, strumming them like harp
strings.

She turns. It is she who touches him. She puts her hand to his cheek.
He is warm, familiar, his hair smelling of the mountains. He closes
his burning, alien eyes, and now he is almost Dasya, his smooth
cheek a perfect fragment of the past. She sees him in his desert, his
excruciating solitude. The burden of his sorrow and of his wings.
His secret, all along, all through the war he planned with Tav, the
private knowledge that he had so little time. She seems to see him in
gardens, dim rooms, forests, always alone. But we were never alone,
when we were together then. Never, not even when reading or playing music, or asleep. By the dead fountain we stood whispering hand
in hand. The fountain was white, like a swan. He opens his eyes. She
is shocked again by their smooth darkness, darkness all the way to
the skin. She trembles. He has not touched her yet and everything is
lost, the world is made of fire, the seas are molten glass.

"Dasya. Dasya. Love . . ."

Will it be like this? Is there now, in his carven face, the mark of a
terrible tenderness? A human emotion returning to him, stealthy as
a frost. A passion, a sadness, something the gods have never known.

"Siski." But he cannot speak. He lacks the structure now to form
clear words, to say more than the poorest, most truncated things.
"Siski." She says it with him, repeats her own name, her mouth in
time with his. Beautiful, horrible sympathy of the body.

His face. His dear face, here beneath her hand. The same face, only now with the budding horns, the deep indigo lips. Sigil of the gods. Tattoo. The color has bled slightly, under the skin, tiny threads about his mouth.

She strokes his cheek. Reckless now, she moves closer to the heat of his body. He closes his eyes again. He's trapped there, pinned, as if afraid to move, to lose one instant of her dazzling caress.

The fires. The seas of glass.

But there were lamps hung on the houses, shadows of trees. There was a library. There was snow.

She sees him in his blue jacket. He reaches to pull a book from the shelf. Evening light on his face. Outside the window, hawks.

In the desert there are empty places, but once we were not afraid. We rode through noon. You sang, *My heart is white with love.* And at last when we reached the shade of the trees you opened your book, your finger against the grains of sand whispering over the page.

Open. Read this book. Here is your Dreved history. Here is the history of the time before time. She leans on his chest, her cheek against his skin. His hands are in her hair. Hot kisses falling, horses, lamplight, pearls. "Siski. Siskiye." She can no longer tell the direction of the sky. She thinks, We are falling toward the clouds. But once we were in a desert, we rode horses. There was a lamp on the stable door. In another dusk a light like pearls. "Swans," she whispers. Swans were flying. There was a beautiful river of broken ice. She hears, very far away, the voice of her cousin, her love. She cannot understand the words. He is not trying to form her language now. He is speaking the language of paradise.

There is still time. She raises her face. If now I am to die it will be here, in this place, here where I belong. He gathers her close, and a kiss delayed for years blooms like a candle's flame, throbbing among the walls of the ruined temple. The *surudin* withdraw: there is no knife, but only flesh. And holding her tight he sweeps from the room, he bursts between the pillars, up now, up, her boots torn off, a laugh torn from her throat, and there is green about them, and sky and sky and sky.

Glossary

Aimila—a flowering shrub of Nain, similar to hawthorn

Aklidoh (pl. aklidai)—a Kestenyi monastery housing devotees of the goddess Roun

Amadesh (Kestenyi)—a kitchen and storage area

Arilantha—a stately dance

Artusa (Kestenyi)—a corral

Ausk (Kestenyi)—clan

Avla (Kestenyi)—a ballroom or large hall

Bais—bread made with chestnut flour

Bamanan ai!—"May it go out" in the ancient tongue. An expression used to avert evil.

Beshadun (Kestenyi)—a female bandit

Bildiri—used to describe the mixed culture that has developed in parts of Kestenya

Bolma—an Evmeni narcotic

Bredis—a low stool stuffed with straw, commonly used by scribes

Bul—a type of popular song, usually a drinking song

Dai—term of address for an unmarried woman

Dakavei—a children's game played with a ball and sticks

Darwad—leader of a town council

Diali—a Kestenyi stringed instrument similar to a lute

Difleta—liqueurs served after a meal

Em—term of address for a married man

Eseila—a vigorous Olondrian dance

Faetha (sing. and pl.)—a table covered with candles and lamps, typical of Nainish homes

Femka (Kestenyi)—an awning

Feredha (pl. feredhai)—a Kestenyi nomad

Gaisk—Nainish herb brandy

Hetha—an aromatic wood

Hoda (Kestenyi)—heavy porridge

Honith (pl. honitha)—a Nainish pastry, often stuffed with fruit
　　or cheese

Ilok (pl. iloki)—literally "great bird." A species of giant hawk.

Kad shedyamud (Kestenyi)—What barbarism!

Kalidoh (pl. kalidai)—Kestenyi: a mystic

Karafia—the "Night of Tears." The massacre that ended the
　　Kestenyi rebellion during the reign of Eirlo the Generous.

Karsavi—a sweet wine of Nain

Kebma—a flat Olondrian bread, traditionally eaten at dusk

Kib—a board game played with stones

Klugh—a traditional Nainish dance

Limike—an Olondrian musical instrument similar to the dulcimer

Lokhu—an aviary

Londo—a gambling game played with ivory dice

Los—peach liquor

Mardh (Kestenyi)—foolish, hopeless, ridiculous

Milim—a narcotic leaf

Misar (Kestenyi)—a plant with poisonous thorns

Mun—term of address for a married woman

Oinov—a preparation of medicinal herbs used especially in the
　　treatment of fever

Omi—"hands"—the card game of the Olondrian aristocracy

Ous—a dark beer

Raush (Kestenyi)—cured meat

Sadh—a traditional Kestenyi dance

Sama—a grain similar to millet

Sein—verse. Used of religious texts.

Shambus (pl. shambusna)—a wild sheep of Kestenya

Shedyamud (Kestenyi)—barbarism

Shedyun (Kestenyi)—barbarian, savage

Sovos (pl. sovoi)—an overseer or steward of a large estate. Used mostly in Kestenya.

Stedleihe (Kestenyi)—honey beer

Sud (Kestenyi)—prince. Suddi—my prince. Sudaidi—my princess.

Susa—a drab Kestenyi bird with a harsh call

Tanbrivaud Night—the last night of the Olondrian year, traditionally marked by pranks and masquerades

Taubel—a bowl employed for divination using the reflections in water

Teiva—an alcohol made from figs

Teldarin—"my lady," a term of respect

Vai!—"fires" in the ancient tongue; an exclamation of wonder or surprise

Vallafarsi—the Olondrian holy book

Vanadel—a type of popular song, often a love song

Vanathul—the "Song of Thul." Composed by Ravhathos, this is the most famous work of Olondrian epic poetry.

Acknowledgments

Many people helped to make this book a reality. As always, I thank my parents for their love and their infectious joy in language. Thanks are also due to Gavin J. Grant and Kelly Link for supporting the Olondria project; to Kathrin Köhler, my partner in crime; to Lisa Bradley and Mary Rickert for their generous responses to the early drafts of this book; and to Keith Miller, first reader and last.

About the Author

Sofia Samatar is the author of the novels *A Stranger in Olondria* and *The Winged Histories* and a collection, *Tender: Stories*. She has written for the *BOMB*, *Strange Horizons*, *The New Inquiry*, *The Believer*, and *Clarkesworld*, among others, and has won the John W. Campbell Award, the Crawford Award, the British Fantasy Award, and the World Fantasy Award. She lives in Virginia and her website is sofiasamatar.com.

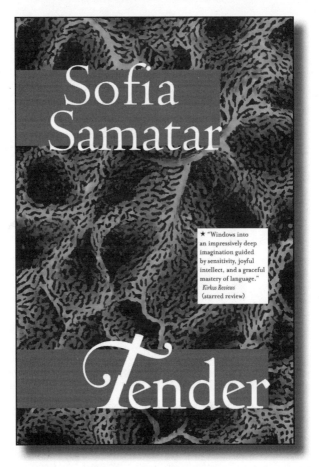

Sofia
Samatar

★ "Windows into
an impressively deep
imagination guided
by sensitivity, joyful
intellect, and a graceful
mastery of language."
Kirkus Reviews
(starred review)

Tender

"Windows into an impressively deep imagination guided by
sensitivity, joyful intellect, and a graceful mastery of language."
Kirkus Reviews (starred review)

Tender: Stories is award-winning writer Sofia Samatar's debut
collection. Some of these weird and compassionate fabulations spring
from Samatar's life and literary studies; some spring from the world.
Tender explores the fragility of bodies, emotions, and landscapes,
in settings that range from medieval Egypt to colonial Kenya to
the stars, and the voices of those who question: children, students,
servants, researchers, writers. *Tender* includes twenty stories, three of
which were included in the first two volumes of the *Best American
Science Fiction and Fantasy* series, and two new stories, "An Account
of the Land of Witches" and an expansive novella, "Fallow."

hard cover · $24 · 9781618731265 | ebook available